DuOPolis

By the author of

The God's Cycle

Maine Metaphor

Gott'im's Monster

And

Fantastic Travelogue:
Mark Twain and C.S. Lewis
Talk things over in The Hereafter

DuOPolis

S. Dorman

DuOPolis

Softcover ISBN: 978-0-578-22407-7
Digital ISBN: 9780463859780

S. Dorman
P.O. Box 172
Greenwood, ME 04255
USA

Cover images © 2018 by Evelyn Yareff, *Creative Memories* consultant. Front cover design, John Dorman.

Back cover portrait: Chief of the Lenape, Lapowinsa, by Gustavus Hesselius, 1735; Library of Congress, public domain

Contents:

\ Timing /

FivePoints Akropolis?

Jay felt herself crawling out of sleep …out of a nightmare. Coming together in solution, bits and particles from the once dissolving periphery of *a dream*. An unfathomably *explosive* dream.

Five teenagers and a little kid appeared suddenly on the moldy old-stone cemetery wall. Through sparse traffic a pedestrian inadvertently happened to capture them on her device. Amazed, frightened, she stepped onto the curb, heading toward the intersection but turned back. There it was, ghostly, transformative! —Frightened, she turned and hurried toward 3rd St.

Jayrai held hands with two of the others on the wall—lightly, but sure. The six had just happened to be here with her on the old stone wall earlier—moments before actually. And now they lined the wall, holding hands. Jay was specially invested in her Arm. The Arm CossycSystems had given her…well her uncle really. He'd paid for it. The Arm was going to make it through.

Now! …Jay's eyes were open. *The first thing was —hands and arms!* Especially for Jayrai, perched with them on the rock-hard wall beneath tall dark leafless trees of the cemetery. —Fingers—yes!! She laughed with delight. "*Girls*!"

Muscles flexing, each FivePoints 2017 gang member checked to make sure of their torsos, legs, hands and arms. Jayrai had loosed her hold on Quadri's small hand to flex her biomechanical fingers. All in working order! "Girls!"

From her perch on the wall between Quadri and Tu she looked next at the sidewalk. Concrete!! She'd been afraid it might be wooden—a boardwalk. Jayrai laughed and looked up. There was the library! Across the street! She sniffed. Of course the sewer smell should be here, but not as bad as 1900 with its horse-pies. —She wasn't smelling it!? Wasn't sewer smell here the moment they transported? The quiet electric vehicles. —Oh That beautiful modern brick library! But… it's closed? —Wasn't it open a minute ago? Five minutes? Ten? …At least it's not wooden and full of violins and musical instruments. Just how much time had actually lapsed while they were in 1900 CE? Only minutes – had to be!

They were not acclimated to the RIT, the *Ripple in Time*. No one could be. They had crossed Times and maybe even multi-Times—the multiverse?! but still, no getting used to it! Or? —could the Time passage itself go unnoticed? For instance, the first time: They had not noticed their arrival from Akropolis 2017 to Akropolis 1900 CE. They had thought they were right here—gaming and witting and surfing—until the wifi and pod phone signals awfully disappeared.

Now everyone was having a variation on Jay's experience. They looked at one another, making sure all the 2017 gang had made it through from 1900. Pomala the albino jumped down, leaned in and kissed Tu, who backed off a bit. All leapt off the stone wall of the cemetery and started yelling, congratulating the air. Pomala apologized to Tu amidst the otherwise general hugging and shouting. Tu was the stoic, not into hugging. "But Tu, Tu, you did it! You brought us back!! We're home from 1900 CE! Home! Our own FivePoints 2017!!"

Everyone screamed. "2017 Rah!!" Even Tu—not the usual for Tu.

He said, "Hacking *Hadesthon* software can be tricky. One glitch kept happening. Shooting Baltoid on Persesus29 fails the first five times, every time, then launches the P29 module gimmex.lld, causing bribell27.xee to gobble mega percentages of its CUP sickles—so, not mega, but you know what I mean. Nothing to do with the calculations, though. The real problem is trying to regard what you are doing as you are doing it. Observation of an event changes it if you are the one engaged in it. You see."

HB answered, "Like I said before, girl, *sure* we know all that dump stuff! We ain't 2017 for nothing." (Sarcasm.)

"I was paying attention to the factors," said Tu. "I still don't know how it worked ... exactly. I've got to study that."

"Got device?" asked Fabian.

Everyone checked pockets for phones and pods. Jayrai ripped open the Velcra™ on the right leg of her purple cargoes, and dug out the z-pod, kissing it. She searched it, swiping. It was on! "We're good to go!" She yelled. She screamed. "Good to go! I've got a zillion messages!" She did a double-take. "Wait a minute! I got *NO* messages! Can't be right! Can't be! You got messages, Pome? HB!!?

Blake Griffin, also known as HBBBAH or HB, had been sliding screen pages, one after the other. "Bogus; bogus; bogus; BOGUS!! BOGUS!!" He started to shiver and jerked his jacket on. He had been sweating a moment before in August heat of the 1900 neighborhood, but now a gust sent chills through him, autumn leaves flying. He said, "I need me some earmuffs, if this November keeps up much longer."

"If they'd fit," said Fabian. He looked pointedly at the big, black kinky broom-cut bristling down-center—from the top of HB's forehead to the nape of his neck behind. "You ever gonna cut that? Me either." Fabian had the shorter buzz-cut version, blond, but with lank hair on either side, like puppy-dog ears. His face sported a couple dimples and small blue tattoos.

"Are we back or not?" said Pomala, looking around at the cemetery back of them, the slow quiet street. She believed they were.

Quadri had picked up her hand again. He was shivering. He asked, "Where's the game?"

She looked down at him and squeezed his hand. We'll figure it out," she said. He continued gazing up at her, dark eyes searching just a bit in his olive-hued face. Pomala's face might have been olive, descended from the Graks as it was. But she was albino, all white, except that she was now mostly tattooed blue. Her white hair and eyelashes were temporarily dyed blue, and her eyes were blue when the contacts were in. Otherwise they were pink. Her hair ascended like a glowing blue gas flame. Quadri's family descended of the Middle East, and yet their skin might have matched if she were not albino. Her skin, Pome liked to say, was descended from the polar bear but had lost all its fur.

"How we gon figure it out, white thang?" demanded HB. "Tu? *You* got anything figured out?"

Tu looked blankly at him a moment, black bang hanging straight above his delicate symmetrical brows and eyes. Then he looked down at his device. It needed a charge.

"Here's an idea," suggested Fabian. "Let's actually walk around and ask somebody. You know, like with our mouths. These guys have ears, 'know?" He gestured to some passersby crossing quickly to the other side of Exchange Street. But none of these fast-walking pedestrians paid attention, or so it seemed at first to Fabe. Then he looked close and thought he saw fear scurrying.

"They must have seen us twinkling back, shouting. A moment ago," he said.

"Right," said HBBBAH. "We just *appeared.* That's bound to scare anybody. I be some scared my own self if the Big Fello didn't pull that number on me, and save us all in Paddy's Pool Hall—1900."

"I don't remember that, yo," said Jay.

HB shrugged.

"What, we've had this conversation before?" She looked down at her z-pod.

"Somewhere or when, before." He puzzled briefly over it. "Get your jacket on, Quadri," he said.

Shivering Quad dropped Pomala's hand to comply, and she stooped a bit to help him. All had worn their jackets tied round their waists in 1900 because for some reason it was August. For some reason it was 1900! August where the *Hadesthon* (evidently) had pitched them into the different era as they played the game here on the cemetery wall in November, 2017. Tu never worked the calculations to figure out precisely why it was August instead of November. There'd been too much going on and maybe not enough battery. Could it, maybe for instance, have had anything to do with *The Hadesthon* slncing of Pluto and the Sun?

"Anyone getting hungry?" said HB. "A man gets empty crossing all that empty on his way through nowhere. Let's go to the SoupMission—make sure it's not Paddy's Pool Hall by some flippin' mistake. That'll tell us what's going on. Pastor Zettler's pretty knowledgeable about soSHmedia and stuff, though he got none his own self. He gets it from your sister, I think." This last was said to Pomala.

"Good," said Tu, "but start sending out now anyway—witter, flumbr, OOga+, all that. Just go fishing on the way."

Now they started toward the FivePoints intersection, still swiping, pushing buttons, surfing... and getting no witts from anybody.

"Look! There's plenty witts everywhere on all kinds of new happenings, especially, but no new witts for me?" said Jay over her bionic shoulder joint to those behind.

"Weird," said Fabian, looking at passersby as they walked down Exchange St. toward the soup kitchen. "Look up, you girls! Everyone's wearing dark clothes. Frowns. You'd say, What's up,?—HB?

HB was mumbling. "Waz up?..." Looking at his gizzzmo8, he wasn't paying attention.

"Pome, look," said Fabian. "Jay!"

The girls looked around.

"Tu?" asked Pomala.

"Tu?" said Jayrai. "What'd you do? All the traffic is almost gone. Everybody's scared and dark. Look, they won't look at us. This-Can't-Be-The-Same-FivePoints. Tu!! Look!" She raised and waggled her bionic hand.

"So, at least you got your arm," said HB, paying attention now. "Just no one wants to look at that arm of yours."

Not at the moment, but often its works were exposed—wires, tiny motors, metallic finger joints, electronics, all. She should wear the sheer polychloroprene covering from fingertips to shoulder beneath her jacket; but she loved the attention and triumph of the works. Some people thought it had been donated but was actually a gift from her uncle. She, however, liked the reputation of donation; she liked hanging out with the poor kids.

Quadri tried to show Pomala his device. "Look, look," he kept saying.

Pome kept looking about her, asking, "Tu?"

"Tu, is this not the neighborhood?!" said Jayrai. "Is this even FivePoints?" She was majorly ticked. "*The Hadesthon* has us on!"

"Again?" (HB)

Quadri wailed. "He says I'm a disgusting troll and he's gonna get the police!" He tried to show the 7qz to Pomala, to Fabian. Everybody stopped to circle him and look.

"Who says that?" asked HB. He grabbed the device.

"Look on the gizzzmo, HB," suggested Fabian as Quadri howled. "Check his witter too, Jayrai.

Quadri tried to get the 7qz back. "My brother, my brother" he cried. "My brother, my brother."

"That's your brother?" asked HB. "Why would Quadrangi do that?"

"That's just it," said Pome. "His brother would not do that. You know Quadrangi would never do that."

"Yo," said HB. "Some trolling hack's just done took over his account then. That's totally off! I don't think he'd let it happen."

"He's right, you know," said Jayrai looking at her z-pod. "Both you. Someone's pretending to be his brother, yo. *That's* the troll!"

"See," said Pome to Quadri. "It's going to be all right, Quadri. There's a mix-up and some bad person is pretending to be your brother. Your brother would never call you a disgusting troll, would he."

Quadri thought. "But he got mad once and said I was a terrorist."

"What were you doing, or what was going on when he said that?"

"I was tormenting him," Quadri admitted. "But I didn't do that before we left."

"You mean everything was OK before 1900 CE?... that would be just a little bit ago...."

"We were playing the game together," he said.

"That's right," said HB. "Quadrangi was playing the game with us, remember? Then the wifi and phone was gone, and we were in horse-and-buggy FivePoints."

Jay said, "But that should only be a twinkle ago, like 15 minutes, not 115 years ago!"

Tu corrected her. "Hundred-seventeen."

They looked dumbly at him.

"That's all you got?" asked Fabian. "A verbal two year math correction? Don't we need an *actual Time* correction?"

Tu looked dumbly back.

Fabian started toward the intersection of FivePoints. "The SoupMission! Pastor Zettler! Maybe Nana's helping out tonight," he added hopefully. "If this is FivePoints, Pastor Zettler's got no wifi, she's got no gizzzmo8 but she's got food!"

"See," said Pomala. "Soup. It's gonna be all right, Quad! We'll be doing homework before you know it."

"Homework!" said HB with distaste. "It better not be history!" He tried to think about today's assignments. "Oh sht!"

"No. Soup!" said Jay, waggling her bionic arm like she does when showing off or nervous. Encased now in transparency, its glimmery wires and circuitry and otherwise hidden electronics would have reassured Quad. He thought, Yes, soup!

But, almost at the soup kitchen on the intersection, and just crossing Third St.—the fifth point at FivePoints—Fabian saw someone steady her pad in the direction of Jayrai, and then hurry up Third. *Whoever—is either angry or scared!*

"OMH!! Comes a shout from one of the long tables as they enter. The place is crowded more than usual. Screaming erupts, a gust of activity and chaotic rumbling as several chairs scrape back and some fall over. The smell is all chicken soup, onions and thyme, which the gang almost don't notice for the turmoil. But right off they see more kids, teenagers, more FivePoints gang than usual in the soup kitchen. Someone was banging on the kitchen wall, Pastor Zettler put a hand on his shoulder, the man jumped back startled and pushed him away.

Shouting, Quadrangi stood. "Quadri! It was you!! Oh my Hal-La!! Quadri! Fabian! Jayrai! What happened! You mean it was really him? Where you been?!"

What's the big deal? They can't know we were in 1900 for, what, ten minutes of 2017's time? Fabian glanced at the counter—where the soup was being served—in time to see his grandma go stiffly to her knees on the filthy floor. He knew what she was doing. *But why?*

Quadrangi threaded through tables, jumped some overturned chairs and grabbed up his little brother. "What happened?" Then he looked at the little boy in his arms and said, "You shrunk! Wait, you're the same, did you just get little again?"

Quadri kissed his brother's cheek. "No!" He shouted. "You got big!"

At that moment FivePoints 2017 didn't give toot what anybody looked like. Home! Ho! Crowding, hugging and shouting, the soup joint jumping and five-highing and/ or ripping:

"Yo-yo!
Y'know!
No mo slo-mo!
No that-n-this!
No fishbone-ham-bone-pig-bone-pork-bone!
CHICKEN SOUP BONE!!"

Pastor Zettler threaded his way through the crowd with Fabe's grandmother, her arm tucked in his. They held hands fast, the Pastor steadying her, but people noticed and gave way for them.

Many friends, a few friendemies and some plain enemies: 2017 looked over people's heads trying to find special someones. But so far the only "specials" were Quadri's brother and Fabian's grandmother. And Pastor Zettler. He shook hands all round in that special way, leftover from old-time 1960's, clasping the hand and forearm of each in turn. He was still an authoritative man, more robust by far than was Fabian's grandmother. Despite the '60's handshake, his hair was short and thick—salt-and-pepper. To 2017 the handshake was old and new at the same time. It was a relief to be "in his hands" again. But he did not stop to talk to them.

The Pastor stepped aside so Fabian could hug his grandmother, and then began speaking to the noisy crowd. Pastor's immigrant roots had been of great, even healing help in the neighborhood. Their descendent now lifted his hands and, speaking in a firm voice, urged them all. "Sit down everyone. Sit back down please and eat the good soup prepared by the brothers and sisters. Please. Please everybody, give our friends a chance to rest, and to eat as well. Afterward we will have the service and listen to what they have to tell us, if they will."

He spared a glance toward them, gauging, calm; and then went on. "Make a seat for each, please give them room either on benches or at smaller tables. Don't worry. If they're willing, you shall hear them, and the service will not be quite as usual... which I know will be a relief to many!"

This brought a laugh as people settled back into their places and began eating again. More soup was coming from the kitchen, great kettles carried out with strong arms of various hue, and placed on boards upon the countertop, an attempt to do the antique "sideboard" (as it was called by older folks) no harm.

Scattered among the friends they'd left behind, FivePoints 2017 sat down. They all looked … somehow these friends looked … different. Distorted. Bigger. *Scary ... are we in the right universe?* But we know them! They know us!

Yet now, for the first time ever they were waited on. Bowls of soup and plates with rolls and real butter were set before them, glasses of milk and bottles of water. Some kids passed their own sodas and colas hand-over-hand to the new arrivals, and everybody was talking at once. Fabian sat on a bench with friends but Nana was by his side. She could not take her gaze off him as others peppered him with questions, boys and girls his own age or a bit older. He joked a lot but said nothing exactly true amid all the obvious satiric exaggerated excuses he was giving for their "absence" —of which absence Fabian himself could make not a bit of sense: It seemed some kids thought he'd been gone two years! At which he made a giant guffaw. But he wondered. People did not look as he remembered—from earlier today? Yesterday...? He felt strange… and creepily younger.

"I knew you'd be back," said his grandmother in a low bumpy alto. "I mean, hoped." She talked with a bit more gravel in her voice than he remembered from—yesterday? —When she'd got him up for school this morning? "I just didn't think you'd look exactly like—well, like you do, she said." She seemed more nervous than before.

He had bent his head to her but now sat up, looking down at her. She looked much the same to him.... Maybe just a bit more worn. Tired? "Are you tired?" he asked. She didn't seem to hear him. Just kept looking at him, her eyes a bit droopy, crows feet surrounding them, wrinkles on her forehead—even on the bridge of her nose between wire rims of her 60's-style glasses. The prescription made them bigger, clearer. He did not expect her to hear—it was just too noisy, but he put an arm around and squeezed her, smiling.

Was it just Jay's imagination or did everything look twice as decrepit as it did yesterday? Everything in this long room had, of course, looked pretty grand and new when it was Paddy's Pool Hall and Saloon. In 1900 it had a shiny white tin ceiling, patterned in crosses. New bar, tables, chairs, gleaming brass accoutrement, spittoons. In 2017 at least the floors were generally swept. She looked up. Dim cobwebby tin ceiling patterned with crosses. Could do with a dusting. Are these people really the same—same friends, friendemies? She was creeping-out. Someone, a couple someones spoke to her and she brought herself back. Yeah. Home.

"Where's Bo?" She asked Trice, sitting across from her. She had to lean in to hear the answer. But that look on Trice's scarred face. What is that? Something is wrong.... something. She stopped eating and fixed her gaze on her friend. "Where do you mean?" Jayrai asked. "What do you mean?"

Trice did not seem to want to say, exactly. Trice. *Trice? Is this even FivePoints? How can there be a different version of FivePoints?*

At last Trice, whose name is pronounced *Treese*, stood up, her long brown hair hanging as she bent to step out over the bench. Trice, skinny as ever if taller, came around the long end of the table and stooped to Jayrai's ear. "He was in People's, but now he's in jail. They thought he did you in. —Your people thought, after I told them about Bo. I had to tell them about Bo, the police. Didn't you know?"

Jay looked at Trice's bony knees, then stared up into her friend's eyes. Trice's hands and face had always been lightly scarred. Jay frowned, looked away. Trice stayed where she was but squatted on her skinny haunches clad in khaki denim, holes in the knees. Then she tugged at Jayrai's brown hair streaked with white. Jay turned back, gaze flaring. Trice backed off quick, but then smiled and said, "Just testing to see if you're you."

"Is it true—Peoples and jail?" asked Jay, thinking of these last few hours spent in such turmoil *somewhere*.

"They say they had to shoot him. Not lethal or anything."

Be back? thought Fabian, a table or two away. *Nana thought I'd be back from school?*

At a table behind him HB, also known as Blake Griffin, was using his CossycSystems enhanced head to analyze the situation. It had been enhanced with software implemented as he was entering puberty. He did the analysis without really attending to it because attention wasn't necessary. When his head got done he would use its software, interfaced with his right contact lens, to flash the results onto the table above the butter knife. He was talking to Quadrangi. "So the po-leese report.... What was that?"

Quadrangi was a much bigger, muscular version of Quadri, who was on the other side of his brother alternately gazing at him and yammering away about 1900 CE—hand pumps, watering troughs, the wrong buildings, can-kicking. Big brother Quadrangi would smile and say nothing or ask a teasing question. He had texted familial others about Quadri's return.

"They got no McRonalds there," said Quadri. "Where would you work? BTW, don't you eat there on work nights? Why are you eating in the SoupMission?"

"No. They got fed up with me." Quadrangi, grinning, did not want to give the real reason. Plenty of time for that later...? He thought about that—Time? HB, he had noticed was no bigger either. He should have been a giant by now. He looked exactly the same as he had that last morning in school. Same shiny black textilite jumpsuit, old jacket, broom-cut 'do, flashing occasional grin. Quadrangi had turned to answer HB's question.

"You guys were disappeared. But you know that? The Pastor says we'll find out... unless you wanna say now?"

HB scanned the summary, projected from his special contact lens onto the whitewashed table amid rows of soup bowls and plates, utensils. These unconsciously gathered analytical reports of HB's were invisible to others. This particular report analyzed every impression experienced since his return. He looked back at Quadrangi and said, "This is 2019?"

"Of course."

"Uh-oh." HB got up and went forward to put his mouth next to Fabian's ear.

"Uh-oh." Fabian turned to look him in the eyes. "Now what?"

"Now we go talk to the brainy guy who got us into this mess."

Fabian stood, saying something to his grandma that she didn't catch. She watched him walk over to the Osiian-Americle boy by the window—the smart one, smaller, with straight black bang, the budding scientist.

Aside, Fabian felt he should caution HB. "Maybe it wasn't his fault, girl."

"Yeah, I know," said HB. Their conversation was covert, close.

"Yo, Tu, guess what?" said HB squatting beside Tu. Tu was sitting on the sill in front of the plateglass window by himself. His preference. He held a bowl of soup but he wasn't eating it. He had abstracted and isolated himself so he could think it through. What was he going to say when the Pastor asked him in front of everybody? Maybe he better go home? He *should* go home.

Tu could *not*. He needed these guys. *And, it was going to be up to him*. HB was here, Fabian stood by. Tu looked up from his bowl, relieved. They were the only ones who could —understand was *not* the right word. *Who* could *ever* understand this?

"I know. It's 2019. November 3rd, 2019."

"Whad y'do, look at the pod—it's working again—Time and Date?"

"No, the battery's dead. Still. Remember? I looked at the calendar." Tu gestured at the big NOV 3 on the printed calendar hanging just below the large soup pans on the counter. "If you look you can see the year right below."

"So... you actually forgot to check a pod somewhere?"

"Didn't you? You got device."

"Forget it," said Fabian, brushing off his buzz-cut. "What are we gonna say?" He wanted to add, And when can you get us back to 2017, but refrained. He looked over at Pastor Zettler, who was still ladling out revival house soup. The place was packed and they kept on coming.

"Guys," said Pomala, coming up to them. "Remember *Akropolis Pop*? Quadri and I were standing right by that window drinking it in 1900 CE." She pointed over the heads of the crowd to the plateglass at the end of the room facing onto Exchange St.. They saw most people were looking at them over their soup bowls, forgetting to eat. People who looked both qualitatively and quantitatively different since earlier in the day.

HB stopped. He looked out the window behind Tu into the dimming November twilight. He was remembering the Fat Man going past on his giant white horse. In August, 1900 CE. He was convinced that Big Fello had averted a catastrophe in his life and the lives of others, his friends, family and companions.

"Pome, it's 2019," said HB, turning back.

She looked at them. *Kids look ... different. Bigger?*

"2019," said Fabian.

She looked at Tu. "2019?"

Tu nodded. "November 3rd."

Pastor had no wifi in here but there was always phone signals. He thought devices were destroying the earth. Literally! She turned the podPhone horizontal. Trice was back sitting across from her, Jayrai was texting her family: *I am right here! Bo did nothing!*

Trice's long brown hair hanging over, she kept pushing it back, and was also texting, but then stopped to nudge her pop-pod across the table to Jayrai. "Look," she said sliding the pop-pod closer.

Jay picked it up. "OMG! OMN! Oh my *Newfish*!! Trice! I forgot all about that! Let me show the girls?" She started to rise, looking for the others —members of 2017— as she had been thinking of them ever since they'd been together in 1900 CE. —The ones who went to old-time Akropolis with her—FivePoints 2017.

"Don't you have it on your z-pod?" asked Trice, reluctant to let go her precious pop-pod. It was a rare gift from the Board of Education, ostensibly to help with homework.

"OMN! It should be! Let me check!"

"I mean it's been two years, so maybe you don't."

"Two years, yo? What's that mean?" Jay's round dark eyes grew even rounder. "You don't mean it's been two years since I took this selfie?!" She sat down slowly, looking at Trice. Trice's hair was definitely longer! Huh? Her face maybe a bit thinner. Even her voice seemed skinnier. Jay looked down at her device, checking images. It was the first image.

An image of the gang sitting on the cemetery wall. The date was November 3, 2017. This day in the SoupMission should be the same.

Trice said, "I've been keeping it on the homepage. Just kept looking at it, thinking about you all. The police have it, too. Gretch said send it to them when word of the disappearance went viral. But, it's strange, I didn't see the image anywhere for a while, and wasn't sharing it. I wanted to keep it just for me. But then the police shared it with reporters to help with the investigation. I showed it to Pastor and asked him to pray. I think Fabian's grandmother was praying."

"Wowsy. You *nevah* pray."

"So yeah. That's why I asked him."

"Two years," murmured Jayrai, staring off. "How can that be?" The last was said in a whisper. She had counted only a few hours spent in 1900 CE. How can that amount to two years? Plus, we all thought only a few minutes —or even *no* time at all would've passed…? She looked for the others, for "2017." Under a wide window in the rear, someone was retching, Gretchen, messy, golden, was moving through tables to help, probably take her (the retcher) somewhere.

Suddenly —a new eruption in the Gospel Mission. Police came through the glass and wood-framed door—plainclothes—the man and woman who were working on the case. And there were a couple uniforms with them, both men. They went to the counter where Pastor was serving.

Then the heavy door opened again and some journalists stood there. A couple recognizable Akropolis video-bloggers were with them, looking about, aiming their devices. Most had never been to the revival house soup kitchen.

Now Pastor Zettler was waving 2017, by the window, to come to him. He looked at Jayrai and Quadri, at Quadrangi, still seated, and signaled them likewise. The packed room became quiet. Hardly a clink of tableware, hardly a cough to be heard. "As you can see, brothers and sisters," said Pastor, raising his sure tenor voice. "The police are here. They've gotten word about the return of our friends and wish to talk with them. Some of you are better equipped than I to summon their parents—." Here came nervous laughter owing to the old joke about Pastor's continued reliance on landlines and snail mail. He was weird like that, most here knew, and was even active in seeing that maintenance of old ways continued, despite local joking, sarcasm and criticism.

"The supper is over. We are out of soup. But you may remain if you will for the service. HOWEVER," here Pastor Zettler raised his voice. "We will NOT be hearing the story of our friends' disappearance. I'd almost say the criminal investigation will be suspended—though I'm not authorized to do so. It's just a surmise on my part. The service is about to begin. You may stay for it if you like, but our friends are going into the kitchen to meet privately with these good investigators."

"Oh sht," said HB to 2017 by the window. They had not moved. "Quick! What's to say? What say?"

"Pastor wants us," said Pomala. We've got to go."

"She's right," said Fabian. We've got to tell the truth. It doesn't matter if they don't believe us. If they want the truth—that's it." He started along the windows toward the doorway where reporters and bloggers stood talking into their devices and aiming for images. The journalists, especially, began pelting them with questions, but 2017, filing past toward the counter made no answer. They did not smile, but looked solemnly at Pastor and the police. Some people were leaving the mission, respectfully silent; others chattering, grumbling, or foulmouthed slamming chairs. The police officers looked hardest at these individuals and the media captured some of the exhibition for newscasts, podcasts, vids and streaming. Respectful departure did not seem to receive media attention. Others, remaining, began singing hymns, softly. One of the journalists, Sheree Kim by name, focused on this aspect and spoke into her device.

Investigator Lt. Horace Hunch, a tall Afrikan-Americle, handsomely turned out in stylish suit and dark fedora, looked the gang in the eyes, each in turn as they passed. In a deep rich straightforward voice, he said, "You will not be questioned until your parents or other adults arrive. Please summon them if you have not done so."

Sergeant Benja Bench was making notes in the Akropolis Police official device on the counter, as each member, including Quadrangi, filed past toward the kitchen. One of the uniforms was video-capturing. Evidently the families were now on their way or were here, as in the case of Fabian, Quadri, and HB. HB said that Pastor Zettler would do as well for him as anyone. He had his reasons for this.

"You are Blake Griffin?" Lt. Hunch was asking, as they all stood in the kitchen around two islands, for cooking and food preparation. Those who had been doing the cooking had hastily cleaned up but would be back after the service. One of these, Gretch, was leading the service in pastor's stead. Gretch was a house parent at Sheltering Cares, who sometimes brought her charges here to "keep them morally real," as she put it. Blake Griffin had lived with them from time to time. He was with them before his disappearance.

"Call me like HB, if you want," said HB. "HBBBAH, *His Big Black Brother Arcturus Hipster*. That's my handle, y'unnerstan'."

"He's a gamer," said Pomala, smiling apologetically at the Lieutenant.

The officers looked at her. They could not help it. She looked a bit like a standing blue flame. Her natural albino non-coloring gave her full-body blue tattooing a slight shimmer of opalescence, and her white hair, also blue-dyed, gave up a similar faint, very faint, glow. Standing behind her the golden Glindora—Pome's sister (in business attire)—smiled. So much leeway had been given this girl by their parents. Sometimes she wondered if they stretched it too far. Did they have any idea how these tattoos would look as Pome aged?

Sergeant Bench was inquiring. She looked briefly at the Lieutenant then said to Pomala, "That's a curious hairdo. It must get a lot of wear and tear. How do you keep it up like that?"

Pomala ripped open the pocket of her pale blue-gleaming cargo pants and pulled out a plastic bottle of blue gunk darker in shade than her tattooed skin. "This keeps it like up all day," she said. "That's where the color comes from, a good touchup, too." She shook the slim bottle, smiling at Sgt. Bench.

The Sergeant was not stylish in appearance. She wore cords and a blazer. As an investigator Sgt. Benja Bench dressed according to the situation, especially when undercover, as sometimes happened. It might be handy to know something about this 'do. But, looking at the bottle Pome had handed her, she said, "It stays up all day? Shouldn't it have run out after two years—or is this a fresh supply?"

Pome looked at the other 2017ers. "So..." she started. Then she stopped. Hymn singing seeped through from the dining room: *Glory Glory Glory I saw the light.*

Lt. Hunch said, "Let's get down to business. He looked first at Jayrai's mother, Nandora, with her round brown eyes, sleek hazel pageboy and slight frown. She had a jewel on her cheek. Perplexed as any parent would be, she wanted desperately to talk with her daughter before all this took place. Then Hunch addressed Jay. "Looks like we've held an innocent man. Where have you been for two years? I'm not asking you to tell me about the others just yet. Where have *you* been?"

Promptly Jay replied. "Gliese 581d."

"How's that spelled?" Sergeant Bench was asking.

"Not sure. It takes a long time to get there and back which like accounts for the time lapse, but actually we were gone like almost no time because that's how stardrives work. Tu?"

Jayrai turned to Tu—who knew everything, or, Jay thought, anything relevant to physics, astrophysics, and faster-than-light; she usually lumped them all together.

Tu looked at her—blankly. Faintly, they heard Gretch's gospel message coming through from the dining room.

Sergeant Bench had been looking carefully at Jay's biomechanical electronic—bionic, for short—arm. She glanced quickly at Tu and tapped something into the device set next to the stove burner. There were six gas burners in a row on the cooking island. The island was still greasy because of the crew's fast exit. Bench had laid down a dish towel to keep her device clean. These kids were so fascinating. She had to restrain herself from taking all kinds of images with her Andreeend Babblet. The officer would be capturing everything they needed to check against the two-year-old group image for comparison when they got done. In a cursory view, they looked the same as that image the Akropolis Police kept coming back to over these past two years.

"Also," said Jay, "on Gliese 581d they didn't like believe we were from Earth. I don't think they believed in Earth, yo?"

"Yes," said Lt. Hunch. He noted the horrified, then exasperated, facial expression of the girl's mother—peripherally—before turning his look on Tu.

"What is this, young man? Some kind of joke, but what kind?" He looked then at the only other Osiian-Americle in the kitchen. Tu's father was also looking blankly, but at the Lieutenant. Mr. Yu looked an older version of his son. They both had the black bang above horizontal symmetrical facial features—eyebrows, eyes, delicate nose, straight slim lips. His black bang had fallen down; usually it was combed back. Mr. Yu wore glasses and a suit. As Hunch recalled, he was manager of the drycleaners up Sharon Rd.

Tu had been telling the kids about this newly discovered planet on the way to school this morning (November 3, 2017). His father had sent him the link. He said, "Gliese 581d is believed to be a possibly extra solar satellite of the star Gliese 581. The third discovered, they think maybe the fifth in order from the star, if it's a six planet sun-system. Believed also to be more massive than the earth, but possibly with surface water similar to ours. It may be inhabitable." Tu was comforted by the info dumping he had such an affinity for, and launched a protracted description of the planet's newly discerned characteristics, including that its eccentric orbit was unconfirmed, and one model suggested circularity, but possibly with orbital spin of 2:1, double rotation every orbit. One day could be as long as 68 days on earth.

The Lieutenant kept his special look on Tu.

"Tu." Pastor intervened before this could try the Lieutenant's patience any further. Bench was not capturing this dump with her data, but just looked at Tu, incredulous, shaking her head.

"The truth, people, the truth," said Pastor Zettler.

The Lieutenant kept his gaze on them. The members of 2017 stood around the cooking island looking at one another, HB shrugging, Quadri holding Pomala's hand. Their relatives were behind them, but standing back a bit. The uniformed officers stood next the food prep island, between it and the oven. One was visually recording with his device. Pots and pans hung above the island but most were now piled in sinks on the kitchen's periphery, a residue of soup drying, and smelling.

Fabian took a breath. He said, "We've been to FivePoints, 1900 CE." He stopped, seeing the look. The look of Lt. Hunch. "Akropolis. Akropolis 1900 CE. I think they called it A.D." He looked back at his grandmother.

"So," said Jay, glancing sidelong at the Pastor, "no time passes when you're in like stardrive, yo... traveling past the speed of light from Gliese 581d. We stayed the same because Time's a slow boat to nowhere."

Nandora trembled impatiently behind her. She was a proud, more exquisite and sophisticated, version of her daughter. That daughter who always insisted on coming down here to be with the mixed classes, lesser in spirit and wealth. One did not give up one's religion, one's cultural heritage, on becoming an Americle! Her daughter wanted to be a barista! Jayrai needed that elegant arm after the accident. It was not a donated trial but the gift of Newfish and the gods… paid for by her uncle. She should stay with her kind—above in Sharon among the highborn.

Jayrai's talk was confusing to some of the gathered relatives, but Zettler, standing behind HB, smiled in spite of himself. He looked across at Fabian, considering. He barely noticed the boy's tattooing, earring, buzz-cut with long blond dog-ears hanging either side of his face. The Pastor was after the eyes. Then he looked past at Fabian's grandmother, small, beyond Fabian's shoulder.

Pastor was aware of Candace Parker's heroic qualities. Both inside and out she seemed as fragile as a very thin globe of glass with fine interior filaments, not too unlike the incandescent transparent bulbs, designed by Edison but now rarely in use. Of his own generation, she was seemingly without Zettler's toughness and strength. She looked bewildered—and anxious, as he had expected. Her ordinary mode now was nervousness, anxiety, but with a continual surprising endurance and sense of stewardship, despite fear. Candace just kept going when others might have stopped.

Fabian, too, was aware of all this as though for the first time. She had changed as he was maturing. But hitherto Fabian had borne the change lightly. His look now, turned again on her, was itself anxious. He turned back to the Pastor, then to the Lieutenant. His grandmother stepped close, and said in his ear, "I trust you."

Then Fabian said, "It's true. We've all been in 1900 CE. FivePoints. Ask us anything. The soup counter in the front was a bar in a pool hall. A building over there across the street was the new grammar school, I think they called it. A mural of industrial Akropolis was being painted inside. When they tore it down a couple years ago it had a mural of Native-Americles." He gestured past the closed kitchen door in the direction of the CossycSystems building across Sharon Road.

Encouraged, Pomala pointed to Quadri's shoe. As she explained, others stretched or bent forward to see it. "That's horse doo. We did try to keep him out of it, and once washed his shoes in the pump. Raise your foot, Quad. Let them see and smell. …But maybe it'll be gone when we get back to 2017?" Pome was inexplicably hopeful they would get back to 2017.

Quad put his sneaker on the stainless steel leg of the island, as high as he could reach. His big brother leaned forward to look and sniff.

"Smells like." Quadrangi said it a bit doubtfully, his handsome olive brown face screwing in disgust. He shook his head. "No doubt it *is* sht."

"Tu?" said Pomala.

Tu, of course, was blank. But this time his blankness came, oddly, from embarrassment. He could not bring himself to testify about all the possibilities teeming in his brain—all the whys and wherefores jostling for his attention.

His father behind looked blankly at the top of Tu's head, wishing he could penetrate to the interior and establish... findings... degrees of.... Everyone looked blankly at Tu, waiting.

"Uh."

HB shook his head. "Uh?"

2017 laughed. A giant eruption, snorting, knocking against one another, doubling over. Prolonged grinning, wiping their eyes. Maybe not exactly the neighborhood they left earlier in the day, but here was some relief to be had. Quad didn't get why they were laughing but laughed for joy anyway. Quadrangi got it, smiling. Zettler kind of got it, but everyone else looked on, puzzled.

"So we better go back to Gliese 581d, girls!" Jay raised her arm, wriggling fingers, exultant. She looked at Lt. Hunch and almost raised an eyebrow, but, on seeing the look, thought better of it.

"Okay —*girls*," said Sgt. Bench. "First, how's that sht—whether horse or not...." She squatted, looking at it, caught the whiff, stood, and said, "Yes. It's got bits of hay or fodder or whatever... but... that could come from farm country back of Sharon. Girls." She waved in the direction of built up shops and malls westward, well past FivePoints, where barns stood full of the harvest southwest of Akropolis. She looked at the Lieutenant, then went on. "Anyone can look up the history of this town, its architecture—pictures of old days, the lot," she said.

Then —silence in the kitchen. A faucet dripped into the cluttered sink.

"I've probably got the proof you need."

They all looked at HB. The tall black kid with taller-making broom-cut, its shaved sides. That sleek black textilite jumpsuit. Not a bad-looking kid.

"Right here," he said, tapping his head beneath the outrageous 'do.

"OMG!!" Pomala squeaked.

"OMN!!" Jayrai sang.

Fabian smiled. He was so relieved. He turned to Nana, smiling. She smiled back.

Tu said, "Genius," very subdued.

The Documents in the Case

SBC News:

"TRYING TO COME UP WITH WAYS TO HELP, THE PRESIDENT PLANS INVESTIGATING AND INVESTING.

"Denying responsibility for policies contributing to what he calls, 'a disgusting, rat-and-rodent infested mess of very dangerous and filthy cities in the Untied States Of Americle.' He says he is 'ready to help fix this.' "

"DON'T BELIEVE EVERYTHING YOU SEE IN VIDEO."

"Famous author of dystopian fiction, George Orville is cautioning the USA on its use of 'Fake Keeps.' Saying that Fake Keeps are denying our nation its truthfulness, Orville also calls attention to the fact (as he calls it), that people are beginning to call black people white, and white people black. Califlower People have also begun to express tech corporations' imposed algorithmic designations requiring everyone in the State of Califlower to call men women and women men whether they identify with these designations or not. Califlower people, he warns, are now required to call people *person* and they *it*. SBC News is currently mooting such changes to incorporate these policies in its reportage: the consensus here is that Orville himself is a Fake Keep."

Sitting in their office, the FivePoints lieutenant said, "Probably some unreality TV… put on by one of those bloggers. You don't spend two years of your life doing it, but there is the temptation afterward to fake and capitalize on something like this."

"So… the APD is being had? Put on?"

"I don't think that will happen." Lt. Horace Hunch did not bother looking up from his report on the screen.

The sprawling FivePoints precinct station was in a newer building—same spot as the 1900 station—beige brick, and not multistory. A low building, on Exchange St., squat on two lots where the other had been tall and narrow with stables in the back for entrance or exit onto Third St.. Now sQuad cars exited from the parking lot on 3rd, but there was the sQuad car entrance on Exchange also. Downhill of the station, FivePoints actually had six streets coming into it, if you counted the alley intersecting at an angle with 3rd behind the soup kitchen.

Lt. Hunch and Sgt. Bench were talking it over, waiting for the full report from CossycSystems. Blake Griffin would be at Cossyc ... at least overnight. Now these FivePoints investigators were going over everything, examining the images in overhead fluorescent but subdued light also reflecting from darkened windows. The first image was received of Jay's friend Trice two years ago; and here was the new one, with video. Quite the puzzle. Analytics was giving it a thorough run-through. It might be—. They had to assume it *was* a hoax. Particularly they thought the second images and video were hoaxing.

Hunch said, "We might put in for some of that new FakeDeep Analytics, but maybe not. Expensive. And the woman who submitted the vids—nothing suspicious there."

His fedora on a shelf by the entrance with Benja Bench's bag, Horace Hunch's jacket draped the back of his chair. Their shoulder holsters and guns were there. A low hum came from a large room with its own individual cuboids. The smell of pizza drifted through. Their own office looked across the parking lot, diagonal to the garage beneath its solar array, where one or two cars were charging in the pinkish glow of a sodium vapor light. The detectives had now gone over testimony inventory gathered on the first disappearance two years ago, along with what they got tonight from the kids and those same friends and relatives.

They went back to the first selfie, and then new videos of these kids sitting on the stone cemetery wall. In the vid this wall was empty—then—suddenly filled with five strange-looking kids, kids that looked exactly like those in the original selfie. But now their jackets were around their waists. The woman who'd sent in this clip, and one other clip of the kids walking toward Sharon and Bechtel, said she'd been capturing the empty stone wall because of its legend—meaning the kids' disappearance from it sometime after the selfie was taken exactly two years ago by the girl with the bionic arm.

"So yeah, if anything is going to make that wall truly legendary, this will." Lt. Hunch said this in complete disbelief of the video. "Whatever the outcome of forensics on these images coupled with the Cossyc reports, we'll suggest parents keep these kids apart until the mystery is solved."

Bench agreed, adding, "They'll hang out online no matter what...."

"Yeah. Still it will be some sort of marker, an encouragement, guidance for the parents. It helps when someone with authority says, etc.."

Sgt. Bench looked over at him, grinning. "We are the law," she said. "Can we get some of that pizza?"

He was nodding, with the look.

She scraped back her chair and stood by the window ordering from the PisaPizza appe. "It's part anchovy, right?"

Now he smiled.

"Wonder what's going on at home right now?" she said on finishing the order. She too looked out at cars coming and going via Third.

"You're not talking the Buster-Benches, I'm assuming."

She turned back. "Right. The 2017 kids—everyone's calling them now. See?" She showed him *flashTag2017* on her Akropolis police encrypted device.

"Who started that," he said. "Before, it was *xxxdisappeared.*"

"It's new. Let's see…." She scrolled back. "Surprise. It's the little boy's brother."

"The Palacestonians? Family from Palacestone?"

Bench confirmed. "The parents are. Came in the eighties, maybe mid-nineties? Nothing explosive. Not a whiff of anything terrible." She was playing with words. "Naturalized. They just want to live. Enough strife, not enough room over there."

Hunch nodded. As a youth he had volunteered at a camp. Kids from Asreal and Palacestone. Asreallys and Palacestonians. Bonds had come from that. Friendships, lasting bonds back in their own hometowns. But it had to be done in this country... away from all that violence and suspicion. "We talked about this before," he said. "Remember the CaShatan camp? In the country. Rural town south of here."

"Yes! It must've been something! Anything different about your being Afrikan-Americle working with them?"

"No. It was something, though. Too bad."

"Did it stop?"

"Like." he said. "It could start up again." He gave her the (barely speculative) look.

"Don't look at me." She stared at him. "I'm 24/7 with kids already; starting to wonder what's going on at the Buster-Bench household...." She looked down at her pad. "We need that pizza!"

The first *flashTag2017* copied to *xxxdisappearedAkropolis*. The messages went paired like that for a while but then *xxxdisappeared* went dead, or, as some put it, disappeared; and all the speculation went to *xxx2017FivePoints*. Quadrangi posted frequently that first evening, but after the initial public claim to the 1900 CE visit, he did not quote his little brother and forbade him to post.

They were in the bedroom. "You can't make me not post," said Quadri, grinning.

"Wanna bet? What do you think that thing between your back and your legs is for?"

"You mean this?" said Quadri, bending over.

Quadrangi obligingly kicked his rear. Little Quad went sprawling into the cat. It sprang up mewling and sprinted out the bedroom door.

"You've got to clean the litter box in the hallway," said Quadrangi. "You haven't done it in two years."

Quad grinned. He was so happy! Tumbling and giggling! Home tonight after a very trying day. Then he stopped. "I'll be playing the game and waiting on the wall across from the library for you to pick me up in 2017."

"What?!" *Not good, not good!*

"Two other things?" Quadri said.

" 'K...."

"Where was our apartment earlier today? And—if I clean the litter box can I post?"

Quadrangi picked up his little brother who'd just been lounging on his elbows, and placed him on the twin bed that the boy claimed to have slept in the night before—not two years ago. Then his brother said, "Get under the covers, and I'll tell you a story about the *Black Ages in StanaTerk*. You can do the litter box tomorrow and we'll talk all about it then."

StanaTerk had always been a hit with little brother. Ghouls, ghosts, vampires, infidels, clerics, and Martians. The infidels chop off people's heads, and the clerics put them back on their shoulders. The Martians are good aliens fighting monsters under the earth. The *Black Ages of StanaTerk* was a game Quadrangi was always writing software for. He'd been working on it since before Quad's disappearance, and had tried everything out orally on his little brother back then. Big brother had kept it up while little brother was *disappeared*, believing it would help the family and himself. Then the quality of the game improved. *Because a fictive Quadri began figuring in the story as one of its heroes.*

When Quad was settled down, head on the pillow, Quadrangi said, "My latest creation is called *Kwad the KonkerEr*. He spelled out the name for the little boy. "The clerics all want Kwad the KonkerEr to grow up and be like them so he can help people be good, and fight the head-chopping infidels. But Kwad wants to align with Martians, thinking clerics aren't mysterious enough. You know what mysterious means, right?"

His answer was prompt. "It means things we can't understand. Like FivePoints 1900 CE. There are houses where this apartment's supposed to be. That's mysterious, right?"

From: HBBBAH@hhhadesthon.net
Subject: incarceration
Date: November 3, 2019 9:48 p.m. EST
To: Fabian

Look at that date, girl! We've got to start the Hadesthon again! Do you realize Pluto is a thing again?! In the game dwarf pluto had to be in sInc with the sun. Or was it vice-versa?

Techs aren't here to do the head download, so shrinks been grilling me like a common criminal.

[Here Fabian imagined the evil satiric grin HB sometimes pasted on his face.]

Just got word the police saying no RL meetings? But nevermind, tomorrow will begin operations of the insane asylum on me. But I won't forget our purpose: 2017. Back to 2017!

[Another imagined evil grin.]

What they are going to find—it's all true! Then **they** will go crazy stead of me being crazy.

It's fun here, tho. You saw me going off with the pastor. He comes back tomorrow. Good thing the service was all broke up and you didn't have to stay for it. It was weird telling all that stuff in the kitchen with hymns coming through. Glory glory glory.

But nothing on the internet. Viral is seriously bad. Tell everyone 2017. Give *no* thing! This be all private e-mails. Fact, don't know how long they'll let me. But. Here's the thing. I DON'T WANT TO E-MAIL either. Cuz they are reading this RIGHT NOW—OK kidding but they will be, the shrinks. WON'T YOU!!?

So basically, this is my first and probably last till I get out. Keep it all in the family, so to speak. You girls are my family now!

Quadrangi is all right tho, and Quad needs him. Look at that! I'm thinking of little Quad. This IS big.

Gotta go get grilled some more.

Love, from 2017,

--HB

[Fabian replied: 'K. Is versa a vice?]

From: Fabianthe60srockstar@hhhadesthon.net
Subject: your guess is good
Date: November 3, 2019 10:00 p.m. EST
To: Pomala

See HB's below. Pass it on. It's just for us. Like he says, Don't share. Only 2017 and Quadrangi. Nana asked me to stay away from you all but I said 'K cept e-mail. Said she wouldn't care but the police suggested it so....

Realize, when he says pluto's a thing, he means it's upgraded to planet again. Note the game changes since 2018. We hope this will not make getting back to 2017 any harder.

Quadrangi said he is for stopping the witter and bunglr and wahzoo and all, so that's good.

It will all work out tomorrow but enjoy the melodrama tonight. No group mailing, either. Just this one-at-a-time. Pass it on.

Fabe

From: Pomeagranite@hhhadesthon.net
Subject: it's just us
Date: November 3, 2019 10:02 p.m. EST
To: (Jay) TheArm@hhhadesthon.net

Please tell Tu via independent e-mail and forward HB's memo (below). See, it's almost like we are under siege except not. Tomorrow will iron it all out and we can figure out how to live here now. How are we going to do that, BTW? Can you believe that date? We've only been gone a few hours! What? Our friends are two grades ahead? Truly bad stuff is going on in their lives -- pimps and porn. Witter says the Prez is a bully so they can be too! He's Big Sister and says chartreuse is pink and it's 2084 and they can say whatever they want, true or not. There's mass shootings with military weapons in restaurants, schools, stores! Opod epidemics, poor kids tracked and watched on free devices from school, kids in cages on the border, moral enforcements, our PresiDent an unreality TV star, the Vice PresiDent a Chrustyun! Old people want to go the prison for better healthcare! --And I was just thanking Tu earlier today?!?

Now he has a new version to work from!!? But how could he help it?? Totally how?

Analyzing HB's reports! Next they'll analyze my blue hair goo.

There's all strangeness in this. What can we do?

--Pomala

PS my sister says we've got to keep apart and I said, e-mail? And she said better not, then *OK*. So here it is. Guess what? Sis says malls are dying! Can you believe? Just a few hours and death to malls! We can't stay here!

From: (Jay) TheArm@hhhadesthon.net
Subject: it's just us
To: Pomeagranite@hhhadesthon.net

calm down, pome. it's not as bad as someone you like being in jail.

(Concerned over Pomala's uncharacteristic tone, Jayrai texted HB and Fabian.)

Jay: pome doesn't sound like pome. What should we do?

HB: Don't start.

Fabian: What's she sound like?

Jay: like me, only with morals.

From: (Jay) TheArm@hhhadesthon.net
Subject: info dump please
Date: November 3, 2019 10:17 p.m. EST
To: (Tu) lighterthanfast@hhhadesthon.net

see stuff below.

WHAT IS GOING ON? pluto's a planet again!?

they actually put up condos where the baptist church was in sharon! and that was like only 6 years old and now it's like *wrinkle wrinkle* here's a showboat.

you've got to stay up all night and work those calculations again! no way we can stay here. my mother was all set to let me barista before we left and now she's dead set *NO!*

[Author's note: Jayrai's mother was never set to let her barista.]

pa-leese! back to 2017! so what if it smelled rather sewerish. it wasn't as bad as 1900 and

creepy everyone else is two years older! tu, did you get mocking e-mail? why is up with that? pome says it's the new normal president. so it's okay to rant and bum. pa-leese!

2017.

i'll take any sorta dump.

--j.

here's HB's:

[Not duplicated here. Author's note. (Frequently indicated with brackets).]

From: (Tu) lighterthanfast@hhhadesthon.net
Subject: encryption
Date: November 3, 2019 10:30 p.m. EST
To: Quadrangi@blackages.com
Cc: Quadrangi@hhhadesthon.net

[Quadrangi had set up hhhadesthon.net for communications between friends, using his thirdhand server. Because of spelling configuration, *hhhadesthon.net* is not in violation of trademark prohibitions.]

First, I already had the info on The Hadesthon.

Second, with regard to the other thing, I got the encryption you mentioned and it's okay but not the best. For one thing, if they used laser or acid on the casing and then used digital probing to read bits and bytes where fused to the hardware to get algorithmic code combinations, sure they might upload to computers and run the millions for pass-coding but it could conceivably erase all auto functioning and then be worthless to them.

OTOH, anything simpler might accidentally trigger destruction with mega-code guessing, memory erasing that could actually give them the unlock segment's memory, making reading or copying untenable.

You see what I mean. And none of this will be necessary after they analyze HB's reports.

I think your own mind will process all this virtually incalculable experience, including processing Quadri's own verbal RL info dump, esp. If he remembers and tells you everything. Pay close attention, but probably it will look different from everyone else's experience. No one's will be exactly the same because that's physics (real life), but we were all in it together. HB's report will speak for itself and everything will be believable to 2019 tomorrow.

I've got lots more to say but thinking is actually better, so I will sign off till much later and just lie here thinking for now.

-- Tu

From: pomeagranite@hhhadesthon.net
Subject: to FivePoints 2017
Date: November 3, 2019 10:45 p.m. EST
To: TheArm@hhhadesthon.net

2019 *is* definitely creepy. Have you seen the latest social media sites? bitter is one. pulpitBully is another. Only bad stuff is allowed. You *have* to be mean. It's mandatory. If you say something nice you are marked and told you have bad manners and don't follow the rules. They say stupid stuff like it was better when the sewers were busted so this city could and should smell like all the stinky stuff that comes out of us. They say porn is good and prudes are bad and should be dressed down. CAN YOU BELIEVE?

I'm with you now. Tu *must* get us back to 2017 so we can stop all this from happening. (Why do you keep talking about a bo?)

Love,

Pome

From: TheArm@hhhadesthon.net
Subject: Re: to FivePoints 2017
Date: November 3, 2019 10:48 p.m. EST
To: pomeagranite@hhhadesthon.net

I'll tell you about bo. But pome!! did you forget the little girl?! so, i remember her. iirc she was autistic and you wanted what? To help? --you almost kept us in the past, meaning 1900 ce, by trying to bring her back with us. am i remembering this wrong? because if i am please set me straight. fabian actually saved us from your making a BIG mistake remember that?

now listen girl no interference no matter what. we've got to leave it all to math, science, meaning tu. IF we're going back, it's got to be him. he's all we got to get us back and when we get there (if we ever do), then we'll see how it all plays out.

i admit it's bad in 2019, but who knows if our absence for two years which was like only about two actual minutes (i'll let tu figure that out) may have pushed everybody over the brink.

look at me i'm a nervous wreck because i don't know how in hecktor i'll be reincarnated in the next life. ok that's a joke, but still.

and yes, we need JOKES so let's work on that. K?

back at you. ♥

From: Fabianthe60srockstar@hhhadesthon.net
Subject: Re: to FivePoints 2017
Date: November 3, 2019 10:50 p.m. EST
To: TheArm@hhhadesthon.net

I agree. Pome should *NOT* be making plans on how to fix the new evil.

What we've got to do is pray like to everybody and I'll pray to God. That seems somehow familiar but I don't particularly remember praying before in 1900 do you?

From: TheArm@hhhadesthon.net
Subject: Re: to FivePoints 2017
Date: November 3, 2019 10:51 p.m. EST

To: Fabianthe60srockstar@hhhadesthon.net

that's you? i can't believe you suggested praying to my gods but ok! that's good enough interference and won't mess with tu. i think we'll be on the safe side with that because we don't want him getting religion. i mean paying attention to his cultural heritage. see, if he sticks to science that doesn't get all mysterious almost like being reawakened or confusioned, and we will also have our eggs in two cartoons instead of just CD COMICS, DUPERMAN, robin and whatnot.

while just letting tu tackle it, one thing i think we'll have to guard against and keep talking to each other about is what happened. we got to keep remembering 1900, horse and buggies, because already i feel it kinda slipping. i don't understand the little girl hand thing and stuff or anything but. know what i mean? it was an actual thing and if we aren't careful we'll get so used to this 2019 that we'll give up getting back to the right time. do you think it's important?

but it's gonna help somehow if people even believe us. that will help keep it firm?

-- j.

From: TheArm@hhhadesthon.net
Subject: to FivePoints 2017
Date: November 3, 2019 10:53 p.m. EST
To: pomeagranite@hhhadesthon.net

remember the muscles on the native americle? was that some kind of guy?! gorge-e-us to his moccasins! he just stood there, watching everything, right? what was he doing there?

Pvt txt from: @pomeagranite
To: @TheArm
He was with the vaudeville, I think

Pvt txt from: @TheArm
To: @pomeagranite
oh yeah! weren't we supposed to be from the show too?

Pvt txt from: @pomeagranite
To: @TheArm
Even the 1900 police thought we were.

Pvt txt from: @TheArm
To: @pomeagranite
Cc @Fabianstar

yeah but actually we were from gliese 581d. ha ha ha. 1900 still thought people could live on the moon without ventilators, suits or anything!

Pvt txt from:: @Fabianstar
To: @TheArm
Not all of them. Besides they were our ancestors (some of them). Well, not yours [Jay] but yours probably thought so, too.

Pvt txt from: @pomeagranite
To: @Fabianstar
That's right yours came from North Regina and mine from Greice.

From: pomeagranite@hhhadesthon.net
Subject: thank you
Date: November 3, 2019 9:00 p.m. EST
To: sis@hhhadesthon.net
[Author's note: This is the private e-mail address Pomala's sister Glindora uses to communicate with her, and occasionally other friends of Pomala's.]

Thank you so much for being the one with the police tonite. I've been trying to help Mom and Dad understand all evening. But they are just so glad that almost nothing else matters right now. The police of course weren't sorry to see someone from the mayor's office. It's handy to have sisters in suits in high places. ¤☺

It's hard to believe, I know. I can't explain it. I told the truth because that's what Pastor wanted. Maybe also because of the Bishop [Sirifim]. OK, because *it's true*. But how can anyone believe it? If it didn't happen to them?

I keep thinking of trying to take the whole neighborhood back to 1900 CE just so they could see it, how very cool it was. And didn't our ancestors come from then? And we are still here partly because it's right and partly because the housing got better with gentrification (uphill) and condos and subsidized and stuff. I mean the mayor's office has a suit in FivePoints. :-)

Love you!

From: TheArm@hhhadesthon.net
Subject: Bo
Date: November 3, 2019 9:00 p.m. EST
To: pomeagranite@hhhadesthon.net, Trice@hhhadesthon.net
i have to battle mom over bo passive-aggressive, but i'm not giving in. no matter what. i will meet him in his neighborhood somewhere when i get the chance. but so far he has not sent. i can't believe she got him jailed! how is that possible? i mean laws, judges, smartfones, smartpolice??

JUSTICE. think about it. six people missing and somehow he's implicated? so bo and i did go missing that once -- you don't know -- but they did (mom and uncle) and and SO WHAT?! six people! with the selfie to prove it! i didn't know his record, but makes NO DIFF. i cd hurt him anytime i want with this ARM.

Pvt txt from: @TheArm
To: @Beauroogard
so. well. you there or not? free now. so.

[Partial record of private communication between Glindora and Pastor Zettler. For diary entries, mostly on the subject of her sister Pomala's disappearance and reappearance, this conversation was recorded on Glindora's IntellectuaLphone and voice-recognition digitized as text, along with corrections and punctuations,. The Pastor was speaking over his landline phone the evening of November 3, 2019.]

Pastor: The people here need my help with the basics. That's the mission, what I work on. They're not affluent enough to identify with anything but food. Shelter, a safe place to sleep. We're trying to clothe them. You know this.

Glindora: …So, yee-es.

Pastor: I don't think I have anything personal against what kids call transganderism. I don't much care for isms, even my own—Aviangelicalism. I want to make friends where I can. But I don't want to encourage personal confusion, and have to think of the *whole* Mission, not just what bathrooms the PresiDent wants. I've got others to consider. And One in particular. I need to respect everyone absolutely.

Glindora: You're saying God— or people?

Pastor: To both, yes. And to the family.

Glindora: So think about it anyway? Don't be daunted!"

"Me? No. Well, maybe. Distracted maybe. The culture is.

Glindora: And thank you so much for taking up this other problem, Pastor. Pome's problem, and that of 2017 kids. So glad of these conversations ongoing since the disappearance [...].

Pastor: [...] I'm hopeful we'll get to the bottom of it. I mean, you will. The police, maybe. The press, I hope not. [There is no digitized record of the smile in his voice.] But it doesn't matter if I don't understand it, or the city doesn't, or even the neighborhood. If you all, meaning the kids and their grown-ups, can understand, find out -- that's the important thing. It must be understood. One thing that troubles me -- the year 2017 itself. Have you noticed they seem to expect to go back to 2017? What can that mean?

Glindora: Don't you think the CossycSystems report might shed enormous light on this? After all, we've seen incredible results with this implemented technology before now. I've been watching the Post's journalistic features on this, and the accuracy is amazing. They followed one of the elderly recipients around and reports he was able to download on his condition as an elder -- and it was confirmed by Cossyc as accurately detailed.

Pastor: I admit to being curious. I don't say that's a good thing. We'll have to wait and see. You know I was never in favor of the experimentations and hated to see it happen to Blake. He really is one of the best kids I know, but even if he weren't I would not want it for him. Or anybody.... But I'll get out of the pulpit now. It already *is*. Of course that won't stop me from trying to make it *not* in the future.

Glindora: well, you're good in the pulpit... but I guess I'd better not say that right? [The smile in her voice was not digitized.] Again, thank you for taking this up.

Pastor: They just came right into the soup kitchen. It all just happened. I shouldn't be surprised, not with my beliefs and all the things I've seen happen over the years --

Glindora: and been involved with!

Pastor: -- but it was a thrilling moment, and one we can be amazingly grateful for. Candace Parker was. But she was also half expecting it. That is -- I should say -- she was hoping they'd to be safely returned -- whatever the cause was. Gretchen has told me -- she's a house parent at Sheltering Cares, if you recall -- she's told me her kids have been praying for the safe return. That's a long time for kids to keep praying -- two years. [...]

From: pomeagranite@hhhadesthon.net
Subject: Bo
Date: November 3, 2019 9:00 p.m. EST
To: TheArm@hhhadesthon.net

I know you don't want me to say this but you know how I am. I care about you, Jay. I don't want The Bad for you. So here goes:

I'm kinda with your Mom and uncle on this. I mean it's not good what happened to Bo but I mean it's not good either for you -- hanging out with him.

Pvt txt from: @TheArm
to: @pomeagranite
busy busy busy busybody!

Pvt txt from: @pomeagranite
To: @TheArm
Of course. I'm me aren't I?

Pvt txt from: @HBBBAH
To: @Fabianstar
Guess what? They's so invested in this case the techs are called in to upload my downloads tonite. Think I'll sideload em for kix.
(I'm not forgetting our quest for 2017. Give Tu some nudge.)

[Excerpt from] **Summary Report for the police**, 2017 Disappearance, November 4, 2019.

By Dr. A'bram Van Helsing, Ph.D. [Author's note: Dr. Van Helsing has doctorates in mathematics, science, applied science, software engineering, psychology, psychiatry; having also D. Lit, D.M.A., D.S.Sc., D.B.A., D.I.S., A.P.R.N., R.N.. Dr. Van Helsing's technology (implicitly) is on trial in this case.]

[...] The technical aspects of this case have presented no difficulties, and are routine. The subject, Blake Griffin, was under our technological/ psychological oversight until his disappearance two years ago on November 3, 2017. He knew what to expect in the way of procedures; or to put it in his colloquialism, he "knew the drill." Briefly then: Blake Griffin projected his report, of what he determined (in my paraphrase) comprised the last several hours (meaning 11-3-2017, onto the receiving wall where it was simultaneously uploaded to data collection. This is a conglomeration of various types including, but not limited to, video, audio, biometrics, geographical (including mapping), diagrammatic; and other sensory data, such as tastes, smells, and unusual noises, all of which have been translated to digital code, where it was cross-reconfigured for our interpretation.

[...]

A brief summary of his experience shows it beginning on the Glimmerdale Cemetery wall in sounds of a jet streaking overhead, possibly from Pittsbury whilst he is looking down at his digital device during gameplay of a certain level of (2017 version) *The Hadesthon* (see notes below for its description). Immediately on the tail end of jet engine sounds he hears the clip-clomping of hooves, and thundering ironbound wooden wheels on cobblestone, notes the cessation of wireless. The sewer smell increases in volume. He had not consciously noticed this before, though it is evident in his download report that his olfaction transmitted for neural registration/ interpretation. At that time (2017), Akropolis was undergoing scattered but citywide sewage repairs or preparations for them. This report shows an exponential magnitude of increase a thousand percent parts per billion, corresponding with the state of Akropolis in 1900 CE infrastructure (surmised).

This is the beginning of his experience, in brief. From there he begins to see a definite projection of Akropolis in this earlier time, and this report shows a projection of his companions taking part in it with him, registering their own observations and oral exchange with one another and with him. It records conversations in video, etc., with various citizens of Akropolis 1900 CE. All are collected in aggregate (see report Griffin 1.b., for the list/ analysis.) Blake Griffin had been chosen for the trial 2.6 years ago because he was extremely healthy and level-headed. Also, his genetic material was good and his (since reputed deceased) mother signed off on the trial for a monetary consideration.

This reportage is troubling, as the organic hardware/ software implant *may* be shown deteriorated at best, corrupted at worst. The possibility of time displacement is not ruled out, however. The plan is for a thorough review of this report, coupled with extensive interviews with all participants in this apparently unusual, perhaps mass, projection. (Provided it is not the corruption of Cossyc biosoftware.)

[...] There can be no doubt that CossycSystems will receive all facts, presented with ongoing interpretations, of this mysterious disappearance/ reappearance. Two of its clients (one Blake, the other [**redacted**] have taken part in the disappearance, so it's up to us to derive conclusively what has taken place. Questions to be answered include, do the clients show any signs of physical regression from their current ages, as popularly claimed. Using technical mechanisms/ techniques devised or developed since their disappearance, the full report should not be long in coming; to the satisfaction of all concerned. The interviews, however, will be most extensive. These also will soon-after be data aggregated to yield abundant, detailed, and we hope conclusive results. [...]

The night following the first report, Lt. Horace Hunch and Sgt. Benja Bench reviewed it together in their office overlooking the station parking lot and garage, the aroma of fresh tea and teriyaki drifting in. Now they were analyzing the positions of 2017 kids sitting on the wall as shown in the selfie (claimed) taken the day before yesterday, before (supposedly) they disappeared into 1900 CE.

"CossycSystems' abbreviated report does not mention the Griffin kid's analysis on this point, whether anything changed before the 'move to 1900.' " This was Sgt. Bench's contribution to the conversation. She did not believe in the transition, of course, but was curious about the official analysis, whether it proved (in any way whatsoever) viable.

Lt. Hunch said, "On this video, forensics analyzed frame by frame, looking for editing, distortion of any kind. They were unable to determine, in my book, whether the Glimmerdale video was a hoax."

"That's not what they said though," the other reminded him.

"Finding nothing still means inconclusive. And, after all, a hoax is only a hoax."

Sgt. Bench shrugged, extended the small white container.

"Teriyaki?"

"No thanks. Pizza's better."

Lt. Horace Hunch files his second shift November 4 case-closed report ending in these words: "Subjects are back under the care and authority of their parents or guardians. Pending further findings of CossycSystems, coupled with possible and/or indications of criminal intent or confessions, this case will not be reopened.

Pvt txt from: @TheArm
To: @Beauroogard
nothing on soSH. can't find you. don't be mad, yo?

The Media Gives It a Try

From *The Lamppost*:

EUTHANASIA IS THE LATEST CRAZE. AKROPOLIS ELDERLY JUMP ON BOARD.

"In a very humble gesture, Akropolis seniors at The Akropolis Living History Center have admitted their uselessness in feeding the poor, owing to a lack of flavor and fat, coupled with an annoying toughness, which prevents them from having any appeal to the palettes of the hungry.

SBC News:

"The South Regina House of Representatives has issued a statement regarding their recent vote on abortion. 'We do not want all this protean life to go to waste and cannot, in good conscience, use its protein cells for experimentation. Therefore we are authorizing all aborted fetuses in the state be given to the state's industrial chicken farms for utilization in feeding chickens. These eggs, in turn, will be donated to feed the poor and hungry of our state.' "

The Sheltering Cares housemother was trying her hand. Gretchen's plan for *Sad Magazine* submissions was to appropriate everything because this is what satirists do. Her tribe, she called it:

"The million-dollar lobbyist of the NSSA has vowed to use student protesters for target practice if they follow through with plans to protest at National Sling Slot Association's regional headquarters in Follywood, Califlower, and in Faxfair, South Regina."

Saying they needed more time, CossycSystems changed the plan, so 2017 had to wait another day for their interviews.

When Pomala jumped out of bed, she wanted to touch the high plaster and patterned ceiling. Everything in her gentrified room was just as she'd left it to go to 1900 CE—white French provincial chest of drawers, dresser, framed mirror, all curvy with thin gold scrollwork. Even her wardrobe was white French provincial, full of her crazy clothes. She was neat, her room was neat for Mom and Sis had kept it just so—though everyone said she'd been gone two years! Crazy! Crazy.... But still, they *had* to get back to 2017!

She picked up the phone. Tons of new messages she wasn't going to answer. Sis had kept the service going though it wasn't the slightest use in 1900 CE. Crazy! Pomala had spent an afternoon and evening in 1900 CE and no one was going to tell her different.

"Jay!" She nearly screamed into the 8phone. "Can you believe?!"

"Thought you weren't gonna talk to me like this," said Jay. "Or anyone."

"Oh yeah, that's right! Gotta go! See you on witter!" Pomala pressed *end.*

-- we need new clothes. (Jayrai was messaging.)

-- Right. (Pomala sent back.) -- ours are baggy and ugly. Everything is skinny now. Cargoes must go--except I can't afford it. Not going to ask Sis or Mom. I didn't grow. These things still fit.

-- gotta go eat then go to cossyc. CU there!

-- Maybe. Not sure how's gonna work.

Pomala put the phone on the dresser, went and showered, dried her hair, dressed, then began working on the 'do in front of the dresser mirror with its curvy white and gold frame. She thought her 'do ought to go flat, just drip onto her blue tattooed shoulders (now hidden under her white blouse). It was hard keeping the hair up, and this was bound to be a "business" day. Not going to school; plus having to talk to professionals. She brushed it hard, 100 strokes this way and 100 that. But she was thinking.

Was there a dream?

It wasn't set in the year 2017, she knew that much.

She tried to remember. Were there strange people in it —but where was she in the dream? Was she even in it?

It made no sense. Now it was vanished. She knew she had dreamed something, but what was it?

Pome's hair was down and colorless, her clothes more formal, subdued. Her blond sister was dressed as usual in business attire, rather silvery and with a blue bowtie. As assistant to the Mayor of Akropolis, it was not unusual for Glindora to be stopped for an interview on her way to the car, but today they were walking together down Sharon Road to CossycSystems, and Pomala was the target.

"Was it really an out-of-the-body two years?" asked one teen blogger.

"Where were you really?" said another, faintly accusatory.

People—teenagers, adult reporters—were streaming, witting and pixing and trying not to fall over each other walking backwards downhill on the sidewalk; traffic passing by on the workday morning down Sharon Road.

"Did you see any rubber barons or take part in labor riots?"

"What did people sound like? Did they talk different than today?"

"Where were you guys hiding all this time? Out of state?"

"Did you get to ride in a carriage?"

"Aren't you supposed to be in school?" asked Pomala, though she and Glindora had rehearsed it all—no talking. They just smiled and kept walking, sometimes stepping gently around a more persistent path-blocker.

"Where's the blue flame?!" Someone shouted.

"I left it at home!"

Glindora nudged her and they kept walking.

Tu stared with unconscious sympathy at his father's back as the man opened the door for their exit. So far, the two had had no real conversation about either the scientific or the fantastic nature of the experience. Conversations among the three family members had been subdued, mundane, despite the silent glow in Mrs. Yu's features.

Mr. Yu had spent his savings in Osiia on passage in a cargo containership for himself and pregnant spouse. Tu's mother. He had worked his way up to the managerial spot at the FivePoints DryCleaners. Tu thought his father had counted himself fortunate to be alive along with his wife and one incipient child. The only child they'd been permitted in Osiia. The voyage in the container had almost killed them and they'd been abandoned with others in their container, half-starved and filthy, at the industrial docks in Groverland, thirty five miles to the north of Akropolis. Mr. Yu was a brilliant man who was always busy in his spare time teaching himself everything. His prize son, Tu, was going to have it all through the miracle of hard work. Tu was going to learn and theorize and calculate like no one in the family had ever been permitted to do technologically or academically.

Tu had no concept, but thought that Mr. Yu probably was not considering personal history as they left the apartment and headed for the stairwell. Tu had no idea what was actually in his father's mind at this moment. But Tu himself was taking all this into calculations for the coming confrontation with CossycSystems and their team of analysts. All this familial data and pressure to respond well was not what Tu wanted. He wanted to stay in his room, thinking and working the numbers, theories and formulas, the game configuration. They needed to get back to 2017—and fast. It was up to him. Virtually hug the hardware, glue his eyeballs to it. How can bodies "move" through time. Do they dematerialize? What does dematerialize actually mean? Is it the same as de-configure? Turn into particles, numbers? The same as teleportation but moving from "time" to "time"? Would being able to "watch" it happen change it in some way? Probably. —Really he wanted to understand what had happened *before* talking about it to those professionals. ...For the first time he considered running. Just running anywhere.

Then he looked at his father's back—thin, tidy—firm-framed, wearing a Western-style business suit. Knowing this small frame was hiding... something... not happy.... Yes, not happy that was the phrase. Yu was so relieved to have Tu back, but still. And perhaps his father also wanted to figure it all out, and run the numbers on it.

They entered the stairwell.

"We have nothing to say," said his father as they emerged onto the brick and gravel pathway of the complex.

"I have nothing to say," said Tu to the reporter confronting them.

Already the Big Quad was having to coach Little Quad in tech changes since his disappearance two years ago to ...wherever. "*Hah-laa*!" Quadri shouted into his device. "Which way should we take?"

"Don't use that name, Quadri," said Quadrangi. "It's disrespectful. Use *Massasappa* or something. And don't ask it to be your friend or make decisions for you. Got that?"

"Why?"

"Use your own mind. That's what it's for. Be responsible. I can tell you this responsibly because you're little and I'm older with more experience—and I'm your brother, not algorithms, not artificial, software or metal, but intelligent in the image of Hah-Laa."

The two brothers were coming down 3.33 street, a.k.a. 3rd-and-a-3rd Street, also 3⅓St.. This peculiarity of naming was the developer's way of signaling both humor and getting correct placement in the city catalog of drives, streets, boulevards, alleys, pathways and lanes. Many of the old houses on the hillside—one-through-three blocks over from Sharon Road—had been demolished to make way for subsidized housing: tall concrete apartment buildings with brick façade. The Palacestonian brothers' family had moved in after living briefly in one of the former old houses, itself subdivided into apartments on the spot where there had been a backyard with garden and grapevine they had lovingly tended. That site had housed the *Leg Bone Diner*, circa 1900, on the first-floor. Circa 1900 CE Argus

Griffin had been arrested and falsely accused of rape. After the turn of the 21st-century, Quadrangi had lived there with his parents, but little brother Quadri had always lived in one of the new subsidized apartments with his mother and father and brother. Other siblings were grown and on their own. Other immigrants of various cultures were also living in the 3.3 complex.

One of these was Sebastian Cruz who was walking with his Palacestonian acquaintance downhill toward the FivePoints intersection. He held his z-pod in front of them on a clip-pole. Sebastian was familiarly called Basti in the neighborhood. Now, skipping school, he tried to get the Palacestonians to stop for an interview on their way to the CossycSystems complex. Basti was hoping to blog it this afternoon, at the latest, and just needed a bit more content and a small amount of *Boogalooging* to succeed. This was very big. He may get a shot at the *LampPost's* blog list or even a slot as volunteer feature writer if it was good enough. Then he could work his way into a paying position (he hoped). Now he peppered the brothers with questions.

At first Quadri wanted to say he needed to get back to 2017, but big brother nudged him. Quadri tried to answer questions directed at him, but Quadrangi told him to stop, with a quiet low-key apology to Basti.

"Of course I'm going to report from his angle, Quad," said Basti to Quadrangi. This name—Quad—had always been a neighborhood problem, being habitually confusing among the various parties. Generally the little kids called Quadri Quad, and his big brother Quadrangi (unless they were trying to self-elevate in the unconscious pursuit of esteem). The big kids called the little brother Quadri, and big bro was Quad. Adults stayed out of the morass, in addressing each by his given name.

They kept walking downhill. Wind gusted heavily about them, scattering dry brown leaves escaping up from the cemetery below. Basti's mic picked up these sounds but he would not realize it until later.

"I appreciate the concept," said Quadrangi, "but advise you to give careful consideration. It depends on whether you want to be a blogger exclusively or become a reporter. The *Post* seems particular about keeping their content professional. OTOH, I wouldn't want you bending over backwards to go the other direction where Quadri is concerned."

"Why not?" asked the little boy, unsure exactly what this meant.

"Because I care about you, eDweebe. You've been through enough."

Quadrangi was uncertain exactly what his little brother had been through but that was not his call. Although he might have to come to his own conclusion at some point, he postponed it as long as he could. The only concrete facts: he'd been gone two years, looked the same, and was full of outrageous talk and questions. Maybe Cossyc could do tests on everybody involved and see for sure if their bodies had aged. Everybody looked freakishly young and entirely normal, at the same time. Quadrangi's memory seemingly had no way of schematizing the data as Tu had suggested. In fact, he wanted to *stop* thinking about it.

At Candace Parker's request, Pastor had accompanied her and the teenager. As he crossed the intersection with Pastor Zettler and his grandmother, Fabian looked much as he did the day before yesterday in 1900 CE. Like the girls, he had worn cargo pants with pockets for his digital device, sunglasses and wallet, and had worn his jacket. (Unlike HB who wore black jumpsuit, and Quadri who had worn jeans, jacket and T.) In 1900 Fabian had played kick-the-can at night—near this very intersection with one of his North Regina (what he might have called) hillbilly kinfolk. He had not known this relational and salty fact. There had been horse muck, huge sewage smell, and rubber factory fumes smelling like rotten eggs because, as the 1900 kids had said, the wind was wrong that day. August! On the first night home he had spent his 2019 bedtime messaging 2017 and telling his grandmother all about it. Wrinkly and twinkly, she had just looked at him through her wire-rims, smiling and listening, so very glad to hear it all. Everything. She had even asked him questions.

Not like the questions he was getting just now before the signal changed for their walk across Sharon Road at the intersection. Ignorant questions like, "What does horse poop smell like?" And, "What kind of deodorant did they use?" "What did it say on that can you kicked? Didn't they just have glass bottles back then?" And, "Who was PresiDent then—John P. Kennedy? Where were you when he was shot?"

On and on these questions.

He yelled back (because HB was for eliminating the use of the word "guys,". "It's past time for school, girls!" But smiling. Always smiling. Fabian was having a good time.

Pastor Zettler, whose own grandparents had crossed this same (but vastly different) neighborhood intersection, just charged along as fast as he could manage with Candace on his arm, while Fabian turned back and forth, jiving with these kids and one friendly reporter. Sheree Kim of the *Akropolis LampPost* was asking, "Someone said this was where the pool hall was. An Irishman owned a pool hall on this intersection didn't he? Where the SoupMission is now?"

"I don't know about an Irishman! The bartender was Afrikan-Americle. HB thought maybe he'd been a slave!"

"OMG!!" Some of the kids squeaked. The three black kids with them were suddenly silent.

"You mean as a kid?" asked Sheree Kim, an Osiian-Americle. "He was a slave as a child?"

"Coulda been," said Fabian. He looked curiously at Sheree Kim. Something familiar?—but not.

Pushing into his right side, Fabian's favorite bully issued a challenge. Billy H., he noticed, had gotten even more bullish over the past two years. Briefly he wondered if it was because Fabian himself had gotten smaller in comparison?

"—Where were you really, liar?!"

"Gliese 581d," said Fabe.

Someone asked, "People say you want to go back to 2017? Why is that?"

"Were there video games in the pool hall?" said one girl hurriedly. "I hear there used to be big machines for gamers." This was from Shiley, the first black girl to recover herself. She was grinning like she knew something, looking sidelong at the bullish. She stepped away fast as he tried to trip her.

"No, but they had pinball. Evah hear of that? The big thing was pool tables. Amazing play there. Balls ricocheted every which way—like kids scattering when the can was kicked out here on Sharon Rd.."

They came now to the side door of the main building on CossycSystems' campus. It was covered by one of the uniformed digital-badge-wearing greeters, who looked down at his device when told who they were. He frowned at the other kids who would not go away. The pastor knew the man and other working class staff only. All were expected but went pleasantly through the formality of announcing their purpose and appointment. All would have to fill out forms, all parties not already in The System (as it was sometimes called). Many underprivileged kids in the neighborhood schools had been genetically tested through a benevolent grant from the system.

Jayrai shouted as she emerged from her uncle's sleek dark car in the side driveway by this entrance. "Girls!" The driver got out to open the back door for Nandora, Jay's mother.

Everyone had arrived for the group interview. This was to be followed by individual interviews with family representatives present, and these, in turn, would finish off with separate interviews. Finally there would follow in late afternoon a group interview again—without family this time—more or less as a formality. However, information might be forthcoming even from this roundup.

Pomala, wearing her hand-me-down retooled business suit, was in the foyer peeking out from behind the greeter. "Jay!" She said as her friend came up. "I can't believe! You're already wearing the skinny!"

CossycSystems Gives It a Try

The PresiDent Witts on his role as Entertainer-in-Chief: "I'm much more attractive then Littler ever was with his fancy-dance mustache and bright red Kaustica. You won't see me turning a cross on its side, either."

From the *GleeClub WebBlocking*: Atheists believe there is no God.

From OX News: "We oliveatists have to provide the pylon social platform in order to avoid frittering precious tech resources and time on social issues. Class disparity, workers and jobs, are beyond our purview." So said one underling top official. Top officials of top tech entities met last weekend at a top resort (unnamed for reasons of top security) to play golf and form a unified consensus regarding their very fine corporations.

After filling out digital forms in the lobby, the group walked labyrinthine corridors past experimentation rooms with interesting projects ongoing. One of these was wide open—at a corridor with corner tables where workers tried virtual imaging hardware. Eyes and foreheads were covered in dark opaque insect-like gear without antennae. Rapid conversations pursued around the large room. Another spacious room, closed but visible via a giant digital monitor as they passed, showed itself virtually empty of real people. Headless robotic arms moved about, doing tasks. A disembodied recorded voice explained as they passed by that these were the brainchild robotics of Dr. Sadzman Dazel, which were able to stitch live animal organs. Several doctors oversaw the process from a glass gallery above, watching screens with the option of looking below on live operations. Some of this tissue was that of embryonic unnamed animals.

Pomala shivered as she went past. Grown-ups doing things that aren't right... *and when she got to be PresiDent*.... But... she went back to wondering over the first room they had passed. Never had she seen such headgear before—and yet, ignorant of its hidden operations, she was struck by how familiar it seemed. If she got a chance she must ask someone here about it. *It all seems so very near, and yet strangely as distant as some galaxy far far away*. She said something to sis and Jayrai who walked the corridor with her on either side. Jay's intentional mother was already in the seminar room, awaiting them.

"It was in the *Lamppost* several months ago, I believe," said Glindora. "The headsets can be used in game playing, or for certain kinds of training, both military and flight; and other kinds of training, I think. Even football coaches are using them now. This, after a struggle with the old guard who didn't even want algorithmic decisions in the draft, or micro instant replay of plays on the field."

"Jay?" Pomala turned to her friend with the beautiful EastA'ndian features and bionic arm. "These weren't here in Americle 2017, were they? But there's an awful lot of tiny new phones, too. I'd remember I think. Do you?"

"Nah. Nothing I'm aware of. It's fun, but I don't know.... Should we go back to 2017? These are completely unfamiliar, and remember I was here at Cossyc every day for a while. But I don't think they were anywhere in the world except gleaming in some digital software guy's eye. I'd remember, Pome."

"Everyone, please remember that these conversations are being audio-visually recorded to help our analysts, especially with regard to the analysis of Blake Griffin's report."

HB muttered. He happened to be next to Fabian, who sat in front of his grandmother at the oval highly polished table in one of the larger seminar rooms at Cossyc. Pastor Zettler sat behind HB. Legally adult at age 18 (and so a voter and required to register for the draft), Quadrangi was there to represent his father and mother whose Anglish was a second language for them. All accompanying adults sat in comfortable upholstered chairs along windows and walls behind their charges. On one wall at the head of the table was a giant screen. Two analysts in white lab coats stood to either side.

As HB muttered to Fabian, Zettler began thinking of kings' couriers who traveled over the kingdoms delivering messages and decrees. They did not write them but simply delivered the messages.

"I did not report anything," HB said under his breath to Fabian. "My head did all that and I just carried it around like some messenger to this strange new world. And btw, when are we going back? Got to get Tu to tell us."

Going back? Pastor Zettler started at his words.

Light fell into the room from one side along with the flickering of stop-and-go traffic. Tiny plaques below colorful metallic window frames indicated that a donor corporation was benevolent but anonymous. All large windows in the building were a gift from an anonymous, apparently unrelated, tech start-up. This FivePoints Akropolis medical organization was a combination of largess and investment. Its mission was wholly tax-deductible. Science and altruism were among the overall goals, as was profitability. This plan was facilitated by legislation swiftly enshrined and implemented after turn-of-the-millennium. Reportage from the *Akropolis Post, EHio.com,* and *The Groverland Elaborate Dealer* showed—at the moment—that CossycSystems was virtually scandal free. No small feat in the 2019 finger-pointing culture.

His mother initially okayed HB's part in trials. There was a time of testing before this great Sharon Road medical and experimentation would be considered proved in the eyes of the world. The adolescent HB had said, "The world got a lotta eyes. It should be okay." But now the world was waiting, breathless, to find out if he was two years younger than everybody else in this 2019 world—or simply a hoax.

Standing between the giant screen and gleaming oval seminar table, Dr. Van Helsing spoke. His white lab coat was open, showing dark T-shirt, red tie, and jeans. An Afrikan-Americle with receding hair, he eyed them cheerfully. "We will go round the table and ask each of you to respond to this brief sketch." Then he put on his glasses, pressed a button on his device and lit up the screen with brief play from HB's report. Scenes were abbreviated, and Dr. Van Helsing spoke of having each instance—by frame—numerically analyzed, charted and navigable. Afterward the youths sat quietly, amazed, and thinking. Their family members had been sitting forward, hands clenching chair-arms, or fingers locked fast together. They were stunned—even Fabian's grandmother, who had heard it all from him in great detail.

Dr. Van Helsing said, "The participants shown were instructed by police to eschew speaking to one another, and we thought it had been agreed. But you have been speaking to one another, have you not? Maybe not face-to-face or orally, but nonetheless...."

"See, wha'd I tell you?" HB murmured to Fabian. "At least I don't think they broke into your gizmos or etc...."

"Now," continued the doctor, "please begin with HB and go round the table. Is this what you remember, each? Does anyone have caveats... or an outright disagreement? Are there discrepancies? He looked at FivePoints 2017 over the rectangular frames of his glasses, then removed and quietly set them on the table.

"Pretty much," said HB loud enough for the ears of everyone. Except for his words, he had not been in a single scene but... everyone else had. It was all from his point of view. An apparent aberration but maybe not, one special scene had been completely omitted from the report shown on the screen. That needed to be corroborated by the others or it might be evidence against the 1900 CE experience.

Round the table they went, each agreeing in turn with what they'd just seen. There were few caveats from other points of view, and HB's thoughts as reported during the adventure were brought up from time to time by Dr. Van Helsing. Then he said, "Now we go round again, and this time I ask my assistant, Dr. Helda Vansing, to put forward a question or two."

The quiet-spoken Dr. Helda Vansing of north R'opean descent

stepped forward. She had been standing to one side of the screen, watching their faces and making both visuals and notations. Her lab coat was buttoned. She wore stockings and dark blue pumps that Pomala had instantly admired.

Softly she said, "I'd like to know how you all came to be together that day, seated just so on the cemetery wall. Were there any changes prior to or after Jay's selfie was taken in 2017? Remember, this is all to help us understand. CossycSystems is vested in this because it is our software/ hardware on trial here (so to speak). You are not on trial or anything silly and have our best hopes for the outcome of this mystery."

Dr. Van Helsing also smiled and nodded his agreement. The kids look blankly at one another. Sitting the wall *had* seemed a crucial point relative to *The Hadesthon* for their return, but….

HB said, "It was just a day before yesterday, not two years ago, so I remember it like it was yesterday. We just like happened to be there. And, we want to get back."

The others nodded.

"But what does that mean, "happened"?" asked Dr. Vansing. She was ignoring the part about getting back. "Details, please. Details."

"I don't actually know," said Fabian. "Isn't it in the report?"

"Unfortunately HB—that is, Blake—was not tuned in for that part. Apparently this part of the episode was too ordinary to activate his hypo—what we here call—his infra awareness.

Looking at the smallest member, gently Dr. Helda Vansing said, "Quadri, you can call me Dr. Helda if you want." She smiled encouragement. "Why were you all there on the wall at the same time?"

Small and dark in his black T, Quadri sat on his chair, elevated with extra cushioning. Arms extended across the table's surface, his fingers played nervously. His brother reached from behind and stopped the small hands. Fortunately Pomala was sitting next to him. She took one hand in hers and, with an encouraging squeeze, held it under the table as the conversation continued.

"The game like," Quadri said softly. This was the second time he had spoken. Earlier, Dr. Van Helsing had not pressed him beyond his monosyllabic "yes," given in answer to the question about his memory fairly matching that of HB's report. His brother noticed the kids were using the word "like," a lot around the grown-ups. They had done that with the police, too. *Nervous*.

"You came to play a game?" asked Dr. Helda.

Quadri looked at Jayrai.

Jay said, "Hey, right Quad. I was playing (and checking the soSHmedia) and you wanted to play too. We played *Twinkle-in-Time* and watched the other game. *Wars of WorldCraft*. Fine. But," and she looked at

Dr. Vansing. "We just happened to be there at the same time. It's not like we all decided, 'Hey, let's meet after school,' or anything. We were all just there. Right?" She looked around at the others.

Fabian said, "The library was across the street." This was a reference to wifi access.

"What about you, Tu?" said the doctor.

Tu gave her the blank look, then said, "I was reviewing scientific information—on quantum teleportation and what might be involved with that. And we were playing *The Hadesthon*. Fabian, HB, and I. That is, I was keeping my eye on their play."

"Was the teleportation info for school?"

"Er. No."

"So no homework going on at the library after school?" Dr. Vansing smiled. "It all just happened to happen. There was no cultic thing going on with these games?" She looked at them pleasantly. "No secret conversation on soSHmedia, e-mail, anything."

"No daajavooing—no nothing like that," said Jay. She had that serious look she wore when joking.

"Especially not with someone named —whad you say his name was yesterday—Bo," said HB with a smile.

"Nope," said Jay. "No need to bring him into it." She was saying, partly for her mother's benefit—whose tense presence she felt behind her.

Dr. Van Helsing came forward. "Pomala, you were apparently the first to notice the change in your situation. Is that right? You first saw with attention that it was, as you all purport, 1900 CE?"

"That's right. I like tried to get their attention because I thought I was dreaming or going crazy. And I still don't—"

"We still don't unnerstand. Y'unnerstand? Even Tu, who is supposed to like have the goods on all this. Apparently he's as clueless as we are." HB stopped, then said, "But I'm not giving up on what happened. You got it all there, and they agree with me and we ain't sayin' otherwise, even though y'all like crazy for saying it's 2019."

"That's right," said Fabian. "This is supposed to be 2017 but something has snapped."

"Does time make a sound when it snaps?" asked Jay. "Shouldn't it go like ka-boom or something? Or is it like when you're out in space—soundless?"

Behind, her sleek mother, wearing a dark merino woolen suit, looked away at nothing. Nandora's hands were clenched together in her lap. She and sat straight and demur. Jay sensed her on edge, but would not soften. Each of these EastA'ndian-descended was equally hard.

"All right, then," said Dr. Van Helsing cheerfully. I guess that does it for this roundtable session. We will now break up into individual family groups for our next go-round on this phenomenon."

Reminded of the audiovisual recording of these sessions, Tu and Mr. Yu sat alertly in comfortable armchairs in a small windowless seminar room. There were cups of fragrant green tea on the table between them, and delicate floral images asymmetrically arranged on the pale walls. Tu's tea had honey. When not drinking tea, Mr. Yu's hands were folded in his lap. Tu's hands clasped the chair arms just above his knees. Neither showed restive signs of nervous energy, but neither did they sit back and relax, though it was suggested by Dr. Neee that they do so. Dr. Neee was larger than the other two, his features fuller. His expertise lay in understanding of spiritual states. Dr. Neee did not press them in the matter of his suggestion, for that would cause the reverse effect.

After obligatory casual remarks, especially between Mr. Yu and Dr. Neee, the doctor asked Tu about his interest in quantum teleportation. Nothing could have relaxed Tu more. He would not be bringing up his attempts to get the gang back to 2017. There was to be no talk, for the present, about his unexplained time travels. *Unexplained.* The experience itself had been described in the earlier session but its cause was something he had yet to understand. Tu was going to dedicate his life to understanding, but talking about that aspect now was not possible. He seriously doubted that CossycSystems, aided by all its experts and technology, would ever understand. It was going to be a project for Tu alone... but.... Tu glanced at his father. (*There may be some discussion there*. Perhaps even a sharing of information? To this point they'd had no conversation about the nature of the experience. Tu had been busy thinking.)

His father nodded a very slight indication that he should proceed in response to Dr. Neee's question.

"Quantum teleportation involves moving quantum bits also known as qubits." Tu did not wait to see if his interlocutor understood the references. In trying to understand, he benefited much from his own monologues and rarely checked to see if others understood. Also, it did not occur to him that an intelligent Dr. Neee might not follow his brief (as Tu conceived it). And, with few questions, it seemed that he did.

"It is communication exchange between two atoms. That is, exchange is limited to this and can't, so far as we know, occur between molecules. Only information is moved so it's not actual transport though it will move a qubit, or qubits—of info—and not actual matter. No physical particles, in other words. And these can't be duplicated. In other words no copies are made. Their discovery went from single photons, moving in the exchange, to small particles. But keep in mind it's not the *material* but *info*—from atoms, electrons, ions, and even superconducting. The qubit only *encodes*—so it's limited. At least that's how I understand it now. I only downloaded the information the day before yesterday. He said this apologetically, and Mr. Yu nodded his approval even though his son had forgotten for the moment that this was a direct reference not to 2019 but to November 3, 2017.

"Thank you," said Dr. Nee, looking directly at Tu through his serious but prosaic horn-rims. He was not taking notes, nor had he any babblet, or screen or device of any kind. He sat across from them, speaking softly and with short frank questions. "Now, if it's not unpleasant to speak of, tell me what role, if any, you may have played in the episode under our consideration. Some of the others indicate your superior knowledge of events under the rubric of physics and vRPGs. How do you understand your role in the unfolding of the experience? I will be speaking in a moment about other possibilities but this is a point helpful to our studies, please." He went quiet, looking directly at Tu with a pleasant attentive expression.

Tu looked at his father. Mr. Yu nodded slightly.

"I have almost no idea."

"Almost?"

"It was fortunate that the battery on the z-pod went only just after I did my calculations to figure out if we were in the right configuration, right place at the right time—according to *The Hadesthon*."

"On the cemetery wall?"

"Yes, relative to our reality—not as game. There was this glitch happening over and over again. After calculations, winging Baltoid on Persesus29 faulted five times, each time, but then launched the P29 module gimmex.lld, which caused bribell27.xbe to wolf mega-percentages of available CUP sickles—to put it mildly."

"A bit more than *almost*. ...Sounds like an idea," suggested Dr. Neee. "What does it mean?"

"I was applying indicative calculations to functions of *The Hadesthon* in an attempt to locate our place in the continuum, or hoped to relocate us there. You know *The Hadesthon*?"

After an attentive pause, Dr. Neee said, "It is a digital game? A V-role-playing game?"

"Something like that, but without much character-playing. We don't play character roles so much as investigate western EndTime phenomenon. Players are not too concerned with ego-enhancing identities but with finding out what's happening in space-time, starting out in this solar system. The first phase is to investigate thoroughly our own system, and find enough understanding to get us past the last planet. Of course Pluto is not a planet but the fact that he was once considered one after his exciting discovery... and then was downgraded to dwarf or planetesimal is a very telling feature of the game in 2017. By its name—that is, the game's name—you can see that his role is larger than any *Hadesthon* non-gamer would appreciate. What with being on the edges as fair-sized body—or wanderer as the planets were sometimes called, in earlier times. But now in 2019 he's upgraded again to planet. How does that change things? There's lots of, multitudes of bits, in the Oort cloud within and beyond, of course, and our system is locally highly influential, always minutely changing."

"Thank you," said Dr. Neee. "Now you say you have almost no idea, and this is all you have. You have no assurance that this played a part in your mysterious disappearance. Is this correct?"

Tu looked at Mr. Yu. Mr. Yu slightly nodded.

"I don't *see* how it can have. It is beyond me *at this moment*. I tend to see features of the game as analog for our experience, especially with regard to western and scientific history, but beyond that... it is beyond that. It was real. We—some of us—think the reality was influenced by our playing the game. However, few outside might conceive it so."

"Have you ever heard of any others being so influenced by this game? Or had their lives affected fantastically by it in any real way?"

Tu was silent. Then, "No, of course."

"We are Osiians. Why would it interest us to play this western game?"

Tu was silent. Considering. He did not look at his father.

"Because East and West are one in the solar system, one in real science. Plus, all scientists from wherever theorize and search out reality.

"So, East and West are lately met in the solar system?"

"Yes."

"How do you answer the skepticism abroad that you did not go to 1900 CE. That this is an unreality game you are all playing for attention... and eventually a creative contract of some sort? For instance, sales of this game will be magnified in the spreading of this information.... If your thesis becomes known."

"I will answer by saying that it happened. And your tests will prove, or at least give evidence, that we have not aged. I don't know what to think about the economic thing. Maybe it's not so important."

The important thing is for me to figure out how to get back to 2017.

"Thank you," said Dr. Neee, and presented his next question.

Meanwhile, Quadri, Quadrangi and Dr. Vansing were talking together in a virtually identical seminar room next door.

"What was it like in the Leg Bone Diner?" She asked with subdued cheer. Quadri shrugged. It seemed he didn't know how to answer a "what did it feel like," or "what was it like," question. She asked specifically, "What did you eat at the Leg Bone Diner? Anything good?"

Quadri liked Dr. Vansing and was comfortable now that there was no group, just his brother and the good doctor. "Biscuits and gravy. Something crunchy, meat I think," he said. "And soft white stuff in a bowl. He said it was gritty, but it wasn't." Quadri licked his lips. His dark eyes sparkled. "I could eat more," he said.

"Where was the diner?"

Quadri, small in his chair, said after a pause, "I don't know."

"Was it, for instance, on 3rd St.?"

"Maybe." He shrugged his small T-clad shoulders.

"Could it possibly be where the apartments are?"

"That's right," interjected his big brother. Remember you were asking about this after you came back? Maybe you were thinking it was on the block where we used to live. Before you were born."

"Before I was born?"

"Yeah, eDweebe. You were born, remember?"

"No."

"So, I do." Quadrangi grinned. It was a teasing superior grin.

Quadri grinned back.

Dr. Vansing said, "Do you remember what you talked about?"

"When I was born?"

"While you were eating in the diner."

Quadri said, "Tu said there were brains to get through.

"Hunh," said Dr. Vansing. "I wonder what that means?"

"It's like when you say about the particles and lots of space and that's us." He was talking to Quadrangi.

"Oh, branes!" his brother returned. He looked at Dr. Vansing. "He's talking about membranes. The probability of other dimensions particles can visit. Kinda like borderlands or biological osmosis or something. Slipping through membranes. You know?"

Dr. Vansing smiling said, "No. Not really my field, though I'm all ears if you want to talk."

" 'K, you got me," said Quadrangi. "I don't know either."

They smiled together, Quadri looking from one to the other.

"Do you remember anything else about the Leg Bone?" she asked.

"HB said they weren't related."

"You mean to HB the boy—the big boy—who made you food?"

"Yes. So, maybe just a little bit. I can't remember." Then Quadri brightened. "He said he would be able to get born."

"HB?"

"Yes. HB would be able to get born."

"That must have been a relief."

"HB was relieved."

"What was he like? I mean the big Leg Bone Diner boy? Did he do anything besides fix dinner?"

"He said it was supper. He washed dishes in the kitchen, singing Pastor Zettler's song."

"Pastor Zettler?"

"He means one of the hymns they sing at the soup kitchen."

"Which one?" Dr. Vansing knew what he would stay. So far Quadri's memories fairly confirmed the data from Blake Griffin's report.

"Onward Christian warriors," Quad began the song and kept singing a few lines till he could not remember them any more. In fact, there was no great precision in his singing: "... marching off to war. Chris Jsus on the cross going on ahead...." He stopped and looked at her to see if he got it right.

Quadrangi smiled.

"Yes," she said. "That's very good. What else do you remember?"

"We couldn't drink the water. It might be sewage."

"So then?"

"HB asked for beer and he told us to try Paddy's Pool Hall for beer. Pome and I had Akropolis Pop."

"Where was Paddy's Pool Hall?"

"Where the Gospel Mission is."

"On the corner of FivePoints?"

Yes. Across from the school."

"You mean where this campus is? Where we are now?"

"It looked different. There was the big picture with smoke and buildings in it."

"A mural on the wall?"

"A big picture on the wall. HB says we are going back to 2017."

Quadrangi did not want to hear that.

In the next seminar room Glindora listened as Pomala shared her adventures in Akropolis 1900 CE. Some of this had been shared with Pome's sister the past couple nights but this was Sis's opportunity to hear it over, regulated by the examiner. Dr. X, was a woman with white spiky hair and square red-framed classes. Her jowls were evident, powdered and slightly rouged; her face looking squared. She'd glance over her shiny frames at Pomala, then look down at her babblet, then up again with more questions in her soft modulated voice. She focused now on Paddy's Pool Hall and what had happened there.

"Basically I was watching over Quadri. The place was so full of life and activity and there was alcohol of course but no one kept Quad out and we could actually have had beer or ale but we had Akropolis Pop. I was floored to find out we used to make our own soda and cereal and car tires and lots of other stuff right here in Akropolis. Maybe even our own underwear. How was that possible?"

"Maybe you could tell us?" This was a Glindora's interjection.

"I wish I could. There was this kid there who was really good at explaining everything about Akropolis 1900." Pomala took a sip of her Dieet Cooke. "He wore a cute sailor suit with short pants. I think he was the son of one of the magnates who made it happen. I don't think it was a multinational corporation connected to Osiia or anything and he seemed very poised and self-assured like someone from OOga or MooZon—for a kid not much older than Quad. His brother was injured in a riot and he felt somehow responsible."

"Riots were mentioned in HB's report," said the examiner.

"Yeah," said Pomala, smiling at Glindora. "Wonder what the Mayor's office would do if that happened now? I think that was a lynch mob riot or a worker riot—I'm not sure. It may have had something to do or been related to HB's fear that he wouldn't get born. Because of the violence against his ancestor—well he was worried about it, but it turned out all right on that account. We tried to reassure him that of course he'd be born. He was born, so that's that, you know? I was worried on his account but not because of that but because he was so concerned. He was very agitated till he saw the Leg Bone Diner report. He was a bit disturbed later, too, but it was for some other reason."

"What was that?" The examiner was reading her babblet with care.

"I'm not sure actually. It seems like a lot of worrying, about everything, ongoing."

"In the town, with your companions, with yourself?"

"All of that. Especially us. We were sort of detached from the goings-on in 1900. Just, looking at it all, speculating and amazed. Plus Native-Americles."

"Tell me about them."

"They were there. That seems funny. But everyone said they were part of the show. Vaudeville, it was called, maybe. But I don't know. It seems like the one didn't understand our talk. Anglish. The one we saw watching everything seemed very stern. And he was young so that seems strange. He had outrageous weaponry and only a skin for his you-know-what. You'd see his thighs and sides of his butt and almost everything. We thought he was gorgeous—Jay and I. He just stood there, watching everything. Everything."

She smiled at Glindora and said, "The policeman was cute too. I think he was Irish. He had red hair and wore a hat or helmet like an old-time Anglish bobby in Londinium. Dark blue. And had a short thick stick he could conk a criminal or rioter with. You might talk to someone about those uniforms. Ours aren't as cute, Sis."

Glindora smiled.

"Tell me about the little girl," said the examiner, tapping something on the babblet, then swiping. She looked up, then over the shiny red frames.

"She couldn't or wouldn't speak. I thought she was disordered and that we could help her today. I wanted to bring her back with us but everyone was either against it or not thinking about it. We could help her today. ...She was not part of the show, you know. She was a target of violence at one time and needed counseling. Maybe had no parents. Something stopped me trying."

"Now, on the order of your seating arrangement on the wall. And also as to how you were stopped from trying to bring the girl back with you. This is a bit fuzzy...."

Nandora and Jayrai sat in comfortable pale chairs at an angle from one another, a low table with tea things between them.

They had Dr. Boko for their consultation: talking about Jay's experience in 1900 CE in order to benefit CossycSystems technology, software programs, and reputation. He was a rotund Afrikan-Americle man with massive white lab coat unbuttoned over a black woven shirt-front with gleaming round silver-edged collar. He was positive and expectant, talking pleasantly with them on opening the conversation, a regulation Cossyc babblet on his fat knee. He sat across from them, a tea table at his right hand. Reaching across his large front with his left dimpled fat hand he'd grasp the cup, set it on his other knee then back onto the table. He was aware of tension between mother and daughter, and did not refrain teasing it out from time to time, in order to improve Cossyc's understanding of the 1900/2017/2019 situation; trying to get at the truth. The kids seemed obsessed by a hope of going back to 2017!

Later it would be evident whose side he came down on with regard to its reality, but this had nothing to do with his liking for the familial one over the other. It may or may not relate to his findings for The System. That must be balanced, objective, thorough, and as tellingly accurate as possible. Peer review must be without sloth … or fraud—the toughest assessment.

Young, imperious, with a beautiful jewel in her right cheek, Nandora sat poised. Her voice was contralto, blotting harsh edges from her declaration: "She is pulling one of her tricks again." Nandora implied that it was part of Jay's casual rebellious nature and its consequences. "I'm almost sorry we gave her the arm. She has been bolder than ever. If we'd left her without an arm after the accident, she would be more humble and attentive than you see her now. Haughty! Falsely continuing in her make-believe with these friends. You *must not* let them get away with it. CossycSystems must stop indulging this nonsense." Her sleek pageboy hairdo swung its neat curves under her uplifted chin. She gave Dr. Boko a brief round-eyed gaze full of fire and contempt.

He smiled pleasantly, but she had turned swiftly, and did not see. "We'll see what we can do with you, Jayrai," he said cheerfully to the girl.

She almost smiled but scowled at the floor instead. "I don't look older, not gonna lie." She said it under her breath and looked up at him. "Got questions, Doc?" She was not going to bring up getting back to 2017. She wasn't sure she wanted to go back.

"The library was where, when you first looked up from your device?"

"Gone. It was Gustav's musical instruments or something, in an old building. I looked up from surfing OoHaHaPlanet and *pfft*— library gone."

"You took the initiative to go ahead of the group during the initial consternation."

"To show off the blessed bionic arm." The unbelieving Nandora was ironic.

"And HB was behind on the street at that point, I think," said Dr. Boko. The inhabitants of the neighborhood reacted how?"

"I scared all the derves-devils out of them. They kind of backed off, y'know? When they saw the others coming they ran off in all directions like light particles after the BigBang. When they came back I told them where we were from."

Dr. Boko grinned, flashing white teeth and mirth in his dark eyes. "Gliese 581d," he said.

"Yeah." She smiled.

They talked a bit about some other incidents, both at the FivePoints intersection and at the grammar school, site of the current CossycSystems.

"Now, skipping ahead," said Dr. Boko. "There is something of a discrepancy in HB's account. Maybe you can help us iron this out." He looked across to Nandora, speculatively, then back at Jay.

"Did you notice anything special about your pool hall experience. Anything exceptional?"

"Other than men wearing gold watch chains, playing pool and singing off-key? Or racist talking? Or drinking? No."

"Nothing exceptional before, say, going out to play or watch kick-the-can?

Jay thought a moment. "There was a pretty interesting dispute outside on the corner, I think Pome said. That's about it—other than legally I got beer." She glanced at her mother. Who glared at the wall's symmetrically placed pastel pictures.

"HB seems to think otherwise."

He waited.

She sat thinking. Thinking, then slowly shaking her head. "Nope," she said finally. "I got nothing more."

"Now, the order of your seating arrangement on the cemetery wall was changed just before your appearance in 2019."

"Quad wanted to sit between Pome and me."

"And Fabian was on the other side of Pomala."

"Yes. I think that's it, because he squeezed her hand. That I remember. We were all holding hands and he squeezed so hard she yelped."

Five people attended for Fabian's record of 2017's 1900 CE experience: his grandmother, Pastor Zettler, Fabian himself, Drs. Nicole Rostof, and Baron deVill. Here seating was also comfortably arranged, the room larger. Again there was tea, green tea as appropriate for this a.m. session. Nicole Rostof was a very tall pale woman in her thirties, with a sheaf of dark hair pulled taut from her thin glamorous face and trailing down her long back. She sat tall, but not regal or intimidating. Her field of endeavor was paranormal studies and her reputation for exactitude was legendary. For instance, her mind was inflexible on the logistical positivist law that "a man could not exist in two separate places during the same period of time." Dr. Rostof could not be got round by fraud or fun, and was especially careful of the latter because all reports indicated that fraud was unlikely but fun was not.

Dr. deVill's field is the study of immortality. He is the Cossyc colleague who frequently published on the thesis that humans are born with the death drive—first explicated by Dr. Duerf (who cited it as an individual aberration for those who had lost pleasure in living). However, Dr. deVill's thesis is that the death drive is *en mass*, common to all, self-treated with pleasurable pursuits. His techniques are in quest of the common good. *Heroic*, for him, is not hubris, but the verbal emblem of passionate pursuit. On meeting him, one feels his charisma and scientific passion instantly. If one approached without potent credentials, he could be rather cold. He would warm up on learning the professional purpose and identity of his interlocutor. He was engaged in problem-solving. Life was too short to waste time.

Dr. deVill sat at an angle to his colleague, the small table between them, while Fabian, his grandmother, and Pastor Zettler sat opposite, tea table before them like a hub of this seating arrangement. Before long Dr. deVill stood. He walked round the company quietly before standing behind his chair for the remainder of the session. Alternately intently or abstractly gazing, his glance was not always trained on anyone in particular, except when Fabian was speaking. Dr. deVill was curious about Fabian after seeing the video and HB's report. DeVill's presence, always dynamic, remained impossible to ignore. He was hypnotically handsome, fair, with a gaze extremely frank and penetrating, his features lean, hair close-cropped above cheekbones and brows. When speaking informally in company his humor, charisma, and dynamism were potent, but subdued. His public speaking was likewise but commanding.

Dr. Rostof introduced him saying that he was her guest at his request, owing to the special connection he evinced for this field. She knew but did not mention his field. "He may pop in on other sessions with various participants in our ongoing investigations." She did not mention that Fabian's session was of peculiar interest. Later this fact might play an important role, but for now he kept silent on both his field and motive for interest in 1900/ 2017/ 2019.

Pastor Zettler shifted in his comfortable chair and looked over at Fabian, then back to Dr. deVill, who walked around the room, hands in the pockets of his jeans, his white lab coat open and wrinkled at the hips where his thumbs rested with quiet nonchalance. Pastor Zettler had, of course, heard of deVill and read everything he published with great interest; plus any reportage, whether in the *Akropolis L-Post* or the *Groverland Elaborate Dealer*. Both papers carried all news relevant to CossycSystems and its projects, and various news services had largely reported this scientist's doings. He spoke regularly on the globally renowned FRED NatterHour. The pastor had a radio where he listened to national and global news, and even had a ham radio to converse with others on short wave. When younger he listened to both *Radio Cowmosc* and *Voice of Americle*, so he could think better. He did not want to be an ideologue; he wanted to think and so needed all sides of everything going on. Zettler recalled hearing about the first all-news station, XTRA—out of Mexico in 1960, the first 24-hour station. But he had no television, computer, or mobile device. He had seen pictures of Dr. deVill in the papers again and again, but this was the first time he had seen the much regarded scientist in person. As the interview with Fabian progressed he watched deVill speculatively from time to time. Dr. deVill observed Fabian more closely than did the glamorous doctor doing the examination, paying careful attention to Fabian's actual account. ...And to the teenager's grandmother who was subdued and small in the corner of her chair. She did not drink her tea. Nor did other participants drink their tea.

Dr. Rostof, candidly looking at him, said, "I'm particularly interested in the physical qualities of your experience, Fabian. I'm very interested in the willing suspension of disbelief among my colleagues, and among your family members. Physical particulars will facilitate my investigations enormously." She paused.

"So, what would you like to know?" he asked. "I mean, I know it's hard to believe. I'm actually hoping it doesn't get any harder." He gave his buzz-cut a couple quick dusts with his fingers. The sides of his 'do were shoulder length, but the top was short, a strip of fluffy blond buzz down the middle.

"According to our investigations thus far, HB has not aged. It is reported that you all seem much the same as two years ago on your disappearance. All this will need to be tested using Cossyc's scan and metabolic-time-dating, if your grandmother and your companions' guardians agree, but I'd like to ask you a few things in the meantime. Did you notice any physical peculiarities?"

She waited, hesitant to lead Fabian's testimony. When he said nothing, she asked, "An instance might be irregular or unexplained slowing or quickening movements in your observations of others or of animated things? Sensations of reversal—people walking backwards—things moving up when it's normal to move down like water rising when it should fall? Events looping—happening over and over? I realize these questions are piled one on the other, but you will be further interviewed again and we will take more time going over your answers, in detail. Until then does anything stand out? Perhaps an unexpected silence, or a weird sounding. Perhaps unpredicted stasis, something meant to be animated, perhaps, peculiarly standing still. Anything at all that comes to mind." She watched him expectantly.

He brushed his buzz, glanced at Dr. deVill behind his chair watching.

"If it comes out in a rush all piled up, that's good, too," she said.

Finally he answered. "Everything seemed as normal as you'd expect of a workaday world in a different time. Like the early 20th century. I don't recall peculiar sensations or anything. It's really hard to describe the transition because it didn't feel like there was any—in my body, I mean. We were 'there' all the time like normal." He indicated air quotes. "Almost like it would happen in this room right now and we wouldn't feel it. We'd be sitting here like this and then 'stuff' would change and we'd be like, 'how'd that happen?' If you can see what I mean."

He tried again. "Like why is this other stuff here instead of these nice tables and chairs?"

Dr. Rostof nodded, smiling a little. She seemed to like that. "We might call this a transposition," she said.

"I think that's what they call it in vRPG's, too," he said, a bit relieved. "You've got to be able to act but sometimes you're suddenly acting in a different place. But the same place, if that makes sense. Everybody you're with is. It won't be just you."

"Anything else?"

He was quiet. He stopped looking at them, leaning forward, hands clasped between his knees; staring at the carpeting.

"There was something right before the end of 11 p.m.."

"11 p.m.?" She knew what this referred to. It was in HB's report.

"The clock was striking." He looked up. "Yeah, we were almost getting back, or hoping to get back, and something... something...." He stopped on the word.

They waited. He could feel his grandmother thinking, "I trust you."

The expectation in the room, however, was too intense. Too conscious. Finally he shook his head. "It's not there," he said. He had to grin.

Then he stopped again. "It *felt* almost like a fail forward.

"*Fail* forward?"

"Like when the GM lets you fail forward."

"The GM?"

"The GameMaster. The game story is not shut down, walled off, blocked, ending in failure. Instead the story goes elsewhere than what was coming—or expected. But that's all I've got. Nothing but a feeling. No concrete stuff to go with that."

CossycSystems' logistical positivists were excited and very wary, especially the more religious (humanistic) among them. Every scientific logistically verifiable assertion is justified and rational. Solely for this reason, metaphysics and theism did not figure into the rationally justified. Van Helsing, given his training and education, would not begin from the bias that time displacement was impossible. Scientific, mathematical, technological, his whole background was against the mystical (which he had also studied), yet he would never begin on the assumption of impossibility. Absolute time dimensionality must be questioned. His attitude was more truly scientific than those who dismissed any evidence of time displacement. At the moment, his white lab coat open, revealing dark T-shirt, yellow tie, with blue jeans, he sat asking HB about volition.

We are looping back to yesterday, in our narrative of the FivePoints 2017 kids who were displaced from 2017 to 1900 to 2019. Here we find HB in the seminar room with Pastor Zettler, Drs. Neee and Van Helsing sitting on either side of him in comfortable chairs around the tea table. The author should have worked back through this narrative to a previous textual scene, correcting a misleading idea that, prior to his appearance here with Fabian and his grandmother, Pastor Zettler had no known associations other than guards, maintenance, cleaning and culinary staff; or that he had not met these learned scientists in CossycSystems. As we see in this scene, that would be displacement—which Cossyc has not yet proven. *However, the **copy error** will serve a demonstrable purpose.*

Time, the reader recalls, is a tricky go-round. While turning or swiping a page, he or she moves through the narrative without the necessity of a reality loop. In moving forward or backward through a book the *narrative, **only**, does the looping*—the reader does not. Readers remain comfortably in place, wine, coffee, or chicken soup to hand, perhaps looking up with a smile recollecting in tranquility that they are reading. There is no need to relive all over again an endless cycle of looping Real Time. The reader may stop, put down the book, lean over and take up the cup. "Ah," says the reader, "I am reading." When again the reader lowers her gaze, she sees that the narrative is exactly where she left it on setting the book down to pick up the cup and say (with a sigh), "Ah I am reading." To the reader it feels as though the narrative is static, dependable, indispensable, all manipulability gone. "Ah," says the reader on seeing the line she just read in its place before the next line, "Ah, I am reading." One sees in this narrative that Time itself has no sway whatever over the everlasting and dependable narrative. "Ah," says the reader—

"Will you shut up!" said HB.

"I aks you please stay in your universe! My hands be full with the Cossycs and this idiot report! Get on with it!" He muttered: "I could use me some logic!"

He grinned at Dr. Van Helsing with his string of degrees leading back to the ancient and decrepit 20th-century. (Who later made careful note of this particular incident, perhaps relevant to cultic investigations.)

"—But I fails to see how it's gonna help, if you unnerstan. You got two witnesses: us, and the report. From what you showed us, everything is on the up and true, according to your organic artificial combo software/ hardware."

Dr. Neee and Pastor Zettler smiled. Dr. Van Helsing, sitting directly across from HB was surprised by this outburst in answer to his question about volition. Then he also smiled.

"We are doing the best we can, Blake. ...Is there anything in particular you'd rather be doing?"

"You mean than sitting here in these dopey cushy chairs trying to help you figure out if we really went to 1900 CE? Anything. Just about—except get my head beat by some bully club. The cops in 1900 had night sticks and now they got tazzzzzers."

Eyes gazing through small horn-rimmed glasses beneath cropped salt-and-pepper hair, Pastor Zettler interposed, "I've never had this opportunity before. Would you explain how HB's head works? Given his background, it must have seemed chancy to make so great an investment in installing the software. He's told me about the surgery and adventures he underwent to have what might be called enhancement of the brain's computer qualities, including its coherent abilities. At least this is my understanding of what I've been told." He looked at HB sitting next to him, with that big black broom cut, his dark eyes fixed on him. "I got that right?" said the pastor.

"If you want to call having your skull sawed an adventure.... But yeah, I remember being excited about it, all the attention they gave me. It was— different from the usual having my head hammered for other purposes." He looked at Van Helsing. "I was more comfortable, sure."

"It was a hardware/ software trial, and he was volunteered. All I can say is, CossycSystems was willing to take the chance. As you just heard, HB was too. Legally, his mother was." Dr. Van Helsing was from a struggling background and he was also Afrikan-Americle. He said, "Of course it was more uncomfortable for you. My background wasn't so painful, but I had some of it... on a micromanaged level, you might say."

Then he addressed Pastor Zettler's question. "I've heard of your concerns—or would it be more accurate to say, your interests in retro—analog communications?"

"Both. That is the positive way of saying it."

"So that I want to reassure you that we have no interest in using HB in an algorithmic *commercial* capacity. We are not interested in creating a world or people in which every suppressed or unthinking desire is fostered and fulfilled for money. A world full of adult babies is not what we're after."

"But I think some of your investors would disagree?"

"Perhaps, but they are not running the Institute."

Pastor Zettler decided to go no further.

And Van Helsing was quick to add, "Of course we developed such organic software/ hardware in the interests of applied science, technology, and profitability for our investors, but the purpose is the prototype. HB was the first, and there are now others walking around town with the same capabilities. But to answer your question, the simplest form is briefly put. We can be more detailed if you wish, but in the non-oral verbal form of your choice. It's best to give the outline quickly here since our session is for other purposes. But again, briefly:

"There's a popularly mistaken idea that the human brain is like a computer, artificially intelligent, but in fact it's rather otherwise. Our brains do not warehouse words and terms with instructions on how best to use them. They don't make and store intricately detailed visual images long-term. Computers do these things. They process computationally. Our patented semi-organic programs are a development of what the human brain might not otherwise do on its own. Organic is key. Until now it was not possible for the organism to process encoding to be used as a computer does—those organic patterns of zeros and ones we call bytes and bits. Software moves the patterns or data to various storage areas and can copy or reform them creatively, upon command. They can then (sort of) spit out the summary report. HB's eye, aided by a special contact lens, is also enhanced for reading it, and we are able to transfer, download, these reports. The rules are algorithmic and coordinate to enhance the brain's more limited capabilities. And these reports can be dense or lean as needed.

Pastor Zettler said, "Curious word, 'limited.' But doesn't that mean giving precedent to the *different* way, far less natural or human?"

"It could, yes. It all depends on what is wanted." He looked at the subject, Blake Griffin.

There was a pause. Then Dr. Neee, one of three Osiian-Americle colleagues at CossycSystems, contributed briefly to the conversation. As he began, HB recalled that in 1900 the word for Osiian was *Ohrental*, or disrespectfully *Chonk*.

This Osiian specialist's expertise lay in patterns and divisions of human wholeness—not solely its psyche, body, or spirit. Some of his colleagues chose to study and experiment in these areas individually. Human biology had the interest of Dr. Baron deVill; Dr. Nicole Rostof studied the paranormal, spirituality; and Dr. Duerf cared only for the human psyche. Dr. Neee's concern was for the holistic interconnectedness of all three. He called it the triune being of humanity. Pastor Zettler would have approved Dr. Neee's concern.

At this moment Dr. Neee tipped toward Dr. Rostof's end of the spectrum. He looked at HB, not to further ascertain the boy's inclination in the matter. He felt that what HB wanted would be lost in the labyrinth of the system, and that he would learn either to keep it close, or become enmeshed—less and less himself. Therefore, despite his colleague's interest in the combination of technology and its end-user, he asked, "Do you receive impressions? If so, do they come more or less than formerly? That is, before you took part in the program?" He knew his question was of particular interest for Dr. Van Helsing's technology but that was not why he asked.

HB was giving him a look straight out of his friend Tu: Blank.

Dr. Neee said, "By impression I mean some sort of quiet impress."

The blank look continued.

"Something... maybe rather companionable that is perhaps not precisely inside you... but close enough so that you would know not to look around for its source." HB was about to burst out with a smart remark, but the blank look was replaced with a thoughtful one.

After a pause he said, "You mean something like... like something the Big Fello might be interested in?"

"Big fellow?... interested in?..."

"Yo, you know. Big Fello. God. Your conscience, maybe."

"That is a very very good start on my question."

Dr. Van Helsing had leaned forward just a bit. The warm-toned LED light shone off his dark forehead where his kinky crew cut receded. He said, "More *now*? Meaning, did you have this before we schematized your brain with our technology... or is it since then? And as Dr. Neee has asked, how do you rate this difference if there is one?"

Blake Griffin's dark gaze, almost always fierce and attentive, withdrew. He was transparently thoughtful, remembering. "Just scattered times," he said finally. "Before and after. Not a whole lot. —Of 'impressions'," he said without sarcasm. "Yeah. I get 'em."

Headlines and Headaches

For context, below find a sampling of Northeast EHio and interWebs reportage and opinion.

From Chrustyuns Today: "ATHEISTS BELIEVE IN ATHEISM."

"PRESIDENT CLAIMS HE 'DID NOT HAVE GENDER WITH THAT WOMAN IN THE STAR OFFICE!' "

"BIG PHARMA PAYS EGRESS TO LEGISLATE TAXPAYERS PAY FOR OOPSYIOD EPIDEMIC STARTED BY PHARMACEUTICALS."

"WE CATEGORICALLY DENY THE PRESIDENT ORDERED THE BREAK-IN AT GATEWATER HOTEL!" *The New HAmsterdam Times*; byline, Chesley Stalled.

"Saying, 'I am not crooked! It's documented!' the PresiDent refutes knowledge of the break-in, allegedly in order to spy on the Publican-and-ReSinners campaign before the last election. 'That never happened,' he said on Witter yesterday. 'Same with the Octagon Papers break-in. That never happened. Besides, we don't need to break into bricks-n-mortar buildings, we have software for that.' "

"2017 HAS A GROUP HALLUCINATION!!" "2017—DUPED BY A CULT!!

"Citing discrepancies, an aberration in Blake Griffin's head data is reported, indicating cultic activity may be associated with the disappearance and reappearance of FivePoints neighborhood kids."

"COSSYCSYSTEMS IMPLICATED IN ITS 2017 ASSESSMENT!" "COSSYCSYSTEMS BETRAYED BY ITS OWN BIOTECH!"

The above is a sampling of interWebs and other reportage and opinion, in conjunction with CossycSystems' official assessment of the famous 2017 FivePoints neighborhood youths reportedly missing for two years.

From one story:

"A medical and biotechnology institute announced findings that an Akropolis neighborhood group of youths, known variously as the 2017 gang and FivePoints 2017, suffered a perhaps cultic inspired hallucination and possible kidnapping by persons or entities unknown. The Akropolis police have reopened their investigations into the disappearance and reappearance of five teenagers and one child of various ethnicities. CossycSystems is rumored to experiment on children with anti-aging formulas and technologies."

This article from the *Akropolis LampPost*, also known as *The Post*, goes on to rehash those rumored adventures, coupled with an official report by CossycSystems. CossycSystems gave its considered diagnosis without implication of its organic software/ hardware, but with an examination of other factors represented thus far in this narrative. According to a spokesperson for the institute, Blake Griffin, a.k.a. HB, a.k.a. HBBBAH, a.k.a. etc., used Cossyc specialized technology to record a mass hypnotic episode perpetrated by a person—or persons—unknown for reasons as yet to be determined. An implication of perhaps a sinister organization or even a rival biotech firm has been hinted. This testing is now focused to examine if aging has occurred in these youngsters, with the possibility that aging may have been delayed or prevented by some corporate entity—or entities in collusion—against its possible competitor, CossycSystems. Owing to fierce competition in the field, corporate espionage is a very real possibility, they say.

The following conversation took place over the phone days after its initial family interviews on the campus of CossycSystems.

Jayrai spoke low into her new MyPhone "Pome! I'm going crazy penned up in this apartment building! They've taken a prize bull and shackled it! I'm going to run away for real if it doesn't stop! There are guards and everything!"

"Calm down, Jay. I'm here. So, I mean, so, you know I'm here for you as best I can be under the circumstances." Pomala was getting ready to walk out the door and go down to FivePoints.

"But you are free to roam around! The doormen simply stand and won't let me pass, while calling Uncle's henchmen to come get me!"

"I'll have my sister ask the mayor to call them and express your need to get out." Pomala's voice was soothing, calm and reassuring.

"That'll never work—even if he'd agree. The mayor's skin is darker than hers. She'd never tolerate the interference. I'm going to get out if I have to bleach myself white as you—have you studied how you got to be albino, btw? I'll dye my hair blond. I'll be silver-white. No one's gonna recognize me! I'll steal the maid's clothes."

"But what about your arm? Everyone recognizes your arm."

"I'll leave it behind if I have to!" (Still low, but spoken with a touch of hysteria.)

"Go out one-armed? Oh Jay!"

Pomala was glad that Jay had not seemed to consider using it on the doormen, and determined not to bring it up in case it was an oversight.

"She's been plying me with gadjets and appes but won't understand that I've got to get out! *Out out!*" Jay growled.

Pomala began to wonder if her room was monitored. *What about her phone?*

"Are you in your room now?" she asked.

"I'm sitting on the folding table in the sub-basement. The laundry! She never comes down here."

"Er. Do you think she bugs you?"

"Haven't I been saying?"

"No—I mean *security*—extended to bugging the apartment, the laundry?"

"Oh sht! Wait till I turn on the dryers!"

There was a pause, followed by the hum of dryers. Evidently she turned all dryers on.

Far downhill from the suburb of Sharon (where Jay lives), and just below the gentrified section in which Pomala lives with her mother and father, HB and Fabian sit in the empty hall serving the neighborhood as dining area in the Gospel Mission. The street outside plateglass windows fills with traffic, stop and go. It has taken some doing but Pastor Zettler, aided by responsible neighborhood sentiment, has convinced CossycSystems to release HB. HB is staying with pastor in the apartment overhead on condition he does not go back to what is calling itself his family.

He felt better being with Pastor Zettler and helping in the soup kitchen. He might have pled to go back to Sheltering Cares but wanted to stay where he was, on this corner of FivePoints with its wider freedom and neighborhood traffic. To good purpose, rules at Sheltering Cares were rather strict.

Following their general cleanup of the hall in preparation for lunch, the two teenagers sat drinking Ko-kola from cans, talking. A cheerful clatter of cooking utensils, pans and crockery, came through from the kitchen along with sounds of good-natured banter. Once in a while someone would come out and pile plates or other things on the counter.

"Have you had a chance to see him?" HB was asking about Tu, the boy wonder who could do all kinds of headwork and absorb the most useless information in the universes but apparently had no clue on how to reverse time to anybody's satisfaction. HB said, "Somebody should figure out time in case of zombie apokalup and the whole world has to go backward just to be safe."

"Nobody is seeing Tu," said Fabian. "He's holed up with his mom and dad and won't come out till he's got it solved. It's a good thing they are keeping us out of school until after Thanksgiving."

"Yeah it's all good—but I miss the fun I'd be having messing with everybody's heads."

"Speaking of which, are they going to let you keep yours now that it's determined defective?" Or it it? Maybe discrepancies don't count?

HB shrugged. He said nothing.

Fabian backed away from the subject. He felt HB's discomfort—maybe it *wasn't* defective? He charged ahead on a different track. "Will we keep believing?" Fabian asked. A definite subject-change.

"It's not belief," said HB "We were there. We start saying, 'do we believe?' We're already not believing. As for your first question, I don't know." He shook his head.

It took a moment for Fabian to realize he was silently laughing. HB's big black 'do twisting as he turned his head sideways up-and-down.

Then he said bright as the full moon: "They got these things called 'terms and conditions.' Ever hear of that?"

"See it all the time. Don't read 'em. Most people click on through. I'm still under 18, for one thing."

"Are you? Sure? —But not a good idea, girl. Do a search on the word *change* in terms of service. Reams of meaningless words you're agreeing to and one sentence is all you need to know. They promise nothing and you promise... you're agreeing to anything, past present future. You are serving your term. Like in prison."

"Really?"

"I don't know *what* they'll do but basically, according to this, we—you recall I had a mother —we agreed to anything." (Said with an evil grin covering, Fabian knew, oceans of pain.)

"Uh. Does that mean they own your entire head?"

"Basically."

Fabian went silent. Someone came out of the kitchen.

"Hey, Bruster," said HB.

"Hey bro," said Bruster. He was muscular, tall, tan, cheerful and brave as one that big can be. He was not reckless.

"What's on the menu? Not smelling the chicken, bro."

"You would not believe the great truckload of stuff we got from the farmboys!" He set the giant kettle on the board. Bruster referred to the farmers in homeboy vernacular. He was one, and relished the good-natured kidding they had ongoing between them. "Wesley brought in hog parts—but that's not the thing. We got stuff in storage now like you won't believe. Winter squash, apples, potatoes, carrots, onions. Sweet potatoes!!" He smiled gigantically, revealing a dimple in one cheek courtesy of a driving iron. "Shelf-life almost to eternity." He went back through the swinging door for more.

"You don't usually see him here for the noon meal," said HB.

"There's lots of stuff you don't usually see here now. Lots of little stuff."

"You mean 2019 stuff. It's weird. Think we'll get used to it? That's what I'm afraid of. You know what pastor said last night?... He started talking about an Emily."

"A what?"

"That's what I call it." HB stood and went over to the counter; Fabian followed. HB dipped the ladle and came out with a very colorful bowlful of soup. He dished, and handed the bowl to Fabian."

"Thanks."

HB got himself one and they went back to the table. Bruster came in bearing another big one. "What do you think?" Bruster asked.

"Too hot to tell, but it's pretty," said Fabian.

"Pretty?!!" Bruster laughed all the way back to the kitchen. Then he stuck his head back out the door and said, "I'm telling that one to the farmboys!"

"It's the big stuff pastor's thinking of," said HB, blowing on a spoonful.

"An Emily is big? Like a large woman?"

"Yo, I'm kidding, Fabe."

"I knew that."

"He means an anomaly. Like when you've got a big black woman and someone says she's a small white man and everyone else has to go along with it—legally. Just until terms and conditions change."

"Uh, what?"

"Pretty soon the whole world's got to go with what everyone else is imagining. Like a terrorist imagining himself doing what God says when he's murdering. Or—"

"—Or something. Who would *do that*?" Fabian wondered.

"People get over an Emily."

"You mean absorb anomaly. Any kind of anomaly, you mean?"

"Just the ones sized and shaped like a small white male Emily who was originally big and black.

"LEAD POISONING IN AKROPOLIS EHIO!" *The New HAmsterdam Times*; byline, Chesley Stalled.

"It's been determined that high concentrations of chlorine used to keep water clean has been leaching lead from aging pipes in Akropolis EHio. Papers filed by regulators have shown that domestic water tested in homes reveals lead at acceptable levels. Citizens and scientists at the university school of engineering are contesting this. Chlorine reportedly is a poisonous, corrosive and gaseous greenish element of halogen groups, highly reactive as a product of sodium chloride electrolysis, used mainly in drinking water purification."

"A'NDIAN FALLS HYDRO-ELECTRIC DAM TO COME DOWN!!"

"SENIORS CLAIM: 'BIG INSURANCE PAYS LEGISLATIVE STEWARDS TO FORCE OLDSTERS BUY MEDICAL INSURANCE!!' "

(Still in the Sharon sub-basement with the busy hum of electric dryers.)

"Your Mom will let me come visit though, right?"

"Maybe if your sister comes?"

"She's awful busy. The Mayor and all."

"So I'm breaking out. My plan is to stay in the cemetery."

"No!"

"Yeah."

"No!"

"Yeah."

"But where in the cemetery? And how will you get out?"

"I told you—disguised. I'll bring everything I need down here in laundry baskets... and I'll change in the sub-basement bathroom just to make sure."

"Your arm?"

"Part of my disguise will be gloves, the jacket ... and I'll put it in a sling."

"But where will you stay?"

"It's just temporary. Permantly temporary if necessary. I'll just flit around the cemetery. Everyone will be spooked if they happen to be there. —And I'll sleep in the portico on the musical mausoleum if it rains."

"But it's going to snow, Jay!! It could snow as early as Thanksgiving! It has before."

"Pome, I've been having brain waves! Do you realize I'll be 18 in less than a year?!"

"OMG!! OMG!! That's right, Jay. If we don't get back to 2017 we will be grown-ups in no time! —So not no time, but you know."

"That's right. And she won't have a thing to say because it's legal. I'll remind her that she cannot go according to the tradition in the states. She's got to go by the law, Americle law.... And... I just realized I can renounce *Narva* in the tradition and go my own way. I can go searching for *Komas*! Yes! I can realize my true self! Oh Pome! This is it!! I think I don't want to go back to 2017!"

"PRESIDENT CONSIDERS DITCHING THANKSGIVING!!" *The New HAmsterdam Times*; byline, Chesley Stalled:

"In an unprecedented move today, the PresiDent of the Untied States of Americle announced his thought-provoking plans to overturn a centuries old tradition—calling for what he terms a 'new tradition' to be instituted in Thanksgiving's place. Citing outmoded forms as a thing holding us back on the world stage, the executive branch today begins pushing both houses of Egress to replace the old holiday with one more in line with our world as it is today. 'We don't need Thanksgiving anymore,' he said at a news conference in the Gray House today. "If I have to issue a proclamation, I will!"

" 'You mean the holiday, or just thanks giving, period?' shouted longtime correspondent, Thomas Helen.

" 'Both! We are yoogely way past that,' he responded with a thrust of his lower lip. " 'What we need now is a holiday to show the world I and we no longer rely on myths of the past, however great people thought them then. I'm proposing to Egress they come up with a referendum proposal for a contest to find our new holiday.'

" ' Don't you mean to *found* a new holiday?'

" 'That's another useless out-dated expression,' said the PresiDent, whose hair was purple today. 'Next! Burni Baunders!'

" 'Mr. PresiDent, could you expand on why we no longer need to give thanks? And could you suggest what you have in mind—what kind of qualities you'd like to see in the new holiday?'

" 'To answer your second question first. I may or may not answer your first question at all if I don't feel like it, Burni Baunders. Remember, you are just a sensationalist newsperson. You don't speak for the people like I do. I was elected, you weren't.' Then the PresiDent stopped, seeming to consider his answer, or possibly trying to remember the question. Golden hair draping close to the podium, an aide whispered something in his ear. He said, 'I think the best kind of holiday would no longer relate to the Native Americle thing. And it should highlight the self-made nation we are today. Like any good entrepreneur, we used our bootstraps and here we are. Let the winning contestant choose some kinda day that makes us feel great! Again we are great!! We built a yoooge wall. We are yoooge! …It's got to be something like that.'

" 'Mister PresiDent! About the current state of our infrastructure—'

" 'My father, the PresiDent in the 1950s, did such a great job building our roads and bridges and sewers and water treatment, etc. that we won't ever need any work done on them. —And don't forget! My father was a very smart man! He made fun of his opponent, Steven Adlaison, for his intelligence and position papers, and that was a very big thing to do.' "

" 'Mister PresiDent! You've never responded to our questions about you former career acting in old westerns. How exactly did that career fit you for the highest job in the land?' "

" 'The fact of my roles in the historical gold rush westerns made me eminently suitable for this job. No one denies that!' "

"He looked over at his aide, and stepped back.

" 'That's all we have time for!' said Priscilla. She gleamed into the camera. 'See you all next time on *Ten Questions for the PresiDent* !' "

The two Palacestonian descended Quads came in from the street shouting "Hi's" and walked over to the spread on the counter, talking loudly to Fabian and HB. Others came in off the sidewalk. Sharon Rd. outside large windows was full of swooshing traffic, stop and go. The place began to fill. Quadri and his big brother sat across from them talking. Conversation turned to big changes noticed since Time-change.

"That was a week ago, not two days ago," said HB to Quadri.

"It was?" said Quad.

"Two years, actually," said Quadrangi."

"Yo, whatever."

"But whoa," said Fabian. "My grandmother was watching the new PresiDent. Her lips were moving, you know how she does sometimes. But how did that happen? He's like the big kids beating up on the small kids at school."

"That's nothing," said Quadrangi. "He wants to deport my parents and all their children. He's got this giant wall building the length of the border with Candia, trying to keep out low-cost pharmaceuticals. And he's got the Egress water-boarded to make them craft laws to get Candia to pay for it—or at least their drug companies."

HB said, "What about boat pharmaceuticals? Drug boats? How's he gonna keep *them* from landing? We got like three pretty long coastlines between Candia and Middle and South Americle."

"He wasn't even here a week ago. And neither were drones but they could use them, too. But anyway, he doesn't seem smart enough to figure that one out," said Fabian. "Maybe it's an alternate time *and* universe?"

"Hey! You can't say that about the PresiDent of the Untied States."

They looked over at a man sitting next to Quadri, two plates of bread and butter, soup bowl before him. He was rugged and disheveled.

"Why not?" said HB.

"It's unAmericle that's why."

"So's the PresiDent apparently," said HB.

"Well, maybe, but it's the way he said it." The man turned to Fabian. Can't you say it without sneering?" He took a gigantic bite out of a bread and butter sandwich. Half the sandwich went in that bite.

" 'K," said Fabian. "I'm sorry. I didn't realize— I didn't mean to say it like that. I mean I guess I shouldn't use that tone."

"Like do you mean he could say the same thing better? Nice?" asked HB. "It's more like Americle if we speak things nicer?"

"Yeah. Like that." The man picked up his bowl and sucked leftover broth, gulping it. He picked up the rest of one sandwich in a dirty hand and finished it in one bite. He looked at HB's big 'do. Then at Fabian. "Are you the disappeared kids?"

"That's us!" piped Quadri unexpectedly. His little boy's face was dimpled and brown, dark eyes shining.

"The man looked down at him. "Where were you all that time?"

"Right here, I think," said Quadri. "Only it looked and smelled different. The cemetery was only a little different. It didn't have music. The stone walls looked different. And the trees. They were different. It was hot. They played pool in here with long sticks and a green table with holes in it like a golf course only smaller." Quadri had seen the golf course on the hill. Quadrangi caddied there.

"I know what you mean," said the man. "They say in the old days this place was a pool hall. Probably my great granddad shot pool here."

"What's wrong with your eyes? They're bleeding."

"Nah, just bloodshot."

Quadri looked up at his brother.

"I'll tell you later," said Quadrangi. He looked over Quadri's head at the man. Still chewing.

"DOMESTIC-RATS CLAIM TORTURE IS NOT BEING USED ON TERRORISTS."

"SENIORS CLAIM: 'BIG PHARMA JACKS UP PERSCRIPTIONS OWING TO PHARMACEUTICALS LEGISLATION.' "

"But why are you so dying to get out?" Pomala was on the sidewalk on her way downhill. "I mean is it something in particular I can help with? How can you want to be in 2019 even as an older person if everything, and the whole world too, is so much wronger, Jay? And potentially older. We aren't really any older."

"It's what we get to do I care about. Like, I want to see Bo. I have not heard from him at all! If I use the maintenance entrance in disguise, I'll be able to go look for him."

Pomala began stalling at mention of The Bo. "Speaking of maintenance, what about maintenance for your arm? How does that work?"

"I've got some prep items for it, you saw me use them before. But if anything goes really wrong there will be Cossyc for that. I don't need her, uncle, Sharon, any of it."

"I just had a thought. —If we get back to 2017 at the time we left you won't have to worry about Bo. —I mean in the way you're thinking of. I mean the worries in 2017 are still something, I think, but at least he would not have been hurt, arrested, put in jail for two years like you said."

Silence from Jayrai. The dryers hummed. Pomala was almost down the hill to the SoupMission. She thought she might see some of the other 2017ers for a conference. Would Tu be there, for instance?

"So yeah," said Jay after a long pause. "There's that. So much to think about.... Where are you going right now?"

Pomala did not like to say. Finally she said, "I'm almost to the um point of my errand." She grimaced over her lack of forthrightness but did not want to hurt her friend.

After another pause, Jay said, "Tell everyone I said 'hi.' " Her tone was lackluster, not quite glum. "But, please let me know what Tu's got. I'm not hearing from him."

"No one is, I guess."

A couple buses at the intersection drowned out the dryers. The girls said goodbye.

"But call me! Call me! When you get there! I want to hear!"

But Pomala had slipped the wePhone into her pocket.

The swishing traffic was stop-and-go at the intersection where FivePoints traffic-light held sway. Pomala considered the difference between 1900 with its chaos—clopping, clattering, thundering wagons carts carriages and antique new autos; horse-and-riders: comparing it to 21st-century relative quiet in the electric traffic of Akropolis. She entered the Gospel Mission and found the noise: chairs scraping, talk cheerful for the most part, and *loud*. Only one person was acting out and a volunteer was with him. Though she did not expect him to be there, she looked the cacophonous room over for Tu. No Tu.

"Hey Pomala!" Fabian stood and beckoned her over. "Join 2017!" he said as she wove her way through benches, tables and chairs, smiling and talking to others of her acquaintance in the neighborhood. The man who recently corrected Fabian's tonality, when speaking of the PresiDent was still eating and did not seem inclined to move. Fabian tried to give her his seat.

"I'll just sit over there after I get some soup," she said, indicating an empty spot on a bench by the kitchen door.

"Yo wait," said HB. "You girls all wanna come upstairs so's we can talk? We're about done, White Thang, so get some soup and we'll go to my new digs with the Pastor. Guaranteed he's not gonna care!"

"Aw *right*!" Pomala smiled. Her hair was long and white today. She was still with the cargo pants despite the utter lack of fashion. Today they were purple-pink, highlighting some of the lines in her overall blue tattooing and pink eyes. She left her jacket on and went to get soup.

Upstairs, standing near the shortwave radio in a corner by the door, they all waited to greet the Pastor who sat on the couch talking on his old black rotary phone with someone about the water situation. He motioned them to sit. Quietly they seated themselves about the coffee table where HB, speaking low, gave them a mini lecture on short wave radios and how they made wifi a future possibility. The room's windows faced on two sides toward the intersection, buildings across Exchange and Sharon visible. They could smell the kitchen, still cooking beneath rooms where Pastor had his own kitchen and contiguous study. In the latter room he often met one-on-one, or with a couple or family, but he also had his books there. Pastor's books were very important to him. Many of them permitted entrance to realms where he might rarely glimpse or experience a longing he called *sehnsucht*. "Inconsolable longing," as one of his favorite authors put it.

HB had quizzed him on it. "What *is* zaneZuckt? Something that happens when you read and eat peanut-butter on white bread? You go in your head to like a cookie factory in Churmany where your ancestors came from, or something?"

Pastor Zettler had smiled, his glasses reflecting light from windows overlooking the neighborhood. "Well, I wouldn't mind that. I might get some kind of joy or longing out of being whisked that way, but so far—no. In fact, conceivably some might be more prone to receiving it that way. And I've never heard of anyone else getting it from books, though very probably they have. I've heard of it coming through nature's exquisite beauty or her wild power. Or from being among people when it expresses itself that way. Through people. Hard to predict I think. But one never knows. It's hard to pin down, in part because generally it comes long enough to notice and then usually, though I've heard of exceptions, it's gone again."

"So it leaves you longing and then it's gone? Or does it just stick to the roof of your mouth so you remember?"

Again the Pastor had smiled. "Sehnsucht may actually be absolute, infinite and permeating, but people only rarely know it's there. Permanent joy with a transfigured sense—of longing."

Now he hung up the receiver and greeted them, then left to get some soup and lead the afternoon service downstairs. Pomala had arrived with her soup.

"What was that about water?" she asked of HB when Pastor was gone. "Sis says it's bad."

"No mind stuff on that," said HB.

Quadrangi thought he was the only one somewhat up on that, and was about to say so but Fabian said, "My grandma was talking about that. They got some kind of leakage or spoilage or something. Toxic metals in the water. I think that was on the news too. We're not supposed to drink tap water?" He looked at Quadrangi. "She's been buying water at the store, says someone's been donating gallons of water here from someplace."

"Yeah. There's a breeheehee on this but nothing's certain except it's bad. Seems they keep kicking it around with a lot of political stink, so to speak. Rumors on dimWitter say it stumped our growth and made us hallucinate 1900 CE."

Quadri said, "Is that the reason it smells bad when we turn on the water?"

"Yes! That's it! So, I mean, maybe it's where my headaches are coming from," said Pomala apologetically. She still had her soup but did not do much more than hold it.

"Makes sense—" said HB. "Wait! That's wrong. I was about to be sarcastic. I mean, Sorry to hear about the headaches and—How long's it been going on?"

"I wake up with them," she said, then stopped. "You know what? I've been having the strangest dreams—and we're all in them!... Only we're not.... But our thoughts are."

"Sense?" suggested Fabian.

"It's hard to explain, but I recognize everybody by their thoughts. You, me, Jay, HB, Quad, even Tu. If you can believe Tu. So not his thoughts exactly. But Yes. These are strange dreams. And other people are in them—or at least one other—and he has thoughts. Or maybe he *is* the thoughts. —I told you I couldn't explain it."

"Back to my sarcasm," said HB. "Maybe dimWitter is right."

"At least headaches make sense now," said Pomala. "There's bottled water in the fridge. Maybe I need to stop brushing my teeth."

Quadrangi looked from one to the other, then at Quadri then back again. The brothers smiled at one another, alike enough to be twins with a very long gap in the gestation of each. Handsome, dark, with skin a rich olive brown and a dimple in the right cheek of each.

"We couldn't drink the water," said Quadri. "Fabian told The Leg Bone big kid we couldn't drink the water and we had to go get Akropolis Pop downstairs here."

"Right, Quadri!" she said. "That's why we came to the pool hall—because they had no sewer infrastructure and people got sick probably from bad water.

"Like here now, only different," said Fabian. "The neighborhood smelled like sewage and horse crap. They had no good sewage system and all that. They started back in 1900—started the sewer back then—but it got old and so needed fixed before we left 2017. Then the sewer got fixed while we were gone to 1900 for a few minutes—"

"—Two years," said Quadrangi, looking at Quadri.

"—and now it's something else. Bad pipes, I guess."

"The water main," said Quadrangi. "Let's wait and see how long *that* takes."

"Yo plenny room for sarcasm," said HB. "But about that!" He gestured across the street. They could see tall asymmetrical Cossyc campus buildings, very elegant and accented with brass-framed windows in large-grained granite and concrete, iron and steel—designed by the best firm of architects in Groverland to the north. "All that biotechnology going on and we got bad water! Point? Anybody see a point to this?" Then he muttered, "Of course Pomala's gonna do something about it, being related to the mayor."

Pomala smiled at this sarcasm.

"Maybe it's because we were gone for two minutes," said the small Quadri thoughtfully. As though he had been to the University of Akropolis Engineering School studying not only everything that had been said, but Time, dark matter, the mechanics of biotechnology and the Akropolis infrastructure.

Before his brother had a chance to correct him, Pomala said, "Maybe he's right?"

"Huh, what?" said HB and Quadrangi in unison.

"So of course it would take them two years to fix the sewers and for the clean water pipes to go bad from corrosion or whatever but we know our experience—for sure—" she glanced at Quadrangi—"and just maybe it has something to do with the twinkle-in-time. You know—the ripple, and—"

"—Don't tell me," said Fabian. "You're going to fix it." They could almost see him face-palming.

HB said, "I wouldn't go that far, but ... we wouldn't have to *do* anything to repair it, except be *when* we belong."

"I'm sure *Tu* could fix that," said Pomala. Finally, relieved, she dipped her spoon into the bowl and came up with soup.

"Jay still held captive by evil uncle and mother?" asked Quadrangi. Just to change the subject.

"Yeah. Wish we could all go visit her. She wants to escape, go live in the graveyard. We could send her our thoughts. *Ooops*. She wanted in on this." Pome felt in her pocket. "Fabian, did you say to pray the other day? She could use some. Some guidance. Would we have to pray to *Newfish* I wonder?"

"Me pray?" said Fabian. "You must have me mixed up with Nana." He smiled and shook his head, blonde "dog-ears" swinging.

"And don't be goin' into my thoughts, girl," said HB. "That's some kinda danger zone. Even in your dreams, hear?" He muttered, "You got this way of messing with stuff."

"Maybe the Pastor could help with the prayers."

"There you go," he said, meaning, *There you go again*. "Just eat the soup."

The singing began down below, drifting up through apartment registers. It sounded pleasant when it drifted instead of being directly next to you from Wilfred Woses' or somebody's mouth.

Pomala stopped eating. "Do you ever feel a longing for something and you don't know about it or what it is or why you have it except you see or hear something and there it is?"

"A kind of 'unfulfillable longing,' " said HB. "No. But Pastor Z was talking about it. Why? You get some from that soup?"

"Oh no," she grinned. "But I might have got some from you. From you all. Maybe it was in my dream."

"Here we go again," said HB. "What I wanted to know—and I asked him this—'If its not consoling—that means you can't have whatever-the-ffuts—then why would you want this longing?' "

"So he must have said something to that. He wouldn't just not answer such a great question."

"Yeah. Of course. But it left me with an unconsolable longing."

"Oh quit," she said. And Quadri piped: "What did Pastor say?"

"That it's *better* than fulfillment."

"Like Moozoon's MarketPlace?" said Quadrangi. "They just don't send you your package and you feel all fulfilled?"

Fabian said, "Yes. It's better in *this* life."

Pomala said, "Having it's better than its being fulfilled...? Maybe…." She thought about it.

"In this life," said Fabian. "In this life."

"There you go with the Nana," said HB.

"Do I go there a lot?"

HB thought about it. "I'll get back to you."

"TWO DECADES RUNNING!! GROVERLAND, AKROPOLIS, TANCAN!! DECLARED MEDICAL TECHNOLOGICAL CAPITAL OF THE WORLD."

An aged wooden building, not quite as old as the neighborhood itself, it had character. There were old photos on Pastor's walls showing the rural charm of the area just prior to roadhouse construction. Later, upper stories were added as were neighboring buildings possessed of a small-town feel. GlimmerDale Cemetery, diagonally across Exchange, its gate out of sight of Pastor Zettler's living room windows, had started as the Akropolis Rural Cemetery over 150 years ago, serving the town proper which stood uphill on what was then Stock Exchange St.. Seven hills comprised this part of the county, with rivers, lakes and streams watering the whole. Canals had been built back then to accommodate trade between Groverland on the Great EHio Lake and the much smaller Akropolis. Sometimes now, especially, Blake studied these framed photos showing fields and the dusty intersection, a farmhouse, barn, a shed. Often, now that he was here, he'd stay away from the service downstairs. Pastor had no problem with this. He was a believer in freedom of will.

HB would look with consideration and wonder on the earliest photos. There were some circa the time of their visit (as 2017ers) in 1900 CE. He now recognized places and buildings he'd seen in person for a very short time a week ago. Looking at the black and white images helped him *remember* in his own mind and being—without the aid of CossycSystems. He had been afraid 1900 might vanish, especially since Cossyc was doing its best publicly to make them seem unreal; but was now hopeful these memories would be sustained.

Heads bent, 2017 sat silently swiping, scrolling, occasionally keying, in the old faintly musty-smelling room above the mission hall. A distant voice was speaking. "A writer of fairy tales, novels and sermons, a wise Scotswoman from the 19th century—." Silently, 2017 continued along their digital highways and byways. The distant voice asked, "You know what the 19th century is, right?" Drifting distant laughter … and a faraway voice called out, "Yeah—from you!" More remote laughter, then, "This Scotswoman once said, 'We don't break the law of gravity, we break ourselves upon the law.' We don't break the laws of physics, people, we can only break our bodies on these unbreakable laws." The room above the sounding sermon was bright from horizontal contiguous windows on two sides above the busy intersection. Pastor's strong voice came up, distantly but distinctly, through grates at either end of the room. They sat in the old couches and armchairs, grouped round the coffee table, so it seemed he was there among them, but disembodied, remote as a ghost.

"You can't repent of breaking yourself upon the law of gravity and have any effect. You can repent of breaking yourself on the moral law to some considerable avail. This is our part in the keeping of universal laws."

Only Fabian was intently attending, while doing a video search on hang-gliding.

Pastor (distantly): "We can't change gravity, but work with it. Use it to teach us how to make and maintain safe bridges, for instance. Work with it. The moral law—we can change its outcome through repentance. Maybe that's working with it? Maybe even part of it?"

Suddenly Quadri looked up and said, "Is gravity the moral law?"

HB murmured without looking up. "If it was, we might be able to get out of this 2019 fix with ***one of us repenting***."

Pomala was chuckling, still looking down at her wePhone.

"He's kidding, Quad," said Quadrangi. "But it's a good question."

"Right," said Fabian. "No telling where repentance might lead...although Gram would say where."

"Could lead to Tu's bedroom," muttered HB.

"Fix is a curious word," said Fabian, flicking a gaze at Pomala. "It's some mess you get into.... Then you try to fix it. Sometimes a bigger mess results."

Pomala was still chuckling. "So sometimes not." She said, looking down, "Jay is refining her plan of escape to haunt the cemetery. We ought to do something."

"You, you mean," said HB.

"I don't know," said Quadrangi. "…Should we be equating moral and physical laws?"

"Yes, definitely," said Fabian. "We definitely should."

"I mean it's a good analogy but. How else?"

"Both are real." He had just been watching a man drop off a cliff with para-glider lifting, stabilizing gloriously, buoying him into the air above a mountainside. "Both are invisible to us." Fabian turned the device to show him.

"So yeah, I hear your idea," said Quadrangi. "You're saying work with laws so you can 'see' them. For instance, if I take certain materials out of the ground and work with them according to physical laws, I can end up going 60 on a highway. Say, no problem, I'd take iron ore with cranes and trucks and process it with other tools made according to process laws... and you go through this whole chain of physically working with laws, and then you're doing 60. See that, Quad?"

Quad looked at him. "Out of the ground?"

"But say," said Fabian, "you're doing 60 in a 35 zone and someone gets hit. Three invisible laws there."

"Three?!" said HB, getting involved. "Wha-chu-talkin?"

"So the Council or somebody wrote down a law they agreed on, while only making it visible on paper and in a court of law."

"Or something," said HB. "This is giving me a headache. There's no end to this stuff—and believe—I've got the head to analyze if anybody has. I guess you can go all day."

"Which brings us back to the water," said Pomala.

" —Water?" said Quadri. "It goes by gravity—doesn't get broke?"

At the same time Pomala said, " —Tapwater. "We could fix that.

"Somebody could."

"A whole lot of somebodies would have to," said HB. "Not some little ol' white thang."

"So," said Fabian, "she's got this big sister... wears a suit... works for the mayor."

"But that's in 2019," said Quadri. "I thought we had to go back to 2017 to fix it."

"I'm not letting you," said big brother, who was still perplexed. He did not yet have a fix on this very strange problem. He was at sea, no compass. Locked in a containership like Tu's family. To escape that, Quadrangi thought, *Tu might need some company*. Or maybe they should kidnap him, take him bowling or something. They could pretend to be plumbers and get Jayrai out in one of —in Bruster's van. —Uh-oh. Cultish much? They just happened to be there and they are turning me into a follower.

"Hey," he said, "did you know they verified gravity waves, the gravitational wave, that is, while you were gone? Of course it's not as big a deal as turning your eyes into a mouse. They did that, too." His dimples deepened. He flashed his perfect white teeth. "At least they're saying it's so, and they were there so they should know."

"Here we go," said HB. "Where's Tu when you need him? So does that mean we go through the particle or wave thing with this, too?"

"Like with the photon?" said Fabian. "So is the graviton particle or wave?"

Quadrangi said, "Actually, it's a peep."

"A peep?" said HB. "Gravity is a car over a cliff *and it's a sound*?"

"New discovery since 2107."

The telephone on an end table rang. He reached over to pick up. "Pastor Zetler's, Blake Griffin speaking.... He's preaching now. ...Yep." He hung up and scribbled something on a pad by the phone.

In other news, religious organizations are converting in a flood of cooperation with trans-young people self-identifying as young. "We want their souls to be saved before they die, and this is one way to go about it," said one magneto-church leader who humbly asked to remain anonymous in order to highlight for the purposes of emphasis on the new doctrine itself.

Being (Somewhat) Human

From *Chrustyuns Today*: "The WitterVerse is an angry God, holy and envious. Who can know it?"

From *GleeClub WebBlocking*:

"Finally! The Chrustyuns are doing something we lefty Politically Righteous can get on board with! Pile on! Support the Chrustyuns in their pursuit of Chrustyun purity. Bootface data are rolling in: more Chrustyuns are supporting the right to reshape their good news to whatever suits! Embrace your new brothers and sisters and whatevahs, fellow PR's. GleeClub WebBlocking is totally willing to turn Chrustyun with this latest trend. Let's do it ye almightys! We are there! We are here! We're everywhere! (Come and get it.)"

From *The New HAmsterdam Times*: The bill mooted by Egress, allowing for adoption and adaptation of fetus parts, would permit a different classification for a-woman's-right-to-choose clinics. Under this bill, if passed into law, agencies such as Moloch's Abortion Clinics would, as their new promotional scheme suggests, be able to call themselves the Moloch Adoption Agency. The bill, hotly contested in the Saneist, will come up for a vote after the 2019 Egressional break known as the Thanksgiving holiday (also mooted). Various stages of embryonic development, such as zygote, blastula and others will be included. Living cells and tissue would then be humanely allowed for these adoptions. Used for purposes of that wonderful abstraction we call "the good of all humankind," it is hoped that after this change these institutions will no longer be targets of conscientious protests.

"So we got our plateful," said Lt. Hunch, as they entered the building—a former YWCA with swimming pool somewhere in its bowels—now housing Sheltering Cares and other ventures, both charitable and for-profit small businesses. They were about to interview the housemother, Gretchen, currently in charge of abused and homeless youths at Sheltering Cares.

"Yeah, pizza and sushi. What a combo," said Sgt. Bench, striding beside him in corduroy slacks and blazer, her hair braided, pinned up in a coil.

They spoke of two new investigations for the city. The precinct wanted in on both. One of these was the cultic kidnapping; the other corporate espionage. CossycSystems had suggested the first, and virtually stepped aside, leaving the APD with relevant documents —scientific findings but nothing substantial with regard to allegations. The institute was also proposing active investigation of the latter, though they claimed to have little in the way of evidence to offer. These cases could be related. It was up to the city of Akropolis and FivePoints Police to find out. And, evidently, CossycSystems was pursuing the case privately with its own or contracted investigators. They weren't saying much. The institute was secret, and proprietary in any of its dealings, despite prolific public relations. It was rumored they suspected another biotechnological institution, a competitor.

Lt. Hunch, the tall Afrikan-Americle stylishly turned out in dark suit and fedora, spoke in a rich voice and clear-cut style. They sat in Gretch's cramped office overlooking Cheddar Ave.. Below its windowsills were shelves crammed full of books and the odd ancient game console. They noticed a foldaway bed up on one wall, hardly likely to find room for opening in here without shoving both desk and folding chairs either into the corridor or atop the file cabinets in a pile. Sgt. Benja Bench imagined these chairs on top of the desk and thought it might do, barely. And how to get out the door? She was thinking of the fire alarm.

"So I can see your reasons," replied Gretchen. Gretch had colorless skin, ready smile and brassy disheveled hair. She wore a long-sleeved T, and less than fashionable but convenient cargo pants with lots of pockets.

Hunch had been apologetic—not the usual way with him, taciturn and focused as he was on any case before him. Gretch did not go on, but waited for him to continue.

"We know you," he said, toying with the fedora. "We've been here. We bring them even before Child Protective gives placement. We don't want to see that partnership end."

"Oh, I totally believe you." She grinned. "I hear you're even investigating the SoupMission. ...It's just plain stupid. You'll forgive me." She grinned again.

"Agreeed," he acknowledged. "But we've got to go through the... steps." He did not say, Go through the motions. Though he strongly believed in them. He was going to be thorough.

"Just a few questions for some of their friends or acquaintance—and you happen to be one," said Bench.

"But we need this systemic touch. We've got to know who all is supporting the two places."

"I know. You need clues." She grinned, eyes flinty. She was having fun, mocking them. "The neighborhood scientists think the neighborhood Chris Soldiers are up to no good. They want to make sure we don't steal their military secrets. Classified."

Lt. Hunch almost smiled. "I wouldn't go so far as to say the scientists. Maybe their paycheck people, the ones who keep the research going."

"Including the taxpayers," said Gretch, rather slyly he thought.

"Yes," said Sgt. Bench, "the ones who pay us to investigate."

"Ooo. I think I see a conflict of interest," said the housemother.

Hunch admitted to himself that he was beginning to have fun.

"You know we are independent of any religious organization. We have to be. Though some—who will remain nameless to protect the innocent—" (she grinned again) "some here *may* believe. Chris Soldiers may even believe crackpot ideas."

"Like what, for instance?" said Bench.

Lt. Hunch had hoped she might.

"Things like, all our thoughts and movements are tracked by a superior intelligence. Or that we are made out of and have our existence in something we can't see. Or that all our skin pores and hairs on our heads are algorithmically countable. —Or there's an abyss where things are sucked apart and spun into some other type thing-being. Or there was an event horizon called 'Let-there-be-light!' Or that maybe it's possible for humans to be immortal! —Crackpot."

"Aren't those just scientific applications and findings you couch as religion?" asked Bench, getting with Gretch's program.

"Exactly. The scientists and technologists have stolen from us. I think you should be investigating their backers. Its ancient stuff people used to believe till the last 200 years when progress took over, so then they couldn't believe until the software and scientists said it was all right to again. Big Data. *Not* Big Daddy. Forget Transformation. *Transhumanism*!"

"So... you admit you may be one of them? One of those religious crackpots, as you put it, those with steal-able secrets?" said Bench.

"... I may be. But I did not kidnap or hold Blake Griffin (lately) without permission. Anyway, CossycSystems did just fine rearranging Blake's head, didn't they? The church did not do that. A business concern did, but not us.... Or Whomever," she was careful to say.

"But," said Hunch, "there have been suspect things, and that continues. Things like racism, stake-burnings, torture-testing, slavery, bullying and bigotry."

"Yep. Some people certainly did those things in the name of whatever. But then there's what we're no longer supposed to call PC, not bad if it had stopped before acquiring its totalitarian control, bullying and bigotry. I didn't like it when the Inquisitives and Poritans did it, when the segregationists did it in the 19th, 20th centuries. PR copies that. It's like they all have the same religion: mind-control bullying and bigotry, which attaches to whatever current cause you've got. Anything to corral me and force me to 'think the right thing'. "

"I could call you on some of that, maybe," said Hunch. "What about the wacko religious cults."

"Got me! But we don't steal software and hardware to stop aging. Look at death—it's a given: Aging stopped! So we aren't against aging; we welcome it. We agree with Dr. deVill: 'Oh death where is thy sting, oh grave where thy victory?' Experience of our immortality comes after death. Your immortalist over there... he'd start a cult if it would help him...." She gestured downhill in the direction of FivePoints and CossycSystems. "But he doesn't need a cult, does he? He's got FRED talks."

"Can you e-mail me a list?" Lt. Hunch was just about finished with this.

"So you want me to spy round religion looking for cults from my contacts? How bout I check out that eternal cloud of witnesses Witter is so proud of?"

"I guess we can do that for you with the list."

"OK, I'll send a list of churches and other institutions we work with. ...You'll notice CossycSystems isn't one of them. Even though it's just like religion—except You are in charge! Cultural appropriation alert!! You made yourself and can confess/ absolve anything on soSHmedia in any blog venue, mode, appe! (Grin.) And don't forget MammalZon's biblical fan fiction! One's voice calls stuff into being and it appears on the second day: 'Buloxi,' order me a sink plunger!" Her tone became bland. "Tech is the manipulative attention police, totalizing all thought like Outer Manchuria before the fall of the Whirlwind Wall. —Forget 666. The prophet obviously had a couple dozen 666666+ in mind: Every human's got to be numbers to buy and sell. That's why the soup kitchen's full. They want to eat without being a hundred numbers."

"That woman makes my head spin," said Sgt. Bench as they walked down the hallway.

"Clever; but overreaching." said Hunch. "Devalued clever—InterWebs oceans of it. About worthless now."

"2017 KIDNAPPING DISPUTED BY VARIOUS FACTIONS, CHRISTIAN CULTS IMPLICATED."

From a clip of Sheree Kim interviewing Dr. Baron deVill, posted to the *LamPPost wwwwww.*: "This is not about healthier lifestyles, injections or surgery. Not about extending life mechanistically, so as to enable the onset of dementia and other deteriorations. That's no mandate. *Reversal* of aging attacks those dissolutions before they start. And it is possible, as well, to deploy the experimental stem cells in a commingling which will result in this reversal I'm speaking of."

"Thank you very much for coming, Fabian," said Dr. deVill. "It wasn't mentioned in my request, but Dr. Rostof thought you might be amenable to hearing something of my plans."

Fabian noticed he did not say *our* plans as most Cossyc doctors did. *Plans?* Fabian did not have quite the easy feeling the other doctors gave him. Of all these clinicians or researchers investigating 2017's "case," deVill was most like Fabian in possessing looks and cultural charm. Dr. deVill was handsome, fair, lean; and dynamic when he chose to be. But he could stop you with a glance, whether in friendship or folly. Fabian was laid back, nominally the go-to guy among teens in the neighborhood, and did not like to push anything. Dr. deVill never seemed pushy. He did not need pushy.

"But before we get to that, let's refer to the conclusions CossycSystems has so far drawn with regard to cultic possibilities."

For the first time, deVill looked over at Candace Parker. Fabian noticed. It was a brief look, hardly a glance, but assessing. Candace Parker wore bifocals, was wrinkled and slight. She had shrunk with age and seemed fragile, often hesitant.

Cossyc administration had its own building, even more elegantly outfitted, also for meetings with business clients and investors. Other buildings housed laboratories loaded with elaborate hardware, and software invention terminals; seminar rooms for colleagues to meet and discuss. Situated with others between corridors in the main campus building, this consulting room had no windows. They sat together in one of the tiny tastefully furnished rooms. Fabian had a vague sense of all this and wanted to be in some other setting besides this small cramped room with the larger-than-life deVill.

Simply, waiting, Fabian looked at him.

"You are aware of these?

The boy waited. Cultic possibilities. He did not want to be disrespectful but had no idea how to put it. "Not really," he said at last. "I mean we don't think so, but we also know that you do. CossycSystems does."

Dr. deVill smiled with his eyes. "So we just agree to disagree?" It was pleasantly said. "It's very good that you continue upfront, open about your position." Then he said, quite unexpectedly, "To tell you the truth... cultic doesn't concern me. I'm not interested in that end of it."

Candace seemed to sit up a bit. She leaned forward slightly. She had never seen or heard the FRED NatterHour, so Candace was suddenly learning to see the child he had been in this astute precise man before them.

DeVill noticed her attention but did not look her way. Fabian wondered, for the first time in his life, if she could see as well as... well, as younger people. Of course she had been young once. Everybody had. She wore glasses now but he recalled youthful photos of a beautiful vigorous girl hanging out with friends in glam cars. He looked back at deVill, who except that once, earlier, seemed not to notice her in the consultation. Faintly he wished he would.

"You and your friends' familial witnesses have all been quite cooperative in helping me determine the amount of aging, allowing the technicians to do their work of extraction, imaging and analysis on a range of biological properties. We are aware that these show a distinct correspondence, even (to my mind) a complete confirmation of a non-aging event."

He stopped, and Fabian nodded.

"Where we differ is in *how* this was achieved. You all have your own idea, on which your friends agree, based on your perceived experience...." He looked with deeper penetration at the boy. "Now, after all our tests and analysis, and my own careful survey... now for the hard admission." He smiled easily, with a touch of dryness, saying, "You have not aged that I can perceive, and I have no ideas on this. That is what makes it interesting to me."

He did not say, *No ideas on how to stop aging*. Dr. deVill worked on engaging problems until they were solved or implemented, and then he lost interest, moved on to the next. He had no idea how *these kids* avoided aging over a period of time in which children and adolescents should develop powerfully. It would be of interest to discover organic technologies already capable of performing this event, and determine relationships to his techniques (in development). Minute changes in aging had occurred in the last few days. Otherwise these kids had not aged since November 3, 2017.

Fabian did not smile. He did not wonder about lack of evidence. He did kinda wonder that Dr. deVill would admit it. He was pretty sure everyone else in these buildings would not have. CossycSystems would probably never admit they had no ideas.

Dr. DeVille stood and walked behind the pair in their chairs: grandmother and grandson. Fabe turned to look up at him as he spoke. For Nana it was not so easy. She half turned, one ear tilted in careful attending. As Dr. DeVille continued, Fabian glanced at her. Her posture was not as straight as he remembered from earlier in the month, or the end of October. He wondered if she was growing a hump of some sort. He'd seen this sometimes on old women. But he wasn't sure if it was happening to her or just a bit of something along with the two-year apparent loss of height.

"The plan is for age to be a measurement in time, not a measure of diminished capacity. We used to dream of using embryonic stem cells for the reversal but that has proved unnecessary. I have proved it so, as now have others."

Fabe saw him carefully assessing Nana as he came around again to his chair.

"The stem cells of immature rodents have been used to reverse aging in those of their species who were dying of various maladies. So you can see what a breakthrough this has been.... What I'm hoping," he said as he sat down, his penetrating look very much focused on Fabian. "...What I'm hoping for, is not so much the reasons behind your long period of not aging. This has proved so and will be studied... as it may be... but my own concern at the moment is with a trial I have in mind."

He waited a moment, then spoke again quietly. "I would like to make a trial on you and your grandmother. The trial for renewal of life in your grandmother."

Surprised silence.

Nana shifted slightly.

Fabian said, "You mean using my blood? My stem cells?"

"Yes."

"What exactly are stem cells, anyway?"

"Living cells capable of sustaining and restoring bodily tissues. Some sources include umbilical cords to be discarded—the blood in these. But also in human bone marrow, which in particular deteriorates with age." He went on with this a little, but Fabian had stopped listening. Dr. deVill understood this as Fabian turned to look at his grandmother. He smiled at his Nana.

After a moment he said, "Ha-ha, what do you think Nana? Can I save you? Can I make you young again?"

Also smiling, she said, "Well we have to think about it. …Do you think we might have a glass of good water?"

"I mean," said Fabian, "what a thing to do to me! Am I supposed to say, no I'm not helping you stop aging?" She was bending her ear to his mouth on leaving the building close to the traffic of Exchange.

"Yes!" she said. "Should I be Countess Dracula? Yes!"

They were about to cross Sharon at the intersection of FivePoints, on their way along Sharon toward their apartment up beyond the 3⅓St. development.

"That was one shrewd cookie!" she said, holding his hand as they crossed before waiting traffic.

From Dr. deVill's recent speech given at the *Institute for Social Supreme Science*: "There are enormous implications, politically, morally, economically, socially; all coming with renewal of life. The aging classes will look and feel younger than their numerical ages. Babies will be born to far older women. Many more generations of families will be alive together. Explosive populations. We need to think about the implications."

On watching the clip later Fabian quipped. "Don't you mean someone else, not we? Then, texting, 'I don't think he's really going to think on that--other things on his mind.' " Fabian was private-messaging HB.

"Scientist not social engineer." HB agreed.

"Like the social engineer who wants to move all people in rural areas of EHio into the cities, Nana was saying?—there's a man now trying for it."

"Yeah that."

"She says people did that on their own in the 1930s, left their well-water behind. No engineers. They got none at Cossyc?"

"Software, not so much social engineers. But they use social scientists for propaganda, iirc."

"What'll they drink if they come?" (Fabian)

Jay had neural control with sensory input. A sleeve pimpled with electrodes sent signals from her chest muscles, software interpreting, to move her hand. She'd had to learn the method, teach the muscles, but now she no longer had to think about it. Jay was *TheArm.*

Housekeeping was gone for the day. She huddled by the concrete wall on a bench in the sub-basement, imagining flitting from marker to marker, stone to stone. GlimmerDale was going to be her turf. Had to be, had to! Only there in the cemetery would she have the freedom needed to be Jay! To be *TheArm*. The only problem was.... The Arm. She stared at it, flingers flexing.

It had given her a new life. But now? Now that she was on the outs with Nandora and Uncle... now the arm was *nuisance* and she was in the laundry. Why couldn't the dimwits at Cossyc see that there was no way she could be gone two years without arm maintenance! Wasn't that a clue?! Maybe they just lied! Maybe they did know the truth and just won't say!

With this arm she could take out those guards down there!... But then they'd catch her and take the arm away. If she ran off she'd lose all the maintenance and upgrades. Oh woe.

Maybe deVill can print me up a better arm.... One that doesn't need maintenance?

"So hi!" said Pomala.

—Suddenly. From where?

She had a heaping plastic basketful of dirty clothes, her arms wrapped round them, the cheery Pomala smile on her face.

OMN! Jay wanted to say. *OMN!* Her glance might have expressed it. But she was down, so she only said, "Good idea. The laundry."

"Yeah! They never question someone carrying laundry. Not at the service entrance."

Not with that smile, thought Jay. *Not if you're Pomala.*

Pome went to the nearest washer and dumped the basket.

Jay noticed the pink cargo pants among other bits of panties, tee's, and odd—was that a knit vest? "You've got to do something about that wardrobe," she said.

Pome knew about the arm strapped to Jay's upper body. About the plastic knobs and wires and metal components, electrodes, of Jay's special shoulder hidden in its sleeve beneath her sweater and blouse.

"You're arm is a wonder." She came close, picking up Jay's fingers. Each finger was encased in flexflesh the warm color of Jay's skin. It went all the way up and over her shoulder. "It's so strong and beautiful," she said, looking with gentle warmth into her friend's eyes. Jay squeezed Pome's fingers. "You have such a good touch with them," said Pomala. Gently Jay loosed her friend's fingers and using both hands—her own and Cossyc's—wiped under each eye.

"Yeah," she said. "I got the electrodes picking up signals so fine. I just think about it and *zing*. And I don't need to think much anymore. I think; they twitch; and I'm good."

"Yeah. I remember you told me they had to reroute the nerves of your upper body muscles."

Jay nodded. "*Pectoralis major*," she said. Jay was knowledgeable about terms and anatomy. She had to be.

Pome unslung her book bag and brought out goodies. The first she opened was beet chips. Sweet, purple, salty, crunchy. They sat cross-legged on a couple washers, munching. Then Pome opened two bottles of cold green tea. Jay drank half hers. "Got any soda? Got any *Akropolis Pop*?

They started giggling, skinny teenage legs sometimes dangling and banging, still munching on chips—white corn chips this time.

"Girl, I've got to remember!" said Jay, wiping salt from her lips. "I've been forgetting."

Pome nodded. "1900 was what happened to us between 2017 and 2019. This is the glue keeping us together." She dug into her pocket, fiddled with the wePhone. "Look at these. No wait! I'll get the pod—they look so much better."

The girls both got out their z-pods and started watching identical flicks—clips of old fast-moving films showing the chaotic 1900 cityscapes. Carts, people, horse-and-carriage, horse-and-riders moving with some sort of intuitive skill through intersections, just missing one another on the streets of New Amsterdam. Then they searched independently for more.

"See, what I need to do is dream it all at night," said Jay. "That should help."

"Yes, we don't want to live there, we just want to remember, and let that help us get back to 2017. Dreaming is good," Pome said. "I've been doing a lot since we got here. Some stuff seems rather cloudy, but some I recognize from before. Before *what* I don't know, but it just seems very familiar."

"What? Like what?"

"So you know how you dream about people who are total strangers? Like what are they doing in *my* dream? And like I should have some say in the matter? But nope, there they are... and who are they? And we're interacting like a game full of strangers. Say like when we first started gaming with I.E.P.?"

"Yes! Yes! I do know that!" Jay had opened a chocolate-and-cream Wooo-E-Pie. She was licking cream all around the puffy chocolate edges.

"I'm not going to try figuring out how all these images and personal —or maybe impersonal— interactions got in my head, or my mind, or my dream. Or whatever. I probably wouldn't believe scientists on this even. Because. If they tried to explain, it would all boil down to believing anyway. I have to *believe* what they say because I don't know."

"So?"

"So anyway it's more like what's the atmosphere, the drift, the feel? —I don't know what I'm trying to say but, Jay, it has to do with, I don't know. Is it what I feel from the dream or its people?

"Example." Jay was now licking cream from her lips.

Pomala took a swig of tea. "Hmmm."

"Is it like when you see a movie and some things feel creepy? Or some things feel fuzzy-comfy?"

"Yes! That's very close. I think I actually get more of a sense of these things from stories in books. Like there are some books I don't read because of it. I mean too much of the *mean*, if you know what I mean." She smiled.

"Mean-spirited?" said Jay.

"Yes! Characters I wouldn't—like Bishop Sirifim says—invite into my apartment, so why would I invite them into my head? Because books put these characters and things they are doing into your head.... So what are they doing in *my* dreams.... Only really it doesn't happen so much that way in my dreams. Usually they are kinda neutral." She stopped. Her wrist turning, flipping the empty tea bottle around with her fingers and thumb, playing.

"But these dreams are different. I like these people. But like I said, there's actually not a whole lot there. With clouds, stars. Just something quiet, friendly. Kind, even."

"Wow—could use some'a that!"

"Yeah," Pomala grinned. "Next time they stop by I'll ask them to visit you, send some your way.

—Contact. I think they're getting it, said Gneis to his Mam, Mary Bala Jones.

—I do, she answered. There may have been a smile on her face. If she'd had a face.

From Dr. Nicole Rostof's most recent report:

"Subject P. discussed her dreams. These transcripts were shared with Dr. Neee because of his interest in body, psyche, and spirit, and divisions between these three. He may contact her sister for follow-up. I, too, am very interested in these dreams though they lack concrete, personal images, narrative and continuity, which lack might be expected, especially the latter. The primary interest is in their quality, which seems somewhat unique.

"Subject P. is not precise or articulate about these qualities, but her analogies are sufficient. [...]

"Another peculiarity is the intense visionary quality relevant to cosmological equivalencies. She describes a universe—or one might even suppose—a multiverse of vast and vibrant proportions, such as anyone might see in documentaries or phoo-tube clips featuring the interplanetary, stellar and galatic, telescopic views; but with this difference: the objects, systems, suns, nebula, even galaxies, seem personified in her dreams; perhaps a hypnotic residue.

"Not all the dream specimens are like this. Some seem to feature subjective familiar reality of persons going about their lives and play with our subject as bystander or observer. At other times she seems to interact with them, playing.

"This all might be seen to fit in with the—as yet I will call it as per our consensus—surmise. A surmise which indicators show: Namely that cultic hypnosis may be involved."

Dual Dreamscapes and What's Wrong Now?

"CITING SNOBBERY BY RURAL ELITES FOR ALLEGEDLY SUBVERTING ELECTORAL PROCESSES, CALIFLOWER THREATENS SECESSION: FOLLYWOOD CLAIMS IT WILL ABSTAIN."

Here's Gretch in her narrow bed entertaining herself with pen and paper, head bent over her spiral notebook. Gretchen has big plans for these jottings. She hopes one day to submit to *Sad Magazine*, along with some drawings of her own devising.

From the Sheltering Cares housemother's journal:

"Notes to social engineers. We think taxpayer money could be put to better use. Transganderrang at taxpayer expense is a waste of our money. This money might be better used on medical procedures to reshape urethras and bladders of the born males and females who are now elderly. If we do this we will save billions of dollars in nursing home expenses. Think about it. Being younger, you social engineers have not bothered to scientifically analyze why old people are committed to these homes at taxpayer expense. In Dunnny's Restaurants, elderly born women are concerned they haven't strength enough to push a trans-woman aside when needing to get into a stall quickly. The oldsters are bummed about having to cut back on coffee, and are prone to blame politicians for the disparity in socially just use of taxpayer funds."

In other jottings, "The DBC component in legal candybus has heightened complaints about reverse engineering paranoia so necessary to both medical and highflown legitimate pathologies."

Gretchen notes that this one needs work before submission to *Sad*.

Tu came out of the closet. He had gone in there to think.

Dark in there for one thing: just close the door. He needed the dark to help visualize and remember calculations from the latest dream. Beautiful, predictive formulas. Equations. Complements. Nothing concrete in these dreams unless you counted numbers, maths, mathmatical symbols, formulae, as concrete. All abstract except when concretized in these codes, the encoding was itself concrete as such, but not the ideas they represented. Such elegant stuff in those dreams—except they weren't stuff. They were all about pre-stuff—as he thought it. This is where it all began. He couldn't think much about the pre-pre-stuff. He wasn't there yet. It was hard enough just getting this far.

So the closet was good for that and the dream memories. Tu had been holed up in his physicist's cave since the session with Dr. Neee. He was not keeping much track of time here in his bedroom but he was grateful for the punctuation of meals. Sometimes he opened his bedroom window and leaned out. Bracing. Then he'd go check the kitchen for food. Sometimes food was ready, sometimes not. Sometimes his mother was there, sometimes not. Same with his father. He liked fruit and yogurt, juice, so that was easy to fix.

They are going to make you go back to school soon. He thought about it, his hands on the window locks. If he didn't keep them locked, the frame would slide a bit and there'd be a draft. These were the first apartments in development. The contractor shaved corners just a bit. Missing social life, missing school, missing studies, or a girlfriend or any of that was not actually missing anything. If they weren't there it was freedom. Mental freedom. So school was coming. Don't deal with it. When it gets here it will deal with you.

... Unless we get back to 2017. …In the moments of return, I will have to stop watching my actions, forget the observation of them entirely. …Just play ball so to speak, get us back.

... *Of course school will be there, too. But that's different.*

2017 is normal life and he knows how to fit everything, every thinking thing into normal life—at least for now. It deals with you, but differently. He raised the sash. November came in. Brisk. November 2019 was as yet pretty much like November 2017 as regards weather if little else.

He did really like the dream calculations so much better than his own. He was tempted to think of them as his own, what with being *his* dreams. Yes, there was some sadness and something familiar. The sadness was owing to... uh… he'd had to throw out what had gone before. All that work— hypotheses out the window. That was bracing, but not as *the new*. The new—how did that—. So it was familiar but.... Yes. He'd seen it somewhere before and just not remembered it. Which is very strange. …The truth was… hardly anyone was getting anywhere with weakly interacting massive particles so why, anyway, was he thinking —dreaming about— WIMPs?

"So here is one thing I heard in my dream." Pome was texting Jay. "Let's just say his name is Gneis."

"his?" Jay texted her back.

"Yes. Just seems right somehow to call him Gneis even though there's no body in the dream— to say so."

"but what's it like?"

"So kinda cloudy like nebulas or other space features. Nonspecific."

"i so understand nonspecific." (sarcasm.) "so he said?"

" 'Dah is working on it. Dah has no experimental hardware. Dah has to go completely theoretical.' How's that for brilliant?"

"anything else?"

" 'Dah is discovering mind.' "

"no duh, dah."

"But Gneis is helping him!"

"needs help if he's only just discovering minds."

"He says we take it for granted, but our world is largely determined by mind."

"retracting my invite. don't ask them to join my dreams."

WIMPs won't fit the standard model... which doesn't even explain gravity anyway. These were Tu's closet thoughts.

If there was the gravitational pull they'd be one to 1000 times more massive than a proton. If we are talking the world as concrete, they wouldn't connect with us... unless... the weak nuclear force. As things stand now. More pull than gravity, but only moving distances on nucleo-atomic scaling. They could be as encompassing as fog—all around us, invisible. And could not interact with us but... well possibly passing through the elemental lead. That's about it.... I think. They need better detectors to go with these theories. A new generation. It's not so much that the experiments fail as they just pushed out new theories. And one of these is—maybe there's no WIMPs.... But I lean toward... better hardware, look harder. In fact, they are passing through me right now! You know, one of these things (or non-things) could be 100 times larger than I am.... What they need is detecting with a hundred tons of liquid zenon. The experimentalists. I mean theorists are good. Yes. You need those. But a closet can only take you so far.

Tu was getting distracted: *What about panpsychism?* If dreams actually mean anything... or can help, then....

He didn't actually care for that suffix—or that prefix! But what? He had no say in the matter of scientific terminology. Just yet. Maybe later. Maybe—by the time 2019 rolled around.

Tu smiled. Actually. Tu.

The golden Glindora set a glass bottle with label proclaiming spring water by the Mayor's open computer. He did not look up as she stood there, serious, blond, in business attire with a red bowtie.

"Thanks," he said absently. Since the election earlier, he was looking at yesterday's poll numbers. This has been the off mayoral year. Next year he was up to bat again. 18 years and counting. Not bad.

The Mayor was bleak. Everybody in the city was bleak, he liked to say. He used this word on account of the takedown by a white ambassador from Angland to the premiere of Rosydia, a few years back: "If you don't like bleak men, sir, why do you live in Efrica?"

He smiled to himself. The numbers weren't that bad. Yet. —He might have added. But he wasn't going to think about that.

Glindora was still there, though he hadn't summoned her. He recollected her standing by, peripherally. Trim figure in silver. The water? The water!

"Thanks for the water," he said looking up. "I suppose you mean something by it." He flashed the still charming smile.

Imagine that smile 20 years ago, thought Glindora. I was alive. A teenager. Got-to-go-places. Hardly aware there was an election contest. Pomala was not alive. Glindora thought she remembered that younger mayor's handsome black face, slightly high cheekbones, cheerful eyes. The signs and ads, TV. Somehow nicer, more real. A good many people liked him. A good many people still do.

"Yes, Mayor. I do." She said no more. She was thinking, *Medical technology capital of the world.*

"Well I'm working on it. More about that coming up. Keep the sewers in mind," he added. He was wary of presenting an opening: "How's the sister? You are so glad she's back. Saw her looking good on the vids. Got rid of the flaming blue 'do." He smiled. "There's hope for her."

"Yes." She continued looking at him, pleasantly.

"Well you must have something to share about it." He looked at the water and back at her.

"Notice the brand?" She said.

"Well-known. Always has been. I was a kid, etc. eating their vanillas... when I could get my hands on them."

"Yes. They buy raw from that consortium. The one working bleak keds really hard in Efrica." She could get away with stuff like this. Her look was more pleasant still.

"You know, you are good at this. That must be why we keep you on. Anything else?"

"Just the latest on them. Manipulating rural townsfolk... with this and that promise... fluid terms and agreements… you know how they do... to get hold of their ground water."

"By them you mean the corporations—plural. And one way we stay in office."

"Understood." The smile was —no smile.

"So?" he said.

"Kinda underground corporate railroading. Look at this? If I may?" She indicated the screen.

"Be my guest." He shoved back from the desk, looked out the window at the brick courthouse across the alleyway, as she loaded the vid to uUbe of... he looked back at the screen. She moved away, he moved closer, hesitated.

"Play?" She suggested.

He looked at it, at the words under it. PuffyHo clip. Covertly recorded. Of course. This did not used to happen. The Mayor gave it a verbal and the thing moved, spoke.

It was the CEO: "No one has a *right* to water."

There was no more. The Mayor waited, as it played again, and again. He let it go, in part, to see how it was done, production values, others speaking off to the side adding context. The CEO was not misspeaking. There were two clips, actually, from different perspectives or angles. As though devices were digitally recording casually, or inadvertently. He read down to see how it was captured. No clue.

"Dang!" he said.

"Anything more?"

He looked up. "I'll have to think about it." Before she could say it, he said, "You'll be back," and smiled.

She did too. Pleasantly.

The Mayor studied all of that, the water question from that particular angle. What else could he do?

It was not exactly spring water. Sure it was in the aquifer. Of course there's water underground. It couldn't rightly be called artesian welling. They had to drill and keep pumping. They're called drilled wells. So... we don't need just their hills and mountains over houses and hollows. We need all the stuff under houses and farms, and well—hell—who owns all that anyway? Mineral rights they call it. Oh yeah, water's a mineral? When its ice.... Oh Lordy. That vid.... It's like they used to say in church about the housetops. *Sht.* Who's got time for it?

You better have.

He was staring at the bottle.

The sewers, he thought now, had been easier. *That* had not been easy. Expensive but easier.

Maybe he means the Corporation, not people. —But the context! The Mayor played the clips again. Corporations? Anyone? No one? Who's got a right to water? A right to water … or water rights. You just *say* "water rights." That's the phrase you want, stupid. That's how to begin. You could use some political help. He was talking to the uUbe.

Pastor was drinking coffee. HB preferred cocoa.

"What's wrong with Jay's mother and uncle?" HB was asking. He could see the second and third stories of neighboring buildings in the intersection out the apartment corner window, above the SoupMission. It was night. Lights were on in those apartments. You could see people walking around in rooms above closed shops and services. Some walked around to close curtains, pull blinds. In the other direction, directly across Sharon, they saw lighted CossycSystems campus buildings. "That can't be right."

They sat diagonally across from one another, what Pastor Zettler had learned to call cat-a-corner, growing up. Newspapers were spread open on the coffee table before them, rings of cocoa and coffee here and there where the cups had slopped a bit. Lingering smells from the soup kitchen below the next room came up: chlorine, chicken, faintly redolent garbage, very slight.

"She's normal. So is Jay's uncle. They are fairly normal as parent and guardian duo." Pastor sipped his coffee and cream.

"That can't be right," repeated HB.

"I think they could use some guidance, that's all.

"You mean they's ignorant?"

"No. They care. They go about their problem, to which they are committed, wrong. —That's harsh. I might be able to soften it a bit."

"So, to?"

"They need guidance, a mentor of some kind. Jay's not easy."

"Tell me." HB grinned.

"She's The Arm, you mean."

"That. I saw her yank a full-grown man in pain to his knees with that. I was getting beat up myself at the time. Saw her with the corner of my eye. Couldn't believe it."

"May I ask what happened?"

"Said the wrong thing in the wrong place at the wrong time."

"Here? In the neighborhood?"

Again HB grinned. "You might say that."

"You look okay. Sounds like a good story. …How long ago was this?" Pastor stifled a sudden wariness.

"About 117 years ago. In the room below, and the sidewalk."

Pastor's brows shot up past his glasses frames.

"Or 119 years, depending on your POV," said HB.

"I don't recall its being brought up at any of the sessions," said Pastor. He had been to at least three sessions with various people, including more with HB.

"It was in the head report. The other kids were asked about it. Everybody in Cossyc's sights was asked. I think Quadri was the only one remembering; said he was hiding under the pool table. Tu hasn't gone back for a session yet. Don't think he will. But Quad's the only one to remember it. Girl, am I glad he remembered. I mean sir." He nodded toward Pastor and picked up his cocoa as casually as he could.

"Well, what's it about?"

"I keep thinking about it... and all I got's magic."

"Magic?" Again Pastor was wary, still hiding it.

"Yeah. It has to do with the vaudeville—only not that. It was this giant they called the Grandmaster, iirc. Cossyc thinks he's the problem pointing to "cult." I just call him Big Fello. He's like the Game Master. Showmaster is good, too. Like I said, I keep thinking about it."

"That can be a very good thing... not always... but often."

"What's that mean?"

"If you can use thinking to determine. It may be best to stick with what you've determined after meditating it. Not keep chewing the same cud."

"Like they say crows do."

Pastor smiled. "Right. At some point it's there. And then you've got it. Keep it."

Which immediately reminded Pastor of his own struggles with indecision. Many would say it had been a mistake to help his childhood friend pull down her barn. Was it so? Or was his recurring lumbago just another partaking in the Lord Chris's suffering? Was there a choice even now to be made among these thoughts?

HB was silent. Still thinking.

"So I have a thought," he said at last. "I keep thinking it."

Pastor waited.

HB added, "What is it ordinary parents like Jay's mother do... that's so ffuts up?" He grinned.

"She cares about Jay. She tries to make her obey. Tries to keep her out of trouble. Checks to make sure her friends won't mislead her. Education. A good future. That's what guardians are for. This is what parents do."

"But you aren't trying to tell me she does all that completely the right way."

"Right."

"What about me? Will I make an ordinary normal parent—or a good parent?"

"I think you will." Pastor emphasized the word I.

"So, are you under suspicion of kidnapping us?"

Slowly Pastor smiled, his glasses catching gold flecks of light from windows across the way. "We've almost always been under suspicion of kidnapping. Never anything formal like this, however. I have the feeling, from FivePoints APD in their handling of this, that we aren't under any real suspicion. Unless it's their way with every investigation."

"You mean some kinda slippery, a disguise. But what about these other kidnapping suspicions? That's your way of saying something else."

"I've heard about the witting and weblogging charges and counter charges. —We are the bad guys, we are the good guys—that kind of thing."

"You mean kidnapping souls, setting snares for the innocent selfie porno-gophers, transGanders, and perves?"

Pastor smiled. "Well, repentance is saving." Though he didn't always give him the smile, HB could say what he wanted. But. …There was a lot here for Zettler to pray about. "From what I've been told about social mediation, you could get in trouble with parts of that?" he suggested.

HB grinned.

Pastor said, "Ranting, unreasonable extended blog entries about charities like ours. Maybe the charge of ...the price of a meal being a sermon. That's one witt I heard about."

"Not true. I'll witt it."

"No don't, please. There's too much of all this already." He looked seriously at HB.

"UFOLOGISTS FINALLY DETERMINE OCTOBER 1ST SIGHTING WAS ACTUALLY THE PRESIDENT IN A NEW SOLO HIGH PERFORMANCE HYBRID ASCENDING AT A STEEP ANGLE OVER THE CAPITOL."

\ Throw Forward /

Anno Domine to the Common Era

Digger-dog and Girl-boy stood rapt under massive tall trees, woodlands of hickory, horse chestnut, buckeyes maples oaks, thousands standing ponderous above and around them. A woodland deep with mote-shot sunlight and gloom. Quiet, they listened.

The elder youth Digger-dog was lighter than any Americle A'ndian brave in the clan—lighter in skin, but for his brother Girl-boy. Having proved themselves worthy, they had been adopted by the clan. These two had come alone into clan territory, and, after a time of testing, were accepted among them almost as equals. Almost. A day would come when the *almost* might be challenged, thought Digger-dog. His thoughts, when they pass as words instead of images, are mixed of True People's tongue and Anglish which, in 1900 A.D., had been native to him. The lay of land. It was the same at the turn of the 20th century. But, it was now grown in great trees. He did not know the year. True People had not numbered the years.

Girl-boy started ahead, but his elder brother checked him.

"Not yet."

It was said in the tongue of True People, only a breeze in the smaller Girl-boy's ear. His feathers hung low beside it, two jay-feathers. The muscular Digger-dog had two black gleaming long raven feathers, dangling, braided in above his pale ear. The names of these brothers had been chosen for them by the clan, chiefly—in this matter—by Red Fox, under whose tutelage they learned. Having been brought into their midst by Red Fox, they were his charge.

The Native Americle youths who had taken them in had been on a mission to find and bring back the seeming escapee: The Girl. They had thought it would be a search of territory, not Time. The braves came from *Timebefore* and had apparently inadvertently entered the *Aftertime* on account of The Girl. These True People youths had sought her for return to the clan.

Sometimes called Rabbit-Foot-Woman-of-Grandmaster, she also was lighter of skin than the A'ndians, and had been taken in an earlier violent raid on settlements in the eastern mountains. The Girl spoke little if ever. Few had heard words from that still mouth. Her eyes had no look. In that earlier eastern raid, her clan of pale people had fallen. The Girl was not of the crying ones, and so was saved. Teary-eyes could not become True People.

Digger-dog was named by Red Fox for the pale-people trade he had plied before coming into the clan. He had been a grave digger. Girl-boy had been named on account of the Girl. He had been holding her hand when they took her again. Girl-boy was made to cry but he too was saved for the sake of the Girl and for Digger-dog whose brother he was. Digger-dog was good, valuable for the clan, and he would teach Girl-boy what was needed.

They were scouting with two born True People—Walleye-stare and Eaglestreak—who were just this side of the hill beyond, with the girl, awaiting their signal. Here were skunk-smelling leaves yet to unfurl, fern stems tightly bundled, not yet unfolding their web-work. Green thin things pushing aside wet brown dead leaves. The stream at their feet burbled past, spring-swollen.

Red Fox had taken fever. Before his wits withered he had commanded these two braves—*and not Dark Cloak or Quick Claws*—go the rendezvous with them. To *Aftertime*, if possible. Dark Cloak was always the challenge to Red Fox, and Quick Claws was too impatient.

As they waited for the others to come, the two pale braves chewed on pounded roasted handfuls of white oak acorn nuggets with bitters leached out of them. Before roasting leaching was done in ash woven baskets set in a stream. Now, gently, great oak trees overhead were sprouting leaves once more, fine and green, scarcely visible. Mentor of Red Fox, the *Meteu*, whose name is derived from the word meaning drum a hollow vessel with tight skin, the *Meteu* had said they must seek no rendezvous except once in the cycle, at this time of year. Solely in this, the season of planting.

Both were of the Strange People, and Girl-boy had almost never let go the Girl's hand till he came among True People. In the cycle of seasons, two planting, two gathering, two hunting, two fallow, they had been under the protection of True Peoples. Neither boy knew the why or wherefore of *Timebefore* in their lives, but believed and experienced it anyway. The small rock ledge, for instance, there in the distance through trees: The small rock ledge had been part of the cemetery where Digger-dog had worked digging graves in that future of 1900 A.D.. There they would meet the other two braves and the Girl in order to help serve her mysterious purpose.

Girl-boy was A'ndian now. He remembered Ma most but everyone else had faded into the background of memory except James Priam. Digger-dog retained much of what had been—or? What would be? —He would not think of *time*. It didn't matter. The internal combustion engine mattered more. He'd keep that in mind if he could.

The stream at their feet was nearly in course with that they had known, through what, in the years of their joint childhood, had been the cemetery. It had flowed down from Harkins Hill but now looked different from its 1900 A.D. underground travels past alleyways and beneath footbridges or through culverts. But now, in *Timebefore*, the graveyard stream is much the same as it had been, but the gravestones from *Aftertime* aren't here, nor the Civil War dead plot, and The Lodge where funeral showings had once been held.

Or—would that be.... how do you call the future when it's past?

He might sometimes recall that the girl had been little. She was the age of his brother, he guessed. Neither, he thought, were so little now. Strangely, this season had changed from summer to spring when they first came to True People's time. Vibrant stars had been poured into the sky, and no gaslight anymore. He no longer missed gaslight. Or grave digging. Or piles of work always waiting for him.

Work now is slow work. You have to get food but not grow it. The braves (he was a brave) did not grow food. Women and girls grew food. He liked hunting. Eating whatever came to hand in season. Giving the hunt to women to fix after the innards were cooled. He did skin the carcass. Tools weren't the best, but he'd made them good enough, on his own after guidance from Red Fox and Quick Claws and the others. He guessed *Ochquetit* did not escape from the lunatic asylum after all. She seems to belong here, though she'd never been A'ndian except in dress. Sometimes she actually said a word in Anglish.

"Do you remember Anglish?" said Digger-dog to Girl-boy in the A'ndian tongue. Digger-dog was tall and broad-shouldered. His little brother had always been slender and fine. They had moved forward a bit, were now halted in trees near the ledge far below High Lake where stood the spring encampment.

Girl-boy became very still. He was supposed to be still, he knew this but it just had not happened. He lived much in the moment, and always seemed to need his brother's quiet "Not yet." These spoken thoughts of his brother stopped him.

After a moment, he said, "Do you mean this?" He said it in Anglish.

"Yes," returned Digger-dog. They were about to have a soft brief conversation in Anglish, not unlike the one of the year before. Only the rendezvous called forth these joint memories. And Anglish was the only language in which to speak of them.

Girl-boy stood a mite taller, freed up just a bit. He said, "Remember Five Points? The musical instrument shop? Pool hall?"

"Yes, but you should speak quietly."

"You mowed the grass here. Where these great trees are. The vaudeville tried to take *Ochquetit* but True People got her. Now I remember again why we're here. I remember the night when everything changed." His face suggested an anguish not seen since the start of the previous cycle.

Neither spoke of Ma. They said nothing of Ma's shop, the clasp-locker hospital at Five Points. Then Girl-boy said, "You found *Ochquetit* here? In the tool shed? You dug the graves. Here?"

"Somebody had to," said Digger-dog. *Good enough pay.*

No one in the clan called it Harkins Hill, only these two clan members called it that. After scouting below to see none were near, they were to meet at the ledge—the great rock where the girl had been recaptured. Where the tool shed had stood. Now they moved forward, softly.

They stopped—peering about, seeing the sweep of a hawk in sun far overhead beyond the finely budding twigs. Seeing the trot of the flycatcher up a near oak. Girl-boy had more thoughts. "*Tschuppinamen*," he said. "The place is the same but not so."

"Don't think too hard," his brother murmured.

"You see," said the other, sounding more and more like Parry again, "It's just an unusual time. We are like the Girl, part of the clan but taken not from a different place, but a different *time.* A strange time."

"Might be time to shut up." It was softly said.

"But don't you see, Willie, it is like Mr. G.H. Wills' *Time Machine*."

Silence. The turning of the hawk, high; the small twitching tail of a chipmunk in digging out an acorn cache—near to the arrow hand. "Where's the machine," said Digger-dog at last.

"The Girl."

"*Ochquetit* —No machine."

Eaglestreak may have been of an age with the girl. Younger, he was somewhat like Red Fox—who may become a *meteu* in time, sensing things not apparent to others. The Girl had been *Ochquetit*, meaning little girl and now, in height, *Ochquetschitsch*, simply *Girl*. Eaglestreak and Walleye-stare were scarred, one by accident, one by warfare among clans. From an infant Eaglestreak was missing a finger by his own hand. He had been assigned this task, especially for his mystical kinship to *Ochquetschitsch*, the Girl. Walleye-stare is with them for his practicality. Between the three there will be wisdom for the quest, the Girl's task at hand. If they came to *Aftertime*, Digger-dog would lead there. So 'twas appointed.

Now the two True People braves and the girl stood amid tall trees by the stream, having descended Harkins Hill. They knew the hill not by that name, but recall it as being a place of caged animals, such as boars and bison, and in its current identity as last-hill-toward-water, meaning the water of what 1900 called A'ndian River. Both Natives had been desperately ill two cycles ago in *Aftertime* but had since recovered and seem not weakened but strengthened by the ordeal.

"Stop here now," said Walleye-stare to Eaglestreak as the three came among tall girthy trees quietly greening above; but yet out of sight of the small rock-ledge.

Eaglestreak caught the Girl's hand. He was wise to do this from time to time, and in uncertain conditions. One did not know but she might wander off. He more than anyone but Red Fox understood that inner promptings might take her. This is how Eaglestreak thought. Red Fox was not in full agreement though they did not speak of it. To the brave Red Fox she was moved by various and colorful workings not always her own. These came from higher, further, unsearchable regions, and one had to take care. To learn and keep learning; to assume nothing while yet, and everlastingly, striving for understanding.

The two braves and the Girl halted, invisible among multitudes of finely leafing twigs and trees. The former with scarred faces, high cheekbones, and watchful dark eyes; with long tails and feathers, intent. Eaglestreak was the younger and smaller. The hand with which he held hers was scarred by the hatchet. She stared, not as Walleye-stare: The girl stared at nothing, at no one. She simply stared without looking, perhaps not seeing. Perhaps, Girl-boy often wondered, *She is thinking*. Just thinking. Yes, that was it.

But what about? Digger-dog would've answered. And did so each time he heard this. "She can't be thinking how to get the best edge on the adze. Or to coordinate arrow-eye-hand; or the best method and tool to grind *chasquem*."

When Eaglestreak heard them he might say, "She is thinking of the sun." Or he would say, *She thinks of the moon. She thinks of falling water*.

"But Digger-dog," Girl-boy had said in the fallow snow-time just after acorns were readied and cached. "She pounds acorns best of any sqau. She has the right" —and here he tried to think of the word. "It's like the drumming, the rhythm." And he had inserted the Anglish word, last in this line of True People words. The Girl had gone deeper than any, doing the work. None faulted her through envy or malice, because she was simply deep in the task. They made verbal game of her for other reasons.

"Now," said Eaglestreak. Walleye-stare, who searched out all using eyes, ears, and nostrils (now faintly receptive of skunk)— Walleye-stare agreed; and they moved forward. Below them, on the opposite side of this vale the pale braves also moved toward the place.

Digger-dog said to Girl-boy, "Now."

In camp, Red Fox lay stiff on skins, wide-eyed. Bewildered. He was with the *Meteu* under high, pale green, burgeoning boughs.

The *Meteu* had been in doubt of it throughout the past two cycles. The strange pale boys spoke not often of it, but when they did strange words were interspersed with the tongue. Their clothing had been strange as befits strangers—as with the Girl's upon her early capture east of here in the mountains.

Aftertime.

The mystery. All interlopers wore strange clothing. He had listened to strange boys' fragmentary speech-broken tales unconvinced. The tales of Red Fox and the scouting boys were also unconvincing for they were too detailed and imaginative.

In or out of the body, a vision is not like this, piling detail upon detail; more detail with each telling. This was not visionary. It had not the fine tight interweaving of pictures and telling symbols.

Red Fox was a'sweat, starting to tremble. He now spoke from his delirium. The *Meteu* listened carefully and transcribed all in his precise and capacious memory.

(Both Digger-dog and Girl-boy had marveled—True People needed no books, no papers, nor pencils. They kept everything in their heads and tongues, and had a rhythm to carry all they required in the way of documentation or recording—as Girl-boy had taken to thinking of it. He sometimes spoke of it that way. So did Digger-dog who thought of Mr. Edison's gramophone invention and marveled that these people were so talented and repetitiously machine-like in the same way.)

Eyes wide, Red Fox shouted forth, trembling on skins among the tall boles. He shouted upwards into branching treetops. "The interlopers have unraveled, re-woven the lands of True People not with the help of The Girl!!! The Grandmaster wove in the interlopers to make his arrow of time spill forth many peoples, tongues, and works of their hands in his splitting open the earth!!! The arrow flew straight, but its mark was the earth herself and she brought interlopers forth!!! The Girl was none of this but the shower of all!!! She is a shower!!! She is a shower!!! Two others she brought back by mischance!!!"

The Grandmaster again. If the *Meteu* could but have complete understanding. The *Meteu* spoke. "Oh trembling one, are you certain of this? *Ochquetit* brought them? It was not Red Fox himself? Not the scouting brothers of Red Fox?"

Ochquetit brought them!!! She would not lose the hand of interlopers until we took her ourselves on the earth's changing back to our land!!!"

But the *Meteu* wondered whose hold it was. Perhaps that of the girl, perhaps that of the interloper. "Was this the Grandmaster, as you call him? He changed the before- and after-time back and forth?"

"We cannot know this, *Meteu*!! Not but the changing back-and-forth!!

"Yet, Grandmaster is what you surmise?"

"Grandmaster is what I surmise!!"

The old man was in doubt of the Grandmaster. In many conversations over the past two cycles he had asked about the Grandmaster. He felt, and Red Fox had confessed: scant was the translation of "Grandmaster." He had no word for it, perhaps *this* perhaps *that*, but no extant word. Yet each time they talked, Red Fox spoke of him with more precision. This description became as fine, after many such talks, as though the ever fine and finer parts of the sparrow hawk feather.

So the *Meteu* was in doubt of Grandmaster. *This was that doubt he did not like*. Rare it was for him to be in such doubt. He did not like it but this doubt he must embrace.

He said, "Why do you go every year to the ledge?"

"We go every year to seek the confirmation!! And reveal *Ochquetit's* purpose. Interlopers prevail even here!!! and we are Peoples who no more will fight one another!! We will not fight the other!!!"

"Interlopers subdue and prevail, and we, who possess now this land, will no more fight each another?"

"They prevail. We and all True People weep at their victory and are led captive away!!!"

"How do you know this, trembling one?"

"It is shown!"

"How do you know?"

"It is shown!"

The *Meteu* was satisfied now. More was he satisfied than in past debriefings of Red Fox since his return with the Girl to their rapids encampment far below High Lake camp. This time, in fever, Red Fox had spoken with the voice of authority, the upward push needed to convince the old man. The *Meteu* spoke, and repeated everything Red Fox had shouted. He would go into woods far from the encampment. He would make all into the *enchantment* ...for his memory, for Red Fox, the clan, and the nation of True People. Red Fox had said in his delirium. The *Meteu* went deep into the woodland. Deep into memory's enchantment.

Who can say if a young scout knows aught of what he speaks? It needs the authority of fever. Now the *Meteu* will pay careful attention, though he had long been curiously attentive. The scouting would be authorized once more at this point of the cycle.

But, he knew—they are already gone to the rendezvous. There would be a confirmation or Red Fox would be no *Meteu*. And the Girl would be no *Meteu's* helper. It seems to the old man now, as he chants the story in woodland far from High Lake encampment that *Ochquetit* would do more than fulfill the prophecy.... No. *Other she would do*, not more. She was a shower, not strong enough to fulfill! Her purpose was other, not that. Not that. She would show something. *Other*.

~~~~~~~

"Look at the braves over there," said Quadrangi to Fabian.

Quadrangi was definitely engaged in trying to distract any formerly "lost" kid from conversation about that pesky time past (known obsessively as 2017). Particularly distressing was the uncanny 1900 CE. Quadrangi had been round to McRonald's hoping to find work again if business had picked up. He brought back some slightly used food, as HB would call it; bags of mostly condiments and fixings for the mission where, at one of its tables, Fabian and Quadrangi now sat facing one another. They were eating burgers donated by one of the processors south of Akropolis. The buns were past day-old from the supermarket on the north hill of Exchange St.. These burgers were sooooo good.

Wiping his mouth, faintly questioning, Fabian looked up from his burger. Quadrangi? Being ironic? Satirical? Not the usual Quadrangi thing.

"Look behind you," said the other, nodding that way.

Slowly Fabian turned. He never liked the obvious turning to anyone's pointed observation—surreptitious or otherwise. And Quadrangi had been unusually direct.

Fabian looked, and turned back again. He put down his burger, chewing. Thinking.

"So?" said Quadrangi.

But Fabian reached up and dusted his 'do —with greasy fingers! And he had stopped chewing. Slowly he turned to look at Native Americles. Feathers hanging, bow-and-arrows sticking up behind, bare chests under half-open cloaks. Then slowly he turned back to Quadrangi.

"Lordy," said Fabian under his breath. It wasn't that hard to catch even though it was suppertime and the place was filling, doors constantly opening, closing, opening. They could feel dark November chilling the place. Soon the furnace blower would kick in from the basement.

"Lordy? Are you channeling HB now?" asked his friend. "They are for real, you're thinking, too? But maybe they're playing."

Fabian stood, pushed his food across to one of a few empty spaces next to Quadrangi, who eyed him as he wove through the long tables, past ragged grown-ups and small ragamuffins moving about, plates in hand. Someone sat down in Fabian's vacated metal chair. It was Pomala. "Hi!" she said cheerfully. "I get to eat! I'm working here today."

Fabian sat down, diagonal from her. He stared at the youths and saw a girl with them: a few tables over, eating hungrily. One, two, three, tables beyond theirs—deep toward windows facing Exchange St.

He was finished with Quadrangi for the moment. Pomala looked her now-usual self: white hair over her shoulders, white eyelashes, pink eyes.
~~~~~~~

She wore retro-retro padded shoulders—a soft hand-me-down blazer from sis she particularly liked. Fabian said, "Slowly...."

She was still smiling. " 'Slowly'?" She quoted him.

"Slowly turn around and look three tables over. Sitting all in a line, facing us. Eating. It's crowded so take your time." He was not taking his eyes off them to return her quizzical smile. The girl, he saw now, was between two of them, the biggest two.

Pomala turned, with the same hesitation that Fabian had a few moments ago.

She turned back. "They're dressed for a show, maybe?"

"OK," said Fabe looking at her now." One... more... time. And watch out for that OMG, girl. *I mean watch out.*" He looked back toward the strange youths. The girl.

Quadrangi was mystified. Recalling accusations of hallucinatory cultish hypnosis, he felt uneasy. And he was glad little brother Quad was at their sister's.

Pomala had looked and now stared down at her plate, thinking, mouthing *OMG* over and over. She was going to turn over her phone to alert Jayrai. She was going to *OMG* HB. Tu, Quad. *No!* Not Quad. OMG!!

She did none of that. Except the imbecilic mouthing. Then she looked up and said, "But they're not the same."

"Maybe. Maybe they're two years older," said Fabian looking candidly at her.

She had to glance back.

Slowly she turned to him again.

"You know, one of them.... One of them might be kinda an older Parry." The A'ndians wore cloaks, feathers, slung pouches (maybe), A'ndian weapons. Was that a spear on the back of one? "You remember Parry the little sailor-suit boy."

"Doesn't seem as talky."

"Maybe too much has happened.... He might be really maxed. Maybe no concept."

"But you know... the girl."

Pomala turned again, noticing for the first time the girl—who was mashing fries into her mouth.

Pomala turned back. "OMG!" It was loud, *too* loud, she put her head down. Hair fell into the coleslaw. First she ignored it, then wiped the dressing off with her fingers.

It came out a subdued squeak: "She's going to get help!" Pome's eyes held a bit of a pleading look, a bit of the miraculous. "I was stopped from bringing her *and she came anyway*!" A passionate whisper.

Fabian looked at her. "I think she's probably got more on her mind than getting help from us."

Quadrangi spoke up. "Looks like she's got nothing on her mind."

Now that is irony, thought Fabian. *If I got that definition right.* "Were you being funny when you said *braves* before?"

"No, and I'm not being funny now."

Pomala began speculating. Are these the exact ones I saw before? Maybe the boy with wide-set eyes? Yes, two of them were definitely white, but tanned. And how did they all come together like that? Out of 1900 CE? *Weren't the A'ndians part of the vaudeville? What happened exactly? Was there a tool shed?*

So they found their entrance into the new world.

Even the cemetery had changed. Amazingly. Bodies earlier buried had remained in their dust, many of them exactly in place with aged markers as Digger remembered them, but True People found strange music speakers, small ornate structures and other tokens crammed into spaces once open and green. These had been lawns of careful proportion and restfulness in the Akropolis Rural Cemetery. The cemetery now seemed "busy" in the way of strange paintings Girl-boy had seen in print, 1900 A.D., and would later become known as Ubism. There were electric light fixtures along its walks, and its gate and name also had changed. The wall separating it from the sidewalk was only slightly different, older, moldier but also cleaner out front. The sidewalk itself seemed strangely stone-like but continuous without breaks or mortar. Leaves had blown off trees and clustered in curbsides and corners. Little quiet cars, with lights! —zipping around, in and out, when they appeared. Except for the leaves, everything was so strange-looking, strange-sounding. Astounded, Digger saw that and Girl-boy also recognized the now (much older) brown brick building at the corner of Five Points. Paddy's Pool Hall and Saloon. Some Stock Exchange buildings had seemed decrepit and familiar but most were replaced, showing stages of development in the neighborhood.

True People looked around at the place and people moving about, serving, sitting and eating.

"We will have to go back and find the ledge place," said Walleye-stare in response to Digger-boy's spoken concern. They would study all things, but especially that entrance point.

As smiling, strangely dressed people served them and withdrew, their plates were once again full, that is half full, no burgers this time, and they fell to again. Before entering, Girl-boy had had wit to add to his brother's foresight; obtaining information that they would not be charged for the meal. He declared the burgers were like the new food served in the elegant home of his highbrow friends on Cake Eater's Hill—1900 A.D..

"Some of these people remind me of outer space travelers from Gleese 3-something —or what was that planet's name? Remember the space travelers? We saw them at the intersection with Ma?" He pointed to one girl with a bird crest and strange tattoos, wearing black shiny slim overalls. She was upscale, serving. Talk around them, and from those serving, was familiar to him as Anglish. It sounded a lot faster, and many words were different. Were they unfamiliar words or just spoken in a way different from normal usage? Entering primitive history had been a hard ongoing adjustment for Girl-boy. But True People history was in stories, not documents. Stories were emotionally helpful.

His big brother was mechanically minded and might have liked to be trained as an engineer. It would never have worked out that way for him—being the support he was to Ma after the rubber factory accident claiming his father. Suddenly Digger-boy wanted to go back to the cemetery and see what his father's grave looked like now. He would do that when they returned to inspect very carefully *the mystical ledge of rendezvous*. Red Fox had so named it.

Digger-dog and Girl-boy used the utensils next to their plates while eating fries and coleslaw. The other clansmen and *Ochquetit* used their hands to eat everything. Eaglestreak and Walleye-stare looked at the plates and metallic implements carefully after the first round of food. The tables and chairs had been investigated on arrival of course. Food was very tasty and filling. They had eaten ravenously. All had. But then they slowed down. The room held more people than was in their entire clan. But they had seen lots of such strange people before on their first exploration with Red Fox, Dark Cloak, Quick Claws and Deereye. *This is the same place*, Digger-dog had assured them, *only different*. And this was the same place as the clans' own.

Red Fox and Dark Cloak had said this about the first tryst with the Arrow of Time outside the Cycle.

Digger-dog ignored his brother's inquiry about space travelers for the time being. He said instead: "People here are sick. They keep looking at themselves in pocket mirrors."

Walleye-stare leaned over his plate and said something to Digger. "They stare at us. They stare at flat stones like slate. They stare much."

"What are mirrors?" said Eaglestreak, looking past *Ochquetit* and Girl-boy to ask.

Digger had used the Anglish word. Now he explained by describing reflections in still pools of streams, or the smooth surface of High Lake when's no wind. "You see yourself when you look down."

"Yes," agreed Eaglestreak.

"Those aren't mirrors," said Girl-boy decisively in Anglish. "Remember—"

"Not yet. I will see," answered Digger, in the tongue of True People. Then he remembered the gadjets from outer space. He said, "I remember Gleese."

Walleye-stare was handling the plastic bottle of water someone had set by his hand. "*Tschuppinamen*," he murmured.

"It's a bottle of water," said Girl-boy. "But not glass."

"I understand your word for water," he said in the True Tongue. "That is all."

"This is good," said Digger-boy in True People tongue. "We could not drink of water in the stream of the graveyard.

"It stank of chemicals, metal and oils," he said in Anglish. He was the one who discerned how to remove the bottle's covering.

From the *Washington Boast*:

"Akropolis Ehio consumers protest 'the crackdown on cocoa imports made with forced child labor.' Activists gathered outside bottled water plantations carried signs and chanted slogans protesting Ehio DHS implementation of a lack of chocolate. "We can't live without chocolate! We can't live without chocolate!"

Story Hour

The ragamuffins precipitated out of the crowd, filing down basement steps to the story room below. They were mostly silent, subdued given their current situation as mostly homeless kids whose parents remained in the eating hall to receive Pastor's homily. Kids, subdued, clutching the wooden railing, climbing down old dark plank steps, were anticipating the stories. Tonight there would be but one story lengthening, told by various participants after Gretchen set up the premise.

Other people exited by the plateglass door. When the A'ndians saw people leaving like bubbling beads of water through grassy fields, they stood and left with them. What remained behind of FivePoints people watched the A'ndians exit.

The two from *2017* watched.

"We should go," said Fabian.

"We've got to stay for Pastor," said Pome.

Quadrangi shrugged.

Some of those who also left the building were seen to stop at the door and stare after those braves walking past the Sharon Road windows. True People stopped—as though studying traffic lights turning yellow-red-green several times. Then turning the corner they were watched, by those seated in the SoupMission, as they headed past Exchange St. windows through a glow of streetlights. One of the braves was seen gesturing at something, maybe the streetlights lifting like necklaces up toward downtown past the graveyard opposite.

Many people outside staring after them would be back later to sleep in cots or on the swept floors of the hall. It would not be much later, as hours were strictly observed unless Akropolis weather proved particularly foul.

The helpers clearing tables had eaten their soooo good burgers. A few were in process of finishing their water, heading into the kitchen. Drinking water was becoming something precious to them of late, but Pastor thought recyclable glass was best as container. Many had not worried about the taste of the water until word reached them of its dangers. And now they were grateful for Goodwater, no matter where it came from. Some had been reading labels and commenting before Pastor Zettler spoke his first words: the same company that made the greatest vanilla cookies and candy since the Venus candy bar went out of business.

The children generally stayed downstairs until all was ready above. Then they switched places with the men, who would sleep in the old stone-built basement next to a furnace room. It was surprisingly dry down there, mortared, but the foundation stones were huge, dark and square-hewn.

When bustling sounds drifting up through registers ceased, Pastor began his talk.

Then, from the back, "Preach, how do we vote next time?"

Here we go. A serious distraction.

"Well, it helps if you can write, read the ballot. Maybe there's help for the impaired. Know the issues, candidates. Show up. To the polling place."

"So a literacy test? But no, I mean how do *we* vote? —Homeless. No place of residence."

Pastor Zettler hesitated, stopped. He looked around. Others were nodding. All these faces, heads nodding, shades of human persons, many known to him, some unknown.

Slowly he said, "Well, I never thought of these before. But I should look into it."

Pastor began again—on one of his least favorite subjects—he began abruptly. " 'I think I am God.' "

Though Quadrangi and especially Pomala and Fabian had each a desire to follow after the A'ndians and try to talk with them, they sat still on hearing this startling declaration. Candace Parker was quietly going around tables collecting plastic bottles left behind.

" 'I think I am God,' " repeated Pastor, standing before them.

Fabian, while rooted, nevertheless saw the movement peripherally: on the edge of seats close to the kitchen. His Nana sat down on a metal chair, wincing for its hard surface.

Then he saw Pastor smile. Everyone relaxed. Sighing, chuckling or whispering, they were now set to settle into the talk. "I'm quoting someone powerful," he said, and went on. " 'In fact I'm God to my creations,' said this powerful being. This powerful one said also, 'The beings and universes I make will perceive me as God.' "

He paused. Pastor was disciplined. A bit vain, this handsome older man with thick salt-and-pepper hair, a longish crew-cut, wearing rectangular horn-rimmed glasses, long-sleeved dark shirt, and brown vest. Unlike Candace Parker, he could scarcely admit aging. He had nothing in his hands.

"You might think you know who I'm quoting here," he said. "That's because there's only one obvious response in this setting where we eat together and share the gospel. I'd be thinking that myself... if I hadn't prepared this little talk for you."

He smiled again, as did others, and someone in the back near the Exchange St. windows said, "Tell us! Don't keep us in suspense!"

And laughter rippled round the room.

"Yeah!" said another. "So who *is* this great God if not you?! Are we his creatures?"

Pastor paused. "Not yet," he said. "Not yet, anyway." This quieted them. They waited for him to go on.

Hands in his vest pockets, he said, "This is someone whose name you will not recognize, I suspect. But he is nonetheless considered powerful in his field of artificial life technologies. He has said that humans will change through his ongoing technological advances. He has said people will escape their condition—the human condition—with these technologies. Not only will we escape, we will be transformed into something else."

Pastor stood in front of the now empty serving counter before this group initially gathered together for a delicious and special meal. It was several days before the Americle celebration of Thanksgiving, traditional day of gratitude, turkey and ham. This was an eclectic bunch of people, both ragtag and splendidly dressed in what might have been the Halloween leavings of SF costumes. The A'ndian braves had not been much out-of-place here, though others had taken advantage of their unusual facial features, handmade garb and hand-shaped weaponry to grab surreptitious or obvious images of them eating a meal of burgers and fries at the FivePoints Gospel Mission.

"The biotech researcher, together with his fellows, the experimenters, have an even more profound vision of humankind's future."

"Apparently—what you just said—we humans got no future." It was the same raised voice from the back, near the Exchange St. windows.

Someone beside him stood up to speak, and was yanked back down onto his chair.

"What else?" said Pastor to that one made to sit; careful for his voice to carry.

The man responded with but half a voice, a drain on his listeners. "Does this mean *everyone* will be homeless—not just us drug addicts and drunks?"

"We aren't all D&D's," said a soprano voice from a corner table. "Some of us are just trying to take care of our kids, you know."

"Speak it, sister," said Pastor Zettler, smiling.

"OK, let this man go on," said drunk and disorderly. His eyes had the same drooping expression as his faded cammo jacket hanging off his shoulders. A jacket three times too large.

Pastor walked across the front toward the kitchen door, then turned back.

"Another researcher, one more experimental. —And by the way, these three words don't mean exactly the same thing—research, theorizing and experimentation— though they support and partake of each other in certain fields. Experimentalists and theorists research their ideas of course but basically the theorists feed ideas to experimentalists to help make their experiments. But that's a digression. Let me say that others in a different field—that of robotics—have agreed with this grand scheme, and extend the vision to incorporate all of material existence in what some are calling a *conversion of all* from the sun outward.... He wants everything to be thinking, a mind all encompassing, a universe of pure extra-material intelligence. He did not say mindful thinking in which all might move and live and have their being (such as Benjamin Frank said about this great nation when it was good, before it was great) —but he might as well have said these words.... Does any of this sound familiar?"

"It's all your God stuff," announced the man from his seat at the rear table beside the three-sizes-too-small guy.

"Too many big words and ideas." This was said by a brown Palacestonian old man from a corner in back by the FivePoints intersection wall. "Where's your gospel?"

"Hang on. It's coming!" Pastor turned to reach for his scriptures on the counter and, holding it up, gestured toward others piled in corners. "Just in case you didn't bring one," he said smiling. "It's going to be in the fourth gospel, chapter 3, verses 4 thru 8. And in Zeke 37, verses 1 thru 6." Two people moved to grab one.

The man beside three-sizes bigger said, "Seems we can't get rid of God, but seriously, Preach, what's biotechnology got to do with us? Only the haves are in trouble with this. Not us. You got to pay big bucks to have yourself transformed into something not human... and go on living forever I suppose. I'm losing my teeth here, and they just aren't interested, are they?"

Another voice, from the front table nearest the door, spoke up. Evidently someone had slipped in, and was leaning against the table itself, legs crossed, turning to look from Pastor to the guy in the back. "You just don't understand their program! You are the perfect specimen for this show. They want you, believe me. It's us they want —first anyway! Just until they can get the bugs worked out. Then the Big Bucks can come in and be safe with it. Listen what I be telling you, bro." He shook his head, big black broom 'do glistening.

Pastor looked swiftly at HBBBAH, who had come from the street. Maybe when the others left—he didn't know, hadn't seen. Zettler had left HB upstairs and guessed maybe he had heard the beginning points of the talk through the registers. Only a guess. There had been no entrance from the apartment to the former pool hall for many a year, though at one time stairs led up from the kitchen. The old wooden stairs were still there, now stacked with supplies of one sort or another to the boarded-over flooring no longer permitting access above. Climbing up, you could bump your head on Pastor's apartment floor.

Pastor turned back to them. "This is a story of immortality," he said. "In the past especially, scientists could be quick to rule out the storytelling nature of their designs, but often science is telling itself stories. This is how things get done, and incidentally stories are the way to market and control ideas and technology."

"As well as politicians and politics!" (Voice from the rear.)

In attribution, Pastor now noted that he had cribbed some thoughts from the Rt. Rev. Clive Staples's slim volume called *The Abortion of Man*. Then he said, "Perhaps this was hyperbole on the part of the speaker, meant to encourage his fellows in the field, but this scientist spoke truer than he knew, if so. He may be thinking that all this is 'us,' but really, it will be 'controlled' (which is impossible because of unintended consequences), controlled by only a few, and these of course may have their disagreements, so what happens to control? Science, when thorough and precise in its studies and experiments, and honest in its presentation of these, does much to discover and improve. Take the incandescent light bulb up there." He gestured. "Fabulous, much effort and dedication in that. And then, moving forward, (as you see the SoupMission hasn't completely yet), there issued florescent, halogen, and in due course the LED, each one superior to the last in energy conservation, especially, and quality of light. Our scientists are excited. It's not wrong that they should be. But they will watch dismayed as the excitement slips away into other hands, the hands of corporate greed and financiers."

"I'm partial to torchlight and sconces, myself," said the more educated of the two men in the back. "You can ignite it with wax, flint, and steel."

"There's an anachronism in there somewhere," said the mother from her corner. The man glared, then smiled, at her. There were gaps in his teeth.

"Corporate greed is just a buzz-word for corporate greed," said the man in the back.

"What about financiers? A buzz-word for financiers ain't it?" said the other.

"Stock-holders," said the first.

"Back to the immortalists," said Pastor.

Fabian glanced over at Nana sitting next the kitchen. She looked back at him. Turned her whole frame to do it.

Looking at her, smiling, he leaned toward Quadrangi and said, "My grandmother's been talking to Pastor. I think that's what some of these religious people call some Cossyc people."

"—Immortalists?" Quadrangi was whispering. "Is it the one you talked with there?"

"I don't think so. He seems more into serum or bio than digital, but yeah, he's an immortalist."

The Pastor kept talking.

"This is how the history of applied science looks—when it's history. And this might be a good place to distinguish between proof and evidence. There was plenty of evidence for the incandescent light bulb in hundreds of trials, but no proof until, well, what you see up there. But what do we see on *looking* ahead, instead of behind us?"

"Prediction?! Witchcraft?! Prophecies?!"

Smiling, Pastor looked at the bigger D&D. Then he looked over at HB, and said, "We see an attempt by a few to control the future."

"With stories?!" This was the mother.

"...With stories."

Later, parents went to join their children in the basement, and the single men had spilled outside onto Sharon, into the glow of street lamps. But some of these went into the kitchen instead to see if there were leftovers or anything more to do. As usual there'd been a couple songs and a prayer to send people off with. Quadri, as Quadrangi knew, was initially at their sister's, so he stayed on with Pastor, Pomala and HB to move things around until the little boy came. First, rattling and scraping, they rolled and piled tables and chairs against the wall shared with the kitchen. Next push brooms came out and two giant dust mops. Pastor always took off his vest and rolled up his sleeves for this. He could be a bit of a dandy, and his friends, the kids especially, sometimes kidded him for it.

"Look Pastor! I'm starting a referendum on abortion."

Instead of looking at her babblet, Pastor looks at Pomala's half-blue smiling face, her pink eyes. She has startled him.

She swipes the babblet, holds it up. "Here's another one: on controlling guns and lobby people making money."

"You mean *against* abortion."

"Of course."

"How old are you? You might need your sister's help with that."

"I'm 15. Going on 16." She smiled.

Ugh. She's still not in 2019. But he was relieved that she seemed involved in these current problems.... Well ongoing long-term but still—2019. This might anchor her in reality.

Fabian and Candace Parker had taken leave before with a bit of chat—not much. Candace really wanted to get home to their apartment for tea, a book or two, and then—joy—bedtime. Around then Fabian would've been catching up with everybody via device. It was too late to see what became of the A'ndians, but never too late to chew that over. He had to get Jay and Tu in the loop about them as well.

The children had been singing and listening intently below stairs to the ongoing story Gretchen had initiated with some of her teenage charges. The tale would be slightly disrupted when movements upstairs and the parents' descent took place. Quadri and his big brother would at some point be among them.

But first one of Gretch's charges led the children in a song, one of Pastor's old acorns.

"Ah, the Lord God's good to us!
And so we thank Good God!
The rain and sunshine, apple trees!
The Lord God's good to thee!"

The kids liked this one with its several verses, sometimes, not always, ending in *thee!* Or sometimes *three!* One adolescent changed the ending to *sneeze!* When the first version ended a child asked about that word *thee!*

"What does it mean?"

This little girl was the niece of the woman upstairs who had stressed her situation, and that of others like her, who had no living wage for raising families. The little girl wore third-hand clothing obtained through Clothe-Our-Kids, and had to sleep on mats in the SoupMission nights; and eat charity suppers with her cousins and brother. Her name was Shimila. She was pale and quiet but has fuzzy screaming red hair, legacy of her dead mother and living absent father—both of whom had fine soft red hair.

"I thought *the* meant what I say when I say *the clock*."

"Yeah," said her brown-haired, slightly older brother, Shemp. He had been emboldened by his sister's speaking. "Like when we say *the dog, the hamburger*. Stuff like that."

The Sheltering Cares teenager who led the singing immediately said, "It means *you!*

"Me?" said Shimila. "Why me? Why doesn't it say Shimila then?"

"Yeah," said her brother. "Why not somebody else, either? Like me for instance. It could say *the Shemp*." He said this seriously but his sister smiled. She almost kissed his ear, but they had no home so she didn't.

"But it does say you! You are thee."

"I'm the? —The Shemp?"

"No-no. I mean thee means *you* in a slightly different language."

"Kinda like Songish maybe," said his sister.

"In Songish it's *el* or *los* or *la*," said Hibotchi of Sheltering Cares. Eyes slightly long-tailed; except for the cammos and long-sleeved T, he looked just a bit like two of the braves who had been eating burgers upstairs.

The song-leading teenager, whose name was Shylane, thought about this question for a moment and said, "*You* in old languages, old Anglish languages. So for instance," and here she looked at Gretch who sat cross-legged in the midst of children sitting on floor mats. "... For instance you might say, The Lord God's good to me, meaning you, Shimila, and you Shemp." She looked at the two siblings. "OK?"

"Nope," said one or two.

"Got it!" said several voices.

"Thanks for that, Shylane." This was a prompt from Gretchen.

"Thanks, Shylane," said several kids.

"Later you'll learn all that stuff about grammar and punctuation," said Shylane. Then cringed when someone said, "What's punctuation?"

The singing went on, and then the story took over.

Gretchen's shoes were off, stocking feet treading on mats. She stepped through the kids saying, "This is a story about a monster with a chest full of water." She stood before them now, not far from the bottom of the stairs. "And no, it doesn't keep water in old treasure chests, or some kind of chest where you put clothes. I mean it keeps water here." She tapped her rib cage suddenly with her fist. "And no I don't mean these," she said, tipping her fingers toward her breasts. "These, as most of you know, is where milk is sometimes kept."

"For babies!" said one boy nearby. He grinned. Proud of his understanding.

"That's right! And we want it to be safe for babies. So mom needs safe water to make her milk safe."

During an after school snack up on Cheddar Ave. before herding her Sheltering Cares teenagers down to the Gospel Mission, they had planned the evening's storytelling for these kids. Sometimes the teenagers have a soup supper and help out in the FivePoints kitchen. Sometimes they make meals at Sheltering in the basement kitchen where once the Y had its cafeteria. Sometimes meals were contracted out from here for Sheltering Cares and other ventures, both charitable and for-profit small businesses now in the building.

Gretchen wore a pale shirt and dark vest (not unlike Pastor's), beige midcalf-length jeans with multi-striped socks tucked up under them. She had no need to stress the entertainment value of these stories, but sometimes she had cautionary words on what these should be about, and what they might want to avoid. She wanted to avoid the explicit and deep suffering some kids (including her charges here) underwent at the hands of evil (usually but not always *adult* hands). The time and place for personal suffering narratives came generally, but not always, one-on-one, in counseling with licensed volunteers. Gretchen was but one of these. Her office was shared by other houseparents on a 24-hour rotating basis. The volunteers (granted small stipends) have jobs, family homes or apartments of their own.

"OK," said Gretchen, explaining tonight's premise to teenagers in the currently deserted old Y cafeteria. "We've talked about the water situation here in Akropolis. Now it's time to get this baby some kick-ass attention. Okay, that was unfortunate language," she said. "I shouldn't put it that way." It was a moment before this fault registered with these teenagers, though the verbally smarter kids got it right off. Some slower kids had other than verbal talents, some of which registered better in the sensitive-toward-others category.

"We want the gov'mint, as stewards, to think and act on the bad water, and there's nothing like a story to help with this. Except—"

"— Except making them drink it," suggested Hibotchi. He was dark-skinned with smooth very black hair, whose butt was parked on one of the basement cafe-hall tables.

Gretch had not noticed till now. "Get off the table, Botch," she said. "And clean it before you leave. You've been sitting Great God knows where in those cammos and we've got to eat off that."

"I've seen you do this," he said.

"And you've seen me clean it, too. Onward. Think of stuff about a monster with water in its chest. Make it imaginative, slightly foreboding, but not too scary. Remember the situation, and that these really are some little kids. It doesn't take much."

"But why do they need to know about this if they can't fix it?" (Hibotchi)

Skinny Trice was texting over by the closed counters where food would be served. Metal panels had been rolled down, hiding the kitchen from view. Trice had patched the knees of her secondhand slink-jeans with canvas painted in glorious reckless colors. She was wearing a tam over her long straight hair. Now, on her device, she was getting Jayrai up in Sharon to give her some ideas.

So far their conversation went:

Trice: Any ideas?

Jay: i'm thinking.

Gretch said, "One day these kids will be grown and have power devolve on them, if we do our jobs right."

"What does devolve mean?"

"Transfer of power. You could use *evolve to* if that works for you."

"You mean, 'One day power will be in *our* hands and *we* got to care." This was from Pristine, sitting in a metal chair next to Hibotchi's knees. She was an Afrikan-Americle, with beautiful large eyes and hair in a huge black frizzy pom-pom pulled to the back of her head. Hibotchi still had not budged off the table. Gretch threaded her way through tables, people and chairs, took his hand and helped him off the table.

The group of eleven brainstormed for awhile, loosely. She told them not to set anything in stone because it was ideas—not narrative—they needed for prep work. Then she dismissed them to go up and do homework till time to go have supper.

She heard Hibotchi say to Trice as they flew up the stairs, "You might use that gizzzzzmo to record it is so we can plaster it on puters and phones all over the city."

With her unkempt brassy hair, Gretchen, looking messily glorious as usual, smiled. She called after them. "Better share that with me, first!"

"So you see," said Gretch to the grinning boy, then looking round on them all. Kids were grouped cross-legged on mats pulled to the center, with Sheltering Cares teenagers sprinkled among them. There was a faint scent of must and the blower could be heard in the furnace room behind a closed-door. Cots were stacked against one old stone wall. "Basically good things, like milk and oxygen or air, are supposed to be inside people. But water is a good thing, like milk and air, right?" She cocked an ear toward them.

"Yes!" "Milk and air!!" "Water!" These responses were heard among the confusion of piping voices.

"Actually, water is not meant to be in people's chests. It could mean they are drowning. So water in someone's chest is bad. But in a monster's chest it's even worse because as everyone knows, monsters are not good. Monsters are frightening, harmful, greedy and evil. And this monster doesn't seem to be drowning. So how did this good water get in such a bad place?

Anybody got an answer to this?" She looked at a few of the Sheltering Cares' teenagers.

But instantly Quadri raised his hand and spoke from his place on a mat near the edge of the group. His brother was just coming downstairs after helping to sweep, arrange sleeping quarters for kids and their mothers. The smaller Quad waved to him, saying, "Maybe the monster came with bad water from 1900 CE!"

Teenager big bro, who had sent him down here when he came to the SoupMission, did not like to hear this coming from Quadri. He did not want to hear anything more about 1900 CE, or anything 1900 bringing monsters. He did not want to hear any more about some mission to return to 2017! Though he would have to own himself playing some part, maybe a big part, in his little brother's developing imagination, maybe even something to do with monsters and alt realities—still, he had no wish for 1900 or 2017 CE. He just kept shoving that by each time it came up. The odd thing—if there could be anything more odd—was the ordinary happening of that November 3 day two years ago, when Quad himself had been on his way down to meet his little brother on the GlimmerDale cemetery wall. What could have been more ordinary thing that? They'd been playing the game together. He was between buildings, almost to the street. Earlier he was going to be there as a surprise, but had happened to be somewhat late. The strange disappearance had *all* just happened. And just happened to happen *without* him.

How had that happened?!!

And why? There must be a why. Was there a why? Was it a cult?

As Quadri kept speaking, Gretch glanced at Quadrangi, who had gone to stand by the boy.

Now he squeezed onto a mat on the edge of kids beside Quadri, who said, "1900 CE had bad water! Jay said we couldn't drink it! They had beer and we had Akropolis Pop—Pomala and me."

"But you didn't actually see a monster though, right?" At mention of 1900 CE Hibotchi had gotten interested. He was asking.

Quadri thought for a moment about all the things he had seen there. At last he said, "There was a giant horse drinking from a tub outside the soup kitchen."

The teenagers in the basement laughed at this incongruity and some of the younger kids picked up on it. Even Quadrangi smiled just a bit. Gretchen continued keeping her eye on him, gaze drifting back to him as the storytelling continued.

Her kinky pom-pom bouncing, Pristine got up and said, "You know, that's not too far off-point for a story. It so happens that when the Americle metro areas started building infrastructure, some kind of bad thing was used to get the water to people. Something called lead. Now, I'm not saying a monster shipped or anything, but. What if the bad thing used just kept getting worse so that it began to *seem* like a monster was hiding somewhere, maybe even infiltrating our supply without being visible. Say all this started happening, it got out of hand, and now we need a monster-herder to get rid of it?"

"Get rid of water, or the monster?"

"Maybe both."

"So, we're going to need that water, but we need to make it good. So, all good," said Gretch, "but it's not quite a story yet."

"Yeah," said Hibotchi. "That's more scientific stuff, like how it's applied to the stuff needed to make pipes, and turns bad (scientifically proven) and stuff."

"Important stuff, though," said Pristine, her dark eyes agreeing, "and it *would* support Quadri's theory."

Quadrangi's head flopped. He did not want 1900 CE in the story!

"Tell you what," said Gretchen, "we'll move on from there because now that we know *how* the monster got the bad water here, we can leave that aside and move the story along. The monster has *bad* water in its chest, his form is hidden or nebulous—that means atomized—that means scattered. Hidden and diffuse, but still monster."

"Does it have a head?" someone asked. "What does it look like?"

"That's my part of the story," said Hibotchi. He jumped up looking around at the kids. "You see why I don't like it to be pipes or a system or grid work. I want it to *look* monstrous. …Although ancient peoples might think that monstrous enough." His black eyes beneath a hank of straight black hair smiled directly at Quadrangi, with whose game creation he was familiar. "This monster lives under the earth at first so when he gets up with that chest full of bad water he's all dirty, right? Stuff from the earth is how you get dirty? Earth, actually."

"Right! Smoke is dirty, said Shemp."

"Smoke is from the sky," argued Shimila.

"But how did he get to the sky?" asked Hibotchi.

"From burning stuff."

"Right. Stuff from the earth. Everything we burn comes somehow from there. Trees, oil, gas, paper—that comes from trees.

"Yes!" said the kids. Small Reese, her hair clipped back with a barrette, said softly, "Burnt houses come from trees." A couple kids went quiet remembering how Reese came to be here. Three old houses converted to apartments went up in smoke. Scary.

"So, if it's to be a story, we need monster-herders. Who would they be?" asked Shylane. "What would these herders look like?" Shylane was asking the kids.

"They should wear gloves!"

"They should use dogs!"

"They should have whips!"

"My idea," said Shylane, "is suits."

"Spacesuits to protect them. From the stuff." Shimila was just saying.

"You mean the chemicals? That's good, but these monster-herders come second. In order to get them on the job, wearing protective suits, we need people wearing suits and ties and shiny shoes and cuff links to get them started. These people are called stewards."

"Our teachers wear clothes like that," said the boy who knew what breast milk was for.

"Bosses!" exclaimed an older black kid, adolescent, skinny with a stand-up fringe and smudged glasses. "Hire and fire!"

Gretch spoke up. "Not exactly, Garr. In this case the suit-wearers are Egressional stewards of the herders, those who labor wearing safety suits and pay them to be infrastructure stewards."

"Huh?"

"It's complicated and outside the simple story we're trying to tell." This was Embla interjecting. She had a juicy idea and wanted to get on with it.

"We'll come back to it, during questions Garr," said Gretchen.

Trice raised her hand. She had been reading her pop-pod and had something to insert, aware this might throw the story into alt-story-time. But with encouragement she'd been receiving (from Jay) wanted to give it a try.

"Hold that thought, Em," said the moderator, signaling procedure. She was not rigorous but resorted to this as a check from time to time. "What have you got, Trice? I know you've been huddling with someone on this water-monster story."

Trice was more reticent than others in the group. Sometimes she received a championing reward. She stayed where she was, cradling her pop-pod.

"What if... what if...."

"What if's are good!" Hibotchi shot this in to help her ignite. "The fantastic and spacesuits, so yeah we could use more. We could use fictional science. What if...?"

Trice charged. "What if the monster oversaw the tools or weaponry? I mean the things herders would use against it?"

"Explain?" suggested Gretchen.

"Say the monster has secret factories in an alternate universe."

She looked at her gizzzzzzzzzmo, intently reading, then back up at Pristine who was making a face. —Kinda, *huh?* kinda face, Trice thought. She looked at Gretch who gestured for her to proceed.

"So, everything in the alternate is shotty. They don't know how to make good stuff there, or if they do they reject quality... in favor of greed...."

"What have greed and quality got to do with each other?" asked the moderator. "Like quality versus investment? Versus bottom line?"

"So, like that. Yeah. The monster told 'em to make things cheap so they wouldn't work good but everyone else thought it was fine—in the alt, that is—because it made more money. They weren't thinking these things won't work good …like the monster was thinking—just, we get more money this way."

She looked down again, then back up. "I like this idea—do you? We could call the alt universe Shotty Landz."

"Trice, this is a good addition," said Gretchen. "What do you guys think?" She looked around.

Hands were going up all over. Kids showed excitement with nods and smiles, hand-clapping.

Gretchen smiled at Trice, ignoring ideas in the flow for the moment. Trice was trying to say something.

"Not my idea!" She cupped hands to her mouth.

"Whose idea then?" asked Hibotchi.

"Someone...."

"Yeah?"

"... Who came here from 1900 CE."

They glanced toward the brown dimpled faces of the Quads, large and small. Quadrangi protested. "But that's when things were made better than they are today! Heavier. They did not make infrastructure cheaply back then." He had learned this in the high school industrial technology course.

"Maybe it was solid stuff, but they were ignorant, or there wouldn't be lead corroding into the water," said Hibotchi.

"They should have understood precautions with stuff no matter how ignorant, though," said Pristine, shaking her head, pom-pom swinging. She was taking the same course in school. "But they took none—all the polluted water they made."

"OK, OK," said Gretchen. "This all requires nuance we don't have story-time for."

"What's nuance?" wondered Garr. He wasn't embarrassed to ask even though he was an adolescent.

Onward went the story. After story hour, songs and prayer finishing, kids and families filed up the dim wooden stairs, lit by a single 60 watt bulb.

Hibotchi wanted a word, so the brothers Quad stood back on the landing as he said, "What about a little game-creation? Would this fit for an episode of *Black Ages*?"

Quadri piped in like lightning. "Yes! It's a job for *Kwad the KonkerEr*! *Kwad the KonkerEr* could wear a suit and get spacesuits herding. No, wait, could I be a herder? Spacesuits have more action?!"

"We'll think about it," said Quadrangi to his friend. "Could you do it yourself if it won't fit? I'd give you pointers."

"Yeah, but the hardware…" said Hibotchi doubtfully. His pockets were empty.

Rendezvous

now they'll have to believe us. (Jay)

I don't think we should use this for that. (Fabe)

This might help us somehow get back to 2017. The primary concern. (HB)

But how did you know about the A'ndians, Jay? (Pomala)

i saw them. (Jayrai)

But you are permanently curfewed. All day every day. Till school starts for us. (Pome)

think about it. (Jay)

Oh yeah :-) *Who was it sent this?* (Pome, looking at the image of the braves just sent to her GRABBag.)

(Now HB was seeing it too. He'd been upstairs before slipping out, had missed seeing them in the mission.) *Yeah, I think it's them—older yeah.*

pix from trice. and she sent this. (An image of A'ndians outside the horizontal plateglass, pointing at lights.)

Pome: *Maybe they need our help.*

Several messages:

no.

No.

No.

No!

Still, (Fabian) *we've got to find them.*

A few moments pass.

what's going on? (Jay) *please.*

"Please?"

! Jay?— with a please!

Please?!

Please?

(Barrage of question from 2017)

Who **Are** *You?* (HB to Jay)

A Delay.

Alright (Fabe) *we are planning a meet-up. HB and me only.*

How do you find them? But they don't know! (Pome, objecting)
Are you sure? (Fabe)
Those A'ndians smart, you know. Remember? They almost got us! (HB)
no. i don't. (Jay) *you say stuff I got no clue on.*
So somebody *almost got us, I be sayin!* (HB)
maybe the show master? (Jay)
Maybe the girl? (Fabe) (Pome)
The girl? Whatchu talking, the girl. The game, say. THE GAME.
Where's Tu?
Probably hiding in his calculations, his mathematica, his particles, 0s & 1s. (HB)
Yes. (Pome) *He's trying to dream into us.*
oh please. (Jay back to normal)

Pastor was on the phone with Pome's sister, asking Glindora about things. Surprised, she says, "I don't actually know about the homeless, but I'll look into it for you."

On the other subject, Glindora is glad about Pomala's quest—seems a gain for her sister's 2019 acclimation. "But I'm for choice, a woman's right to choose. It works by conscience. ...The taxpayer has a right to register their choice in the matter. Personally, not being an activist, I'm interested to find out which, either way, is in the majority. Also personally, you know why I think about this... *issue*."

He looked at her. Then remembered what she'd been through. Perhaps was still going through. He was silent. Neither his nor Ortho — she'd had counseling outside the faith.

He said, "Of course."

There was a pause. He said, "Well, God does not coerce."

She agreed, but. "Still, there are consequences."

Pastor nodded and stopped. He did not know what to say.

"Pome does not know," she said. Then, "The Bishop might be able to do it but Pomala can't. She's too young."

The ledge? Still the ledge.

The giant rock, turf-covered mossy, moldy in wet weather, heavily spotted with pale lichen and brown rock-lichen ledgy. The GlimmerDale board were currently in process of debating the ledge. Good-humored, Glindora joked that the City had no problems so pressing.

At meetings: Should it go? Should it be cleaned? Sandblasted? Chipped apart, scattered with plaques throughout the grounds? Dynamited? Anonymously carted away? Organizational debate was how it began: It should stay. It should not be cleaned, should remain natural. Not broken up, or scattered. A plaque on it, as is. Persuasive reasoning was put forth for each suggestion on dealing with the massive rock. Administrators, while certain of its historic importance, were unaware of any possibly mystical qualities. Such considerations would never come under its purview.

Then things got heated. "Sometimes this happens on boards. Even over things like rocks," said Glindora to Pastor over the phone. She was on the board but was not particularly heated. Zettler, her sounding-board, was listening on the rotary phone, seated on his couch by the end table.

"What did you contribute?" asked the pastor, turning toward movement on his periphery as the old knob rattled in the wood paneled door.

"Sometimes it's just—we want to keep the board going instead of we want to achieve its purpose. Which in this case would suggest no change at all because the ledge, as is, suits the quiet role of the burial ground. Quiet? you'd say, yes they should stop with the piped music in spring, summer, autumn! —Or, even as we lower a loved one, are they trying to tell us we don't have death after all?"

HB was slowly disappearing beyond the door. His pale hand flew out, waving.

Pastor said, "Hold on," covered the receiver and said, "HB."

HB stopped closing the door, stepped back in from the hallway landing. Pastor did not look pointedly at the couch, but HB, sensed, yes, maybe pastor was looking at the couch, just not with his eyes. HB came and sat on the old couch.

Hand still cupping the receiver, Pastor said, "What's up?"

"You know those A'ndian-dressed critters tonight? Down in the mission?"

"Yes, I recall."

"Seems we might know them, Fabe and I ... and we stopped to hear *your* talk," HB was very careful to say, "and they left before we got a chance to talk to them."

"So what now?"

To Glindora he said, "This will take a moment. Should I call back?"

"You and I need to talk about the disturbingly causual group effort to 'get back to 2017,' by-the-way," she said. But if this is about the A'ndians, Pomala thinks he should go. She's been very open with me about it."

"Is she going?"

"No way!"

"Heh."

Pastor looked at HB. "Go ahead, Blake." *Blake* was what he used to deploy authority. "But be back in half an hour. Forty-five minutes at most. Can you do that?"

"Will do."

"Whether you find them or not. There's tomorrow."

"Tomorrow? You sure about a tomorrow, Preach? There is gonna be one?"

"Half an hour. Got your watch?" He said this to suggest a look at his watch.

HB raised his fist and shook his arm. "Ten-thirty," he said. He grinned. "Yo, your gift-watch says there *is* real time. I'll be here then."

"For you, tonight there's time," answered pastor.

Thoughts emanating from Tu's closet:

Could we be messages? That is, is it possible for us to be messages? What if... conceivably... what if... theoretically... what if we are sendsible*? That is, the sendsible, as yet undeveloped in 2017, but in the theoretical works... what if the webbing of certain communicatory particles theorized in the science and in fiction were capable... or contained the capacity.... What if in our real life it was possible through the sendsible... to instantaneous travel between here and there — however mysteriously linked here-and-there? Even the same universe: here 2017, there 1900 CE. Then we could be that message. Forget the moth-eaten wormhole. You wouldn't need that.*

You'd need, at first, hardware detection, the dark matter detection of of of its uh clumps, no clouds. We already had the dark matter detection going on then. These machines might conceivably be capable of being *transport, transportation of beings —instantly—incoherent "clouds" of dark matter.*

Tu was aware of affixing air quotes around the word *"clouds"*.

Naturally we call them channels. This is not new but exactly — channels? — that's the question. You move between universe and universe, time and time, —no problem. But the trick is coherently*. One comes down on the side of infinite velocity, yes, but* to be the message*. That's the thing.*

... What could be urgent or useful in any message between stars or galaxies or universes? Or times? It's laughable. What's the point? If HB were here he'd come up with a dozen, and we'd all be rolling on the floor. Maybe for an order of milk, or visit from an ambassador — 11 years' travel to receive it. Meanwhile the spaceship lumbering through space at lightspeed. Or you are stationary, space-time warping all round you. — Point?

Tu did not seem to realize that, while 2017 rolled on the floor, he would be looking on.

He merely looked blank as he sat here in the closet, now with the door open letting in the swath of white light from a small LED by the bed. Shafting across the interior closet wall, hanging shirts, his knees and thighs, leaving his Osiian face in the dark. In twilight under the sloping ceiling. But inside, where his microbial and molecular life pulsed, and his atomic structure (with great tautness and care), did not flinch as interstellar universal subatomic particles shot through his material form: *There* he was smiling. A giant face smiling tenderly at his new friends.

He had never loved them like this. Hardly knew them. He recalled how they were just there on November 3rd. Everybody appeing and gaming, and Tu studying the possible info downloads to help him work out that afternoon's problem. The one before the sounding jet in the sky with its luminous trail, loss of wifi, the stench of horse manure, the boardwalk below the cemetery wall.

But. What good will it do, this theory? We are the message coming from, belonging in, 2017. And we want back to 2017, but I'm supposed to get us there and it's not like the Iron Range is going to invite us to come unravel and be detected. They won't say, Would you like to step into our liquid argon bath? WIMP nucleon scatter sensitivity, at intersections cutting through objects to the longest axis, will be just what we are looking for in you people!

If one were there to see: Tu looked blank.

What if HB were here (wistful). *I could just about crack him up...? Or could I? This scenario might. —But could I?* Too much jargon.

He climbed out of the closet. Went over to the light. On the night-stand was a message.

Aiii! messages. He checked the last message first.

"OMB!" He said it aloud but in a whisper.

Really?

He swiped back.

OMB.

He did not even reply, but took a step, reached the doorhandle. Stopped. What would he say to them? How could he get out of here without upsetting them?

He glanced over his shoulder at the window. There were lights on in the tiered uphill neighborhood.

Was that some—maybe another—dream a little bit ago? Pome says something about dreams. Too bad dreams aren't sendsibles. Or?

Two flights down, but from the ledge not much of a leap to the fire escape. He thumbed the window locks open, shoved up the sash. Brr. Jacket? On the hook by the kitchen door. —No jacket. He took out a sweater, closed the top drawer. Pulled an extra shirt from the closet. Dressed. Looked at the time on his new q-phone, slipped it into his pocket.

Climbed out. This would not have happened pre-November 3rd, 2017.

From his bed in the darkened room next to Tu's, Mr. Yu was aware of the opening window... then the leap across to the fire escape outside. He sat forward, saw the dark shape of his son begin its descent.

Mr. Yu had been sitting dressed in the dark, thinking, waiting for his wife to finish up and then they would have tea. His shoes were off, legs outstretched on top of the covers; not thinking of atomic physics, as Tu. ...But Mr. Yu had been thinking of the Oorrt Cloud surrounding the solar system, with its nebulous astro-debris, small and large; and of its likeness to earth-launched debris, nearly half a million bits of space junk orbiting the earth; the debris of satellite, rocket parts, tools, and all manner of bits and pieces circling, circling since the mid-20th-century. *Vanguard*, he thought, had initiated the Americle portion (nonsegregated) of the junk cloud traveling, orbiting at approximately 17,000 mi. per hour, depending. There are various elevations, some in the thinnest of earth's upper atmosphere, and some undisturbed by its friction—higher, further.

And then he heard the window open. He saw the leap, against night's ambient neighborhood light, sat up in the dark room craning to make sure of what he saw. Then he jumped from bed, slipped on shoes, opened the door, light from the kitchen striking into the passage, his bedroom. He went in to his wife at the sink, small, smiling kindly on him, as he embraced and murmured something. Something about needing to check on the press. Had he left it on? —he thought so, yes, kissed her, she turned back to the sink, and he stepped to the door, looked over his shoulder as, bundling Tu's jacket in with his overcoat, he passed out toward the landing. He would be back shortly. That had been his promise. And he would correct his lie, tell her the truth then.

Lightly jouncing, he hurried downstairs, hopeful of no injury to his son on the ground below that last section, the folded flight of fire escape. But he saw the empty ground in the alley and, donning his coat, started after. Mr. Yu was determined not to lose his son again. He felt in his pocket for the q-phone. Yes, it was there.

[Translation from the dialect Osiian] *Tu had never been able to explain... the strange disappearance and reappearance. Tu and his new friends, for I never heard of these friends before the Cossyc meetings, though maybe yes I saw perhaps, I saw them wave, one or two, in passing it was, surely. I'm certain the young black man with the big hair, yes. Then the mayoral assistant's sister. Were all stolen? Or just a few? Or just Tu? But surely, as reported, all were unchanged from their condition two years ago. Even their clothes were the same, not a day older or worn. There is certainly experimentation here. Successful. Biological. There is conspiracy.... Surely CossycSystems only has the hypnosis, the knowledge, cosmically hidden (till now?) for such experiments. And they are still hiding these. Surely.... still....*

But he felt Dr. Neee to be trustworthy. *Dr. Neee surely was an honorable man.*

He fished out his phone and, in the light of 3rd St.'s connecting driveway, as he hurried down hill on the curve between apartment buildings, he thumbed and searched the green, white, and red lights; then speed-dialed to the new phone he had given Tu since the boy's return. His son still had his 2017 devices, but it would take a new phone to make Mr. Yu secure of Tu.

[Translation] *Surely he's at the intersection by now. There must be pick-up interference in interception of Tu. The boy had not once disrespected me. Not so this evasion! this is someone, some entity—sinister!—who can say? Who can say?*

Mr. Yu kept the phone to his ear as he looked left and right—toward all alleyways and up driveways in the complex —all the way down to the street. Then, still listening, hearing no signal of messaging, still with the phone tight to his ear; feet tapping pavement, still watchful of movement, the scarce quiet traffic of Third onto Exchange, the few pedestrians. *Now at the corner*. He stopped. Oh this quiet traffic. In Osiia it had been noisy, internal combustion engine, making pedestrians safe by its sounding. Exchange ran up hill, dark alongside the cemetery, glowing with street lights on both sides, and buildings mostly closed on the right, but still throwing off light onto Exchange. He did a double-take.

There on the dark side!

Someone was climbing over the GlimmerDale wall. Down there along the thoroughfare across from the library. It had to be Tu. Had to be Tu. *Now*. Now Mr. Yu was quietly leaving his voice message. He did not shout—but ran across to the sidewalk opposite.

Tu Tu. He wanted to call out. But he did not. He went on. Lightly tapping the sidewalk with his feet, running.

— *Can a smell smell a smell?*

Pomala was having a dream. Somebody named *Dah* was going to help them get back to 2017?

"Of course not," she answered. "How could it?"

— *Say a clump of dark matter was part of a smell or say within a smell. Or a smell was partaking unbeknownst with dark matter.*

"So I'm not smart enough to know but that does not seem unreasonable. Do you mean without the other knowing about it?"

— *Knowing is a strange word. A good word. It implies mind. A mind.... It's not so much that the smell is dark matter and dark matter is a smell. It's more more like both are... just there.*

"Oh, okay. In the same place?"

— *Roughly speaking. More more like in the same space. Or place, either one.*

"But does it smell the smell? Or just be not part of it... or part, depending on what this all means. It could mean a lot, right? Or... does it mean anything?"

— *Let's just say there's more more dark matter than your kind of matter, your material matter, body, refrigerator, trees, that sort of thing. A lot more. In fact, we WIMPs predominate in both universes.*

"Predominate? Hmmm," said Pomala, "am I supposed to be having this conversation with you? —since I'm so not much?"

Pomala was talking in this dream with what looked like a pale starry bit of heaven. However it was mostly like a dusty pale starriness. Some bright pricks of starlight or galaxy-light here or there within the dust. A massive pale glimmering bulge in the nightish starrish non-earthish heaven. Her dreamy interlocutor looked like this. She could see no planets nearby. She tried to stretch out her hands but all she saw (or otherwise distinguished) was bluish dusty shimmery, with what seemed light blue star-scattering. The juxtaposition of the two talkers seemed somewhat binary.

She said, "Or by *we* do you mean, you and me? You and somebody else? A bunch of somebodys? The whole of dark matter?

— *I think we've had this conversation before. Or at least that's what I was going for. Remember the WIMPs we talked about?*

"Yes. Weakly-Interacting-Massive-Particles. Right?" And she was thinking, that's big — I actually remembered that, that wholly technical thing!

— *So so that's us. Me. Kinda sorta here with you. Like you — and them — were kinda sorta here with us. Before. In 1900 EE. Only then <u>you</u> were the WIMPS, not us.*

"Don't you mean CE, 1900 CE?"

— *No. Try to recollect this. Mam and I are alternate universe, alternate reality. You're going to have to report.*

"You mean report to FivePoints 2017?"

— *Yes, FivePoints 2017 CE. Remember this sub-sub-sub particulate.*

Pomala laughed, her starry twinkly dusty blue-ness spreading and contracting as she said, "I so like when you use that word! Like we're something the EPA should clean up. We are carbon emissions. But our 2019 PresiDent thinks we're insignificant."

— *Off-topic*, said Gneis, pale and sparkly.

"But *you* made me laugh. I didn't do it."

— *Tell me this. Do you recall SiXPointz at all? HiTopOLis?*

"It seems familiar. Let me think."

— *Can a think think a think?*

"Please. I'm obviously a thinking think or we could not talk.... So WIMPs is familiar."

— Good! How about Berle? Sheesh? Are they familiar to you? Or, do you recall you once told me — do you recall being a smell? A burger smell? Did you not say you smelled burger in our SiXPointz apartment?

"I may have. Let me think." *How can I remember weakly interacting massive particles but not this?*

Laughter! They were laughter!

"So. I do think Jay said we had no butts and no noses, couldn't smell. —I have my assignment. I'm to remind 2017 CE about 1900 EE. Remind FivePoints about SiXPointz, Akropolis kids about HiTopOLis kids?"

— That's right. The W —

"— The WIMPs! We were WIMPs once."

So so. Very good.

"Anything else?"

— Aren't you supposed to be checking your messages?

Gneis would wait till next time round to remind her that Dah and Claude and Sheesh were all little more than a centimeter away. Even though SiXPointz and HiTopOLis itself were no more. But still they were harvesting cornfields east of those decimated places.

— Your friend Jayrai did have a dream, by the way.

"Why is the library always closed now?" Quadri was asking his big brother. They were in their shared bedroom in an apartment high above Third's offset intersection with Exchange. Curving drives were below the window, 3rd St. was at the bottom, mostly hidden from view; but sometimes the glow of headlights ascended there between buildings.

Quad, in his pajamas, looked at the bigger Quad. Who was still dressed in black jeans and black T.. They had been talking, gaming, and looking out the window. Popcorn was in the big bowl on Quadrangi's lap. Sometimes the little boy would dip a spoon into the olive oil and yogurt their mother had prepared for the family. It was very thick yogurt piled high. She kept the culture going and always had fresh.

"It's not always closed. Just more than before."

"A lot more?" Quadri had white creamy yogurt at the corners of his mouth. His brother cleaned them off with a cloth napkin, then poked the boy's cheek-dimple with his finger. They smiled on one another with dark eyes. Their grins were very white between full dimpled cheeks.

"So, yeah. Maybe a lot. Library money's not there."

"I know that! They keep money in banks. Library's where they keep *books*, wifi, computers —stuff like that. And you can read in the library if you want. I liked the *Poky Little Kitty* books a while back. I guess I was a little kid then."

Quadrangi suppressed a sigh. He said, "Picture books with some words are good, and when you can borrow them it's even better. I actually went there to read, especially when—" he stopped as he was about to say, *you were gone*. "People would be there milling around but no one bothered me. I just dived right in and read. I did software developing there using an application program interface with access to the DPL of Americle." He began thinking of Hibotchi's problem.

"I could read, and kids didn't pick on me there. No teacher to say I had to read this, not that. Like I could read the *Greatest Melon That Ever Lived* instead of about what they grow in some country. Say, Skandia or some place. I liked our librarian. She had big eyes, big pink glasses. Is she still there?"

"Yeah, when it's open. She volunteers now, maybe gets this thing called a stipend for pay. And has another job. She's trying to get a business going. Maybe something online. Maybe a used bookstore."

"She doesn't tell me what to read. She might show me something. Sometimes it was good."

Quadrangi's head was down, checking messages. "Bedtime!" He said abruptly.

"Huh? No way?!"

"Way. Butt in bed."

He put Quad under the covers, took the devices and bowls, opened the door and set them on the hall table, came back to turn off the bedside light. He bent and kissed his brother's forehead. Touched it lightly with fingertips. "Kwad the KonkerEr." He whispered it, stood there smiling down. Then he went out and pulled the door to. But not all the way. Some hall light slipped in.

"we were in this place called shotty landz. every thing was junk. some monstrous things in that dream. kinda went with the monstrous story trice was working out with sheltering cares. she was able to use it." (Jayrai)

"I had another dream!" (Pomala) "Maybe they're related?

"quit that!" (Jay)

"Okay I won't say that."

"right. then i won't shut off."

"Like you would."

"i'd just go over to everyone else. i need me a shot of the hadesthon."

"Be careful. We still don't know what's what."

"so what's the dream --but what's up at the cemetery? did they end up there?"

"If you don't know, I don't, but that's my guess based on last messages. They were going in. You got that, right?"

"yeah --that's where i'd be! god, do i need this arm?"

"Yes, Jay, you do."

"don't tell me --you dreamed you smelled like burgers and fries."

"Ha ha! :-) Close. I dreamed I was dark matter talking to dark matter. Can you believe?"

"no & don't ask me to."

"No, I mean can you believe I dreamed it?"

"so go on."

"So this other dark matter wanted me to remember EE."

"are you screaming? is that a virtual scream we're supposed to use now? eeeeeeeeeeeeeeee."

"1900 EE, not 1900 CE."

There came a pause.

"i do have a memory of you saying 1900 EE, once. loud, like you were scared. at least i think it was you."

"You see, we were wimps."

"don't rub it in! if cossyc could give me a non-maintenance arm." Jay was thinking with longing of some sort of cemetery rendezvous. "you could go, pome! disobey, disobey."

" 'Get the behind me,' the Bishop would say."

"but he is ancient, not postmodern!"

"Hee. All the more reason to obey."

"if it's dark matter how could ya see it to tell? what's it look like?"

"I don't think it looks like anything. In the dream we were like star clouds or nebula or something. Like you see in Bubble Telescope pix. So, you know... dreams. What was your junk-monster dream like? What did the monster look like?"

"he lived in a factory with a big yellow and orange sign over the door. it said, junk-monster factory a.k.a. shottyLandz.

"Did you go inside to see it?"

"he looks like a giant made out of children."

"What?! That can't be! Back a few messages you said *we*. We were in Shoddy Lands does that mean me too?"

"a bunch of us were just there."

"You mean 2017 were just there?"

"not sure who all but it wasn't just us. other people were there --from the same place, an alt-universe i think. think it was more than an alt earth." Maybe an alt reality.

"You'd expect an alt-earth in a dream. Everything alternate. I mean a monster -- made out of children. Is there anything less monster-like than kids? I mean comparatively."

"at first he looked like a monster made out of children. like frankenstein. sort of all put together out of these children -- like they were part of his body, anatomy -- arms and legs hands and feet and stuff."

"But then?"

"then he just sorta fell apart, that is the kids came apart and were sitting on the floor, working, or at machines. making shotty stuff. it came out in-line, like factory stuff. robots carried them away."

"The children. Carried the children?"

"no. stuff."

"How can it be monstrous if it's made out of children?"

"he's hurting them."

"Who were the other people, the Shoddy Lands people?"

"various and sundry. they said they were from hi-topolis -- wherever that is."

"OMGOMGOMGOMGOMG!!!"

"big deal?"

"Jay! That's where the dark matter is from! His name is Gneis. He told me to remember it but I forgot!"

"sht!" (Jay)

"I better e-mail Tu, maybe private message. Just like... just like... — Tu, what's up with dark matter?"

"if you want but i'm done. too creepy for me. if one more person hooks up with my monster-dream i'm gonna..."

But Pomala was off her. Pome was on the scent: *See what the Native Americles, the A'ndian braves think about this! If I ever get to talk to them.*

Mr. Yu was delicate about his dignity. Except when it came to his son's welfare. He hesitated at the exact spot (as a near estimate) by the GlimmerDale stone wall. Then he climbed over, coattails dragging. It was his best overcoat, the only one in fact, a distinguished looking winter coat made of coarse dark wool, lined with what seemed like satin but was rayon. He thought it wise to conserve so much—no soft woolen overcoat, no real satin. Now the rayon was damp from the stone wall but he would not notice until later, at home.

Surely Tu could not have gone far? Why? Why was Tu in the cemetery? His brave kidnapped boy. Why?

Mr. Yu looked ahead into darkness, letting his eyes adjust, but he went forward. Gradually ambient light from the neighborhood on his left filtered down, and he was able to distinguish flat stone dedications on the ground. Beyond these were chiseled stones, shaped and refined. Some seemed quite old, he noted in passing. Maybe he should take the path over there? That would keep him from obstacles. From Bechtel Street, on his left above, golden glowing came down through gaps in great buildings. Windows there shone faintly. The ground on that side sloped darkly upward toward them. A stone wall up there was much taller than the one on Exchange St..

Earlier in the evening one of those graves had been frequented by a gravedigger from 1900 CE. The gravedigger had never heard of the Common Era, and knew his history as Anno Domine, and the year as 1900 A.D.. He never thought of any history but Western history. The world had been too big and far away. In fact, all the graves in that section had been dug by him. But this particular grave was one he had dug for his father at the age of 14. It may have been his first grave. Willie, as he was known then had been forced to work another job beside the one he did with his mother at the Clasp-locker Hospital at Five Points Akropolis. His father was killed at work in the rubber factory owned by Priams.

As Willie-Digger-dog he was astonished at how little the gravestone had weathered. Mr. Priam had been right about the slate: Slate was better to retain engraving. The factory owner had bought the gravestone and had it etched and installed after learning about Willie and Willie's new job. Mr. Priam made sure of the Clasp-locker Hospital for Mrs. Wilusa, Willie and Parry's mother. It was all hard work, but the family fared well afterward, maybe better than others in the neighborhood, and, of course, better than the immigrants and most of the colored people. Other grave markers had not endured so well, Willie saw as they moved down the grounds toward the ledge.

Across from the ledge he expected to find the Civil War picket fence and gate. That was going to be his first landmark, those graves of the Civil War brave. The paths had changed somewhat over the course of the two cycles they'd been gone. Now he remembered he had changed his thinking. He didn't like to, but it was necessary: apparently he'd been gone over 100 years since 1900. It had to be so.... Except he still held out hope they'd get back to the further greener past, those taller trees.... These trees, while giant, were sparser than in the A'ndian forests. If only True People did not become too interested. Even Parry, his normally timid brother (timid since the initial time-change) was too interested in this awful place. As they passed down through the grounds and graves, more than ever Willie was convinced of greatness in the green primitive age they'd been living in for two years. Parry, he knew, had been terrified but that had passed. Parry was changed, humbled, and had lost a lot of his social—what?—energy maybe, since they'd come among True People. Energy was beginning to seem something different to Willie who had been so mechanically minded in 1900 A.D.. Willie also thought that Parry was missing all the reading.

Parry was trailing behind the braves, trailing behind the girl, even his brother... thinking about all he had lost and how much his imaginative life had suffered since the loss of Five Points 1900 A.D.. He tried hard not to think about Ma, but he could never forget how smart and imaginatively rich he'd been, and all that sharing of literature with his friend James Priam. It was a kind of grief, and different from that he felt about Ma.

The imaginations of True People just did not interest him as much. He thought he had this in common with Nathan Hawthorn, one of Americle's early literary pioneers. Just no sympathy with their stories. Still, he admitted to himself now as the others went on ahead—the stories of anthropomorphized inanimate objects, animals, and landscapes were better than nothing.

The dark shapes of young men and the girl, bobbing before him down toward the stream, were receding just a bit.

Hurry!

The Suffering of Trice and Other Mysteries

Yesterday they had talked about the possibility of bio-printing with layering of cells to conceal burn wounds. Trice had been reading about it on her device. Gretchen had also read up on the procedure at CossycSystems website. Stifling her reluctance, she needed to know if her charge had plans to do this, or wanted help getting in contact. But Trice had said she was no longer undecided and would not go for it. *These burns will remind me.* Trice did not want to forget. They *might* have no power over her now.

"What have you been reading, Trice?"

Today Trice was a bit wary. Trice was usually wary. Trice thought she was always wary, but it was not so. Oddly, she was best able to let down her guard in a crowd. Among big doings. It was in tiny spaces, the intimate—there she had the trouble. Oddly, alone, too, wasn't as bad as one might expect given her history. She wasn't alone often now. Was it something to be grateful for?

She was in a tiny intimate space straddling a metallic chair in Gretch's crammed office, the volunteer's metal bed folded upright against the wall. Not many had seen this space—if space it was—with the bed down. Her charges would know the secret: Where did she put the other stuff? —desk, chairs, computers and assorted personal belongings. Most books were stacked on shelves under the windows overlooking the traffic off Cheddar Ave.. But there were piles on the desk as well. Very nice smell in here, for Gretch had started with the holiday candles even though Thanksgiving—still on option—was several days off.

Gretch had once explained the opening social question: "It's a space in which to start a conversation. But actually, I just like books and want to hear about them. Get others' take, and learn a bit about what my friends like. It helps me understand both my friends and the books."

The books Trice liked were all good. All good books and stories. Full of people doing things, having relations, as many good experiences as possible. Gretch had been surprised to learn from Trice that she could handle being alone... given that as a baby she was put, alone, in the cellar of an old house—the house-turned-apartment-house where her parents (if that's what they were) lived. Gretch knew that the basement happened whenever baby Trice cried and they could not get her to stop. How does anyone make an infant or toddler stop crying while *doing the hurting*? Those choosing to hurt tend to think, *nuisance inanimate object*, though it lives and moves and has its being. It's what you do with a broken useless can opener—fling it against the wall.

Because this kind of treatment occurred in close helpless places, among two or three giants—maybe four or five depending on who else was there drinking or drugging—. The intimacy factor was large in the event. LARGE. This is how Gretch sometimes parsed the situation out of which her humble charge had come. She had first learned this stuff, not from Trice, but from the Department of Human Purposes, where Trice had landed after a near-miss. As a smallish child. Filthy, bruised, broken, covered in impetigo pustules, cigarette burns (some very fresh and infected): Scars from these were still visible today. Later extended foster care. Not exactly loveless, not exactly loving. And frequent new foster siblings with frequent changes of foster family residences. For a while, on the verge of adolescence, it was the city protection ward for Trice, and things started to look up when Aviangelical youth group kids would happen by, or extend invitations. After that it was Sheltering Cares with its individual care. Over the first months, in small horrible bits at a time, Gretch had heard the personal embodiment of this tale from Trice herself.

"So yeah, but you never ask what about games or videos?" Trice was venturing here. She had noticed. Books. Always books. She glanced smiling, sidelong, at Gretch.

"Books are where your imagination comes into full play. Or, let's say, fuller play.... You've noticed you have to work at this sometimes?"

"Yeah depends on how easy they make it."

Her long lank hair, in contrast to Gretchen's brassy dishevelment looked sleek and lithesome draping her slim shoulders. The wrists and arms of her longsleeve T. were patched with colorful scraps from ragged garments found in the discard bin at the Salvage Army Store. Her knees, also patched, stuck out on either side of the chair, her hands clasped in front of her over its metal back.

"You mean can the author yank you in with the first sentence? Example? What about current reading?"

"Amazing, but Mrs. Spiel actually got me interested in a real old-time book with lots of drama and Anglishness and landscapes like you wouldn't believe. Or probably would you?" She cocked her head—that sidelong smile.

"Ha ha. I think I know this lady. Let me guess. I'm always exhilarated by what that teacher can introduce to readers. Something by Charlotte Brunty? The *June Air*?"

"That's it! It's just really good. I can't wait to be alone with it tonight. So you know what I mean about alone."

"Just you and the story even though roommates and other things, happenings."

"Yeah so it's good you make that space for us where we *have* to be quiet. You've said 'quiet!' And we have to concentrate on something... which means get into it and let it get into you —in a good way. Thanks for that." She looked directly at the housemother with the *we-are-here-together* special eye contact. With Gretchen she did not have to keep her gaze indirect as when, in echo, someone was demanding to know what Trice was looking at. (Trice had been looking up at the one who was talking to her, the one fueling-up ready to scream.)

"So June had the suffering childhood. Is that reading going okay with you?" They talked a bit about the suffering of June Air's childhood and how the character dealt with it, its parallels with those of Trice, and contrasts with that of the author. Gretch was able to fill Trice in on parallels and divergence as much as she knew about author and character. The housemother talked a moment about issues of power and control in the novel. She cautioned Trice about the melodramatic crafting of adult life as the story would unfold.

Gretchen stood to hug Trice. "Maybe only a chapter before bed, then sleep? Rest, Trice. Go to sleep, okay. No more monsters. You and your friend stop dreaming of monsters."

Trice nodded, unlimbering from the chair.

"Get to bed, Trice!" Gretchen smiled softly. So did Trice, smile sidelong in its wreath of scars and draping hair.

The desk was piled high, so when the girl was gone, Gretchen shoved the furniture around and stacked chairs in the hall by the door. She pulled down her bed, opened the covers to air. Sat, got out a magazine, opened it. There was Chris. The page next to him was folded down for easy access to this image. She sat on the bed gazing at the image of Lord Chris's suffering as they beat him.

In *Believers Arts* magazine she'd found this recent fine-art depiction of a densely muscled man thrown down, his arms over the thorny, crowned head—bowed—his muscular arms trying to shield it from blows. What came to mind was the picture of Trice's head, crowned with burns and pustules, from a photo taken on her entrance into the system. This photographic image now before her was of dirty charcoal on paper, faint patches of smudged color here and there, widely spaced. It was intimate close work. You could see the muscles, but not the sadistic inflictors of this beating destroying these human features.

Gretchen held the magazine, searching the depiction, her hands clenching. Some she knew would be moved by this image, as was she. Some, she gathered, would use it with morbid heavy libidinous lust. *The creator creating the world!* Her hands clenched the magazine. She wanted to scream her monstrous anger into the night. No more monsters for Trice! *Stop stop stop the monster.* She whispered it very small. Stop the scream, God. Please. Stop the monster scream....

Looking left to right and back again, Mr. Yu hurried along the dim path, clutching Tu's jacket. His Osiian-Americle eyes had adjusted to the ambient dimness and glow from Bechtel Avenue above. The path wove among gravestones and tall trees in elegant long curves. Just passing the Civil War dead and cannon, its plot no longer set off by white pickets as in 1900, Mr. Yu looked down toward the gentle slim stream and saw movement. Dim figures, perhaps, moving against a backdrop of darkness surmounted by trees and glow from high above. Up there, he knew, stood old mansions now subdivided into rooms, lofts, apartments. The crazy streets up there twisted this way and that—but in fact it was only one street. People called the neighborhood Krazy Knoll because of that street. He knew the nickname from his position as manager in the dry-cleaning establishment at FivePoints. But Krazy Knoll was far enough and high enough that GlimmerDale sank large and dim, and here and there outcrops or small knolls and marble or granite tombs stood, throwing deeper shade.

And, in that shade, he saw them, maybe three figures beyond the distant tiny footbridge below him, moving deeper into shadow.

Tu is with them. Tu must be with them.

He did not cry out but stayed with the path, weaving his way down toward the small stream. Beyond, ground began rising slightly again.

"This's turning out to be a regular sandbox," said HB.

Fabian said, "Wouldn't that be an irregular sandbox though?"

Shivering a bit, his arms wrapped tightly about him, Tu had to agree with that. If this was anything it was nonlinear gameplay. The challenge of getting back to 2017 was definitely not linear or fixed. Some overarching cosmic order permits multiple sequencing, each of us choosing the path to explore its cosmic environment to imagined optimal effect; but ultimately with probabilities simply and arbitrarily side-questing in hyper but—by no means optimal—contingent subplots.

Having satisfied his thirst for explanation with these tentative thoughts, Tu went on to correct for push back. "Cosmic ordering" was beginning to sound like Fabian's belief in God. He knew about this though it was never explicit (that he could remember). And Tu was *not* ready for that yet. *If ever. Probably never.*

They came up to a rock ledge. HB said, "Yo, this ain't workin', hear what I be saying? Not working." He looked at the lit dial of his watch.

"So yeah, not," agreed Fabian. "Any ideas, Tu?"

But Tu looked at him blankly then shifted gaze toward the ledge. Fabian was leaning against its cold face. Just a shoulder. He closed his eyes, yawned and shrugged off, giving a glance at Tu.

Tu looked at the rock face where it had recently been cleaned—preparatory to what? He opened his Q and shone light on it. Only one small part had been cleaned of lichen and mold and moss. Water dripped down here and there. He was clearly considering. The others followed his gaze.

The ledge was taller than a teenager. It formed part of a slight knoll, sticking out of overtopping earth. In all their youthful isolated forays into GlimmerDale they had never noticed it before. Tu had probably never been this deep into the metropolitan cemetery, which had once been the Akropolis Rural Cemetery —smack in the undulant farmland edging a fledgling canal-building mid-19th -century small town.

The three stared at the strange fresh symbol chiseled into the face of this great glacier-hewn sandstone, not recognizing it as a rock that had backed an ornate 1900 tool crib—initially a showpiece for the wealthy bereaved seeking a proper place for their dead. Those 1900 wealthy would have known of this rock with its ornate tomb—those living on the historic Knoll high above with its mansions and carriage houses in that earlier century. They had attended the mansion marriage-ceremony in which the inventor of electric light had made his vows. But afterward, at the turn of the 20th-century, this former mausoleum had been the tool crib for Willie Wilusa's workaday tools, shovels, rakes, mowers, buckets, and other grounds keeping tools.

"The braves. They must have put that there," said Fabian.

"What is it?" asked HBBBAH. "A fish? A snare? A Native Americle eye? What's that an emoJi of. What does it mean?"

"Those are the same questions," suggested Fabian.

"I'm not getting an answer to either," returned HB.

"Maybe the important thing is what you said first—that *they* put it there." This was Tu's considered contribution.

"They used a knife of some kind," said Fabian. "Did anyone actually see their knives? Were they made out of stones?

"We saw their longbows and arrows. I think at least one had a spear." This was said by HB, who was fingering the fresh primitive strokes. "Definitely not steel. Not iron."

"There's something important here," said Tu, capturing an image, "but we aren't going to parse it now." He looked at everything carefully, memorizing the sensual qualities of this emblem, and its surroundings. "I think they did not clean this first. Someone else did. Chemicals seem to have been used on it." He sniffed again at the scrubbed cold surface.

Someone behind gave a gentle cough. Tu closed the phone, cutting off its light. They turned.

Mr. Yu stood there, shadowy dim in ambient light, small in his dark overcoat. He held out the jacket. It was then Tu realized he was shivering.

HB did a double-take. As Tu grabbed the jacket, Fabian held out his hand, saying, "Hello Mr. Yu."

Taking it, "Hello," he said softly. "Fabian."

Silence took hold for a moment.

Fabian said, "You're probably wondering what we're doing here."

Mr. Yu did not look blank. He smiled slowly. "Yes."

Since having numerous talks with Pastor Zettler, and seeing him at the initial Cossyc meeting, HB did not need to wonder why Mr. Yu was here.

Tu was stymied, surprised, and blank as usual. He slipped into the jacket but then groped to pull down sweater and shirt sleeves stuck up inside its arms.

Mr. Yu did not glance at his son.

"So, you see, sir," said HB.

"So, we thought," said Fabian simultaneously. He half-turned and pointed to the carving. Tu fumbled, opened and shone the Q on it.

Mr. Yu looked at the picture blankly. Tu thought his blank look assessing, the others just thought it blank.

"I promised Pastor Z...." said HB looking at his watch." —Think I'm late."

"Yes?" said Mr. Yu.

"Better go now," said Fabian. Tu closed his Q and they all moved together toward the glimmering stream.

Weaving their way silently back up through darkened grounds, Mr. Yu walking behind, Tu was thinking of this event, the etching. Then he started thinking about the history of cybernetics and how anthropologists conceived the ideas of application to social science... which wasn't much of a science at that time. Probably still is not. It was feedback loops of course. Feedback loops with information on behavior in society, its symbols, and human beings themselves. All organisms contain feedback loops. It's universal.... And can be modeled mathematically.... And....

Mr. Yu was thinking of primitive symbols in straight anthropological and even artistic terms: unlike his son, who was thinking abstractly, Mr. Yu was after meaning. He had seen the etched symbol before. He had placed such on a book handed to a fellow quiet conspirator. Mr. Yu had never said anything about this episode in his life to his son. He had not thought to. No that was not true. He had thought of it but, in deep consideration, did not act on it. Though in Americle now free to speak of it, he had deep faith concerns for his parental his expressions. So far he had been modeling it. Everything wrapped up in the symbol was part of the reason they had come to Americle. It was the whole reason they had been *able* to.

HB thought, *Are they signaling?* —Are the braves and 1900 signaling something with that snare? Or —?... He was definitely going to download his head info. Also, he was going to be making plans and thinking about the problem of CossycSystems after tonight's revelation in the SoupMission.

Fabe was thinking, *That one symbol looked familiar*. Almost... so, almost? ...It was a believer's symbol for sure. But why was it there? Who did that?

Meanwhile, along with Jay, Pomala was hatching a plan of liberation. Maybe Trice would even be part of it! Yes!

...But *NOT* Bo. No Bo, Pomala was thinking, definitely no Bo.

[Because readers experience narrative time displacement it might be wise to apologize here. This is not about the ***macro*** displacement experienced by our heroes, whereby 2019 CE causes confusion for them. The *mini* type of time displacement explained here is solely for a reader's experience. One technical term for this type is ***micro*** *displacement*, in which smaller amounts of time-action are removed from the chronology and placed elsewhere in the narrative. The reader may recall this happening with Pastor's dual Cossyc visits earlier in this narrative, with Trice's backstory, the Americle exploratory scene, etc.. The micro process described here is not necessarily ongoing but can be disruptive for the reader even so. The purpose of macro and micro is twofold. The macro gives a reader the *vicarious* imaginative feel for time displacement which feels acceptable to him or her. The micro displacement is actually more disorienting: The reader experiences not vicarious but *actual* disorientation. While hasting through the narrative, this literary device helps readers themselves become disoriented and so are better able to understand 2017's macro disruption.]

On their NotRecyclable Devices:
"What did you find out? Did you see them?" (Pomala)
"We found a fish symbol." (Fabe)
"It was a snare symbol. Picture looked like a snare." (HBBBAH)
"Explain." (Jay)
"Something you step in and get caught." (HB)
"no I mean WHAT HAPPENED!" (Jay)

The digital conversation was mostly a five-way but Tu was basically lurking. Once in awhile he clarified. And Quadrangi also virtually showed up.

The outing was described, leaving aside the surprise shadowing by his father out of respect for Tu. The cemetery had been investigated first, and that had proved a good guess, and then the mysterious posting at the ledge was given in detail.

"We don't think they cleaned the spot before carving. Someone else did that." (Tu)

"How big was it?" (Quadrangi)

"Nearly 6 in.." (Fabe)

"About 15.24 centimeters." (Tu—sent simultaneously)

"Here's something." (HB) "It pointed like an arrow in the direction of Exchange St.. Maybe that's significant."

This did not receive a response.

"they went exploring." (Jayrai) "who wouldn't?"

"Right." (Fabe) "They did in 1900 -- probably more than we did. We wanted to get back, esp. after finding out HB was going to make it. They seem to have convinced the white boys and girl to join them in A'ndianland."

"Wherever that is." (HB)

" HB? Make it?" (Quadrangi)

"Get born."

"Little Quad told you."

"Actually," (Tu) "it was his 1900 progenitors who were going to make it. ...There's A'ndianland in The Hadesthon."

"Wait!" (HB) "It's in Grandmasterland. Showman Land!

"You mean Game Master Land?" (Fabe)

This also got no response.

"anyway," (Jay) "exploring."

"We won't find them."

An argument ensued during which HB was absent. When he was back on: "the Game Master had them kidnapped. It's not known how. The symbol is both fish (yeah religious, Fabe) AND snare (A'ndian). It points in the direction of pursuit. Prints in the turf between leaves led back toward Exchange. I got nothing from there."

"This is a head report, right?" (Quadrangi)

"Yo bro. Actually it don't say Game Master. Just says mysterious unknown force. I'm calling it Big Fello."

"Do you mean God the Father, God the Son, God the Force, what?" (Fabian)

Silence.

"Those are all metaphors." (Tu)

"That means we aren't getting hold of this." (Fabe) "Of course."

"Keep trying, though." (Pome)

"btw, what's hah-laa?" (Jay) "has he got a metaphor?"

"He is a metaphor." (Tu) "I mean the pronoun he is."

"Quadrangi?" (Jay) "is destroyer a metaphor? seems like that's all hah-la does now. kinda like *now-i-am-become-death*."

"Quadrangi?" (HB)

"I'm not going there." (Quad)

"My take is. We'll see them. How can we miss? They stand out like sore buttkus."

"Does the cemetery mean anything? The rock?" (Quad)

"Or the clean spot?" (Pome) "I think my sister said something to pastor about changing the rock. Maybe it's the same as the ledge being debated by the board. They probably cleaned that spot."

"Why would they do that?" (Fabe)

"Don't know. Maybe a test?"

"To find out what kind of mineral it was." (Tu)

"Maybe they'll post something." (Pome)

"On their website?"

"On the stone. A placard or something."

"am i a metaphor?" (Jay)

"You are made up of metaphors." (Tu) "And atomic dust."

They rang the bell promptly at 1 p.m.. They had been announced on the intercom by the doorman downstairs, but there was one more security measure. The peephole and bell. They were expected. Invited to luncheon after Glindora had politely requested a visit for herself and Pomala with Nandora and Jayrai. Uncle, of course, would greet them, and retire to his study. He was a very great academic, and professor of engineering and comparative religions at the University of Akropolis.

Afterward the others were sitting in the living room, getting to know one another, sipping tea and nibbling on pastries. This room was spacious, its colors pastel, with wide maple-framed openings to other parts of the condo apartment; furnishings somewhat austere in appearance to balance the decor. Nonetheless, it was comfortable.

Though she had remembered Pomala from the soup kitchen during the first interrogation, Nandora was startled yet again by the ultra white skin, blue tattoos, pink eyes, and white hair of Jay's friend.

But Nandora was gracious. She and Glindora did all the talking, except when Jay couldn't help herself. But she did quite well, considering; seated almost demurely beside Pomala who smiled a lot, looking each speaker pleasantly in their eyes. One hardly noticed Pome's respect so natural was it. (Unlike Jay's—who noticed and owned her own acting from the get-go.)

Of course I respect Uncle and mother and Glindora. Of course! I just don't know how to show it without "showing" it. She was disgusted with her own acting abilities, more with the necessity of deploying them.

"It must be a very great responsibility to be in the Mayor's office... and on so many boards in the city." Nandora was suggesting this. She had no such responsibilities. Jayrai was responsibility enough for 20 mothers! This is an exaggeration. Nandora reminded herself.

In the two years Jay had been gone (without apparent aging!), much time had been spent consulting various investigators, writing letters demanding justice, and with frequent though discreet appeals to CossycSystems Inc. in case Jay had shown up for maintenance. Seeing her again had been tremendously relieving, but she was careful not to show it either to Uncle or Jay. Dignity is very important. The Americles, she found, were sadly lacking in this. Jayrai sometimes teased her mother, calling them the melted pot Americles, the cracking-pot Americles.

Glindora was wearing her business attire with blouse and skirt, low very dark blue heels, ankles modestly crossed, and a bright silver bow tie, setting off her monochromatic good looks. She said, "It's fairly equivalent with any management position. You get immersed in details, tried to swim up for air, while recalling all the while that it's time to be responsible."

"Is it wearing?"

"It would be if I didn't thrive on these kinds of activities. I'd probably quit and work on floral arrangements or something if I didn't feel the passion."

Nandora did not notice that she herself was faintly skeptical about work at a florists'.

"Passion for management?!" Jay looked down quickly. *Grrrr.* Jay had to *grrrr* internally after her flubs.

"Of course she would feel that," said Nandora coolly. "What if you were to manage a chain of BarStucks?" *You seem so interested in running coffee machines.* She might have added.

"Jay wants to be a barista," explained Pomala to Glindora. It was an unusually quick response. Pomala liked to leave room for a person's own response, but in this case....

"That's a very good place to start," said her big sister. "You can learn much starting that way. I have a friend whose father began as a bagger and now owns a chain of P&A supermarkets."

"Goodness," said Nandora.

"Is that Ray Grand's brother-in-law," asked Pomala.

"It is."

This visit went well, and at its end, as they stood by the door, Nandora said, "It was a pleasure to meet you, and kind of you to come. This does seem the best way for our Jayrai to begin again getting out just a bit in this city. Thank you."

"Pomala's parents and I will take care to see they have a great time together during their visit." (If only. If only they would *not* be talking 2017 CE.)

"was that diplomacy?" asked Jay when they were texting to set up a time. "that last thing your sister said?"

" 'Bye now?' I don't think so."

"quit that."

"Actually, I don't remember."

"it was like she said something that signaled different things to each of us."

"Sorry I don't remember."

"Oh Trice, this is so great!" Anyone else choosing these words and tone might seem gushing, but not Pomala. It sounded just sweet and plain. Somehow Jay had not mentioned to her mother that Trice was invited to the overnight with them.

The patchwork girl had come into the gently gentrified living room with its eight-foot high ceiling and maple molding for trim. Standing with the other two girls, she looked around at pale satin furniture, a bit stunned. Then she smiled sidelong at her friends. Pomala had been more of an acquaintance but this was almost instantly rectified.

"Wait till you hear what I've picked for our music!" She said.

"Please don't say the Bloatles, Cyberpuke, chEEse Z, or MetalBlisters," said Jay.

"No no no! Think 1930s! 1940s! Jazzy BIG bands! Swing!"

"Whew! I thought it was gonna be scratchy violins. Maybe hideous bellowing convoluted opera."

"Kitchen stuff!" shrieked Pomala, taking Trice's hand. They ran off down the hall through a pale swinging door, into the kitchen with its equally high ceiling and smell of feta and anchovies. The island was piled with ginger and chocolate treats, fruits, cheese, and natural sodas. They sat on tall stools, listening to Goody Bennyman, Lead Woowis, and White Paulman. Talking like talk had just been invented. Trice was quiet but smiling, absorbing it all. She could not take her eyes off Jay's bionic hand and arm—with all its wires and works on display—perhaps because of Jay's recent extended absences. Trice had recently spent only those initial minutes in the Gospel Mission with her in person—discussing Bo. Next the girl could not stop looking at the glimmering dark appliances in the spacious, otherwise very bright and pale, room. Music sounded as though issuing from the toaster oven... or maybe the mesh-covered overhead cupboards.

Much as Pome wanted to discourage it, they talked about Bo. (Who would probably be gigantic now in 2019.) A couple attempts to moderate some moderation on the topic *Bo* failed, so Pome chose silence to see what would come. There was a lot of *Bo* going on. Bo, whom Pome had not particularly known about in 2017. Bo had been police-shot, in People's Hospital, in the jail, and was now missing. How do you disappear digitally? Behind an alias? Change your identity in 0s and 1s?

At last Pomala said, "The best way to fix poor ol' Bo is to get back to 2017. Don't you think?" She looked at each girl.

She was not unprepared but it felt so: Jay opened her round eyes and her mouth even rounder, but she stopped. She said nothing. Jay?! was silent.

Trice saw it all and understood instantly, but she also shut down. Then the three were quiet.

Pome upped the sound on the pod and T. Dorsey's trumpet came on strong. She grabbed Jay by the hand and both girls began to dance—Swing! (*oh the-music-goes-round-and-round...*) Then Pome reached for Trice's hand and the three were going at it all over the kitchen, round the island, out the door and back again. Jay tried to roll Pome across her back (*I'll-dream-my-way-to-heaven*) but she flew off and both girls slammed into cupboards beneath a set of long night-dark windows above the kitchen sink. They lay breathless and giggling in a tangle, then flopped apart, breathing hard. Trice was holding her sides leaning against the island, laughing aloud.

Bruised ribs, the head-bump and scraped elbow—it was worth that laughter from Trice. "Okay now, we've got to devastate this fruit and cheese," declared Pomala turning the music down. "Get to it!" And they climbed back on the stools. "Enough of the sweet stuff. This is real," she said.

"Pome!" said Jay at last, wiping her mouth on an embroidered napkin. Trice was careful of her napkin, trying not to dirty it too much, and folding it after each use.

"2017— I just don't know!... If you can believe that."

"Nope." Pomala smiled. She winked at Trice who also smiled, sidelong. Trice was wondering if anyone else was here. She heard creaking and other faint sounds in the big old house, but nothing particularly human. Wouldn't someone be down to check on the household abuse?

"I mean seriously," said Jay playing with the utensils in her hand. She liked flipping the knife back-and-forth between deft bionic fingers. It clattered out of her hand onto the floor. Her streaked hair falling forward, she reached down for it, feet and ankles gripping the stool's rungs and legs.

"We could all meet, talk, and it wouldn't do anything," she said. "This problem reminds me of —." She stopped. "Something. Some other thing."

"Some other thing," said Pome.

"Anything more to go with?"

"I feel like there are clues all over the place and I can't get my mind wrapped."

"Me too."

Silence again.

Trice wanted to lower her eyes, and watch them curiously at the same time. She did both— sequentially— watch first, then lower. Then Pome said something she might have been prepared for but was not.

"Dreams," said Pome. And Trice looked up. "We need more dreams."

"No. They are nowhere, Pome. Just more clues to pile up, black herrings everywhere." Jayrai was emphatic.

"But each time ... I think I've really got something."

"Then—you don't. Face it."

"What do you think, Trice?" Of course Pomala was not going to leave someone present out of a conversation.

"Um. Is this about shotty land?"

They looked at her.

"Oh yeah," said Jay to Pome. "I gave her the monster dream to work with for SoupMission storytime. It was crazy, of course. All dreams are crazy."

"Maybe... but I don't think so. Some—maybe only a few—have a good quality. They …they just feel different."

Trice was wishing she could have one of those. She said nothing.

"So," said Pome. "Er. Now what? I don't actually know how to summon these dreams."

"Ha-ha-ha-ha-ha-ha. Good."

Trice and Jayrai were sitting atop stools side-by-side, Pomala across from them, all blue tattoos, white skin and hair; the decimated treat spread between them. Pome took a swig of SimpleSoda and looked expectantly at Trice.

"What do you think of 2017?"

"So. Well. …It's—different."

"Hard, you mean," Jay said flatly.

"So. Yeah. I guess."

"You're just like mystified."

"—Like us," suggested Pome.

"...So, you... don't seem..."

There was a tentative respectful silence.

"Scared," finished Trice. "You don't seem scared."

"Hmmm." Pome was going to proceed carefully here.

"Weird. Weird wired weird! That's all," said Jay raising and shaking The Arm. "Strange, weird, no concept, all that," said Jay.

Came silence again.

"So," said Jay. "This means Pome will not be asking you if you want to try getting back there with us." She looked at Pomala, then at Trice. Then at Pomala again, eyes agleam.

"So…. Would that be—anything?" asked Pomala, slowly, wondering, looking at Trice. Jay shook her head, exasperated.

Trice looked down, then up at them. It was frankly said. Firm. Bold even: "No. No, I wouldn't go back to 2017 for anything."

They thought it over, talked. And agreed that if anything weird happened again, Trice was to remain calm and see how it would work out. She was to be hopeful. Watchful. And she promised to be okay.

After a bit more snacking, and a couple more dances, they went into the foyer and picked up their overnight packs. Talking together, they climbed the wide blonde polished stairs with balustrade, and went into Pome's room.

Pome's mom and dad came to the door to peek in and welcome them. Her mom's hair in pink curlers, her dad in dark dressing gown, Pome gave them each a hug and kiss. They all said goodnight. "Think the kitchen is still in one piece?" They heard Pome's dad ask as the door was closing.

"No way," said Pome's mom, her back fleeting, pale in its wrapper.

The door was closed. They heard movement in the hallway, then taps on the stairs going down.

Trice was thoughtful, sad, but not unhappily so. She felt herself among friends.

What is Okay?

"SOSHMEDIA FAULTS FOLLYWOOD FOR RELIGIOUSLY DEPICTING ABCDEFGHIJKLMNOPQ PERSONS!!"

"NATION'S LEADING ASTROLOGIST SEEN LEAVING STAR OFFICE!!

The PresiDent pushes back on implications for use of gray arts in managing the Executive, saying, "Where have you been, Stalled, that you don't recall PresiDents following their guts? Sleeping under a mattress somewhere?"

PRESIDENT CREATES NEW CABINET POSITION: SECRETARY OF THE DEPARTMENT OF ASTROLOGY, CONSIDERS POTENTIAL NOMINES TO SUBMIT FOR CONFIRMATION BY EGRESS.

Dear Baron,

I hope you will forgive the familiarity. I'm sure you've forgotten I grew up with your mother. [Here Candace stops, trying to remember his mother's name.] Philipa's early passing was a grief to me as well as to you but surely not in the same way, or on the same scale. My name has changed and of course, as you know, the aging has done away with the former me, perhaps as in a molt. [However, Candace was still a Parker.] There is scarcely any recognizing the former me in the current me.

I do want to thank you kindly for the offer to help me through your work. It might encourage you if I could say I gave it much thought but I gave none, though I have given thought to the aging process itself, but in a different way, of course, than that of a scientist. I will share with you because that is what we religious do. Briefly share.

I would like to see it as an adventure but its very qualities virtually destroy these opportunities of the youthful. Working to solve the mysteries concerning these qualities, you are very familiar with all of them. So I need not recite them. However, I understand this process as being, in my case, gradual, a withdrawal of all the vital elements of youth that were not my own but that of Another. Of the Creator. I must be grateful for this understanding bequeathed to me through this very process. Grateful because I've still mind enough now to understand. Be in possession, at least for now, of such ability to comprehend.

The one in whom, as the Scripts say, I live and breathe and have my being upheld me in vitality through various stages and now slowly withdraws that force in order I might try and come near both to understanding and to Himself.

May your mother rest in peace. I hope to rest so with her at some point, young friend. And May God bless you.

—Candace Parker nee [forgetting to include her maiden though it is identical to her married name in her rush to recommend the following works of literature]

P.S. Reading various authors has helped me understand better what this all means. I sometimes a reread Stoyol's *Golovin's Death* but there are many other stories and books of wisdom, Monsolo's *Ekkelesiastes* among them.

Each was silent, looking down at her device, glowing in the darkened bedroom. Each saw the message at the same time. A'ndians sleeping in the mission! Trice was also in the loop to receive from Fabian. The texts flew back:

"OMN" (Jay)

"OMG" (Pome)

"OM" (Trice, meaning Oh Man.)

It was from HB.

[The most comfortable way to deal with micro time-displacement disorientation is to ignore it and keep reading regardless of time passing or backing up. Time will go forward, or time will go backward, but it is the unreliable characters we care about, not displacement. Narrative puzzlement and perplexity do not matter, isn't that right, HB?

Thus, the night before their sleepover, Jay was polishing up consultations with Trice for her story contribution with kids in the basement. When the SoupMission was busy cleaning up and telling stories, *Anno Domine circa* 1769 were surveying the cemetery, then symbolizing the rock-ledge. At some point images of the visiting braves, eating in the soup kitchen, were sent from Trice; causing Jay to stew and chew it over with Pomala via texting.]

Circa 1769 teenagers were wandering FivePoints, exploring the newest form of the neighborhood. In 1900 it was called Five Points. In 1769 *Lands between High Lake and the River*. Here the A'ndians would hunt turkey, grouse and other game; and gather cranberry blueberry juniper-berry, marsh-elder, *quenchers*, various nuts and also may-grass, among a multitude of wild edibles.

Here also the boys from 1900 lived above the clasp-locker hospital in the days of horse and carriage (and the exceptional motor car). Before the old-fashioned clasp-locker hospital was replaced by modern zipper-repair, the establishment was run by their mother, Mrs. Wilusa. With neighborhood kids, they played kick-the-can, nights, in Sharon Road outside the door.

But looking up at the new monolithic structures of the neighborhood, Willie got the willies and would be glad to retreat back to the cemetery for peace of mind. Yet the 2019 area was of great interest to them for its notable changes—as an example of FivePoints' continual transition through time. The graveyard was still the graveyard, however. Though its looks had changed here and there, (it sounded music throughout in summertime) it was still quite fair.

At the moment, as befits a brave on an errand of discovery, he made sure no one watched as he crawled under a few cars to investigate the undercarriages (as he called them). The works were compactly covered, polished, boxy; smelled of nothing —unlike those of 1900 with their combustion parts.

You can't see moving parts! Where was the smell? He looked curiously at the tires, kicking, and pronouncing on them. Willie was the brother who was interested in mechanics at the turn of the 20th century but had thought he might have to work in Priam's rubber factory when he got older. Parry stood by, watching, wishing he could take notes for his brother to peruse when they, when they, *when they…*? What were they going to do? Why does The Girl and her, her, her…figure in?

The born True People, Walleye-stare and Eaglestreak, stood not far off, conferring in their tongue about the formal changes witnessed in their mission through time. If it was a mission *through time to serve the girl's purpose. Ochquetschitsch* was passive, standing with them, her hand clasped in that of Eaglestreak, who was very careful of her.

When they'd come to 1900—with Red Fox and other scouts to retrieve her—for the cycle to which they belonged—in which cycle they fought the Interlopers—she had been harmed by the 1900 man who carried light—for so Dark Cloak had said. That was the time of Digger-dog and Girl-boy; of buildings and horses pulling with great what-were-called-wheels. The little girl, then, had been violently dishonored by the lamplighter. Now they were to keep her close—at all events.

These True People told Willie to quit the discovery of undercarriages, and he obeyed. Willie began his next course, to scrutinize with great care, all electric lights (especially those in color) across the street from buildings where once the new grammar school stood. Walleye-stare and Eaglestreak, became aware when duty officers began to watch Willie discovering FivePoints. "Remember our purpose," said Eaglestreak in the tongue.

Parry, being more knowledgeable in the Anglish, did the talking when, at last, the uniformed pair approached— those whose shift it was to safeguard the citizenry of the neighborhood at night.

"You see, officers," said Parry Girl-boy as they stood outside the CossycSystems campus, great walls of various buildings bounded and woven with walkways and shrubbery. They stood on the sidewalk opposite where the clasp-locker hospital had been on the ground floor beneath their apartment a few doors up from Paddy's Saloon and Pool Parlor. Breath pouring clouds as he talked, Parry said, "I'm glad you asked us what our business is because it gives me a chance to comment on your uniforms. We haven't quite seen this style before, you see. May I ask what prompted the redesign since, ah, olden days? I see, also, you have unusual squarish guns but no billy-clubs. Those hats are quite debonair. And your automobile is very refined. Are those lights on top? One of you is a woman—that is very strange, we did—"

"Parry." said Willie.

"What can we do for you, sir," said Parry swiftly, "other than explain our presence here as part of the vaudeville? Naturally, as traveling folk, we wish to explore when we're not on stage."

Parry relished his renewed confidence, so unexpectedly bestowed. The gift of himself had been returned to him as they began to interact with scattered nighttime neighborhood folk, some of whom were very polite, some of whom were derelict and smelly. He did not have the willies in the least and was glad of the opportunity to employ his literary and imaginative gifts of friendly intercourse with those who spoke his language and might be counted on to appreciate his curiosity.

The boy's cloak was clasped at his throat. His (maybe) twelve-year-old face was dirty, pale hair pulled back in a ponytail. Officer Slim Wilkes noted his pale chest dotted with what looked like insect bites. Bed bugs? Active in November, sure.

"First of all," he said, "you've got to know we don't believe your story about the vaudeville. There is no vaudeville, okay? The closest thing is phoo-tube for documentaries, or maybe boo-tub for your kind of thing. And it seems obvious that this is what you are all about." He would not, of course, search them or ask to see what devices they might be carrying. It was a friendly encounter with adolescents, teenagers in costumes, some sort of coSplay, he thought.

"We could be wrong," suggested Officer Wilhelmina Robust. Despite the name, her voice was a smooth soprano. She had been admiring their feathers. "You are awfully good at concealing your capture devices, if not. Why not just tell us plainly okay?"

The boy looked puzzled. "What's OK? What is a capture device?" he asked Officer Robust.

She saw the boy look around at the one he had called Willie and the —was it?— A'ndian or Mexicola boys, one of whom was holding the girl's hand. The girl had been quiet throughout the casual surveillance. Simply following along, it seemed to these officers. The officers were not used to these types and had conferred together before approaching the five kids. Two were seemingly Anglo. The others could be from somewhere else, south of Americle. Except for a few words with neighborhood others, all had been speaking an unknown language before the officers came up to them. Evidently the girl was speechless—on the spectrum somewhere. Just where, they could not say. Perhaps someone on the Cossyc campus holds the key to their presence? It would not be that far out of the way of things.

"Just tell us plain okay." repeated Officer Wilkes.

"What is plain OK? I would be glad to," said Parry.

"Okay," said Officer Robust, being clear. "Maybe you should?"

"I would be glad, ma'am" said Parry. "What is OK? Gladly I will tell you if you tell me what is OK. See, then I can tell you about that."

The officers looked at one another. A chestnut fringe stuck out beneath her hat, just covering the pale ears of Officer Robust on either side of her shimmery glasses. Officer Wilkes was in possession of a buzz-cut under his hat, so his face and ears were ruddy with cold beneath the street lamp. Both shrugged, turning back to the kids in their A'ndian weaponry and garb. A few more words were exchanged, leading virtually in the same direction. Then the officers took friendly leave, to go about their rounds. Moments later, sitting in the patrol car, Officer Robust sent a brief message with image for Sgt. Bench at the station. Not long after that a report came in of faint light flashing down in the GlimmerDale. It would be a while yet before anything came of that phone call.

Later the A'ndians returned through the cemetery to take their rest, not at the ledge, but beneath a utility overhang with solar panels on the historic turreted and many gabled Lodge. The grounds, they'd seen, were changed in their landscaping fashions of the day. But yet there were many giant branching, oaks and maples and ash in places familiar to Willie from his work on the grounds. But greater. Owing to its historic standing the ornate stone structure, called The Lodge, was mostly unchanged. An architectural monstrosity or wonder, depending on the cultural state of Akropolis's transition; a Gothic museum for the dead and famous dead.

Here, in 1900, Willie Digger-dog reported to his superior, receiving instruction as they stood beneath the portico. Mr. Sneed was manager and, with his family, lived within. He was often called upon to welcome the newly dead, and oversee the ground of their mortal remains. Mr. Sneed had worked with funeral directors and families to acquire plots and see to details. Willie was pleased to find the structure still maintained in dignity, and was glad it now had the overhang where trash bins, electric cables, fuel and plumbing pipes were sheltered. They shoved the bins out and found enough lie-down room in pea-gravel, at last heaping it with nature's bedding, fragrant cedar and fir, masking the smell of trash. Willie was now somewhat requited for the loss of his tool crib at the ledge. As they lay down to sleep on broken evergreen branches, Parry said in Anglish, "What do you suppose OK is?"

Hearing footsteps on the slate pavement rounding a corner of the house, the four youths turned, sat up. *Ochquetschitsch* lay still. They should have posted a watch. Two officers had arrived.

Though eyes of the living may seldom be focused on them, graveyards are secure enough without surveillance apparatus. But, aside from the nature of things, someone from the gentrified neighborhood high above the gentler slopes of GlimmerDale had seen a faint white flash, and called in the report earlier.

In a windowless comfortless room at the station, having come along peacefully as bidden, they were about to be patted down. There were four officers in the room. The braves hesitated, backed up a bit, shifted fierce gaze to the bigger pale youth. "Remember our purpose," said Eaglestreak in the tongue.

"This is what the police do," Digger-dog said in the tongue of True People.

"What was that?" asked Wilkes.

"This is what the policemen do," said Willie in Anglish.

"That's what you said?"

"Yes."

Then Willie submitted, then Parry and the braves. The A'ndian (or coSplay) youths were lightly patted down by male officers; all but the girl who seemed somnambulant. Dark glass ran along one wall.

Wilhelmina Robust waved away the suggestion she might check the girl. The more mysterious braves were scarred, with high cheekbones, eyes fierce and dark with an alien elvish slant. A finger was missing from one. The taller apparently white kid was muscled, had feathers tangled in long hair in a tail. They were all dirty, smelling earthy, almost animal. The incongruity of their presence here in this brick-and-concrete room was striking. No one precisely seemed the leader, least of all the grubby girl. The darker coSplayers would gesture fiercely at Willie and Parry if asked a question of Robust or Wilkes. Then Lt. Hunch and Sgt. Bench came into the crowded room. Two officers left. Bench, at the desk with screen and keyboard, was smiling and dressed in her usual cords and blazer. She began asking questions in a friendly conversational manner, and fielding much talk from Parry.

"So, no place to sleep tonight?"

"We were quite comfortable, thank you, ma'am," he said. After missing his bed above the repair shop at FivePoints 1900 for some time, Parry had learned to be comfortable lying on moss and boughs.

Primitive weaponry was lined up against a wall by the door behind them, including hatchets in a heap on the floor. The eyes of Hunch and Bench occasionally strayed in that direction. A spear with large carefully worked flint tip fastened with rawhide strips, bows, arrows, one knife chiseled all of a piece out of flint. No guns, no gadjets; bags of hide and pale rush lay on the floor among weaponry. These had all been examined before by officers, providing much conversation, including admiration for the artisan carving and workmanship. The braves were deeply into their roles. Now to figure out the game.

"We'll have to see if we can do better for you," said Lt. Horace Hunch flatly in response to Parry's blithe declaration. He was a no-nonsense type, a tall Afrikan-Americle, handsome, with a deep voice.

It was the first time he'd spoken. Parry looked at him in some surprise. Hunch half-sat on a far corner of the long desk, one leg slung over its edge.

Parry looked at Willie, transparently amazed, as if to say, *A colored man in a suit.*

Willie shrugged. He was wondering if this could possibly be a descendent of his friend Aneas, the boy who sold newspapers at Five Points intersection. Could that really be? Could the colored—

—*But they were*. He plainly saw this. There had been two more very brown men in the room, those who had patted them down. But this one had authority over all. How did this happen? This was even more strange than a woman police officer. For the first and perhaps the only time, Willie wanted to go back to 1900—to tell this to Aneas. That would comfort Argus's son. Make up for the trial they had endured when Argus was wrongly accused of the girl's violation.

"Were there—how many cars did you 'check out,' " said Sgt. Bench to Willie. Willie shrugged.

"You don't know?"

"No. Ma'am." He remembered to add the last (as taught by Ma).

Sitting at what looked something like a flat typewriter keyboard, she reached to turn a small rectangular projection screen toward him; showing a sequence of his undercarriage surveillance, continuing there before his eyes.

"Swell!" squeaked Parry. "Astonishing."

"You knew there were cameras all over the intersection. You would not booby-trap cars."

"Booby trap!" exclaimed Parry, familiar with the term.

"Enough okay." Bench smiled.

"OK is booby trap!" He yelped.

"Parry," said Willie.

"We had the dog sniff out the cars. Just in case." She grinned. Benja Bench had the brightest teeth, wore pink lipstick.

"Sniff cars? You mean for OK's," said Parry sounding knowledgeable.

"Okay, so we have Parry, Willie, Eaglestreak— Walleye-stare? —is that right?" She looked at each in turn. "And this is—I didn't quite catch—."

Came a pause, while everyone looked at the most unkempt member of the group. Even Parry paused. Then he pronounced, "The Girl."

"Oh." Bench looked at Hunch. He looked back at her, waiting.

"Has she got another uh *name*?"

"*Ochquetschitsch.*"

"Right. How do you spell that?" Her fingers were poised over the keyboard.

"You see," said Parry, "I haven't quite learned how to spell *Ochquetschitsch* in True People, or even Anglish, yet."

"True People."

He gestured. "Us."

"You mean you're in the same 'vaudeville' with them." Hunch aimed his gaze at Eaglestreak and Walleye-stare and back again.

"In a manner of speaking."

"Do they speak no Anglish or is that part of the draw?... Because if it is.... We aren't buying tickets. Not watching the Tub, not anything but possibly holding you. The juvenile detention center."

"We really don't want to do that," said Sgt. Bench reassuringly, certain of her good-cop-bad-cop ground. "You've all got someone waiting for you."

"Parents okay," said Hunch.

"Parents are OK too??"

"Who are they?" Lt. Hunch's deep voice was as cool—cold even—as ever.

"Last we knew, Ma was the efficient and kindly proprietress of the Clasp-Locker Hospital.... Pa was killed at Priam's."

Was it a look of genuine grief? Or was he "acting"?

Hunch had a thought. "Priam's," he said. "The old, original, rubber factory?"

"I don't think you're old enough for that," interposed Bench.

"It was a long, um long, a long um a long —"

"Parry." said Willie.

Looking back from Hunch to Willie and Parry, she said, "Place was bought out a hundred decades ago, bought again, and again and again etc., then scrapped. There's a museum and offices there." Parry was hang-mouthed, Willie stoic.

The true braves were standing perfectly still, the girl between them. These braves were watching, listening, understanding how much? Bench pushed back from the keyboard and looked over at them. Has it anything to do with the so-called cultic kidnapping?

At last she said, "Do you know Sheltering Cares?"

"It's OK too?"

She smiled. "What a routine." She looked up at Hunch, saying, "If not boo then phoo. I'll check that routine when I get home."

"Stay out of work," advised her superior. He was thinking, *You got the Buster-Bench kids. Do that for a while.* The roster was due to change.

Bench picked up her device and poked it for Gretch at Sheltering Cares.

"She's got no room for the boys, says send them to the Gospel Mission."

"Okay," said Lt. Hunch."

"*Everything* is OK!' Parry made the declaration.

FivePoints 1900 A.D. and *Lands between High Lake and the River* circa 1769 were walked down to the SoupMission. To spend the night.

Later the police would discuss the GlimmerDale flash, and what might have caused it. They will decide to try and pinpoint its location, since they had no evidence here.

"OMN!"

"OMG!"

"OM."

"So," said Pome after they discussed the presence of braves at the homeless shelter. Do you think they were okay with it? Will they be back there again tonight?"

[Remember your micro time displacement, reader.]

"Let's sleep on it," said Jay, yawning.

"Soda?" said Pome.

"Yeah," said Trice, reaching for it.

"Don't go far," said Willie to Eaglestreak and Walleye-stare in the tongue of True People. "Maybe shouting distance of the wall." By this he meant the (current) GlimmerDale wall.

This was said as they stood in Pastor Zettler's living room after breakfast in his apartment's kitchen above the mission. HB and Pastor had cooked and served oatmeal and bacon. Coffee, juice. HB had looked the A'ndians over pretty good as they ate. They attended much to their meal. The all-volunteer mission did not, as a rule, serve big breakfasts. Donated granular bars with coffee might be passed out. So Pastor had invited the coSplay upstairs following a night spent among homeless men in the basement. Both levels of sleeping were watched overnight by volunteers. During the meal in Pastor's kitchen nothing was said about time displacement or anything related to the current strange situation.

experience was awkward. Pastor had sensed a deep hidden restlessness in the two True People, and having no tobacco to offer them, put the problem to Willie and Parry. The latter had been engaging throughout the meal, bringing chuckles to Pastor and Blake Griffin with his OK routine (of which, as yet, the 12-year-old himself was unaware). No one 2019 made the connection that these were 1900 and 1769 A.D.

The girl had come from Sheltering Cares with Gretchen who left her with Pastor. It was decided she would remain with Parry and Willie. "Take care for her," said Eaglestreak in parting (the language was True People). Unlike those of 2019, these A'ndians were fascinated by the dark paneled doors, brass door knobs and stairs. They tried the doors several times, opening and closing, before descending the latter. They turned and promptly ascended again, then descended before going out the door onto the street. Though they had never directly spoken of 1900 together, Pastor was now unsettled.

"Willie will probably go too," said Parry decidedly to Pastor Zettler. Pastor and HB looked at Willie, still standing by the end table, while everyone else, including the girl, sat on a couch or one of the old armchairs. The coffee table was strewn with books, open and closed, a few newspapers. The precocious Parry, Zettler noticed, had been looking at these, but not touching. In the corner stood Pastor's shortwave, out-of-the-way not far from the door. It was not turned on. Willie's gaze went there a couple times but he hesitated to ask about its various components, microphone, key, cables, wires. Pastor saw this and said, "Would you like to give a listen?"

Willie shook his head. Slowly. "Maybe sometime," he said. "It is a new fangled type of Macaroni's wireless telegraphy transmitter where the amplitude is modulated to make signals intelligible."

Pastor had glanced away but now did a double-take, staring at him as Willie said, "I think I will go, Parry. Remember about the girl." Willie's reasons for this were different from that of the others, though each had been charged with her care; Willie by his mother, the other braves by Red Fox and the *Meteu.*

"Of course! It won't happen again, brother Digger-dog," he said, smiling.

HB, considering his forebears, thought he had an inkling what that was all about. He looked sharply at Parry, who said, "I hope that's not OK too."

HB said, "Never."

Pastor Zettler wondered, but bade goodbye to the older boy, inviting him to return for lunch with the others in the soup kitchen. "Someone might have tobacco for them," he said.

Willie's eyes betrayed but a hint of hope. That was the thing missing from their pouches, piled in Pastor's study.

Not good to look for rendezvous without the time of tobacco, he reminded himself. They had not done well last season in growing or curing. There were substitutes, like sweet fern, but not as good.

He remembered thanks "sir," and went out closing the door, then jounced down the stairs.

"It's so odd to be up in Paddy's parlor," said Parry gaily.

"Whatchu mean? The parlor was downstairs," said HB.

"But this is where he lived. His *personal* parlor."

"Oh. Yo. That's what they used to call the living room." He said this flatly.

"Yo?"

"Yo."

"Oh." Parry was stumped.

Pastor shifted uneasily.

HB had gotten born, but that did nothing to remove his anger of what had happened to his ancestor. His head knew how many grandfathers back that was—no one in his family had ever kept track of that—if it was even a family—he sometimes thought in anger. YES! It was the white man!! YES!! Then he looked at Pastor; thought, *Okay white,* and simmered down.

Pastor saw all these looks pass. HB looked at the girl. Then at Parry, who was briefly quelled by fierceness he sensed in HB.

Pastor: "So, Parry. You... you...."

Pastor seemed to be on pause.

"So you knew HB, here? —Blake? — Blake Griffin?"

Parry looked at HB. Again, he was, uncharacteristically, not quick to speak. Cautiously, he said, "I've seen him. You," he said looking at Blake.

Another pause.

"Your name is Griffin, too?"

"Yo."

"Yo. Oh."

Another pause.

"My brother's best friend two years ago was Aneas Griffin. The newsboy."

HB said, "He worked in the Leg Bone Diner, right?"

"Yes. His father and mother owned it." Then Parry said, "Argus was accused. It was wrong." He looked away. He looked at the girl. He looked away. Parry had never known exactly what was wrong. Only that she had been somehow hurt and had to be protected.

"Paddy's was a bogus place and time," said HB.

"Does that still mean counterfeit?" Parry understood and found language changes fascinating. "Did it get any better?" he asked. Parry wondered about the man in the police station.

"Hardly." HB looked at Pastor. "Maybe some."

"Yes," said Pastor. "It means counterfeit."

"And your name is Mr. Zettler."

"Yes."

"Ours was—is—Wilusa. Did your ancestors live here? At Five Points, I mean?"

"They did. For awhile. I came back later."

"Maybe you are related to Dr. Zettler."

Pastor looked at him, astonished. He paused.

"My great-grandfather was a doctor here."

"Did he have Johan?"

Another astonished pause.

"I had a grandfather Johan."

"That was one of Willie's friends, too. They were Churmans—that's what people called them."

Pastor stood and went to the corner with long horizontal rectangular windows, staring down into the morning's busy intersection. He began to think of his study, full of books—and now strange weaponry. High, on the highest shelf in the corner behind the door were his great-grandfather's medical journals, saved from an antiquarian book sale. Excitement was whelming in him. He remembered… remembered… along with lots of findings from medical cases, there were bits of neighborhood life in those old journals. The neighborhood. As it was in the late 19th and early 20th centuries.

"That bathroom is quite stunning," said Parry from the couch.

Pastor seemed not to hear, though he half-turned.

"Yep," said HB. "Stunning."

"You mean it's boring?"

"It's okay."

"Everything seems to be OK now," said Parry. "How do people even know what they mean, if everything is OK?"

"How 'bout stupendous, okay? That do it for you?"

"... Ma gave the girl a bath after we found her getting pelted with garbage. That was several years ago. Maybe two."

HB did not know what to say to this. He glanced at Pastor, who half-turned some more. He seemed now to be staring at the Cossyc campus across the street.

Parry continued. "Our bath was in the kitchen under the sink. I pumped the water. She made me leave and go do something else."

HB looked at him. *Big Fello! you smart, bro. Li'l bro.*

"We got no wimmins here for the job," he said. "You could use one your own self." He wrinkled his nose.

"We might find someone for her," said Pastor coming back to his armchair, Candace Parker in mind.

They all glanced briefly at the girl. She looked like she wasn't there. Just that grubby little, possibly 12-year-old-girl, body. Hair like a mouse's nest. They looked away. Parry looked at a book. Pointedly, perhaps.

"Does that interest you?" Pastor asked.

"What's it about?" said Parry. "Please don't say OK. That's confusing."

Pastor smiled. The cover pictured a beautiful iconic manly form Parry had seen before in some library books. A naked man with outstretched limbs and geometric lines. But this one was more abstracted, more full of lines and enmeshed in a denser more highly organized pattern. The title was superimposed but seemed also somehow a part of the image. Parry marveled at all the images on all these books, at the gleam and shine of them, the array of colors. *The Complex* —at the top, its subtitle: *How the Industrial Medical Complex Invades Our Everyday Lives*.

Pastor gave a very brief summary of the idea.

"Is that anything like Mr. Wills' *War of Worlds*, or *The Time Machine*?

"No, it's not science fiction."

"Science Fiction," said Parry, lighting up a little over this alien term. A romance?" Pastor was understanding more, Parry's cultural context for instance. "Not a novel of any kind. We call this nonfiction, with a sub category of some sort. Maybe science, applied science, science history, social critique. Something like that."

"Oh." Parry was deflated. That means it's hard to read.

"Maybe you would like a bath as well?" suggested Pastor.

"Indeed I would."

"Let's see what we can do." He reached for the phone. Instead of using a big wooden box on the wall with speaker and crank, Pastor called someone on a rotary dial phone. The dial, swinging round and back over the numbers, fascinated Parry. *This must be applied science —nonfiction.*

Parry listened. He had thought he himself might go directly to the bath. But then he remembered the girl. Yes, a lady would be good. The girl was of course ahead of him in line.

HB was going to get out of the way. He said so in other words after Zettler replaced the heavy-looking black receiver.

"Okay," said Pastor.

Hmm. (Parry)

What's Not Okay

From *Chrustyuns Today*: "Children unable to choose their identity are made to lift heavy burdens in school. Teachers assigned to place heavy burdens sometimes drop them by mistake. In order to help their children grow accustomed in the home, parents inquire of state officials where regulation heavy-burdens may be purchased. MammalZon facilitates."

From the Glob:

"The Glob has discovered that last century's prohibitions on moral teaching worked well in restricting the teaching of sexual morality in elementary, middle, and high schools. Citing current enforcement of sexual regulations, and abortion instructions, 21st-century Chrustyuns cry foul: 'Whose morality are you teaching?' they demand."

Dear Author, thanks for reaching out to us. Unfortunately, *Sad Magazine* is no longer publishing satire as we find it in the Old Tastamint. We find God's judgmentalness and mockery of people no longer funny. What we are after now is a quieter more dry and subtle satire, for discerning dry and subtle intellects, based more on the New Tastamint. People of higher AQ's are put off by the easy recognition of satire with somewhat childish overtones. If you can manage something more along the lines of Chris's parables, but more nuanced and staid, we may give it more consideration.

Don't give up! And thanks for embracing our form rejections, as in the past.

As it turned out, Parry got his bath before Candace Parker arrived. Up in Sharon, Jayrai was preparing for Pome and Glindora's visit. Fabian met HB at the intersection. They were looking for A'ndians and waiting on Tu. Quadrangi wanted and did not want to be there for it. But he had school. Mandatory attendance relieved him of choice in the matter. He thought again of how saving *rules* could be. There was, of course, the choice to disobey, but he chose not. Quadri was with their mother, watching her roll ground meat mixtures into grape leaves for steaming. Maybe goat and lamb mixed together. He was eating thick yogurt with olive oil in a wrap.

"It's not too crucial," said Fabian looking up Exchange toward the library and then across the street to the cemetery. "They'll probably be back for lunch." His hands were in his jacket pockets, breath clouding out as he spoke. He was wearing earmuffs! Silver-blue earmuffs! HB smiled. Then he was wishing he had some. If he did he would not wear them like Fabian, cutting the buzz across his head. He'd cut the broom 'do in back with the band.

Meanwhile, Tu was in the closet again, under the hanging shirts, doing research. The main thing was getting back to 2017. He fully intended to meet them at the corner, the library, somewhere along the street as agreed before going to bed, but. ...This dream from last night... or was it this morning... yes. He must not let the adventure take it out of his head... and research was involved. With the dream. The fish or snare (if either or none) would have to hang for now.

He was looking at the SNOWLAB now, Sandman Neutrino Observatory with Lab: 3000 m of overhead rock, effectively blocking cosmic rays. Dark matter is not counted there, that is, it *is* counted in the experiments. *What we want is stuff from another universe, not this one. No supernova stuff. We don't need stars, we need—.*

Tu sat thinking of the dream. It was full of equations and diagrams he couldn't quite remember, though he had a sense that there'd been familiarity with one or two. That was why he was postponing the meeting.

But he was not postponing it. He was forgetting it. Distracted now into the dream. If he could abstract himself into these dreams....

Dreams plural?

Y-y-yes... Yes! He was having these dreams. Pomala, he thought, was the only one having these dreams, but hers were images more concrete. And with conversation! And somehow, he felt certain! These dreams were (at least) not unconnected. But was there rationality here?

He checked the message *jing.*

Tu jumped up, knocking his head on the closet ceiling where it sloped on this side of the shirts.

The A'ndians had slept in the mission! They had breakfast at Pastor Z's! He was supposed to head into the cemetery. Something might happen—they left Pastor's and now HB and Fabe were hunting them.

His father and mother were already in the FivePoints Dry Cleaners for the day. Mother to be home for lunch. He'd be back... Unless they Souped it. In which case he'd message her. Tu pulled on his jacket, left the kitchen, looked at the Q. on his way downstairs. This *jing* now was from Cossyc: they wanted him back. They wanted them all back. He'd have to see about it later.

He came off Third to the intersection. There they were. In front of the library. Now they were jaywalking through traffic. HB in his jumpsuit, Fabian had earmuffs!

"They want us back," said Fabian as they walked the convoluted path down toward the streamlet and bridge.

"They want us, period." said HBBBAH.

The great overarching leafless trees, here and there, were done making oxygen in abundance for the year. November light, the lowering light of the year, showed dull winter-leaf-scattered grounds to best advantage: green turf, and dead leaves, great gray institutional buildings bordering above a large stone wall on the left. Two of which were St. Invincible and the school. What Willie and Parry would have called the new High School. Kids might look down and see them, tiny humans moving toward gates leading onto Market Avenue and also a Boulevard upward to the mansions.

Tu begin thinking of Dr. Neee. He was okay. And his father respected him.

Looking up at the school, HB said, "I'm not going."

"You're not?" said Fabian.

"Nope."

"That's it? —'Nope'?"

"Yope."

"So... you think none of us should."

"Recall what I say-ed."

"Last night after Pastor's talk?"

"Right in the middle of it."

"So this is a stand of some kind? A general stand against... what you said?"

"It's a good enough reason."

"But there's more."

"Yope."

"Tu?"

"You have another reason, more particular," Tu suggested.

"That too. Look, day's gone download my head, keep bringing me back, download some more. You realize. Thanks, BF—they can't do this remotely. Yet. That will come."

"And?"

"And I don't want 'em knowin nothin, 'K.? Nothing. I'm done being spare-a-ment property. Do you realize they own this stuff in my head? They think they own *me*. Seriously. And they're going to make a bunch of little me's, and those kids will be seriously majorly *took*!! Think about it. Do you want your head downloaded remotely by someone else; or some AI?"

He stumbled over the pea gravel as he said this. Fabian almost reached out but refrained.

Fabian said, "They want me to transform my Grandmother into a 29-year-old." He was laughing.

"Huh?"

"I told you about it. I'm supposed to give her plasma or something so she won't age. Evidently they don't want her to die."

"Just her? You look re-dick-lus wit doze earmuffs, girl."

They were laughing, tripping along in the somber-hued neatly trimmed graveyard between ranks of old graven stones. Even Tu was smiling.

"Wanna try'em?"

"Course I do."

Fabian stopped and pulled off the muffs, handed them to HB. "Want me to dress you?" he said as HB looked them over, a bit gingerly Fabian thought.

"Why do you s'pose they want *you*, Tu?"

"They want to figure out this time-transfer-nonaging-displacement thing. Any scientist would. Some, maybe most of them, simply want to de-hoax it. Not the non-aging part, of course."

"Whew, wait till they hear about the braves!" said Fabe.

"They'll prob'ly wanna do spectrum analysis on that girl." With exaggerated but deliberate care, HB placed the silver-blue earmuffs over his ears. Its band was in back, doing little harm to his vanity and 'do. He turned his head from side-to-side, fluttering his dark eyelashes at them.

"They probably just want to pick Tu's brains," he said, starting down the path again. "They got their eye on you, girl. They want you for their own, Tu. Someday you'll be transforming or transmuting or transplanting or transgandering or terra-forming the likes of me.

Tu said, "I don't think so. My interests... lie elsewhere."

Walking backwards before them, HB stepped out in front to show off his new look. "You mean h-beans ain't Tu's thang."

"Sort of. Not."

HB yanked the muffs off and handed them back to Fabian. He stepped between the other two and they went further along.

Tu said, "Pomala has dreams, you've heard?"

"Yes," said Fabian. "Er, do you?"

"Not the same, though," said Tu. "It would be good if HB had some—to download I mean. Give us a report. Then we could compare. See what's there."

St. Invincible's clock-tower bell high above them began to toll.

Candace Parker was in the habit of giving thanks. Some of her recent thanks were for the return and continuing presence in her life of her grandson, Fabian. She had grown up in a big family, and had nieces and nephews in abundance, even to the grand variety. All of these she was grateful for, always. She gave thanks for the Gospel Mission. She prayed for the tap water and electric, rent, and neighborhood, the community. She did not think these would or could go away soon, though she understood she might be wrong on this. The utilities are a matter for prayer. The tap water she gave thanks for was undrinkable. It smelled bad, but you could still wash clothes and bathe. What harm it might do in these activities was unknown by her. …So much to worry about…. She persevered, thinking the clothes might be all right, especially if she hung them outside from the pulley clothesline to dry. They usually came in smelling fresh and nice.

It had been awhile since she'd given anyone a bath. Fabian was a little thing, and the water here was better then. Washing her, she prayed for this little girl in the tub in pastor's apartment. Candace made small almost cooing noises, as gently she scrubbed the palms and fingers of the girl. *Oh her hair*. That must come next. It would be hard on both. She must get something for those bites, too.

Now what might her name be?

Dressed in clean 2019 castoffs, Parry was in the living room reading pastor's books. He looked at *The Complex*, but it didn't really interest him. Parts of it read sort of story-ish but most did not. They might be story-ish about odd machines, but they weren't dramatic like time machines. He picked up a giant dense paperback opened to a certain place, stuck his finger there and turned to the front to begin reading. *The title is rather taking. But it begins reading a bit dry like the other*. He looked at the fiery cover again. What an intriguing title: *The King of the Rings*. Books should begin at the story if they have one.

Pastor Zettler was in the study taking down his great-grandfather's old journals. They were dusty, musty and leathery, sewn together. He had completely cleared the old walnut desktop for the purpose of stacking and laying them open one at a time, covering the surface. Stacks of brown or black leather journals with their yellow pages, open, would help him determine the content of each. Those wholly medical would return to the shelves.... Or... maybe these would be candidates for donation to the Simeon Harkins archives? He stood over them. Hovering. He felt like Augustone in his years without leisure sufficient to read. Would there be time enough to begin?

He looked up without noticing the shelves across from his desk. There was a lot going on. He might have to wait till late tonight. He could hear them beginning for lunch in the kitchen below. That was Hattie Heckster's high-pitched laugh amid the clatter of pots and pans. The low rumbling thunder of Balboa sealed the deal. He would stop hunching over the journals. Now, with regret he stood tall and went to the door. He looked back. He turned and opened the door.

Digitized clock towers poked up from among lower buildings all over the city: old stone, brown brick, spots of character for the worn out industrial town. A good solid legacy for the rusty belt. At one time Akropolis had been aurally punctuated by tolling mechanized clock towers—donated by rubber factories also scattered throughout the city—to help workers without watches or clocks get to work on time. Most had ceased tolling the hours, and some still kept time without gonging. Only one clock kept to the mechanical tradition. That was St. Invincible's tower clock. Knowing the history of technology and applied science, Zettler had thought this appropriate.

Their passing had disturbed the votive flames. The A'ndian braves ran out of the great vaulted stone nave of St. Invincible's and fled down many dark stone stairs, across the stone courtyard to the sidewalk; and turned right. BONG! Bonging the 11 a.m. far above, its sounding shaking them, resonating, resounding: quivers and pouches bouncing, the A'ndian braves ran. Eaglestreak and Walleye-stare, feathers and unstrung bows lifting, almost vanished from Willie's sight as he turned to follow.

Unperturbed by the vast bonging, he ran after them. They'd be headed alongside traffic of Market Ave. down to an intersection of the Boulevard and the cemetery entrance with its cobblestone pillars. So much of the city was still the same town, though he'd noticed in the earlier hour that downtown over the old Canal Bridge was all news to him. Glimpsed as they came out to go up the hill toward the west part of town, sky lines there seemed to tower. He had admitted his curiosity about downtown, but advised against its exploration. The canal was gone! where ran a great highway down below, full of the fastest traffic he'd never imagined, curving through banks between downtown and the Mansions Hill away out of sight somewhere. That part seemed to lead back toward Priam's rubber factory. —A museum? *That direction, anyway. Who could tell if it turned sharply away somewhere?*

They ran back into Akropolis Rural Cemetery and headed up the pebble path along a streamlet toward rendezvous rock. …Around a shrubbery-clad bend in the rock-and-tree face. They slowed down and stopped. Willie was about to explain about the clock but Eaglestreak was already propounding this subject.

"Mighty to slay!" he whispered. "Mighty to slay is that Sounding! It runs through me still. Red Fox told us of it, when first we heard among graves; saying it is the token of passage. That it sounded from the deeps of earth and also high overhead. He said it unwise so to cut the days with it! Do you not remember, Walleye-stare?"

"That I do, brother, that I do." He was subdued, a'shake, as they continued speaking in the tongue of True People.

Willie was thinking how to explain it as just a clock tower, pulleys and chains and a great iron bell. In their tongue he could say nothing of it. He would have to draw a diagram. A picture. He would do this if they found a sand shoal somewhere. Maybe if they followed the stream back toward the river? Then he thought of Parry and the man's books and papers. He could do this when they went back to eat if they were invited back upstairs.

The braves had heard the bonging distantly while in the neighborhood. And even in the cellar of Paddy's the night before. And they had heard it louder on the periphery of the graveyard at times but hearing it inside the church had devastated them, *these worthy worthy braves*! Willie would show them. They would be enlightened, saved from their fears when he taught them of the forging and works. He became almost, not quite, excited in the prospect. Superstition was to be banished once again! And he was recalling Mr. Sneed's reassurance about the turn of the 20th-century, and that the girl they had found was simply insane, escaped from the asylum, not a ghoul or anything an illiterate might think.

"So what are we going to do?" Pomala was messaging Jay after firming up the overnight with Trice. This is just prior to Jay's liberation from confinement. "I'm not sure about going back. What purpose would it serve?"

"i'm definitely not going!... unless --"

"The Arm!"

"not before 2017 anyway.

"Don't you mean after?"

"problem: mother says i MUST. i sidestepped just so i could get out of the house tonight."

"Sidestepped?"

"okay i lied. said i'd go after thinking about it a little bit. what does your ancient bishop think about that?"

"Honestly, I'm not sure he'd care."

"what?! no kidding?"

"He'd probably care if I did it. What would Newfish think?"

"who cares? -- just kidding, Newfish, kidding!"

"The fam says I don't have to if I don't want to."

"lucky you. you've got them."

"So you've got your mother and uncle. They're not bad."

"HUH!?"

"So okay things are not going good right now. Maybe some thanks, it's a little bit better for tonight's plans. You can tell they *care*, Jay."

"grant me they're just WRONG."

"Maybe."

"agggg! side? whose side?"

"Yours. Always."

"so yeah so................"

"So and this is hard but. But being on your side doesn't always mean agreeing with you."

"HUH? please tell me what this means?"

"Suppose this. You are headed for a cliff, while saying there's no cliff. Do you want me to agree?"

"but i can see a cliff."

"Sometimes, yeah. But what about fog?"

"like when you wanted to bring the girl to 2017 and we said don't?"

"Heehee. You're good. But I still don't see --

"because FOG!"

"She's here anyway, though." (Pome texting.) "Maybe Cossyc can help her."

"wow that's right. she's here. if she's still here. does anybody know? she could be gone again."

"Like us? Could we be gone again?"

"one thing -- i'm not bringing in cossyc to help me figure it out! they don't believe us."

"Or say they don't."

"You think they're lying?"

"I don't like to accuse or judge, though."

"right. what would the bishop say?"

"Guess we don't need to check out the rock after all," said HB.

Tu, HB and Fabian stopped at the little bridge. The braves were coming upstream toward them. They were wearing dark scraped skin cloaks and hide britches, bug bites still red on their chests. Feathers in their hair, weapons slung on their backs.

HB said, "I think maybe they understood while I was feeding them this morning."

Fabian called to Willie when the others halted several yards off. *"You remember us from 1900, right?"*

Pastor glanced through the small kitchen window, shouldered the swinging door, and came out of the busy raucous kitchen with a great kettleful of fish chowder. Setting it on the counter, he noticed Candace Parker, the girl and Parry seated nearby at a small table together. He came over to them, smiling, looking especially at the girl. "Well she's almost a beauty," he said.

The girl had shining hair drawn back with a hair band, and wore a clean yellow dress from the castoffs stored upstairs above Pastor's rooms. There were smaller rooms up there. In one dim room, lit with a single light bulb, were neat shelves and boxes of various things, including clothing. The clothing was in good clean condition as the volunteers would accept nothing less. In another attic room were looping shortwave antennas set up for receiving and sending. A 450 ohm ladder-line went up through a crack between window and frame, connecting to coaxial cable between transceiver and the dipole antenna high between buildings. This was for a separate designated band.

"Parry picked out her clothing. I think Heirolynn is beautiful," said Candace Parker. Her bespeckled wrinkled white, almost translucent, skin had a quiet sheen of its own. "Parry looks good," she added.

Looking toward the dark oak paneled counter full of pots and utensils, Parry said, "Can we get some yet? I can get the girl's, too," he added.

"Yes, go ahead," said Pastor. "Chowder today."

Parry rose. "Corn chowder!" He said, and walked quickly to the counter.

"Actually, it's fish," said Zettler. "Well, you've got her name then?"

"Yes. Heirolynn. A pretty name."

"Yes. How did you find out—I assume she told you."

"And Parry confirmed it. Said his mother found out…. That it was her 1900 name…. —Well, she was gazing at the soap bubbles. She seemed to like them. When I got done with her hands she scooped up a handful. We looked at them together. For quite awhile. I surprised myself, actually. I didn't think I could be interested for so long at this stage of my life. Then I found myself telling her all about the soap bubbles. Some things I didn't even know I knew. I sort of put them in words first, like the *iridescence*, describing in words. Such as: they appear changing in color as light, unlike in the rainbow, for soap bubbles, light is sort of interrupted, reflecting in diverse ways off the filmy spheres."

"Is that right? I didn't know. So you simply asked her name?"

"Yes. —And, as you fix your gaze, you can imagine our sort of spherical very colorful universe, with all these lights reaching us—and very like a sphere it is with lights from what we almost think forever, reaching each one of us individually, if we could but observe with instruments or the naked eye."

"Fascinating." Pastor seemed delighted by these correspondences. "Did she say any of that?"

"No. …I doubt very much I'll be able to remember all this later, though."

"Perhaps not," said Pastor with commiserate understanding. "It takes a certain type of mind."

"Yes. And then that mind will age as well, of course."

"Well, I've got to get back. Sounds like you had a fun job."

"Restful, too." Candace Parker smiled and Pastor went back to the kitchen. She looked down on the girl who was gazing at her own fingernails, apparently without seeing. But then Heirolynn turned her hands and looked fixedly at the fresh clean palms and fingers.

Parry came back then, hands full with bowls and utensils, a mouthful of observations. He set things in their proper places. "Must go back and get corn bread!" Plus, he saw he had forgotten a bowl for Candace Parker. As he went he thought of James Priam, wondering if he could be as old as that now? Then he looked over at the counter and saw the hanging calendar, *2019*. Oh yes, 2019. James Priam, his friend, would be 129. He judged Mrs. Parker was maybe half that age. Perhaps? Parry himself would be 129. *How does that work?* He felt twelve years old, but also like he'd lived forever.

Pastor, helping in the kitchen, had begun to think of the rainbow. So it was different in its expression of refraction, but yet it is seen in each individual's eyesight as a unique phenomenon. No one sees the exact same rainbow. Apparently it's the same with these other, these galactic lights? Marvelous. The universe is in the eye of the beholder. ...But that eye. Where did that come from? He smiled.

When he came out of the kitchen later, and holding a tray full of clean utensils then setting them on the counter, he noticed the round table beside Parry and Candace full of young men. He looked at them a moment. There were Fabian, Blake Griffin, and Tu Yu, rather smaller, sitting with the three A'ndians. The latter three looked older, muscular, lean. The others looked more adolescent in comparison. They were talking together and eating, mainly eating he thought. The conversation seemed tepid, far from animated. Parry was more voluble. He had turned in his chair to converse. However, Pastor began to think about age differentials. He wanted to do research on molecular biology on account of the apparent non-aging of 2017. As he went through the swinging door he wondered if his ancestor's medical journals had perhaps prompted him just a bit in this direction? Then, there was also the Fabian-Candace-Dr. deVill intrigue. He grinned at this turn of phrase. Pastor Zettler was sure he himself was now intriguing.

Tu nudged his z-pod in the direction of Willie, who was actively ladling fish chowder into his mouth. Willie stopped, looked down at the device beside his bowl. The other two braves had the bowls to their lips, sipping; also slurping and gulping. A fine treat of corn bread came with this astonishing good food. Of course these interlopers were eating well now in 2019. It was just after harvest, not fallow time, not planting.

During their 1900 visit to Akropolis with Red Fox and the other scouts, summer had reigned. Later, Parry had been keen to tell True People about how things were done in 1900 but couldn't do it in their language. Willie had always nixed the idea. Wait till we learn better, he'd say.

They spoke to one another as Digger-dog looked at the "mirror." Willie had recalled seeing Tu look at one in 1900 outside Paddy's. Walleye-stare said in the tongue, "Be careful for this place, Eaglestreak. We feel it a Place even as our minds know it for a Time. Remember that Digger-dog and Girl-boy are captive to True People's time. We must take care to avoid the snare."

"I hear you, brother," said Eaglestreak.

"I hear you, brother," said Digger-dog while looking down at the device. He said this in the same tongue.

Eaglestreak continued. "Watch for a snare, the fish is safety. We do not know how you and your brother came to be with us, unless it was, as Red Fox said and the *Meteu* suspects—the girl. We do not know how the girl can do this thing. We remember that Dark Cloak, for his curiosity, was in danger of staying behind in your time.

"Not by herself does she this thing. Grandmaster."

"*If* she does," interposed Digger-dog. He said, "Look now. This is how the clock works to make its sounding with the great bell." Carefully, before them, he placed the device with moving images of inner clockworks yielding a redounding BONG. "They make the building and bell and metal chains out of rocks in the earth. For these they use fire and forging. I will tell you about forging sometime —maybe tonight. It will tell in your tongue.

Parry leaned in to their table and conversation, saying in Anglish, "But we made it in 1900, I mean the workmen made it in the 19th century. It's basically from our time. Even earlier, I think, R'opean. Not St. Invincible's design, but R'opean.

Neighborhood children were all in school. Filling, the room was busy but not as noisy as might be expected. Some people held up devices, apparently as though looking at themselves but actually taking images. These coSplay videos were to be shared everywhere for the next year, though most had no idea beyond the next moment. Parry would have so much knowledge on his return; knowledge to think it all out, and tell it before the fire at the High Lake or the Gorge, or even the ledge (if any dared go to the rock-ledge). Maybe he had achieved enough confidence from this venture to tell stories before the fire. But he still needed more ability to speak the language.

He turned back to Candace. "You see, they are learning about St. Invincible's clock tower from the Ohrental's little projections. He seems quite clever with that. I remember the first time I saw him at the corner of Five Points, outside when it was Paddy's. He was afraid of the horse but showed us pictures of it. Swell!"

"Oh my yes," said Mrs. Parker.

He turned back to the others and Candace began thinking of the 1900 problem again. She was concerned about Fabian. …So much to worry about…. She had given thanks and trusted him, but was still very very mystified. Anxious.

The girl was mashing cornbread into her mouth. Parry kept bringing her this treat. Now she was choking. Quickly Candace opened a bottle of water, poured some into the girl's empty chowder bowl and lifted it to her lips. Candace rubbed her back. The front of the yellow dress was now a mess. She would have to help her change upstairs. What about the blue-and-white shift—that might be pretty on her. This time she would follow Parry's advice and mime the donning of clothes as he said he had done …in 1900. She might leave the room after, then return to see if it took, as he said happened at his apartment above the zipper-repair. Candace remembered that zipper shop from her childhood, not the one previous one, the one he called a clasp-locker hospital.

The table where the six teenagers sat was round. HB had a fleeting image of the wow-wow from Native Americle culture but he was drawn in by the commonality between the various parties at this meal. That commonality was 1900 CE, where all had met coincidentally—or not. —Or not—or not—or. Now he was stalled.

Get back to the joint venture, he told himself sternly. He was inadvertently glaring at Parry, the kid. *I'm just not fond of chirren*, he told himself. And 1900 CE's the thing.

Parry noticed the glare. He looked down. *Maybe I better not ask about the OK.* If Aneas was here he could help but he's not so I can't go on with this disturbing question. No one wants to talk about it. ...Maybe it's in one of Mr. Zettler's books? He'd seen the library on the street in a different place from 1900's, which had been up toward Cake Eaters Hill. Parry unscrewed his plastic water bottle and took a swallow.

"I'm speaking Anglish, he isn't."

"how can you understand then? is it Grak? ha ha ha ha."

(Pomala is of Grak descent.)

"Ha ha. No silly, I mean I'm speaking in a language. He isn't."

"what does this mean? he uses sign language? you do sign language?"

"He just sends thoughts, what he's thinking."

"hideous. that means he's a mind invader."

They come back to the overnight topic, but these side conversations continue. [Soon *Now* will be *Then*, and the meet-up for the overnight visit with Trice—who is currently in school—will then be Now.]

"But it's a dream!"

"yeah yeah. what's his name again?"

"Gneis. He says that means stone. I think. I would call what he does ESPkyThingg -- like in the story about the twinkle."

"so he says ha ha he's from another universe."

"Better be careful, it's only the thickness of a fingernail away from us right now. So his dah said. If I've got this right. Meaning, he said his dah said."

"sheesh, not duh again."

" No, Sheesh is his twin brother."

"so no comparison with the nearest star? 93,000,000 mi. away? Or gliese 581d."

"But no heat or light. Only dark matter."

"ahhh. get out the handkerchiefs. does he have a point then? --he can't *be* a point right?"

"Ha-ha."

"so just disembodied."

"Like we are."

"huh?"

"Right now I mean. We are 0's & 1's."

"oh right. i'd like to be more. should we talk larynx-to-larynx?"

"OK. Give me a call."

Pome's phone *jinged.* "Hi Jay! What's up?"

"I like your voice, it's real."

"Yeah, it's real."

"We aren't zeros and ones," said Jay.

"And just wait till tonight! You should see the spread! Actually Mom wants me to go with her now to get stuff, OK?"

" 'K, bye."

[Meanwhile —although we cannot mean meanwhile here since the SoupMission lunch happened earlier—even before Jay and Nandora received Pomala and Glindora for luncheon. —However, this brings in the *idea* of *meanwhile*. What does meanwhile mean? Mean and While? And how about Meantime?]

The place was packed with hungry people and more coming. Many of those who had eaten enough hung around, either greedy for more or for fellowship. Some of these would leave if any of that hymn-singing started. A few slipped into the kitchen to lend a hand or hang around talking, getting in the way. This time it *was* corn chowder—all the fish being gone—the next time Pastor came out with one of the last great kettles. He noticed the Osiian-Americle Sheree Kim, from the *LampPost*, moving around, device in hand. As he set the heavy chowder-pot on the counter with a wince, he heard HB yelling and looked over the heads of others to see him, still seated at the round table. Yelling.

"Okay means okay, okay!!"

He yelled this more than once. Pastor was startled and looked at HB's target. Then he understood. Parry had slumped down on his seat, turned away from the tableful of bigger boys. He seemed to be murmuring to himself, his 12-year-old head bowed, smallish hands folded on the table.

Candace Parker was still sitting with him and the girl, who, in spite of the ruckus, looked absent as ever. Candace reached out a hand to pat the boy's shoulder.

HB looked over and saw Zettler staring at them, then back at HB. Blake Griffin shrugged. With much exaggeration and impatient face-making.

Pastor turned and went back through the swinging door, praying. HB had never had much patience with smaller kids. It was the bully part of him, and Pastor understood its history. HB's history.

Willie stood up, muscular, tall, and looked down expressionless on HB. HB looked at those muscles. *Guy was my size—a week ago, two?* He looked up at Willie, shrugged. Slightly. Willie went to the counter. Fabian was face-palming. Tu, sitting between Fabe and HB, began to wonder what an analytical report downloaded from HB's head would look like. What would it look like as a projection to HB? The A'ndians looked with stoic dark-tailed eyes from one to another and back at the 21st-century youths, then to one another again. Willie came back with corn bread and set it down beside Parry's folded hands. Parry looked at it and picked apart a crumbly piece. Then he used his fork, began chewing, looking around.

Mr. and Mrs. Yu, Messages, and the Groaning

It was etched on a spot cleared of lichen at the rock. A pictograph. They were sure —somehow: Somehow it was a gigantic clue. To what? 2017 boys did not know. No one knew. Not a word had been said about how the A'ndians got here. Fish or snare, what did a symbol matter? Tu and the rest of 2017 knew from their experience with 1900 that these Akropolis boys had been saved from one ordeal of time travel—to the back of beyond—only to land now in 2019. Saved from how their R'opean ancestors had to live. Ancestors who were able to live in R'opea primitively, just like the A'ndian Americles. That was how ancestors survived. Unlikely as it would have seemed to those R'opean ancestors—themselves hunting, gathering, cultivating—they survived just to prepare for the last two hundred years of accelerating civilization. But 2017 might have ended up like Parry and Willie—living with the A'ndians! 2017 were inclined to think that Willie and Parry had somehow gone back to ancient Time and that 2017 themselves had been—*simply saved from a similar feat*. 2017 also tended to think it was Fabian who had saved them with his hand. Or maybe it was Tu with his calculations resolved in the game, *The Hadesthon*. Maybe it was both. They had no firm ideas... except that possibly, just possibly, *just*, the girl had been (somehow) involved. Every time they hashTagged this out (privately) they came up with the same thing: We don't know. *Somehow*.

...And then there were some dreams....

In the evening HB ate upstairs alone...wondering if they'd ever get back to 2017. He did not invite the A'ndians. They'd be there for breakfast. That was enough. Pastor had invited them to sleep in the clothes-stash-room upstairs, and they would be eating soup supper at the mission. The girl was to sleep at Candace Parker's. Candace always slept on the couch but there was a camping mattress on loan for the girl. Fabian had his own room. In the meantime, after soup supper, the A'ndians explored the neighborhood. The braves wanted to see if a captive buffalo was still up above on Harkins Hill, and also the apple and cherry trees. Willie was looking for cherry wood to make Parry a longbow. Ash was good for arrows. Maple, hornbeam, and ash for longbows too, but he wanted something special. Pomala and friends were readying for the overnight and Fabian was eating the evening meal with his Grandmother. And the girl was with them, feeding her face.

Tu sat at the kitchen table with his mother and father, eating a meal the three had prepared together—in stages—in their small kitchen. Except for the wonderful smells and strict cleanliness, the kitchen was barren, its furnishings sparse, of linoleum and metal. Jackets and coats hung on pegs by the door. A small TV set on the counter under a cupboard was on, and the grown-ups glanced at it from time to time. If something interesting came on they watched steadily together. Otherwise they spoke of parks and public gardens and the aquarium. They were eating steamed rice, short-grain, and cimchi with fermented cabbage. There were scallions and oysters, and, for before and after the meal, two types of tea.

Mr. and Mrs. Yu looked up as the PresiDent began making proclamations about Thanksgiving. The tiny television was directly across from them where they sat small, side-by-side. Tu sat opposite, slightly to the right, back to the tube, eating and surfing on the z-pod. He seldom watched TV but took hints from it, now and then, in order to look further into those hints on his device. The PresiDent, he'd heard, had been a yooooge success at detonating ChrisMas through liaisons with the Politically Righteous, called PC in 2017 but PR in 2019. Now Tu watched as the PresiDent continued to test fatuous waters on the abolishment of Thanksgiving. …For some reason Tu's parents had always celebrated ChrisMas. Tu, of course, did not believe in Santi Claus, never had, and neither did his parents.

Reportedly the PresiDent was also a big restroom denier and liked the fact that he had power to outlaw all public restrooms across the nation. Also, he wanted to enforce people asking what to call people and enforce jail if they failed to follow through. (Or was this all parodying he'd heard about on the newly popular and cheeky *Sunday Nite Dead* show?) The PresiDent was, in addition, a big climate-stasis refuter. He was changing the laws in order to protect the Celtic Isles (where his ancestors came from) from freezing over. The PresiDent's favorite accomplishment in his first term was economic: Trickle-up economics was a brain child in which ordinary working people supported the financial industries through sweat equity. Defying gravity, the executive and legislative governmental branches made sweat trickle upwards contrary to the laws of physics, if not political economics. Everyone must pay a choice medical insurer or go to jail until the last quarter-penny was paid. He also liked having the nuke button in the Star Office of the PresiDuncy, and was (reportedly) said to wave his fingers over it from Time to Time. Tu did not know this, but—at the moment of its Thanksgiving proclamation—Star Office thoughts are actually floating in the realm of PresiDent's Day. Changes are afoot. Unbeknownst to the *Sunday Nite* citizenry he is working on it as a surprise. It was going to be an A-maZ-Ing Thing.

As Tu listened, and remembering the rumor about the waving fingers, he had an idea. Maybe this would put his parents more at ease. Their status in Americle was secure, but he thought they might need reassurance on another front. Surely there could be no comparison between the (solely) current gooFy PresiDent and the dynastic monumental Glorious Magnanimous Leader they had escaped.

He found a video of Cim-Jungle-Unc's perfect piece of moving history: inherited dark, out-of-date, perfectly preserved pale blue Olldsmmobile Malibu driving along ranks of dark troops standing at attention, with guns and bright bayonets pointing skyward like vast rows of Auzzzes. Everything in that country was out-of-date... except for the black market and nuclear weapons. Not exactly up to par—perhaps. But … always the threat, along with what was probably botched testing. The Glorious Magnanimous Leader was nowhere to be seen in the vid. It was believed he rode in the ancient dark limo at the fore of the tank corps, beneath a gigantic framed image of his cherubic plump face and bright smile. Fission-colored flags were everywhere and snow fell on the troops who looked thin and tiny if scrutinized.

Tu hesitated a moment to see if his parents noticed him. At first they did not, but then some prompting, perhaps intuitive, perhaps sensory, turned their bespectacled Osiian-Americle eyes his way. Tu slid the device toward them and touched the screen. The vid began moving again.

Came a look of subdued surprise followed by swiftly vanishing horror. They glanced at one another. Mr. Yu looked at Tu, shook his head slightly and pushed it back. Tu was confused. He wanted to apologize. He did so quietly, explaining that it had been a mistake on his part. He stood to bring another dish to the table and pour more tea. His father murmured that it was understandable, and to think of it no more.

The mistake was indeed understandable. Tu had no idea, though. Because Tu had never been told.

"We'd be very glad to have that!" There was a pause. "Yes, I can be there then. Thank you very much!" He hung up, looked back into Dr. Zettler's journal.

The old rotary phone on the end table rang again. He said to the caller, "I thought I saw you down there earlier. ...No, they still aren't giving interviews, me neither, I'm afraid." He hung up.

It rang again. Zettler greeted this caller and listened for a while.

Pastor (scarcely) sighed, and said into the big black receiver, "Do two things for someone else, get some rest, then call me in the morning." He paused, listening. "Yes, come on, they always need someone downstairs. Flo could use a break from the kitchen anytime." He hung up, mentally muttered a prayer and turned back to the old journal on the arm of the chair.

The phone rang again.

HB was sitting—slouching—on the couch, thumbing it, intent on his device. The telephone never rang for HB.

"They'll be sleeping here—upstairs—tonight. I'll vouch for them." Another pause. "She's staying with a volunteer." Pastor hung up.

HB was playing WOWC, and leaving messages with Pome and Jay about the A'ndians. They weren't responding. His latest message received from Fabe said he knew that too. The two were also texting with Quadrangi over it. Pastor was really into his old journals. HB sent this information to Fabian.

The phone rang.

"No, I'm not interested in insurance. Again, take this number off the list please."

HB smiled. Pastor was ticked. "Someone wanted Native Americles info," Blake said about the previous call.

"The police." He opened the brown leather journal again to where a thumb marked his place. It was coming apart, pages loosening from its sewn spine.

HB said, "The other was Kim wanting an interview for the *LampPost*."

"That's right."

The phone rang.

"That must be for you, Blake." He kept his head bent, eyes focused down.

HB reached for it on the end table. "Pastor Zettler's. Can I take a message?"

A pause.

"Tell them he's been enraptured all right."

A pause. Pastor looked over at him.

"Tell them he's been enraptured to hell."

"HB!"

"Tell them they can quote HBBBAH." He hung up.

"It was a *LampPost* dude seeking comment on this." HB swiped back three and handed Pastor the AP story on the man in New Amsterdam who escaped house arrest with bacon fat on his tracking anklet—found lying on his bed. His lawyer was claiming one explanation could be the enrapture of believers. The escapee was a convicted pedophile. "Supposedly he was a repentant sinner," said the youth sarcastically.

Pastor scanned the story, handed it back, went on with his reading.

The phone rang. HB picked up, mimed throwing the attached receiver across the room. He hung it up again.

Pastor stood and went into the study. He left the door open. Reluctantly.

Downstairs, on both levels, they were getting ready to sleep. The phone rang.

In a bedroom of the gentrified house upslope on Harkins Hill (Sharon Road), the three girls would soon discover the news about A'ndians staying in the attic above the Gospel Mission.

"So who is the girl?" Trice asked. She was curious but respectful.

"So she's a mystery, yo," said Jay. Jay was lounging on the bed, holding the device, glancing back up.

They both looked at Jay.

"She is."

Pomala reflected that Jay was not prone to such declarations. "Depends," Pome said after a moment.

"So what do you know, then," Trice asked her.

"I think she's got the worst autism and was probably raped in 1900 by someone. Everyone seems to think it was the lamplighter."

"But first they tried to pin it on HB's ancestor," said Jay. "But that doesn't mean the mystery is gonzo."

This was too much for Trice. "HB's —?" She sat silent, looked down. The 1900 thing. Nobody knew. But.... *These guys are good*, she thought. Had to let time tell. She said, "A lamplighter?"

Pome explained. "Someone who goes all over the neighborhood lighting gas lamps. Streetlights."

"It's his job," said Jay. "A really cool job. I wouldn't mind having that job." She looked at Trice. "You've always been skinny, don't look that much older. We look younger to you? The same?"

"So, shorter. The same but shorter. Tinier even," said Trice.

"Talk about mysteries, girl," said Jay. She smiled. Her round dark eyes narrowed a bit in that smile.

So so, I'm going to tell you a story.

"I like stories so much."

So so, I remember that about you.

"You do?"

Once upon a time some kids visited a strange universe almost by accident. At least they couldn't help it. Partly.

"Huh?"

They were drawn into it as dark matter by a machine. Underground. An underground machine. And then they hung round in that universe for a while. Sort of ooing and aahing and wondering.

"But how did that even happen? It sounds familiar. I may have heard this story before. I mean, read or watched it. Back in the days when my brain was bigger and I wasn't caught up in so much stuff. It's been really weird here."

Your universe isn't as weird is it might be.

"I mean Akropolis. Our neighborhood."

Should I go on?

"Oh please. I could use a good story. That way I can forget the story I'm in."

Pomala was smiling. A shiny blue starry smile. Full of vapor and steam and vacuum and bursting in making, remaking, and onward. Gneis, a burnished sort of nebulous brightness and winking, winked brighter. Both seemed to be laughing but only nearby slowly dancing galaxies, or distantly singing stars, could tell.

So so these kids, sub-subatomic particles which we'll call wimps, began taking an interest in their new surroundings. At first probably they were interested in the subparticle transfer machine. (You know how kids are).

"Are you one? A kid, I mean?"

So so so. Yes. Even my mam is a kid.

"You know, here, kids are also goats. You know what goats are?"

Yes. There's two in my family and friends' farmstead. That is a good analog you've got there.

(More laughter in the starry blue burnished dark heavens.)

"You're smart for a kid! Analogies are fun?"

It's fun to look for them. Like... clocks have hands.

"You mean you can almost imagine clocks' hands making cocoa?"

Not quite. Shall I go on?

"Please. I promise not to interrupt the story again."

The visiting kids began taking an interest in an embodied particular family, then in the family's friends. They even began playing games with them, the alt universe games. One of which was called BABY.

"Wow! Great name. How is it possible for them to play if they are only sub-sub-sub-etc.-subatomic particles?"

I don't know.

"But but the story. You're telling the story."

If I can go on....

"Okay. Tell it."

Let's just say they became a kind of ...pre-material... influence. Especially for one or two who were more involved outside the game. One of these was really interested in the kitchen wallpaper.

"Oh come on! No way! How can wallpaper be an interesting part of the story?"

If it's special, contains important words, and was thoughtfully applied.

"Okay, I can see that. Go on. —But wait! That part is *awfully* familiar. I'm sure I've heard this. I can almost see it! This wallpaper was like pages of books carefully glued or with urethane or something to the walls!"

Yes. This is that story.

"And they kept trying to call attention to the wallpaper!"

Who did?

"The wimpy dark matter," said Pome. "It was like they were ghosts who could not move things around. In our stories here sometimes ghosts could knock on wood or spoil milk."

But the —or at least one of them —could help— one of them — could help them dream.

"So they could dream about the importance of the wallpaper!"

Right.

"That's what you mean, Gneis. Wallpaper!

So so I'm telling the story instead.

"So it's very familiar. Maybe I'll remember when I wake up?"

Shall we go on? —Wait.

"Pome! Pome wake up! Is it one of the dreams?" Jay was nudging her. "You were all excited about wallpaper, talking in your sleep...."

Zettler had gotten sidetracked, transported. He was living before the turn of the 20th century in the growing industrial town working mightily on its slowly extrapolating infrastructure. The medical profession was using its brains and microbial experimentation to understand how disease and infection worked, and how to combat it. And Dr. Zettler was a part of it. Today he might have been experimenting with new molecules at Cossyc. Now he was smiling on his antecedent's description of his son's cap. *My grandfather Johan Zettler's cap.* He had not found the specific 1900 journal.

Reading on, he ruminated. *Hmm.* The industrialists, not the scientists so much, were for it—eugenics. What was not then called eugenics but would be: The good doctor Zettler must understand we are headed that way. The hopeful idea is in danger of being promoted by investment and bigotry. *Oh. Here it is.* ...Scientists are in danger of using their support in order to pursue.... Yes.

Pastor Zettler was between the serving counter and the lunch crowd. He spotted the braves. Apparently they were staying for the message. That was peculiar. He'd had a word with Willie, during lunch, about the old orchards. Willie had seen how they'd been replaced.

"You tore out the fruit trees and cornfields and put ugly buildings and acres of automobiles in their place. You can't grow food on that acreage."

Parry piped, "You always liked automobiles, Willie."

"I wasn't thinking then."

The other braves sat stoically, as though listening. Again, pastor had wondered how much of the language they understood. Certainly they never spoke it. ... Would they understand his talks —ever? But at that point, as before, he was thinking they would leave after eating.

Only, they did not. They sat silent, waiting with others at the tables for the pastor to begin. The street door opened and Pomala came in, quietly taking a seat near the Sharon Road windows. She got out her device in case she wanted to check in with Jayrai.

Came silence as pastor stood there, legs slightly apart, attired as usual in blue dress shirt and brown soft velvet-and-satin vest. In his hands was the open scripture with gold leaf edges. That was not usual. Often he verbally launched and, as holier scripts were needed, simply recited from memory. Today it was an open scripture launch. Directly on the verbal text itself.

And God blessed them, saying, Be fruitful, and multiply....

"This is the very first commandment. Before even, You shall have no other gods before me, you shall not kill, this is the first commandment—made to those biologically capable of fulfilling it.

And God said, Let us make man in our image, after our likeness.... In the image of God created he him; male and female created he them.

Someone spoke from back in the room, by windows where traffic on Exchange St. could be seen sparsely passing. Pastor stopped, turned his face a bit, as though, "Say again?"

"How can I tell if I'm man or woman?"

Pastor did the double-take. Yes. Doped and Disorderly. Zettler paused.

A distant voice from above spoke, "Look in your pants, not your head."

Pastor had been in the zone. Now he wasn't. He looked for the remote voice. Others were looking at the ceiling above him with silent expectancy. What would Pastor say? He looked up. Nothing. Nothing but the grate of the register. Maybe a spot of light beyond. A movement of shadow.

Pastor seemed to look down at the text once more. What to do? He read on, but silently, with his eyes. Then he hesitated, stepped back, put the leather goldleaf book on the counter.

To one side of the lunchroom the A'ndians sat at a round table talking among themselves. Parry leaned forward in earnest, saying, "I've never heard it put that way before. I mean, how do you tell?" He wondered if he might have chosen a dress instead of a plaid shirt and corduroy overalls from the attic castoffs.

Willie looked at him. "That's crazy, Parry. It's as simple as what the colored boy said."

Parry was a bit deflated. If only his friend James Priam were here to talk it over with him.... But he would be 129 years old.

Pastor decided to preach a different sermon. One sketched for a future he'd been considering.

"It's been said that Akropolis is the setting for the Apokalup because our metropolis spreads across seven hills. You've all heard this rumor, right?"

"Only from the crazy believers," said D&D.

"Well, belief is important, Darren. But so is the truth. Truth is more important than belief. Sometimes we need to eliminate belief in lies. Actually we need to eliminate lies. This rumor about Akropolis is bosh."

"But isn't the other lies—about the creation of the world?"

"It depends on how you read it. Remember your literary categories."

"I got none."

"Okay, the story of creation is an ancient creative simplified story of how God calls things into being. It's not a scientific treatise. This is how truth in words works in simplified story form."

"Your prophecies don't seem very simple to me. They are obtuse."

People scattered round at the back began mocking the word *obtuse*. And mocked Darren's use of the word.

Finally Zettler said, "What does obtuse mean?"

Immediately Darren said, "It means hard to understand."

Pastor Zettler smiled.

"So you're saying Onah or Noah, or whoever, didn't have the math to give us that info so he just gave us the story instead?"

"...Something like that."

"So fairytale."

"More mythic. In the sense not of moderns equating myth with lies, but as truth breathing itself through words and metaphors, literary pictures, to enable our imaginations. This is how the ancients did it."

"But I'm just not seeing a picture, no forms, voids, waters. Ups and downs, what's all that?"

That's why we read the creation as forming forth into things we can understand like continents, birds and grasses, people. We see this making out of formlessness. Chaos. We get the sense of God's power and glory, unfathomable except when we see an earthquake or volcanic eruption, a hurricane."

"God invented sex with that first command, you're saying."

"Well, yes, I think."

Trying to top D&D, someone else shouts, "What did God make on the eighth day?"

Darren raises his voice: "Monkey-wrenches!"

Winter and summer —year-round— Paddy's Pool Hall took coal deliveries to heat the building, water from hand pumps, and to fire up kitchen stoves. Coal was delivered by horse-and-wagon in the alleyway, and shoveled down the coal chute into a coal cellar. A coal cellar was partitioned off in stone and brick from the furnace-room and from the larger part of the basement. Here, one day, turn of the 21st-century homeless men would sleep, and children would listen to stories. In the 1950's coal was replaced by a new furnace and natural gas—still in use in an adjacent basement chamber in 2019.

The empty coal cellar had been used in the mid-1960s as a very cool subterranean beatnic cafe and hoot-e-tanny hangout where very cool kids drank soda and chanted poetry, sang hillbilly, and pretended to smoke way more leaf than they had. They also read continuous chapters of *King of the Rings* aloud. Among those who took part were Candace Parker nee Parker, Philip Von Zettler, and some other current older volunteers at the SoupMission. The coal cellar's walls were blackened sandstone, giant stonework carefully built by masons of old. No one in 2019 opened the stout wooden door leading from the furnace room. It would've been found locked.

A hermit of sorts had taken up residence in the dark and dank former cafe and coal cellar. It was still vented, and this hermit was careful to keep candlelight hidden or unlighted during the night, especially as all were readying to sleep. With "lights out," the glimmer might show. Pastor Zettler knew the hermit was there but, so far, had not hindered him. Perhaps he enjoyed listening to children singing, to storytime. Zettler noticed the hermit climbing in and out the old green trapdoor once used for coal deliveries. In the alley. A massive man, dressed like anyone, a workman in dirty clothes, dirty hair and face. That window, big enough for a hefty soul to fit through, had been glazed, letting in light during the 60's but has since been removed and replaced with the old trapdoor. The hermit's presence was a recent occurrence. Pastor began paying attention. He was still considering what, if anything, to do. If anyone else knew of the Gospel Mission "guest," they weren't saying. At least not to Pastor Zettler.

On the back alley way, in 1900, dray deliveries were made and the blacksmith plied his trade, opposite, a few doors up. Today, just outside the back door of the soup kitchen stood metal shelving, a drop-off station for donated canned goods. Sometimes cans of herring or sardines were piled on these shelves. Cans of peaches and pears or fruit cocktail. Even canned evaporated milk, mustard jars, packs of nuts, bottled water were placed there. When these were eventually carried into the kitchen they may have been fewer than originally intended for use in the mission. Added to this was a homemade wooden box with hasp that no one paid any attention to. It was just there. A lock would have made this box conspicuous. Someone might happen along and perhaps find it worthy of stealing for that reason. It wasn't very big. This was the hermit's larder. Sometimes it held homemade goodies separated from those served en masse in the common room of a hall.

This hermit was not …especially… homeless?The coal cellar, until further notice, was his home.

He sat in darkness with the glow of a single candle casting the shadow of his presence, moving when he moved, over blackened stone walls. But at the moment he sat still, immense in the candlelight, his shadow bigger still. A gigantic, seldom moving, black shadow. The hermit sat listening to the distant voice trailing its way, faintly, through vents and registers of the old building. The opening homily wafted remotely toward the hermit's intently listening ears. The hermit was smiling. Like a baby. Innocently.

pome, i think we better consider the cult.

What do you mean, Jay? Not what I think you mean.

yes, that. seriously.

At the moment everyone is buzzing about the trans-gander thing.

in the soupmission? why?

HB threw a bomb, right after I walked in the door practically.

oh fun. what did he say?

So, for one thing he's not even here and people don't exactly all know it's him. Pastor was trying to preach about procreation, bodies and all that. I can't tell if he intended all this -- I don't think so. No one's listening to him since the bomb dropped from overhead.

live and let live. Shehe and herm.

We don't have those terms in 2017, Jay. If you've noticed, HB seems to think they don't let live.

so THEY couldn't live for the longest time. …so about the cult?

Nope!

it's your dream, know?

So?

maybe it's some mind-hypnotic auto-suggestion. (Jay)

I don't get it. (Pome was tapping away by the SoupMission Sharon Road windows.) Pastor's changing the sermon topic.

so, what if we WERE imprisoned two years by a non-aging cult and just don't remember and now a weird dream--um--figure is trying to hook us back somehow?

Don't the A'ndians, Willie and Parry actually disprove that?

no! they could be part of it!

What? The non-aging part? They are bigger, older. You haven't seen anything but images. Believe me, they are older. Willie looks totally alien and other but Parry is wearing a pink plaid shirt and looks a like bigger version of himself. Remember how he wore a sailor suit in 1900? The two A'ndians are ones I don't remember seeing. We saw one, the really scrumpshy one on the grammar school corner -- remember? (Pome)

yeah. beautiful! but.

How can they be part of it? How do the dreams work in all this you mean?

wallpaper, pome!? Seriously? wallpaper?

So it *does* seem familiar, Jay.

maybe the room we were held in was wallpapered! maybe we had nothing else to read and had to read wallpaper over and over! maybe there's monsters and robots and children locked up with us and we had to tell stories about wallpaper!

Jay Jay this was nothing like that! I mean the dream. The dream was nothing like that. I keep trying to tell you what these dreams *feel* like. I can't get it across. They just feel really loving and good. Wise even.

not all shotty and stuff, yo?

No.

ever?

No.

okay, pome but i still think it might be a possibility. like what if the cult was magic AND wise. Or sciencey AND wise? huh?

I'm not saying it's impossible. I'm just saying... not. I just think it's okay. The dreams. Even the mysterious um mess. Poor Pastor can't seem to finish his sermons. He's going to have to come up with new subjects, or tactics.

Two cameras had been added to the west side of Exchange Street between Cheddar Ave and the FivePoints intersection at Sharon Road.. The GlimmerDale wall and gate were now secure.

"So we've got to look at these kids again."

"The disappeared-reappeared nonaging."

"I went over the inputs this morning, much of it pure non-point speculative hooey."

"Whooo-we." Sgt. Bench responded with a grin. Bright pink lipstick dotted a front tooth. She was dressed in her usual cords and blazer, tags of nut-brown hair curved around her ears.

He continued. "About the only thing we can trust is the Cossyc stuff. The science I mean, not their motives. They are self-interested. Whether or not they had anything to do with it. And we are still waiting on them."

"They're going to make us all young again. Dr. deVill, anyway. Overreaching. Your favorite term." She smiled.

"Some of us aren't really interested." Lt. Hunch said, "Those experimentalists/ theorists are probably all contributing to that work in one way or another. In whatever capacity the research of each can add."

They sat at desks, screens loaded with data, desks scattered with paper cups. His desk was at an angle to hers. The cups were on Bench's desk. Hunch had a ceramic cup he rinsed, used over and over for the purpose. Sometimes his dark eyes would peer into it, black nostrils flaring, sniffing. A year or two worth of stain buildup, inside and out. Bench would poke fun. He would remind her to trash the litter.

Lighting in the office was subdued but for the screens. The ambient glow of surrounding cuboids. The halogen gleam of the yard pervading through windows. Patrol cars coming and going.

"We should add the coSplay to the mix." Hunch was turning to look at her, dark eyes intent.

She looked over at him. "Why?"

"You didn't see this? From yesterday." He turned his screen.

"Nope."

Six boys, the A'ndians and FivePoints 2017 had been videoed coming through the GlimmerDale gate together out onto Exchange St.. Not far north of the station, actually. Nearly across, diagonally, from the library. She clicked and there they were on her own screen. "Looks like they went to lunch?" She keyed in the intersection vids to follow. "At the soup kitchen. The girl and younger boy weren't with them."

"They'll be somewhere together. Remember, Zettler's got his eye on them."

"Right. They won't get away." She smiled.

"So what's up?"

"*Hmm.* Wonder if Sheltering Cares—our character Gretchen—knows anything about the connection? Does this question mean you got no ideas, Lt.?"

"So far the only thing I've got is we need to talk to the GlimmerDale board about more security."

She looked from the vids showing these kids' entrance into the mission. Just before noon yesterday. *What would they have to talk about?* Obviously they met to talk about something. ...Or at least ended up doing so, if meeting by chance.

She might have been surprised to learn. The conversation was about clocks. Mechanical clocks, towers and bells. A'ndian death-rite customs, such as the image of sorrow, and ochre face-painting of the dead; Willie refraining from interpreting. Grave digging with the shovel; machines like backhoes, and coffins made out of non-corrosive metals and concrete bunkers to protect them from overflowing water tables. What else would interest young men? All these curious workings of infrastructure, engines and *things*.

The same afternoon, Pastor was thinking about Willie and the apple trees, the acres of cars. Young people might like to talk about the mysteries of nature coupled with super nature... but only if it's not happening to them? …Or maybe 2017 and …the others… are speaking of it together? Otherwise people talk in the abstract, in speculation, marveling over mysteries in which we are not directly involved. Uninvolved, we'll talk intellectually, earnestly, about these with our friends. We like the what-if, the science and speculative fiction.

Back aching, Pastor wonders on all this. ...With his own lessening physical power, onset of decline. And it's getting harder to preach his sermons since this 2017 mystery happened in the neighborhood. However, he has found the journal germane to these mysterious questions. Tonight, unless he has an emergency, a parishioner with a problem, the recurrent lumbago worsens from the kettle-carry today... tonight, in the old journals, he was going to find out—

Something.

Pastor Zettler might not find mention of Willie or Parry. So far he had not. But this was going to be... what? ...Journals dedicated to medicine, pathology, research, and perhaps those neighborhood doings or illnesses in 1900 CE? There's always something going on in any neighborhood. Always. And if Dr. Zettler was recording the unusual, as shown heretofore, it was about to show for this very special year. Tonight.

Mystery solved to be, proved or disproved.

He almost smiled to himself, standing at the deep steel sink in the kitchen. He washed pots in greasy water up past his elbows. The sink had been refitted with faucets, since the hand pump when it was part of Paddy's Saloon. He was in here alone, trying to think things through. Pastor was going to have to talk with HB about the PR. Pastor needed help. Yes. Maybe HB was going to give it to him. Just by letting him bounce these concerns. These verbal hits would at least please HB. Pastor was in need of counseling.

Then he heard it. *Again.*

He had heard it before.

A kind of distant *basso* groaning, a ragged weeping. Very remote. He would never have heard it if he hadn't at times been alone on the main floor. No one would hear any of this sorrowing when the building was working and full. But now even the hum of refrigerators or blower on the furnace could not drown it out.

And this was another puzzling—no, perplexing—concern.

"Akropolis—did you change the name to Gleees 786g or—was that what you said?" Parry was asking Fabian. Supper was on the table all across the hall. Some time-displaced persons were eating together in the SoupMission. "I find it rather comforting that the hymns are pretty much the same. Why are letters pushed together? Shouldn't it be Soup *space* Mission? This is a different time. Sometime in the future?"

"You only get one question at a time," said HB. "Why are you wearing a dress?"

"Someone gave me permission."

"Who?"

"That man back there." Parry pointed to the D&D at the rear of the hall beside plateglass windows. At the moment, head bent, D&D was all over the AI digital counseling appe Cossysuc had given along with the device. Counseling—by artificial intelligence whenever he needed it.

"Parry, he did not," countered Willie. "You have to change back right after supper."

Parry looked at HB. Parry said, "OK, Willie."

HB grinned.

Parry smiled. They were going to be friends?

Fabian swallowed a mouthful of meatballs and spaghetti. He said, "This is Akropolis 2019. Jay—you remember Jay?—she was kidding when you saw her in 1900."

"Kidding is a nice word," said Parry.

"Nice is a nice word, too," said HBBBAH.

"One thinks of lambs. Lambs playing together."

"Butting heads," said HB.

The true True People, Eaglestreak and Walleye-stare, listened intently. They ate spaghetti, alternately slurping from the plate, and using big spoons—soup spoons for the meatballs, red sauce dripping from the corners of their mouths. Two feathers each hung from their thonged dark hair, and did not fall onto the plateful.

"Nice is nice?" said Walleye-stare to Eaglestreak, not in the true tongue.

"Yes." Willie answered in Anglish. Then in True People he said, "We do not mean this. This is not a word for us."

Two strands of spaghetti slithered up into Fabian's mouth. "This is the future," he said. "For all of us. We're not supposed to be here, either."

"What do you mean?" said Willie, a bit challenging.

Here Tu spoke. "We are meant to be in 2017 and came from your time—1900 CE—to 2019. This is the wrong time. In other words, we are displaced by two years." He stopped as though his meaning were clear.

Fabian said, "He means we experienced a twinkle from 1900 *A.D.*" — Fabian emphasized the A.D. in order to make plainer for Willie — "to 2019 instead of our own time, which is 2017. Same time of the year, though," he added.

"A twinkle," said Willie.

"That's a hand-wavy word for WE DON'T KNOW," said HB.

The A'ndians listened intently, dark eyes roving from one speaker to another. Eaglestreak, especially, tried to understand—but also to remember in case he had an opportunity to report to Red Fox or the *Meteu.*

"Actually, it's not," said Tu. His blank look enhancing and dignifying each word, he went on to explain Steinein's semi-special theory, in colloquial terms but heavily nuanced; and also some alternatives.

Willie listened intently. The others tried and gave up. Fabian said, "Maybe I'm getting it." HB said, "Maybe not."

Willie said nothing. He was wondering if this is the kind of thing you could diagram as with the clocks.

Pomala came over to the table next to theirs, her white hair just caping slim shoulders, a smile in her blue tattooing including pink eyes and white lashes. She carried a plateful of spaghetti and meatballs. There was but one meatball on her plate. A very small meatball. She was going for vegan. Slowly. She sat down with Candace Parker and Heirolynn. Pastor Zettler was with them, listening intently to the conversation next door. Hearing was not that easy in this noisy place. Maybe he should have his hearing tested? All the critics sitting nearby began silently protesting the head-hopping going on—as though no head-hopping would make for better storytelling. Had Parry been able to read their minds, he would have wondered what Mr. G.H. Wills thought of it. Then Parry would have decided that this authority had shown what he thought of it in his works. Pomala spoke to Candace Parker and the girl, then got out her gadjet to converse simultaneously with Jayrai. Who was still imprisoned in her lavish tower, longing to escape.

Jay: they've got out the BIG GUNS!! cossyc!!

Pome: Let me check that.

She tapped her e-mail open, saw the message, sent back to Jay: We'll be right over! Ha ha.

She reached and slid the babblet across the next table for the 2017 boys to read. To pastor she said, "From sis. Cossyc's getting us to go back for more testing. They say our no-school-till-after-Thanksgiving pass will be revoked if we don't. Everyone's asking her for interviews. She says no. Maybe Cossyc leaked it?"

"Is that right?" Pastor smiled.

"What will HB do?"

"I'll get my own Big Guns!" He said from his place at the table. An empty plate was before him. And he had picked it up and licked it clean after seeing Eaglestreak and Walleye-stare do it. "Yo, can I have your Tom-hawking thingy?" He was asking Willie. "Or maybe you could give me a hair cut with that?" He looked to the weapon in Willie's hide belt, holding his deerskin britches in place. They were a thing of Willie's devising.

"What for?"

"You just scalp me. Split open my head and remove its contents."

Everyone was smiling. Everyone 2017, 19, that is.

Fabian said to 1900, "It's a long story. Maybe HB can explain over breakfast sometime. But, basically, he's kidding."

Parry said, "You mean like when the other girl—the big girl with a strange arm said about Gleeeese 877a? Or whatever it was? Was that an outer space arm, or an invented mechanical arm? Willie says it was."

Pomala nodded smiling, looking down at her device in hand again. To the others she said, "Jay says she'll go back only for arm maintenance and upgrade, not the psyche stuff, the 2017 testing. She actually wants to go back to school so she can get out and start living. She says being in a tomb has made her defiant."

"Jay? Defiant?" (Fabian)

Everybody was laughing. All but Candace Parker, *Ochquetschitsch*, Willie and the other A'ndians. Parry laughed because he wanted to be in on jokes. Even Pastor Zettler was laughing.

Jay: and BO might be there! he'd be stunning—2019 version—i think.

She did not want to appear needy by texting around on the subject of Bo. And no one in the neighborhood was spreading news on the subject.

Pome was talking to Pastor. "Guess what? The Bishop started a petition for me! Churches are becoming signing places. ...So, for voters. Of which I'm not."

Night of The Girl

Quadrangi came in the mission's street entrance on the opposite side of the hall. He stood surveying the crowd. Several people close-by hailed him, but he waved and kept scanning. Then he saw 2017 and the A'ndians on the other side, not far from the swinging kitchen door. He threaded his way toward them and sat down at Pastor's table. Zettler had moved to the chair at right angles so Quad could stay close to the roundtable.

"Aren't you eating spaghetti?" asked Pomala, mouth reddish in her slim blue-tattooed face. She wiped at the sauce with a napkin provided by CLICK, the Northeast EHio grocery-and-goods chain.

"Naw. Had my meal." He nodded vaguely to others at Pastor's table. "Just came in to see what you're doing. —The Cossyc news." He looked over at the others—his real interest—who were now flinging comments and questions at him. The overhead light was dull and blinking. Light in this corner away from the windows was a bit ghostly.

"We're sending Quadri back to school," he said. His dark eyes tossed a challenge —just a bit. "We've had it with 2017 and just want him to get acclimated. I don't need to ask what you guys think. You'll be sure to tell me... in exactly..." he looked back at the clock, pointedly, then said, "now."

"But what about the bullying," suggested Pomala, who was trying to text Jay about it at the same time. She put down the babblet and looked at him.

"We'll handle it."

"But he's little," said Fabian. "Littler than his classmates."

"Not so. Recall: he's in the same grade as when he left two years ago. What you're expecting—till Thanksgiving—is only a reprieve. Quadri's got new classmates and will be studying pretty much where he left off. Also, remember, he's Kwad the KonkerEr. The kids in his class will be in awe."

HB said, "He won't escape his old classmates, bro."

"But they know I'm here. His abject *genii*." He showed off a knotted muscle far greater than any at the roundtable could manage, excepting the A'ndians. "He just rubs his qz-phone and I'm there wielding sword and shield."

"I could use me sum-a-dat." HB was grinning.

"I really don't want Cossyc scrutinizing Quadri. He's had enough. But what about you guys?"

They started talking it over, Pome texting with Jay. After a bit Quadrangi quietly concentrated on the A'ndians and 1900 CE, whom he had not been next to till now. They seemed totally in character. …A smallish boy with long light brown hair and feathers —wearing a dress? If Quad remembered right, this wasn't an A'ndian that had been kidnapped —at least in their coSplay— and this was just a white kid from the old century? —if what 2017 said was true. He had not made up his mind on all this... and... didn't see a need to. It kept coming up, but.

Then—looking back at his own table—he saw The Girl. Hairs on his nape rose. Quad's armpits gushed sweat, a shiver chilled his backbone. *The Girl.*

He looked back at the gang.

He would not look at her.

He would not.

He jumped back into the conversation. But as he batted the Cossyc stuff back and forth, he was thinking of Quadri's talk about The Girl. Like lightning sparking the neurons of his brain, every weirdness the little boy had expressed lit his thoughts! *Ghoul! That's what we call them.* They like to say *zombies* here in Americle. Zombies—so popular! No way this girl can be popular. Why why—what's up?

Everyone from now, in 2019, is troubled but these guys don't seem concerned except they want back to 2017. Quadrangi shivered. But before leaving the Gospel Mission he would be calmed. He would even look over at the girl again, and again, without too much trepidation. He began thinking hard about it, became subdued listening to the others. Even wondered how it might be applied to the game, *Black Ages of StanaTerk.* If the terrorists were ghouls—deadlands ghouls—that would be more effective, he thought. In real life terrorists looked hyper alive—he had no doubt.... But really... weren't they already dead, the Living Dead? On the inside they were dead.

Once, when he looked at her, he imagined…. He imagined being alive. Hyper-living. Feeling life surging through him, through the tables and chairs, the hands of the others, faces, the the *the Everything*. What if—inside she was a galaxy, swarming with lights? What if she was busy helping make suns and stars, and planets teaming with life. What if, what if—

He stopped. *This is crazy. Stop now Quad. Stop*.

He tried to stop, to listen and take part. Like when his little brother would start on 1900 CE. He succeeded after a bit. For a little while.

Later he stood and took his leave, head teeming with ideas. He looked back over his shoulder as he went. There she was.

Above, the overhead light—dull and blinking, a bit ghostly and pale.

He threaded past people, tables and chairs. He stopped at the door and looked back at her tiny white staring face.

Creepy. *Creepy*, he thought. And went out into the dark-and-glowing dead-leaf scattering wind.

As he walked up toward the condos, he was met by Basti the blogger beneath a streetlight at the corner of Third St. and one of the uphill drives. Device in hand, he asked Quad about the school-threat rumor. The complex loomed above them, lights glowing.

"How'd you find out—already!"

"Good question! I'll try to trace that back, track it down. A journalist would."

"Good. Let me know. So we still got nothing to say. But—you might try doing research on time-displacement as prep work for your story. Just keep the pot boiling so to speak." Quad did not want to discourage his friend.

In an apartment above, Tu was researching theory, experimentation and protocols for metabolic time-dating—CossycSystems' ostensible reason for their call-back. And there would be a lot of biometrics to gauge on everyone except HB. They were going to add to the 2017 data. …Looking for something….

Mr. Yu stuck his small bespectacled head through the bedroom doorway. In a beam of light from the bedside table he saw his son's bent legs inside the open closet door.

"I think you were interested in weakly interacting massive particles, dark matter?" He'd overheard something about this from his son's friend Pomala while working in the dry cleaners today. She was smiling at him while talking with her relative.

Tu stuck his head out. "Yes!"

"Using the weak nuclear force a bit stronger than gravity, only active across small-scale atomic nuclei? You knew they aren't finding any evidence now?" Mr. Yu meant since 2017. "I won't say the theory's collapsing. They seem to be, well, quite in the dark." Saying it, Mr. Yu almost smiled. "Well anyway, they're planning a new generation of detectors. You might try a search, and then theorizing on your own a bit."

"Yes!" Tu did (almost) smile. This is good, he thought. You take what is *now* and go on from there. ...Even though... possibly *I'm* evidence of WIMPs?

Meanwhile, downslope of the 3.5 complex, in his apartment next to the alley above the SoupMission, Pastor was head-bent at his desk in the study.

Parry was reading on the old couch in the living room. Zettler had received thoughts from HB there prior to the older youth going off somewhere (with his watch). Though in many respects he was still open on the subject, Pastor would begin with a straightforward approach for his next Gospel Mission talk on the subject. Actually, current cultural quarrels had not been the subject of the lunchtime talk. That was to have been a real homily on procreation, and the new birth. It had been disrupted by Darren Dargwood (D&D) and HB. Then he'd made the mistake of switching to prophecy.

But now this, in the study. This is what he had been waiting for! He pored over the hasty hand of his ancestor in old journals on the desk before him. On his right hand was Pastor's own neighborhood journal, where he'd noted down unusual SoupMission happenings and plans. His own journaling purpose was threefold. He needed to keep track, refer back, document everything for another generation —perhaps local historians, and also he wanted talk fodder for his short wave nets. Before HB's arrival as apartment mate and fosterling, Zettler had spent a portion of his evenings touching base with his favorite nets, most of which were located in Northeast EHio, but hams scattered on particular bands might call in from over the border in Candia, and from other states, near- and far-range. One net was almost all pastors of various denominations. Short wave participants across times, bands, nets and topics were usually of his own generation. And when it was his turn to talk, these journal notations gave him something to say. But now he had decided that he was also going to read back to that spot in his own journal two years ago when the gang disappeared, and move forward to reread his notations since November 3 of this year. But not tonight, perhaps.

Occasionally his forebear Dr. Zettler (1900 A.D.) would write in Churman, but early on he had schooled himself to stick closely with English. The doctor's wish, as with all immigrants at that time, was to assimilate, and this was one way to help himself. Another was to speak no Churman to his son Johan. Dr. Zettler made it a practice to speak Churman only with his fellow immigrants as a way to comfort and make things cozy for them from time to time.

... Here is a mention of a *Parry!* Parry? Is this the same Parry sitting in the next room reading *King of the Rings*?!

Slow down....

In the good doctor's hasty hand writing: "Parry met me coming along Sharon after that house call on a case of typhus. This is an ongoing problem and we must keep up the campaign to get the sewers and aqueduct to the river. After that we will see about building the treatment plant. I'm still hopeful that may happen, but it has a way to go yet. Any way, the quarantine was applied.

"Now this is the younger Wilusa boy...."

Parry Wilusa! This Parry Wilusa reading King of the Rings?! In the living room?!

... Slow down.

"... the son of Mrs. Wilusa with the clasp-locker repair shop on Sharon Road. I was called in to see if I might help the little girl come into her care, no one knows from which direction. That is, no one knows where she comes from. She herself cannot say. An interesting case. Some have speculated that she is escaped from the lunatic asylum in A'ndian Falls. I have inquired over the telephone, and found it is not so. A most interesting case. Parry came up later to get a wash concocted for her rash. This is not the rash associated with typhus. Parry says she hears but does not talk. It was evident she does not want to be handled. I took a skin scrape for the microscope slide, my finding for the rash is so far inconclusive."

Pastor read on, losing sight of Parry and the girl in these pages. ... A page or two of medical testing, and cases of what Dr. Zettler said the neighborhood called jail fever (typhus).

Here are Candace Parker's ancestors! The household quarantined with jail fever! Interesting. That part of 3rd St. was called Little North Regina!

... Ah, here she is again.

Pastor stopped reading. He stood and walked about the room frowning, hands clasped behind his back. He went over to the journal-strewn desk and sat down, heavily. He went on reading.

... Here are Blake Griffin's antecedents.

... One of these is accused of her rape.

Pastor Zettler read on.

He stood and, still holding the old journal, stepped to the partway open door and spoke to Parry who was reclining against the arm of the couch, feet up on its cushions. He was wearing the plaid shirt and an old pair of worn jeans, knees bent; holding the big soft book with shining gold fiery ring on the cover propped against a pillow. At first Parry did not look up.

"Parry," Pastor said again.

The boy looked up, his eyes distant, reluctant.

"Parry." Pastor came and sat down beside his stocking feet.

"Yes?" There was a slight frown creasing his childish brow. "Yes, sir?" he said, recollecting enough to get him through an opening conversation.

"Parry..." Pastor looked over at the short wave station, fingering Dr. Zettler's journal. Then he looked back at Parry who was now eyeing him attentively.

"Parry, were there riots? Say, race or labor riots? In 1900, I mean."

"Oh yes. Argus started a riot."

"What do you mean —Argus Griffin? Started—"

"Well, I mean everybody else did. Because they sent him away, I think. Or maybe... no. Because they thought he hurt *Ochquetit*. But he didn't."

"The girl?"

"Yes. I think they were going to kill him but the police sent him to Groverland jail."

"I see."

Pastor sat as though dazed.

Parry went back to the book. The Grey Riders were below Underweather Mountain. It was stony and breezy, and misty below. *They knew they were down there. ... Something was going to happen. Something....*

Pastor sat still.

Thinking.

... He didn't know whether to ask Parry or not. He had sat in on some CossycSystems probing sessions, but he had not probed. ...Cossyc was not responsible for the non-aging (*though obviously seeking a way to non-aging*). Following his hesitations, many thoughts and turnings, Pastor was now simply *believing*. He no longer wondered if they'd been through a cult or acting a play. Here were documents and presences—people, children.

He was optimistic more documentation would be found at the Simeon Harkins historical archive. Even the *Akropolis Lamp-Post* might have 1900 archives. These were evidence for real belief. He was a minister of the gospel, believing in miracles. But, as other thoughtful people, he'd leave the *how* to the physicists.

Parry.

The others, the 2017 neighborhood kids, did not know how they had moved through time. Perhaps it would not be wise to ask Parry how he got here. This leaves aside the ever more perplexing question of how the A'ndians.... Well, it was not good to disturb this little boy, anyway. No matter what-if. Especially if all that's involved is curiosity. The ignoble heart of that fallen quality! Curiosity —so impulsive, urgent, insistent.

He stood and went back into the study. He settled down to reading again. Now also he began copying verbatim, and making notes from his current perspective.

Meanwhile, five teenage males were entering a back alley between the soup kitchen and maintenance buildings associated with the 3rd St. apartments and condominiums. This alley was lit mostly on the south side where plow trucks, pickups, a backhoe and other maintenance vehicles were garaged. All manner of tools, grounds keeping equipment, and maintenance offices were in these long structures, which backed onto storage bays for apartment dwellers and owners; laundries and other utilities. Niche entrances and passages honeycombed the maintenance buildings. Sharon Road shops and businesses had back entrances onto the alleyway. Some of these were now empty, but a few had thriving businesses like the FivePoints Dry Cleaners, a pharmacist, local eateries or cafe, and a co-op for local agriculture.

Above the alley, Parry happened to be on bathroom break from his reading of *King of the Rings*. Actually, he'd been reading the book while on bathroom break, and so sat ensconced holding the book. He had opened the window just a cracked to let in fresh air. After each flush there came a strange metallic smell, but he had fun times flushing the elaborate chamber pot, as he called it. Also, he had found shears in the bathroom and cut off his hair-tail. But now he heard voices down below, and peeked out to see what was passing. He had to raise the sash just a bit more. It squealed and the boys below looked up.

Parry saw the small upturned faces of his friends. He waved, leaning over the sill, saying softly, "I want to come too!"

Willie waved him to come down. "Hur-ry." It was no shout, just two quiet syllables.

Minutes later the shorn Parry appeared at the alleyway entrance and ran toward them. He was wearing a jacket, his hair raggedly cut, and a pair of what he called Levi Strausses. The guys were just past the soup mission but well below the dry cleaners—in conversation about differences in the structures and businesses between now and 1900. Walleye-stare and Eaglestreak listened intently to everything the interlopers said. They were scouts going to report, once the girl brought them back to their Time. Their compatriot, Dark Cloak, had he been chosen for the mission would be doing far more than listening. The two braves had no doubt that Dark Cloak would be off on his own, scouting and would probably not even want the two more obedient braves along. Dark Cloak might act to change Time, unwittingly. Eaglestreak was sure of this, and that Willie and the Late Peoples would be best guides and give wisdom. Even Parry might be useful. May it be.

Parry was swift to point out differences.

"The cinders are gone," he said, on his knees, feeling the flat of asphalt with his hands. "It's plain Willie," he said and stood up. "Hardly any texture."

"Cinders?" said Fabian.

"Cinders from Akropolis boiler rooms. Crushed coal, and ash and burnt coals left from burning in industrial works."

"Like the rubber companies?" said HB.

"Right about here was the blacksmith." Parry gestured toward an open garage of a maintenance building. The front grill of a pickup gleamed there.

This exploration on the part of 2017 CE, 1900 and circa 1769 A.D. might be recorded if these youths were to stray opposite, where maintenance for the complex had security cameras, mics and other surveillance more subtle. If they moved up past the Gospel Mission building and strayed into the area where some shops had given permission, their presence would no doubt be recorded or even observed by security for the 3.5 complex. However, these were not turned on the lower part of the alley. Pastor had declined an offer of free surveillance for his own reasons.

"I recall this path very well from your part of Time," said Eaglestreak in True Tongue to Willie. "I was very ill, yet I knew it well, both before and after. Here we explored after everything changed. Trees changed, land shaping stayed much the same, but these" —he tapped the wall of the mission— "were here instead of our woodlands. There were no graves in our woods."

Parry endeavored to translate for HB and Fabian. He was only partly successful. Fabian said, "Tell him we came here in the cinder Time, too. When the path was not like this here, but like Willie and Parry said. Buildings were changed. We also explored briefly. Then we had to go home."

"He means home had to come get us at a particular time," said HB. "We almost didn't make it."

"In fact," said Fabe with a glance at HB, "we still haven't."

Before this could be translated, "Hello!" called a high remote voice suddenly. They turned. A woman was coming toward them from the alleyway entrance near Third St. and Exchange. As she drew near, Fabian and HB recognized the Post reporter who had earlier requested interviews and been politely declined. Her person was not large. She gave the impression of being athletic in a *roambo arts* kind of way. She would not be timid about entering an alleyway, security or not.

At her approach the 2017 boys recognize her as being mostly 2019.

Fabe said, "Didn't he just used to be Kim Kim, like two weeks ago in 2017?"

Had Jay been with them, she might have said, "She, and yes."

HB said, "My, how two years changes a man."

They greeted her, subdued. FivePoints had not particularly been her beat in 2017. Both boys were wary but not unfriendly. Just a bit stiff. (For them.)

Sheree Kim made a quick decision. There would be no effusion as was sometimes deployed in quest of her subjects. "I happened to see the little boy turn in here as I was coming down Third St. from the police station. I was hoping we might all have a bit of conversation together." She looked at each quickly in turn, assessing, but not obviously so. Her look was simply inclusive. She slipped her device into the pocket of her slacks, with a slight smile for Fabian and HB.

She wore casual business attire, heavy blazer and slacks with a dark beret on her sleek pageboy 'do. Her eyes were slant, like Tu's, fine-looking. She was smart in a way that was easily hidden, appealing, or acute—depending on what was needed. Kim was a professional, very good at catching the faux news scent. She had caught the Mayor being faux-newsy more than once. At the moment, what she wanted more than anything was the *foe*-news-worthiness (or not) of this story. Newsworthy, yes. But in what ways? And who in sht were these coSplays? The police did not know. That much was evident to this reporter.

— Have you ever noticed that your FivePoints neighborhood is really a six-points neighborhood?

Pomala thought about this.

After a moment she said, "So yeah, especially when I was little I noticed it had more than five. It had six: Bechtel Avenue directly across from Sharon Road, 3rd Ave., Exchange Street, counted twice because it ran completely through the intersection, and then the alley. They only ever called it the soup kitchen alley, but I think it had earlier names. The street sign posted on the building says Alleyway. I had forgotten that! You're really into our neighborhood!"

She was dream-talking with Gneis. They were a couple of Bubble space nebula buddies; spacey starry gaseous sparkly explosive stately Bubble buddies. She thought it strange (from time-to-time) that this was such a comfy experience. Every time she had it.

— *Let me see if you can guess what this is leading up to.*

Gneis could be a bit of a know it all... But then... he did seem to know just about everything. And he wasn't even a showoff. He just seemed sort of isn't-it-kinda-cool-we-can-be-friends sorta guy; sorta nebula.

Pomala thought about the question.

"Maybe SiXPointz HiTopOLis? Is that how you spell it?" The tipoff was the giant neon sign in garish star-letters, twinkling throughout the galaxy: *SiXPointz HiTopOLis*.

Gneis smiled his special bronzy star-crinkly smile. It was a calming smile. Aside from its heavenly qualities, it had this sort of spiritual quality to it. You never saw that in her universe. In her universe smile qualities seemed always — what? — deteriorating, sheepish, sarcastic or nasty, cynical or sentimental — always a bit of something mixed into smiles — what she thought really didn't belong in a smile. Just a tinge of something negative that was slightly or hugely off. Gneis had none of this. She felt she *belonged* in the heavens when she was with him… while sensing or seeing his smile.

"So SiXPointz," continued Pomala, "that's a real alternate reality universe place. Is that right? It's your universe?"

— *Yes….*

"And you just pop into ours via these dreams, right?"

— *So so pop isn't exactly the word I'd use — but that isn't important, actually.*

"Tu might disagree with you on that?

— *Of course.*

"Do, do you dream with Tu?"

— *Sometimes. When Dah has something for him. I kinda deliver the message*. Here came another of Gneis's great smiles.

"Can't Dah give it to Tu himself?"

— *Not directly.*

"Why?"

— *Because Dah is in his body.*

"In the next universe?"

— *Yes.*

"Then how does Dah give you the message to give to Tu? You are unbodied, de-bodied? How does that work."

— *Think about it.*

"Oh yeah — the WIMPs. Does that mean you are a WIMP?"

— *Yes.*

"And Dah calls you on the WIMP phone and gives you the message to give to Tu.

(Mutual laughter and smiling explosions.)

— We have this thing — you are familiar with it from your own multi-universal travels — called KythHinG.

"Oh yes, here we call it *E.S.P.-KyThingg*. But it's only fiction. You know — science-fiction."

She paused. Gneis did too.

"So you're saying Dah can ESP-*Kyth*?

— Sheesh does that. My twin.

"That is so familiar."

— Do you remember anything about Sheesh?

She paused.

"He could walk."

They began laughing. It took several light-years for them to stop. *Enough with the side real-timing*, gasped Gneis. *Anything else*, he said.

"Sheesh fed you."

"That's right. I stopped being able to feed myself."

"You and Sheesh would ESP-*Kyth*.... —With GURlee!"

— Yes. It's how we all communicate now through Sheesh who is in the body. Me and Mam, that's Mary Bala Jones, can kythH with Sheesh and GURlee, who both still have bodies in our universe.

"And wallpaper!"

— No. We don't communicate with wallpaper—not anymore. Mam's wallpaper is gone.

"I remember showing you the wallpaper in your sleep! I mean I had to dream-show it to Dah when I was dark matter so he could know what to do before the the the—"

— That's right—

"Before the atomic explosions that destroyed HiTopOLis!!"

— Yes. That was you.

And then?

They disappeared?

Pastor looked up. *They disappeared?* He saw but did not notice the rows of books across from him.

Pastor looked down and read it again. Just that last passage. He had read further, looking for answers, finding none, and had come back to... just *here*. Again and again.

The general 1900 consensus: and his forefather Dr. Zettler had confirmed by quoting *Lamppost* articles—mainly those of a correspondent named Dreiser. The Five Points neighborhood police detectives had gone out-of-state on the rail-lines searching for Willie, Parry, and the girl they call *Heirolynn*. Not finding them. Nothing. *Just disappeared.*

No, something. Simply put, it was believed they had gone on the vaudeville circuit. On their own. Without chaperones. Some said they were kidnapped. He noticed that one quotation from Dreiser included mention of A'ndians.... Curious....

But what to make of that? Anything? Well, maybe something.... Perhaps he could ask Parry after all....

The question, however:

Should he mention any of this to Willie and Parry?

He took off his glasses, rubbed his eyes, then went back to the journal, again reading Dr. Zettler's brief mention of son Johan quizzing him on certain particulars regarding scientific and technological questions. Johan even asked about life on other planets and said some of the vaudeville had claimed to be from other, terribly distant, planets.

This can only be a slight confirmation of 2017's claim to time travels. ... But again. Is it really so slight? There are no descriptions, beyond a vague costuming and makeup artistry. A mere mention of a conversation with an Osiian boy. Osiians were not common, in Akropolis or Northeast EHio, according to this reading, and Pastor's own understanding. But the biggest correspondence in the idea was expressed by 2017 —that most 1900 A.D. Akropolites believed 2017 were from the vaudeville —the newest act arrived with the next troupe on the "Grandmaster's" circuit.

Pastor sat back, his hands clasped behind his bespectacled head. Pondering.

Two of them are definitely full-blooded Native-Americles. Sheree had noticed this right off on seeing them across the crowded SoupMission hall. Even from that distance the facials and fierceness were evident. Now she was seeing a nobility, even. The eyes and cheekbones, the quiet dark forthright gaze apprehending her without display, even as she was scrutinizing them.

She looked at Parry in the ambient glow of subdued alleyway lights.

Fabian said, "We aren't talking yet about the the—"

"About the coSplay—dig?" said HB, channeling somebody in his bold and indignant manner. Then, of course, he grinned. "Like."

"We?" she asked.

No one spoke. Then she looked sidelong at Parry again. "Weren't you one of them? You cut your ponytail?"

Suddenly Willie spoke:

"This is a conversation." It was a question, yet the flatness of tone was a rebuke.

"He's harmless," said HB. "Did stories on it when Cossyuc was doing my head. Harmless, if you actually want all your words recorded and distributed throughout the live long worl'." He corrected himself: "I'll vouch for her." He did not grin.

"Okay. Okay," said Sheree, smiling. "I'll let you go, now." She continued up the alleyway and kept going up Harkins Hill. In the dimness, footsteps echoing, she disappeared as they watched. Maybe she cut through the side alley up past the dry cleaners?

OKOK, Parry thought.

"Big of her letting us go," HB muttered when she was out of earshot. Between all this and CossycSystems, he was feeling himself beset with friendemies these days.

The alleyway was quiet.

Fabian nudged him. "Look." It was very quietly said.

Just there—between the six boys and the back light of the kitchen door; in a shadow below canned goods and donation shelves: There came a noise of creaking and scraping.

A wooden hatch opened. A massive dark head and shoulders appeared —sticking out of a gap or hole in the basement foundation. The boys had fleshed themselves against the wall. The hatch lowered. And now they saw this great head, short dark hair tangled, looking out toward the shelves. Great arms reaching, huge hands gripping asphalt beyond the lowered door, as though its next move would hoist it out the hole.

They could hardly believe it!

Is it actually clutching asphalt?

Suddenly the gigantic head turned their way. Eyes glancing from a dirty face, he saw them. This was no *it*.

He did not seem surprised, however.

In the glow of maintenance buildings across the way, they saw him smiling, each kid peeping out beyond another beside him. The giant smiled slightly, innocently, at each of them in turn.

Then he slid back into wherever he had come from. They heard the scraping and creaking, saw the hatch closing. He was gone.

"Huh?" said HB, stepping out from the wall. For once nothing beyond that one syllable came to him. They all moved. As though breathing again.

It was a friendly get-together at night in the Mayor's home in Sharon with his great great wife serving beer, nothing but, and finger food. The Mayor's assistant Glindora was present. In the kitchen she asked Abundance for wine. They were talking.

In the living room the Mayor was talking with council members, assuring them that the funding was on track, and, importantly, that this lead-fixing was not going to interfere with funding for the dam takedown.

"Both are going to happen. The EPA will not renege on the first project. They will be working with us on both. And of course we will still be working jointly with the town of A'ndian Falls on the project."

"So what do you think?" said Glindora in the kitchen to Abundance as they worked on the trays, sipping wine.

"I think the plaque-in-place is the way to go. I guess that means just you and me?"

"The rock ledge should stay, yes, but I think maybe Westerheim and Bill will go that way eventually —on account of the cost, even though there might be bucks in having new plots to replace the rock. I mean, after all, Thompson and Thompson and Thompson and Thompson and Thompson and Thompson might rather have that."

"You like being silly. Don't you?"

"Well it's fun." Glindora admitted this with her pretty yet pale mature smile. Family mattered: The string of Thompsons was the actual legal name of the Northeast EHio funeral firm, but everyone just called it Thompson. "But it is so beautiful, all mossy and lichened and the grass clipped all round. Trees at a perfect distance."

"Yep." Abundance smiled her great great smile lit by dark eyes in full attractive features.

But on Harkins Hill above FivePoints; on the street running past the Johnny Green Farm historical site—its surroundings built up two or three generations ago—just on that street; in a side row of old houses, The Girl stood on a landing atop a flight of old wooden stairs. It was all in The Purpose. All things. She did not look down so much as out. Did she even see the wall in front of her? She passed down along the right hand wooden banister, slowly. Downward. At the bottom she turned right, away from the newel post. Darkness was in the open door beyond: The door was open, containing darkness where once there was light.

Once, long before this old house had been converted to small apartments, there had been light in that room, and in a room beyond, toward the back of the house: Almost 120 years ago, Johan Zettler had stood at the stairtop in answer to his father's call. "Go get the Wilusa boy, tell him the girl is found." He was careful to use Anglish phrasing, not Churman. Without words, the girl knew this.

"What's wrong?" asked Johan as he descended in woolen knickerbockers, tucking in his nightshirt, Victorian lace-up shoes under his arm.

"The girl was coming along the road just now, she is in there now." Dr. Zettler gestured toward the examination room beyond the reception room. "I will see what I can do, but please go now." In words both Churman and Anglish, the girl knew.

The tall crank phone stood on a small table by the door, but in this case it was useless: The Wilusas had no telephone.

Dr. Zettler did not say that the girl had been virtually naked, that she'd been found crying all the way along the dirt road as he stood in the doorway taking the air.

"Please hurry," he said as Johan hopped on one foot and then the other getting his shoes on.

"Better to lace those," said his father in that Churman accent.

In 2019 the girl turned back toward the front door.

Now here she was... walking, crying, crying along the brick-paved street. This was Harkins Hill. There was an alleyway leading down toward FivePoints. The girl went past, kept going. She turned right at Sharon Road, going down toward FivePoints intersection, crying.

Pastor Zettler was so engrossed in Dr. Zettler's journals that he did not hear Parry leave the apartment. *Where in the world had Heirolynn come from?* He was training himself to use the name Candace had given him.

Yes, evidently there were A'ndians —unusual event!— in town at the time of 2017's visit. And the vaudeville at the Opera House! And now she was here—evidently, (somehow) with them. This was not play-acting. The Girl was the real deal.

But, as he thought of her, he began coming back to the present. He had an impulse to call Candace to see if all were well. Would Fabian be there now? He pushed back from the desk. "Parry." He went looking through the next room and on into the kitchen. Parry wasn't in the bedroom. Maybe upstairs? Are they all in but HB? He stopped in the living room to listen.

Silence.

He did not sit down. He picked up the receiver and began dialing Candace. It was a moment or two before she answered. Quietly. Rather slow of speech.

"So sorry to wake you, Candace."

"That's all right, Philip. Is everything all right?"

"Yes. I've just been reading Dr. Zettler's journals and jotting things down. You knew I had those old things?"

"Probably." She laughed. "Once."

He smiled. "Your North Regina antecedents are in there. Say, I've been thinking about Heirolynn. How is she getting along?"

Candace had been curled asleep on the couch with a light on, and was now on her back staring through crooked spectacles where wall met the ceiling across from her. A faded frieze of roses and daffodils ran all the way round the room up there.

"Pretty good." She fumbled with one hand, righting her wire-rim glasses. "I put her in Fabian's room temporarily while I was reading so the light wouldn't bother her. I guess I fell asleep. Here's my book on the rug." She turned to grope for Stoyev's *Raw Youth*, and noticed the bedroom door open. It was dark there except for light shafting in from the end table.

"Oh wait, Philip, till I go see." She pushed herself up on rickety arms and stood uncertainly. Candace went to look in.

"Oh dear." She half-wailed on her return. "Oh Philip she's gone. Fabian's not here either." She moved her head to call toward the kitchen in quavering voice. "Both gone, Philip. What shall we do?"

"It will be all right," he said calmly. "Maybe they are together, teaching Willie fog-computing or bot-podding, or whatever they've got. But I'll have a look around here. I may have to go out. For once I wish I had a cell phone or something!" He was making light.

"Yes!" she said. "If they weren't so complicated I'd get one!"

The male teenage time-displaced were walking through graveyard grounds again, following the streamlet down towards a new destination: They were planning to take the Aqueduct Trail, cross a footbridge suspended over the river, and continue on to The Gorge Park beside its dam. So far they had not even made it to the GlimmerDale rock-ledge. HB was suffering compunction. There was no way they could execute this exploration and be back in time to satisfy Pastor Z.

Fabian, too, was concerned. If it hadn't been for the girl being with his Grandmother, he'd quit and go home. But the two were together so it was good. And this was *the goods*—for 2017—. So he would not want to be much trouble to her—because of all his disappearing acts. Well, just one disappearing act, actually. If—*when*—he left 2019—it would not be disappearing but reappearing—in 2017! Timewise, every adult, everybody 2019 would already be there.

Willie and Parry, the true braves, him and HB: everyone in the gang wanted to see this particular destination, however: They were going to have the whole story from every angle. Would there be answers in this mini escapade? Probably not, but at least they would have the story. The best stories, his grandmother always said, might not have all the answers.

Fabian was the only one in the group who'd taken the metropolitan parks trail before. He saw in the news that the dam was going to be dismantled. Maybe this year, maybe next. From the conversation they'd had in the alley before starting, he had learned that even Willie and Parry understood the trail and suspension bridge only as a novelty: The parks and the trail and the bridge had no place in 1900 CE. As Fabian understood it from them, the aqueduct was only proposed or beginning in their day. It was planned to take Akropolis sewage to the river on the edge of town. At that time, evidently sewerage found its way on its own, making everybody sick in the process. As a separate issue, the dam for electric power was only just going up in1900!

"Infracture structure," HB had said. "These guys know what happens without it. We had no idea until the crumbles and breakdown of the water system in this town."

The way 2017 was beginning to understand it, these braves have—had—a camp on or near the dam site, The Gorge. It was not their only camp, of course. Willie had said there were others. They needed to change every so often to let the stench of human waste go by. It was their way of cleaning up after themselves, so to speak. HB liked the simplicity of "cleaning up" by not the actually cleaning up.

The plan had been formed on the spot in the alley after the strange encounters. Well—not Sheree Kim so much. Was she strange? Not really. It was the giant. The giant with the smile.

Now the conversation in the graveyard was about the Giant.

"Never seen the giant before," said HB. "Yo, if he's been living in a hole under the alley I knows nothin' bout it."

"Wouldn't Pastor say something if he knew?" said Fabian.

It was night here in the vale but lambent glowing surrounded the graveyard from city heights and the gentrified neighborhood above. The boys were strung along the pea gravel path going down to the little cemetery bridge. The plan was not to visit the rendezvous rock. There wasn't enough time. They'd keep going following the stream. It was going to disappear once they got to the street beyond the GlimmerDale, but Fabian knew where to pick up the trail once they were over the concrete streets, headed along the river above its glimmery shores.

"The hole he's in is below the coal chute," said Willie.

"That's right." Parry explained. "It's where they dropped coal down for the furnace under the building. Didn't it have a special cellar, Willie? Only for the coal, I mean."

"Yes."

"1900 was weird," said HB. "No pipes for natural gas, no furnace duct, solar panels or wind generators. That musta been some bad air in the wintertime."

"It could be bleak," said Parry with one of his literary precocious turns. "Like streets in Dickens," he said.

"It musta been the dickens, 'nough said," returned the other.

"But you keep food cold in the big white box," said Willie. "We had the ice man, every day."

"Where'd the ice come from?"

"They kept it in ice houses along the lakes. Harvested all winter, then stored. It was kept altogether so it didn't thaw much."

"So horses, wagons," said Fabian, remembering the old street from a week—was it!?—ago. "Did you see that smile?"

"The giant's."

"Yeah."

"How could we miss it."

But the truth was: No two boys had received the same smile. Or, perhaps, the same smile was perceived differently by each.

"When we were climbing over the wall, Eaglestreak said he saw the Giant before." This was Parry speaking as they reached the tiny bridge below the rock-ledge. "Walleye-stare also thinks it was the Grandmaster, but Willie and I saw the Grandmaster on stage. He introduced the A'ndians. All of them, as reenactors of the same tableau.... But then again I don't know because he was dressed to the sevens and clean as a whistle."

Eaglestreak and Walleye-stare conferred together. "Ghosts Leaping," said Eaglestreak in True People tongue.

"But Parry," Willie said, "they saw him up close. We didn't."

"But Willie, he was majestic! Don't you recall?"

"I guess he means this giant is not majestic," said HB.

"He did look kinda simple," said Fabian. "And dirty."

"Harmless? You mean. Like he wasn't going to beat you to a pulp with those giant hands?" HB offered his speculations.

Eaglestreak said something else to Walleye-stare, who nodded once.

"You were told not to dance, just stand? That was the tableau, I think it's called." Parry explained: "He told them—the Grandmaster told them—just stay in place. He put them that way. And we saw them in the bushes, well these were stage props actually, and then he explained to us—the audience—what it was all about. —The Ghosts Leaping—I mean. It was going to get rid of interlopers. I mean in history. I mean...

"—You don't know what it means, Parry," said Willie.

Parry laughed. He stumbled along the path and Willie caught his arm, righting him.

HB was not talking about his own perceived encounter—meet-up?—with the Grandmaster—or Showmaster—as he had called him, at least in his own mind. It was not a face-to-face but a peripheral encounter, he thought. Dude was big like that. He still had not decided if it was imaginary or not, even though his head (downloaded) said it was not imaginary. 1900! What a frakking mystery! Quadri seemed to know….

Eaglestreak was remembering. He esteemed the look in the alleyway giant's smile. He was the same and yet not the same. But Ghosts Leaping: *it was foreseeing. For a time to come will its fulfillment be*.

Stairs and doorway, down from his apartment above, opened on Sharon Road. Pastor Zettler stepped onto the sidewalk, lit with the glow of streetlights beside the SoupMission. He had been praying. Where to look first?

The street and intersection were p.m. busy, traffic sparser than daytime, stop-and-go. A few pedestrians loitered or hurried along. Flo, on watch at women's-and-children's overnight, stepped out to chat when she saw him through the plateglass.

"Hi, Pastor how's it going? A mild night."

He scarcely saw her, a big woman in draping shirt, sneakers and jeans.

"Looking for the girl. Heirolynn. Remember her?"

"Oh yeah, the girl—that her name? Kinda well, heebeejeebee—"

"No, autistic perhaps."

"Yeah, no. Have not seen her tonight."

Pastor hesitated.

"Oh wait," said Flo. "That may have been her with Sheree Kim. The news gal."

"Where? Where'd they go?"

"Over there, I think." She gestured across the street to CossycSystems.

"Sure?"

"I think I said 'not'." She grinned. "Do you need help?"

"I think I'll head over." He went jaywalking, passing through traffic both ways.

Wearing slacks, a blazer, and dark beret atop her sleek hairdo, Sheree Kim was walking out the campus gate. "Hi," she said walking toward him. They met on the sidewalk next to the driveway.

"Sheree, have you seen the girl? —the one we have here?" Zettler gestured toward the mission.

"The silent one."

"Yes."

"She's in there now." Ms. Kim gestured toward the campus buildings.

"How did that happen? We were taking care of her."

"Apparently not," said the other. She looked him in the eye.

"But you knew. Were you with her? Why didn't you bring her to us?"

"So, *pastor*, she was crying. I found her coming down Harkins Hill from up there." Sheree Kim pointed up Sharon with its descending line of lights.

"Crying!—but why?"

"I don't know."

Distressed he said, "You might have taken her to Sheltering Cares or, or called the DHP (he did not like saying that). Or the police, even."

"Yes. I might have."

"Please, how did it happen, her going?"

"Someone was driving in here—Dr. X—and we talked.... I trust her. Of course they'd be interested, given their studies, and her state. She thought they might do something to help ... after I told her the story." Ms. Kim did not mention that Dr. X was one who had helped with Kim Kim's transformation.

"What story?"

"Whose hands she's in."

She stood eyeing him. Then relented. She really did not distrust this man. Just that blamed strange religion. But—no—they do good work. *So, no—the religion.* "I just think, pastor (here Kim entitled him respectfully), that they can do something for her. Even the Mayor's assistant—her niece—thought so."

"Pomala? She's a child, Sheree."

"I noticed. But look, call her sister Glindora. But this is a good idea." Her striking Osiian eyes turned back to CossycSystems.

Pastor had been gazing in earnest at her. He dropped his head suddenly. Then he looked back across to the SoupMission.

"I just wish—" he stopped. Not a good thing to say. "Thanks for looking out for her, Sheree. I'll take your advice and call Glindora."

He started into the street and she grabbed hold of his arm just as a car slammed around the corner onto Sharon from Exchange. He stepped back on the curb. "Thanks, Sheree!"

He watched both ways and hurried back across Sharon. He did not hear her call out about Cossyc calling the hospital if need be. Pastor did not even see Flo lean out. Flo let him go.

No.... I cannot... believe.... Pastor was thinking, climbing the stairs. He stumbled back, grasping the handrail, huffing, heart thumping. He needed to put in brighter light here. Cannot believe—not the system. Cannot believe in the system. The numbers they make us. Not that. Not over neighbors. No. No. They cannot care. They can't! *...As numerical system.... not as statistical system. Corporate nothingness.*

He was gasping, reaching the top. The door was wide open. He went straight to the phone.

Stop, and pray why don't you?

Okay....

"Hi," he said lightly when Glindora picked up. "You home?"

"At the Mayor's now. There's a meeting. Nothing I can't miss for a few moments." He heard her step into someplace quieter.

"What's up?"

Pome to Jay: "So what do you think? I think we can help her, I guess?" Pomala lay supine on her bed.

"Who?"

"The girl! Heirolynn, I think her name is."

"Oh yeah, right. I recall something. You thought 1900 couldn't help and you thought 2017 could so you almost tried to take her back with us, that didn't work, and boom she came anyway—what—two years late here? Are we on the same page? What brought this on?"

"I got two calls. Sis woke me and then you called. She wanted to know if I've been talking to reporters and I said just one, but not about 2017. I've been very good that way."

"But you *could* talk 1900? Bogus, Pome. HB would tell you, Fabian."

"I didn't say it was 1900, just said the girl was with the A'ndians. I didn't say anything about them. But they might at least do spectrum analysis? She's asking questions of them now, but I'm being good, Jay really I am."

"But watch out Pome. There's spyware now. Would this reporter use it?"

"It's Ms. Kim. I don't think so."

"And you know all about her right?"

"So no. Okay point made. Stop now."

"To answer your question I don't see *why* the girl needs help! If anyone needs help!"

"Calm down, Jay, I get you, but—"

"She's got people watching over her—friends. Look they're always holding her hand, feeding her, washing her? —anyway, no she needs no help, Pome!"

"So it's not like you—"

"AND she's not a prisoner!"

"But autism—"

"Not a prison!"

"By-the-way." Pomala was desperate to change the subject. "Now this is interesting! See what you think!"

"What?"

"So I just woke up... and guess what?"

"Another d-r-e-a-m."

"Y-y-yes. But."

And here Pomala came completely back. Away from everything else. Considering.

"Uh-oh," said Fabian, spying the parked sQuad car out on Market Ave.. "Better not say anything about The Gorge. The park closes at 9 p.m — and that's in summer I think."

Coming down toward the GlimmerDale gate, they saw two officers standing in the lane below, apparently waiting for them.

Officer Wilkes was eyeing their longbows and quivers as they approached. "Oh yes, our fine feathered friends and their FivePoints cohorts."

With a faint eye-roll, Officer Robust glanced her micromanagement concerns at him. These braves just seemed so much like the real thing—the two with distinctive faces, especially.

HB stuck out his hand, very polite and sophisticated. "Good evening, officers," he said, pleasantly, with a smile.

Below the great church, P.M. traffic was going by on Market, one of Akropolis's main streets—trafficking between downtown and West Hill over a nearby expressway underpass.

Wilhelmina Robust smiled back and shook his hand. "The cemetery is closed after dark, you know."

Wilkes was slower, but forthcoming in shaking hands.

"So, no going back to 1900, then?" he said. "No tunnels from here through the cemetery? Just where d'you s'pose it got to—1900 CE?"

Parry offered his hand. "I found out about OK, OK?" he said.

"Fine." Officer Robust smiled.

Wilkes said, "I presume you have plans, are on your way to a rousing soon-to-be-seen-everywhere-on-every-device exhibition of Buffalo Boys and A'ndians taking aim at one another?"

"Nah." HB was still smiling pleasantly. "It's our night off. Just out for burgers 'n' fries."

"Care to join us?" said Fabian.

"Y'unnerstand we cain't foot de bill fo y'all—be we's be maybe eat together?" HB was charming tonight.

Parry was admiring Officer Robust's trim uniform and hat with its corners and bill—all in blue set off with gold here and there. An official sort of Grecian-looking badge. "Police here used to wear helmets, tall ones. That's a nice outfit," he said. "Why are women and girls allowed to wear pants now? Men and boys don't wear dresses?"

So great at role-playing for one his age!

"Oh yes they do," said Wilkes. "Now. It's really not co-shore but what can y'do — arrest' em? No, we just get with their program."

Wilhelmina was rolling her eyes. "We're on duty," she said, light and smooth. "We can't go eat. Thanks for the invite. We just wanted to let you know we'll be around... if you need us." There was ambiguity in her tone if not her smile.

And the officers did not move on.

"So, thanks!" said Fabian, turning to go up the hill in the direction of the monolithic church, toward the fast food.

Robust called out, "Better take Bechtel back to FivePoints!"

"Appreciated!" called HB over his shoulder. He also gave a salute. Willie, Eaglestreak, Walleye-stare and Parry followed after, eyes on the clock tower emerging beyond tall trees above them. Traffic was passing and they saw the glow of a McRonalds up there across the street. Fabe's peripherial vision caught the fat dark scamper of a rat going into the sewer.

"Don't worry," he said. "There's a way down through there, once we get out of sight." He did not gesture large—in case they were still being eyed by the law. Willie, who was interpreting the interaction for True People, explained this as well.

Later that night they are on the suspension bridge, away out over the glinting river on their trail to The Gorge: an exciting uplifting experience of dark nature glowing with remote town-lights. Wind comes through a vale around and below them—surrounding black hills, light-crowned on all sides. They hold onto cables, metallic patterning beneath their feet clad in moccasins; pretending to dance above the running river far below—a river curving, meeting smaller streams, promising much goodness of life and limb for all kinds of creatures. The two True People, alight with dancing awe, begin to chant.

How the interlopers were so good at some things and—recalling plastic bottles along with the FivePoints explanation—so bad at others. Of course they would have to keep maintaining, rebuilding, supporting, supplying everything continually... instead of just moving camp, or going through thickets stalking caribou and deer. What a strong footbridge—strong night!!

Bong!! bong!! bong!! and on. They hear deep distant resonance of clock tower bells floating out to them high over this wide dark deep ravine.

The time-travelers follow a dark path down, where waters flow between cliffs overhead and a tree-bristling ridge opposite A'ndian River. Lights of houses glow above. The breath of November pours in and out their lungs as they walk. As they draw near, roaring of A'ndian Falls increases. This is the thundering responsible for early-mid 20th -century electricity in the two towns. Dismantling and removal of mountainous deeps of contaminated sediments are planned to enhance metro parks of the 21st

century along the southward running A'ndian River; toward Groverland where it pours into Great EHio Lake.

Pale water flowing past on the river below, Eaglestreak and Walleye-stare are eager, entranced as the falls loom glimmering ahead. In the ambient light from streets and homes above they see mist rising, shimmers of water flowing down over the crumbling dam from the old electric plant out of sight above and beyond. This is the thing they witnessed initially building almost 120 years ago while exploring the time-generated land displacing their hunting grounds and camps.

When first The Girl came to them they lived beneath this massive, tall wall of age-weathered and darkened sandstone. Here *Ochquetit* worked, carefully grinding the corn. They stood and spoke of this in their tongue, Willie and Parry listening. They too know of this camp from their adoption: It had no falls thundering down from above. Instead, rapids hurried with more subdued roaring and foaming among ancient rocks down toward the great turning. And still, until this historic rendezvous with FivePoints, the girl was corn-grinding. Grinding, grinding the harvest dried and kept through previous autumns and winters. Too, she pounded acorns leeched in the river.

Of their number, however, only the two True People witnessed the beginning of the 20th -century building itself in the form of this dam.

When. They knew interlopers would defeat them, bring bondage, bring prison, destroy freedom to travel and hunt and farm where they would. They discovered the strange people would think to parcel, buy, sell, own here and there; not fight among themselves for territory, treat, make peace, live in accordance with what was right in True People's eyes.

And Eaglestreak said, "Grandmaster."

Walleye-stare said, "Yes. Grandmaster."

Each was silent as the river roared down from above. Each was silent, pondering. Then they moved off the lower path, climbing upslope away from those bellowing, thundering falls.

At last Willie spoke. HB was about to question them, but Willie spoke:

"Why do you say 'Grandmaster'?" He was considering the 1900 vaudeville showman, Grandmaster.

Fabian, HB, Parry, and Willie gathered close to hear their answer.

"Grandmaster told us of *Ghosts Leaping*," said Eaglestreak.

Willie said, "We saw *Ghosts Leaping* in the vaudeville at the Opera House.

"You stood in the tableau," said Parry to the braves.

Eaglestreak spoke and Willie translated: "Then also we heard of the prophecy. Grandmaster told us to keep heart through all ... though Ghosts Leaping seems failed in intent and vision. He told us of the Plains and the dancing, and the hope of many nations, meaning True Peoples ... to receive back the land in a manner more fitting, and according to laws unbreakable by men, in learning to be men, true men, to be True Peoples indeed."

"But what does it mean?" said HB. For him the explanation was mysterious, a wonder, and maybe even unwelcome. "Does it mean things will be better —or worse?"

Fabian said, " Better or worse, when? Better or worse how? Better or worse? What does it mean?"

"Yes. Does it look like anything?" said HB. "What does it look like?"

Parry, the boy-child among them, said, "It will be a story."

"Not helping, bro," said HB. "Little Bro." He grinned, teeth flashing in the night beneath this giant dark moldy wall of rock-ledge. He turned slightly, saying this to Parry, when his peripheral gaze caught something. He turned more. "What's that?" He was fishing in his pocket. He got out his device and went up closer. He would gleam the gizzzzmo on a metallic something under the steeply overhanging rock.

"Looks like a plaque," said Fabian. "Oh yeah, I remember. I've seen it before—a historic marker of some kind."

Climbing just a bit more they came to a higher path and gazed at the old bronze plaque fast in this great stone ledge. The mold- and lichen-covered ledge leaned over them dark, casting its great shadow. Above, invisibly, moved the A'ndian Falls night-time neighborhood, slowly, sleepily. Behind them fell the lambent glow of North Hill of Akropolis onto the plaque. But it was light from HB's LED device making the letters plain:

TO MEMORIALIZE HEIROLYNN HAMPBELL

Who, as a child, was kidnapped circa 1765
From a Pensil'swood Rovmorian Mission
And made to work beneath this ledge
in A'ndian kitchens.

Heirolynn Hampbell
Thus was the first white person
To live in the Western Stock Reserve.
This plaque is set in dedication by
Children of the Americle Revolt.

"Is that our Heirolynn?" asked Parry over the remote roaring of falls. He reached up to finger the engraving.

"It must be," said Fabian. He turned to Willie. "But you'll ask what they think?"

Then Willie and the A'ndians stood down a bit off the path, talking. Parry followed.

"*It is even as we know*," said Eaglestreak to them. "*Now she is the Shower. Red Fox has told. Therefore are we come.*"

The others coming more slowly, Parry hurried back up to them,. "Yes! It's her! It's *Ochquetit*! Ma found out her name is also Heirolynn. She was grinding corn here when she left for 1900. It was a mission to scout her out, and bring her back when she got away from them two cycles—years—ago. Red Fox was the leader. He brought back the girl. The Scouts all did."

He stopped his earnest speaking. Then he looked down. "We came, too." He said this in a little voice.

"How did that happen?" said Fabian.

Parry looked up. "Willie opened the doors of the tool shed in the cemetery, and they came out and took her away. You disappeared, the tool shed was gone…."

"What about all this?" said HB, gesturing around, over the two encompassing overhanging metropolises above the falls. The towns of Akropolis and A'ndian Falls.

"Everything changed then. Only the springtime, and everything springtime, was left. The, the woods were huge—bigger than any woods I'd ever seen, and the grass Willie'd been mowing was gone. The tombstones were gone. Skunk cabbage unfurling and ferns and small weird flowers. I guess they were weird—they won't be if we make it back to—" he looked helplessly at the plaque.

"To circa 1765," said HB.

Parry was disconsolate. He did not want to be 129 years old, but neither did he want to be A'ndian.

Ghostly Struggles

KIM'S AKROPOLIS NOTES

In the early hours a coSplay, known as "The Girl" at FivePoints SoupMission, was found crying, wandering on Sharon Road by this reporter. Somewhere "on the spectrum" she was taken into CossycSystems by Dr. X for observation until her parents or guardians could be located.

"HE IS 'NOT A MAN OF SIN!'

"Claiming he is 'not a man of sin,' the PresiDent announced his intention of visiting the Holy of Holies during his trip to the middle-east next month. 'It will be the capstone of my PresiDuncy,' he said in a question-and-answer exchange with Chesley Stalled at the Gray House, Monday. 'The capstone so far,' he later qualified."

GleeClub WeBBlocking:

"Chrustyuns have put out a stunning work of literary fiction while managing, according to their customary line, to weave in the titillating Shaker romance. Chrustyun publishers, generally known for putting out vapid sentimental but tender works of the imagination, have not succeeded, until now, to heft their message of self sacrificial love in such a way as to engage the curious but bored and baffled reader of today. We cynics must acknowledge their effort in the fine, distinguished, and buoying cliffhanger, *What Shall We Have for Lunch after Magneto-Church*?"

PRESIDENT TRUCK, LIKE HIS 19TH CENTURY HEROIC PREDECESSOR, TURNS BLIND EYE TO HIS OWN GOLDED AGE CORRUPTION SCANDAL.

Baunders reports: "Mr. PresiDent, Didn't you say before the election you'd hand in financial reports and tax returns for the public record after you came to office?"

"That was a figment of your imagination, Burni. No."

Jay was in upscale Sharon trying to find HB and Fabian via the usual digital avenues. "i'm going back to school tomorrow, yo!"

She was sending to any FivePoints 2017 who might be in a position to respond. In town, Candace Parker was on her painful knees in the apartment on Harkins Hill not far from the martyred abolitionist's historic homestead. Pastor was down below in his FivePoints apartment above the soup kitchen thinking about his conversation with Glindora. Fabian and the other boys were on the path headed toward The Gorge and falls. It was going to be a long night for them, several miles round-trip on foot, mysterious, but somehow fulfilling.

Earlier: To capture the love of HB and others from 2017, Tu speculates that alternate universe theories vary from universe to universe. Each theory is slightly different, depending on the universe in which you are currently residing. For instance, the universe three universes away may conceive the multiverse as residing in the molecules of ravens with gallbladders. Tu might have to do math on cellular structures and calculate RNA for gallbladder mutations. He begins researching raven gallbladders for particulars in order to have finds for his calculations. The irrationals from 2017, who just happened to be there, are influencing him. He understands this.

But now Tu, in his closet up in the 3rd St. complex, had dropped into sleep. Mr. and Mrs. Yu were at the kitchen table, holding hands across its formica surface, whispering. Across and down the alleyway beyond the maintenance buildings, Flo kept watch over her female flock by night above a cellar where homeless men were laid out, snoring. Or tossing. Turning. Speaking crazy-talk in their sleep.

In the coal cellar next to them a great majestic homeless bum was thankfully daintily eating with plastic fork in his giant hand: from an aluminum tin of oily sardines. It was too dim in there to see much but the fish was tasty, good. Almost as if he'd had a hand in making it himself. His big lips were oily. He did not lick, but mopped them with a KleeNexT from a box on the bench beside his massive thigh. Light seemed almost to come from his smiling eyes, but perhaps it was simply reflecting from alleyway lamplight through the hatch-cracks. Its fit was not quite flush after all these years. Or maybe it had never been so.

Pomala sat on her bed, in the dim room, neighborhood glow falling through tall old-fashioned windows. Ignoring Jay's questions, ignoring all the things she loved about her room—which had remained neat and pretty and French provincial, as it was when she went to 1900 a week or so back. She ignored anything digital. The phone was muted. Two devices were overturned, one on the dressing table, one on the bed. The laptop—she hadn't opened the laptop since school stopped happening, since 2017 CE.

Pomala sat hugging her knees on the disheveled bed, thinking about the Gneis dreams.

This... this... this.... This is what they mean by profound.

When she wasn't thinking *profound* she was going over and over the dreams. It was coming. There was more. She was actually remembering... something... for which... for which... for which.

"Say it!"

For which I had—*no head!*

I had no head when all that happened! No body, no head. How can it be? How can I be thinking of it now, remembering it. *If I had no head*?!

I can't talk about this. Not to anyone. If. If—even if I mention it too *the others*. They won't remember! They'll start thinking *cult*.

It's not.

Gneis is not cultish.

Gneis is... is... a dream figure or a pile of particles—maybe a cloud—yes cloud computing—. No, that's not right. Not exactly. He doesn't need software, a machine.

I was there!

... We were there....

We were, we were, we were—*in the next universe*. Another reality – entirely.

Yes.

We were between 1900 CE and 1900 EE—the other universe.

No—no—no we were *in* 1900 EE, not in between.

Gneis's father and all the scientists—not theoretical—the applied scientists—with the machines.

They sucked us into their universe.

And she was remembering it all: BABY, the game they played about the origins of the cosmos. The gang of kids who lived in HiTopOLis. Porno culture. (*shiver*.) The evil pedophiles, flying cars, leaking sewers, dead bodies... *wallpaper*! Prophecies in book pages pasted and varnished on the kitchen wall of—of Gneis's apartment above SiXPointz.

And we helped them escape!

We did.

FivePoints 2017 helped the kids, the families escape the coughing thundering catastrophic holocaustic bombs!

Pomala kept going over and over it, recalling more and more. And trying to retain.

Maybe I should type this out?

She thought about it.

It was late but she was psyched. She really did not want to lose any of this.

Was she going to go back to school? Or was she going back to Cossyc?

Jing. She snatched up her q-phone. Jay.

Glindora!

"What's up, sis?" she asked.

Pomala listened to the news, to the thoughtful request.

"Yes," she said. "That sounds good. I'll be ready, yes." She hit end.

Pome was going back to Cossyc systems on account of the girl. The Girl.

Wow, she thought. *It happened.*

Help there for the girl? ... *Except now it's changed.*

She got up and went over to her laptop on the curvy white and gold-trimmed provincial dresser. Her bright hair and dim blue face, pink eyes, were visible in the mirror. She gazed without seeing. Then she pulled out the stool, sat, and opened the laptop.

Gneis will be proud of me!

... But wait.

I was *aware* of them. SiXPointz families, kids—all the time in the other universe! Maybe... maybe he's aware of me right now?

She looked around the room, laptop open, glowing. *Are you here?*

She looked at her image in the mirror.

Just in case, Pomala smiled. Shyly.

Dr. deVill was pulling an all-nighter. These were Frequent for quiet lack of distraction or interruption, these midnight hours were accepted practice, appreciated by the System and its many scientists, theoreticians. Especially by financial people who kept the campus fueled for the dedicated productivity of its many experts. This was not an institution embracing ongoing stasis while self-deceptively talking creativity—resulting in a moribund system. CossycSystems, intellectual, disciplined, and creative worked its way through the night on the passionate ambitions of its individual yet connective endeavors.

Baron deVill had perhaps the largest experimental suite on campus. Masses of LED lights gave brightness like day to these cool white- and pale-blue rooms. Its central area opened onto side chambers, double doors open or closed depending on what the bio scientist was working on. While full of gleaming apparatus—such as UVFL20X microscope objective, and smaller binocular microscope with high transmission for UV light of 340 nm wavelength—its *laborare* bench was long and partitioned, but nonetheless highly organized, spacious enough for note-taking on both device and paper. All his data was worked, and orderly retrievable, across all devices; everything available for a glance at any point during concentrated experimentation.

Just off the central *laboratorium*, one cubicle held compact housing for supplies related to tissue culture. Here were refrigerator and CO^2 cylinders, plus a heating block for magnetic rocking. One cabinet held an array of chemicals. Other cubicles with more equipment opened onto the central area. Yet another opened also onto a central circular mezzanine overlooking a grand lobby below where, during daylight hours, sunlight poured in on the concourse of touring visitors and professionals alike. Dr. deVill met with both kinds in this small tasteful room. He would close the *laboratorium* doors behind his empty polished desk. Visitors could sit and talk in comfortable chairs, or he might walk about speaking with dedicated but equally charming engagement, perhaps about the effortless alphabet spelling of gene directions for cells.

Tonight he stood at the *laborare* bench with binocular microscope gazing on minute scraps of cell tissue. Some of the cells were eating, ripping apart other cells in both ongoing consumption and renewal.

He was making notes by the small microscope platform.

A sudden knock. On the *laboratorium* doors leading to the mezzanine. *Disruption*. He jotted. He looked up frowning. Then crossed quickly to the reception area, walked through past his desk and upholstered chairs to the door and stepped out.

Aware of his movement within Dr. X. was already coming toward him from the other door. Dr. X., she with spiky white hair powdered jowls, serious eyes behind red-framed glasses matching her rouged cheeks.

"May I speak with you?" she asked with melodious cadence.

His gaze had just been magnetic, focused. Questing for the sweet spot. She had to capture his interest quickly. The man who reconfigures mistakes in DNA might be willing. "We might try code replacement therapy on a special case just handed me," she said. She would love to see it happen in this mysterious case, and his payoff would be an unusual, possibly exotic, find. She had been going over her examination of Pomala's version obtained at last week. She had an idea. Also there were speculations, rumors and pictures all over the InterWebs, even video: This was not an ordinary case for biotech. Baron may understand these error codes and assimilate corrected versions.

She gave him a brief but close account. "Would you like to come down and take a look?... I'm sure it could wait till morning if not."

Dr. deVill looked back through the two sets of doors at the *laborare* bench and microscopes. "I think I can manage that now," he said. "I'll meet you down there in a few minutes." He turned away.

Sometimes these genes have simple spelling errors. This may be one we can edit. We're editing half these typos now. Autisms will be going under the CRIZPer11 ...change the instructions without snipping DNA.

There was no need of words. They sat gazing at one another, arms extended across the table, holding hands. Both wore small dark-framed rectangular glasses, they were slim and diminutive by neighborhood standards. Earlier Mr. and Mrs. Yu spoke in murmuring tones, but now each was remembering along the same line. Would Tu ever be told of their previous lives?

Were it not for you I'd be dead.

Were it not for you Tu would not be. We would not be here raising our mysterious child.

The first had been Mr. Yu's thought. He was remembering how his believing young neighbor, a nurse in the corps, had saved his life after the border skirmish by bandaging him tightly and begging room on the transport for one they thought virtually dead. All this he was told by a corpsman (also wounded) beside him after they were well away from the field hospital.

Mrs. Yu was remembering his later constancy in crossing borders, bringing her on a terrible journey that must not be denied. He also was a believer fleeing for his life... with the added burden of pursuit by The Glorious Leader whose tutor he'd been. For Mr. Yu—after his near-death injuries—was granted to attend college in GyangYong, and there he had succeeded to a professorship.

The Glorious Leader had not always been so, of course. First he must be a child, like anyone. But he was also the child of the previous Glorious Leader who, in the succession of life, must become the previous Glorious Leader. Saved from the repressive régime, Mr. Yu was now always busily forgiving him. Because the Glorious Leader had no *concept*, was still the ignorant misguided being grown from a child but....

The sole part of the story known to their mysterious unbelieving child was of the arduous journey: first across borders and Osiian countries on the metaphorical underground transport, then being boxed in metal aboard a great containership traveling over a vast ocean and along another, different continental, coast. Tu does not know all. This travail and ardor is what saved Mr. Yu from the cold smiling murderous intent of the fat-cheeked pupil who once respected and even, it seemed, adored him. The monster who was currently glorious, currently fat and smiling, currently test-launching solid fuel missiles with nose-cones of a size to carry nuclear warheads, currently insanely jealous of Northeast EHio and its fabulous Institutes of Medical Industrial Pursuits. These launches are mobile but not road-bound, and can be cold-fired prior to ignition of primary boosters. Mr. and Mrs. Yu had been closely following the latest North Osiian systems developments. Secretly. That is, without Tu's knowledge.

[Translation] "Shall we tell him at least of our faith?" wondered Mrs. Yu aloud.

"At most we shall tell him," murmured her husband.

Mrs. Yu knew all the deep meaning contained in this, as one who had survived solely on such meaning. She did not ask Mr. Yu when this might happen. Mrs. Yu knew that it would happen. And that she would be there when it did. This was the deep meaning requiring two witnesses. Mrs. Yu would be the second witness.

When HB, standing by the A'ndian Falls memorial, was about to shut down, he saw there'd been a message—voicemail. He listened to Pastor Zettler's first request—for info. But there was another message as well. "Blake come back now," said Pastor Zettler. That was all. HB looked at its timing, told the others it was past time to go. As it was, he knew they could not be back till almost sunrise.

Fabian decided to check his phone and heard his grandmother's message. Evidently the girl was missing. Both pastor and Candace Parker were on landlines without answering machines, so it was uncertain if Heirolynn *Ochquetschitsch* was still missing. He checked the timing—three hours—and decided not to call but let her sleep, in case the girl was now back home.

The list of atrocities and crimes against humanity is fulsome, nauseating and long. Beginning with zero freedom of expression, the schools' curricula are comprised of teachings of its glorious leaders, present and past. The *bunsong* system of class hierarchy is composed of two: the elites and those subject to starvation and human trafficking, with many subcategories in the latter. Elites have access to the city, housing and medicine, food. There is no freedom of movement for the massive underclass. Hundreds of thousands have starved since the famine began two decades ago. Citizens seeking escape, shot on sight by border guards. Tu stopped reading on encountering familial detention atrocities. He did learn that prisoners were not informed of crimes they had been charged with.

He was in the closet, device in hand, horribly wakeful, looking up information on his parent's homeland. He had not interested himself in the subject before: except as comedy—fodder for late-night shows, the butt of jokes and cleverness.

His chest was heaving, his face full of water.

Then briefly he stopped to consider his own homeland—Americle—so dearly bought and handed to him. 2017 to be cherished, he thought. Twenty-seventeen.

He stopped and reconsidered. In this 2019, *We are the butt*—globally. twenty-nineteen. Us and them. Will it ever be 2017 again? And what would that mean in light of all this? What would it mean for 2019 if it were 2017 again? … There is *no 2019* in 2017.

"Jay! Jay!"

That had to be Jay! Fabian was calling out across dim misted old gravestones in the undulant older part of the cemetery. "Jay!"

Jay, tiny, dark, had been flitting about in the predawn misty distance, lawns heightened in color, green green green. November was moist and perfectly snowless. The breath of the Warriors and FivePoints gang pouring from their mouths as they called: Even the braves called in imitation, so exhilarated were they all. Willie and Parry would recognize her as they drew close to one another.

"Fabian!" She shrieked. It was a remote birdlike cry. She was beyond the Civil War Memorial graves, running, her arms raised exultantly. The Arm was in the air! A fist triumphant.

They ran toward her, meeting on the pea gravel path below the rock ledge where Willie's tool shed abutted 120 years ago.

"Yo! What you done, girl!" said HB. "Did they spring you?"

"Not exactly." She grinned her false grin, eyes round, brown pale-streaked 'do swinging. "I sprung me! Let me tell you! —What're you girls doing here?! I messaged no one! No one! Thought you'd be in bed, yo." Jay was breathless, mighty.

"We's at de Gorge, girl! Guess what?"

"They're gonna take down the dam," she said.

"Not that," said Fabian.

Jay was looking curiously at the tall A'ndians with their longbows and quivers full of arrows. Feathers of jet and blue hung in their hair beside exotic features and quiet solemn eyes. Then she was taking in Willie clothed in scraped deer hide, wearing feathers and arrows, his long bow. And Parry, dressed in secondhand contemporary clothing. "I remember you," she said to Parry. Willie was older, of course, taller, more muscular, gorgeous. Absolute. And back again she looked at True People braves. She wore no smile but was marveling within.

Willie wondered at his little brother, as Parry stood tongue-tied. Jayrai looked at Fabian and HB. "1900," she said.

"Yep." Said by HB and Fabian together.

"What a *go* to finally see in person!"

"So Pome doesn't know you're out? —Hard to believe."

"I'm fed with the household, yo," she said. "Sharon. Riding with The Mother. So I left."

"What courage! What blls!" HB was heckling.

"You told no one, right," said Fabian.

The A'ndians smelling of forest and earth had moved close to Jayrai, squatting to scrutinize her hand. Jay's arm was covered in shirt and jacket, but that hand! They could see the wires and works of its fingers through the almost translucent sleeve-glove reaching out of sight up through her clothing. Hand by her side, she waggle her fingers for them. Willie was happy to see the hand again. Parry recalled how the kids took off across the intersection in all directions when she came up to them out of 2017. Parry had run! He ran to the clasp-locker hospital doorway, clutching the girl's hand, dragging her. Ma had stood her ground in face of the Arm. Willie and Ma.

"So yeah, no one," she was saying. "But at least I left a note making sure my butt —my Arm—was covered. The mother knew I was going to school and gave orders to the doorman, etc.. I'm following orders, girls. Cossyc says come back or go to school—so I'm GOING TO SCHOOL." She yelled, victorious.

"Kinda early, though," said Fabian, looking at his phone. HB looked at the watch Pastor had given him.

"But I left the note, got on the Metro bus, etc.."

"Where's your backpack, books?" said HB. "Remember them?"

"Oops!" She grinned.

"AND you still got to get back to the foncy-doncy Sharon school by time de bell rang, girl."

She waggled her fingers, magically. "No biggie."

They were walking back together toward Exchange Street, bunched up, no one straggling, Parry half-skipping to keep up.

"You guys are bigger," she said to Willie. "Have you been with them?" Jay gestured to the true braves. "You dress just like 'em."

"Yes," said Willie. That was all. They kept walking. She turned to HB and Fabian. "What's going on?"

"We got an intuition," said Fabian.

She glanced quickly at him.

"We felt the 'inclination,' " said HB, "to see The Gorge."

"What for?"

Leafless trees, tall and girthy, stood out as dark giants in fog. They walked among misty gravestones, newer, and older stones lying like stunted still babies between dark rootstock, roots gripping green turf like great dark claws.

"Just wanted to, I guess, who knows?" said HB. "I never been."

"When we got there," continued Fabian, "lo and behold.... You wanna say?" He turned to HB.

They kept trooping along. That soup kitchen had to open *sometime*. No breakfast but maybe some doughnuts?

"That's where the camp was. That girl—you recall the girl—done been and gone got memori-al-ized."

"Huh?"

"A plaque," squeaked Parry. And he recited its words from memory.

"Holy Cow!" said Jay, looking swiftly at HB. "Remember, I can say that—not you!" She grinned that false Jay-grin. Girl was just SO glad to be loose!

"Think anya des Anglo ghosts care?" said HB with a sweep of his hand.

Think it's true? —That's the girl?"

"It is," said Parry with distinct definition. "OK?"

"Yeah sure," said Jay. "You think?" She asked Willie.

"Yes."

"You think, yo?" Turning, she asked Fabian.

"I do."

"How did you get here? All older like that, too?"

Parry piped, "We lay down by the big rock and fell asleep with *Ochquetit*, *Ochquetschitsch*. The ledge back there." He gestured, skipping.

"That's it?" She said this to Willie as they kept walking.

But Parry answered. "We did it last year and nothing happened." Softly he murmured, looking down, "We stayed A'ndian then."

She turned back to Willie. "But how did you *turn* A'ndian? You mean you all went back in time?"

"They just took us," said Parry. "The girl did."

"We don't know that, Parry," said Willie. He went on ahead of them.

Misty air was brightening, surrounding neighborhood traffic beginning to sound. As they approached the stone wall, Fabian said, "Maybe there's something in a local history book about her." Morning traffic was gleaming beyond the wall.

Pastor woke. His eyes stared at a fitful glow across the ceiling. Traffic, much of it virtually silent (but for trucking) —traffic moved below, lights passing, adding to FivePoint's beginning morning twilight. He would talk to Gretch, DHP, and.... It would be good to see what other pastors, regional, national or international, thought about this taken girl. They will pray. He got up from the couch and stood to see what might be on the shortwave. Had he been equipped, this was one of those times he might've e-mailed one of his younger Pastor associates, got on a forum, or pyked—but he had only the landline rotary technology. He switched on the rig, the yellow panel light of the frequency meter glowing on his Kenword TS-830. He picked up the mic connected to its rig with a coil cord, listening to faint crackle on 75 meters, 3920 khz. He almost tried tuning around the band. Considering. Zettler switched it off. Standing, too clueless to do anything, really.

...Except. Yes. Start the coffee.

Meanwhile, throughout the night, Fabian's aging grandmother was on her painful knees, praying for the safe return of two children. The girl was but 11 or 12, she thought, and Fabian was not the sort to run out into the night for his adventures. She was thinking, always thinking, about the dreadful 1900, the missing boy, his miraculous strange reappearance and his own non-aging. It seemed to her she prayed the night long though she slept some, lying curled, Stoyev's *Raw Youth* clutched, then gradually loosened, at her withered breast.

She woke, lifted her head, a.m. dimness fading streetlight glimmers on their apartment walls. Candace stood uncertainly and walked about, looking around. Then she went into the kitchen to start tea. As she sat drinking tea at the table, she heard the *thud-thud* of young legs taking stairs by twos, energetically climbing to her apartment.

"Hi!" she croaked, when Fabian came in the door. "Want some? Oh, you don't drink tea."

He dusted moisture out of his minibroom 'do. "I will now!" he said. "Guess what? —you'll never." Abruptly he launched, tapping his gizzzzzzmo, "According to HB, the girl's not lost by-the-way, Cossyc's got her. Pome's getting her wish. Heirolynn's her name —oh yeah, *you* said that!"

"Are you sure you need tea?" she asked, smiling, standing. She went to hug him. Smelling earthy he accepted, embracing her.

"Sorry about last night," he said.

"Maybe she's with pastor by now?"

"Don't know—just what HB said here. He's fixing Pastor's breakfast. I left the guys at pastor's apartment steps and came up to see you."

"I'll call pastor later," she said, then paused. "Breakfast? Adventures?"

"Yeah! and a plaque!"

"Wish I had time to hurry uphill and check on archives at Harkins House. They've probably got something on this memorial, no doubt." But—the *captive girl*! Cossyc's got her.

Pastor had been talking to HB who was fixing breakfast for everybody. Willie was helping. Parry set the table. The kitchen was crowded with earthy smelling bodies. The A'ndians sat still, arms upon the table, circling their empty plates. Pastor was interested in all this talk. The one thing he didn't comment on was the Big Homeless, as they were calling the coal-cellar dweller. He listened carefully to their description. Parry and HB did the talking. Both seemed to think perhaps they'd seen him before, and, with the wildness of speculation, talked on surmise alone. Hammering out descriptions of the wildest order—or no—disorder, all tied up in 1900. Oh that 1900! What? *What?*

But HB came back to the archival pursuit. He laid food first before the pastor. He owed Pastor Zettler—keeping him wakeful, probably, and then there was that thang about the kidnapped girl. Cossyc got her in its mouth! She gwone get chewed up, spit out in pieces.

"You might not need to go up there, Pastor Z. I can do a search of that Harkins House archive, bet, on the webs. Strange name, hers, but no stranger than mine. She won't be hard to find in archives history, huh."

Pastor smiled and took a greasy forkful. "This is good," he said. "I don't usually use this much fat or oil, or whatever you used, on my eggs."

HB grinned. "Yo." Meaning, *I know, and ain't this better?*

After the meal the A'ndians left to go sleep in the graveyard. The prohibition about visitation hours had been explained to them, and about the cameras lately installed, viewing entrance and wall and exit points, but they chose to go sleep there.

"We can find a nook somewhere," said Parry, after Willie made his intention to go with them known.

"Well... take those blankets upstairs with you," said Pastor. "No wait. Knock on the door downstairs and tell them I said to give you sleeping bags. But be certain you are hidden from mourners—or they'll take prisoners." He smiled, but, having failed to convince them to sleep upstairs or in the basement, he relented. Verbally. He felt distress moving inside. Videoed climbing over walls with sleeping bags. First Heirolynn—now this. He did not want them going to the DH or other institution.

After the apartment door closed behind them, he said, "HB, go after them and convince them to sleep here."

HB looked at him, hands full of stacked plates and dirty utensils.

"They'll get in trouble. This is getting out of hand."

HB set the plates in the sink and went after them.

Pastor sat there, gazing at nothing, virtually dazed. Coffee. He stood and went to the sink. The brewmaster was on the counter. *Jayrai broke out.* He smiled and turned on the water, but, smelling it, thought better, then started to fill the sink with sudsy water. He went to the fridge for a jug from CLICK.

Jay's plan, apparently, was to use Cossyc only for maintenance on the arm—what her family were paying for. She was going back to school, two grades back. Same size as the new kids she would meet in class.

But he began to feel sorry for those teachers. What an armful! And they would worry most of all about influence on the other kids. What would he do in their place? He thought about that. It was more helpful to him than thinking about the other stuff.

... The best approach.... And kids'd be remembering Jay as big two years ago, and with the news vids, so.... Let Jay talk! That's it.

Finally—teenagers will get some real interest in history out of this.

The phone rang. He grabbed the receiver. "Glindora!"

The Showing

GleeClub WeBBlocking:

"We've found these latest headlines, including, 'Chrustyuns, for love of PresiDent, commit political slavery.'

" 'Chrustyun conservatives make millions on climate unchanged efforts.'

" 'Chrustyuns say PresiDent's racism is not racism but "devalued racism." ' "

The *GleeClub WeBBlocking* will be performing live at the Osten Magneto-Church this Sunday. Be sure to reserve your seats now. In case of hurricane the performance will be postponed."

"Claiming its services 'the greatest show on earth,' one North Regina magneto-church pastor speaks with relief of his "street-fighter of a

PresiDent," and says he wishes the Lord Chris could have been more like him.

HB was saying, "So, yeah Pomala sent me the link for Pastor to read—straight from the EHio Secretary of State website. Pastor's got some hoops but you can vote using the SoupMission as your residence for voting registration."

Darren Dargwood nodded. He had heard.

"So why don't you go with the flood on this other thing?" Darren Dargwood was asking HB in a very sober fashion. HB knew him just well enough by now to wonder. They were having a conversation. Darren was middle-aged, sorta brown, generally unshaven but never quite bearded. "I'm not with the facial hair," he had once declared. His was a good strong tenor, easily heard above the rattle of plates and knives, when he wished. Sometimes it slurred. Often he was dressed in dirty fatigues, whether from the Army-Navy or actual service—he never responded to queries on that.

Someone was in the corner crying, forehead against the plateglass. Gretchen stood there; hand on his shoulder, leaning a bit on the plateglass herself.

"What?—the transgander?"

"Of course. You don't ride the flood with choice, either. So it's religious."

The dark November sidewalk was trickling people into the SoupMission. These two were at the back of the hall, lights of Exchange Street flowing past—stopping and starting outside plateglass windows. Those big windowpanes were old, and had a grungy sheen of their own. This was the same glass Pomala and Quadri had looked through to see Gwendolyn Partum run away from her gas-lamp-lighting father; across the road through scant evening horse-and-buggy-and-horse-and-rider traffic, 119 years ago. *If you even believe in 2019.* (HB)

"Either religion or that fancy head of yours."

"My fancy head got nothing on this. Or abortion, either. Choice—get away!"

"Should I stop now or aren't you going to tell me?" His smile was rather yellow, with two holes in it.

"It's not religion." HB decided on toying with D&D.

"So pastor got you religion and they'll tell you what to think."

"Yo, who tells you what to think?" returned HB.

"Like everybody else—whoever's got the biggest hammer, the most water, the best stocks to hold my feet. And they might threaten to cut out my tongue."

HB grinned. "I'm starting to like this." He was leaning against the windowsill, gazing now across the room at the sideboard, the bar—both it was once called. He remembered that bar and the bartender from a week or two ago. Now it's the 21st century counter and HB had just filled it with the first round. —Stew, of course, big aluminum kettles, full, and piles of biscuit to dunk or submerge according to taste. They could hear banging and laughter coming from the kitchen.

"And?"

"Yo. I trust you, bro. You ain't gonna hammer me, flood me, none a dat." He glanced at Dargwood sidelong, "Maybe the tongue, though?—It's right, what I believe."

"So it's religious! How you have changed!"

"Not on dis. I's always be believin' dis."

"More." D&D dipped a spoon again into his stew, looked at him. Two biscuits were soaking it up and now the corners of his lips dribbled savory brown stew.

"I believes what is, Mr. D&D. Try changing dat."

"So, religion."

"No. I believe what's real. A person's got mens parts—they's mens. Don't use your hammer to put my tongue in your pocket. A person might believe he's a woman—men stuff hanging out—fine. He believe all he wants. Not me. I'm goin' wit *my* wits. It's what's there: Reality, not religion. I got my feelers out for that, but this ain't it. Stop trying to make me say something, believe something that ain't." The rant went on.... "Apparently people are too imaginary to go along with my self-identifying as a smart person. Don't mess wit my head, unnerstan? It's mine!"

D&D was going to say, *Except the part that's Cossyc's*, but thought—nah—he wouldn't.

HB was running: "Why should I go wit someone's imagination when the bulge is saying otherwise? Reality, Bro. Do reality. OK I overstepped me. Sorry. Your reality may vary—it just ain't real. ...You aks me, so."

D&D kept eating. Smiled even, dribbling.

HB went up through tables toward the counter—lined with people dipping or peering into kettles. Next he's be telling me he not Native Americle but Afrikan-Americle.

Can't hep da man. Don't be changing me!

Pomala and Jayrai were out shopping.

Pome had gone to Cossyc with Glindora, submitting to another examination in which she told a very wild tale of becoming wallpaper while visiting another universe—convincing her smiling big sister that she really did not want to go back to school. Dr. X felt a decided authenticity in the account: a reality that was in Pomala's own thoughts. Here X found evidence for the hypnotic cultic kidnapping of 2017, complete with false memories.

With their studies decades ago, CossycSystems initiated the trend in false memories, in all its dense analytic detail, by being first to distinguish and promote the mistaken phenomenon under the rubric of reclaimed-sublimated memories. Cossyc was not the first, however, to disclaim. They did this quietly later, after a herd of lawyers nudged them.

Heirolynn, seeming none the worse for wear, was released to Glindora following Pome's examination. Glindora promptly restored her to Candace before taking the girls down to TanCan to shop in the refurbished quadruple-decker *MammalZon Mall Museum* with a rotating rotunda in its midst. The girls had found that, since its destroying rampage, this digital giant had taken over the bricks/mortar face of the earth since 2017, resurrecting malls in kaleidoscopic ways. And at this very moment, riding with her friends in MammalZon's magnetic monorail between TanCan and Akropolis, Jay was giving a full report of her fun day at school.

"The lessons were a review of something from October, two weeks ago, so—boring. Hideous Anglish classic about an obscure man."

Gently Glindora responded, "You mean two years ago?"

"Yeah, I guess. We must be getting slower at learning."

Jay had also been speaking up in social studies, giving history lessons and asking why schools stopped teaching history since 2017. She actually heckled the teacher for the deletion of history courses.

Pomala's personal invitation to shop, extended to Jay's mother and seconded by her sister, had been declined by Nandora. "I'm quite certain Jayrai will be fine in your capable hands." Released from captivity, Nandora hid her weariness with quiet heroism, then went out with friends up to Groverland and the theater, inwardly relieved; exhilarated even.

Sitting next to wrinkled bespectacled Candace Parker and Parry in his second-hands, the girl Heirolynn was in her usual place with them near the kitchen, gazing at nothing.

Quite the specimen. The girl *Ochquetit*, had been thoroughly tested, physically examined and genetically sampled, every part tallied virtually to within a sub particle of all her atoms. Working in the kitchen with her charges, this is what Gretch said when she heard the girl was sprung from CossycSystems. "But they'll never actually know her as a human person. Fortunately they didn't have time to do anything change-making. They still need 'permission' for that." She voiced scare quotes.

One of the genetic specialists had contacted both pastor and Glindora about the possibility of using *CRIZPer11* to revise her genes. This process had been used (to improve hog genes) …for schematizing to correct and normalize the spectrum in which *Ochquetit* had her being. Great things were being done with *CRIZPer11*, which (a sensation!) swiftly and cheaply assembles RNA biologically to remake till now extinct, creatures like the woolly rhinoceros. Inwardly, pastor was shouting a large NO!, but calmly he said, "No, I don't think that would be right in this instance." Glindora's thought was that it might be good, especially given the fact of the two specialists in charge being concerned to have ongoing dialogue among church and other ethical leaders about the moral value of re-sequencing human genes. She found this generous on their part because many CossycSystems specialists' honestly confessed their atheism, as they attempted to open conversations in this inclusive way. Everything of this sort must be open to articulated, nuanced global dialogue. But, following her usual attempt to nudge a position change, Glindora yielded to pastor's wishes.

Tu came in to join the group but was not eating. He sat with 2017 and 1900 at the big round table next to that of Candace Parker and Parry. Tu would be eating at home with his parents later.

Pastor was moving around the hall, going from table to table smiling, even laughing and trading one-liners; checking on things, talking seriously about concerns of his parishioners and agreeing to counseling sessions. Simply, he was grateful. The girl was with them. Yes, she had been inspected, used for some purpose of which he was unsure, but hoped the science would prove useful and harmless. He did have his doubts about —what was harmless...? Unintended consequences.... He was doubtful.

Now Pastor stood before people who remained after eating. The SoupMission was fairly full, lights of FivePoints neighborhood moving, glimmering into the hall. At Pastor Z's request HB had dimmed the lights as the man began speaking.

"Tonight we have something special," he said, and paused.

"Why didn't you say so before others left?" Darren Dargwood was shouting from the back by the traffic-lit animated windows of Exchange. "That way they might've stayed for that *special* instead of leaving till bedtime or whatever—lunch tomorrow, maybe."

"Why do *you* think?" piped HB from the big round table not far from the kitchen door. With all the FivePoints gangs, of whatever century, they'd taken to calling it King Arthur's Roundtable at Parry's suggestion. At the suggestion of Candace, they also called it Pastor's Roundtable. Pastor's Knights have broom'do's (a couple), feathers in their hair (three), one 'do cut straight across like the old Beagles (Tu); and one a ragged chop-do (Parry). Tonight seven Knights sat alternately whispering and paying attention. Mostly the A'ndians and Willie paid strict attention. The whisperers lamented that Jay, Pome, Quadri, and Quadrangi weren't there to complete the mythic assemblage. The girls were going shopping!

Sitting at table next to them with Candace, The Girl said nothing. She had stopped crying after being abandoned to Dr. X.'s care the night before. It was thought that the white rooms and labyrinthine pale-colored passages of the campus buildings had quieted and shut down everything else within her. Dr. X. had put it so to Pomala and Glindora as she sat with them earlier, taking digital notes and recording. Now *Ochquetit* stared quietly into the atmosphere of all being and knowing. It was not known if she gained or lost anything by this. But Candace was greatly relieved on other grounds, silently and continually giving thanks for her release and presence at the table.

"You'll say because he's not like that." Darren Dargwood answered HB's question.

"He's not manipulative, you mean."

"Depends, I guess." D&D smiled a holey smile, looking around for anyone agreeing with this dubious response.

"No!" Several shouted at once.

"Can I get to it?" asked Pastor. "Like I said, it's special. People in the kitchen already know about this, and you may have seen a few new faces here tonight. Am I right?"

"Yes." "Amen." "Hear hear." A few other affirmations were shouted as well. And regulars were looking around the hall at people they'd not seen before. Tu's gaze was still on his device, scanning calculations.

"I came across some interesting history of Akropolis today. Or maybe I should say pre-Akropolis history. There wasn't a lot to go on, but Marion at the library on Exchange Street helped me discover some things I hadn't known." Pastor gestured, smiling at Marion who was at table in the hall with them. "This is a history involving both our R'opean and Native brothers and sisters in the Lord *Chris*."

All eyes in the hall turn toward Eaglestreak and Walleye-stare, who are instantly aware of attention paid them. "Remember our purpose," warns Eaglestreak in the tongue. "Her purpose. These do not know."

Parry quickly leaned over to the roundtable, whispering. No one knew of time travels (imagined or otherwise) in connection with these braves, or with Willie and Parry. Rumor was this cohort was in character and costume for some purpose yet to be revealed. Parry did not do an adequate job of translating Pastor's words. Willie leaned in to explain these words and others Pastor would say tonight.

"It's not widely understood or remembered that some Native peoples were converted by Rovmorians, a branch of Christianity from Rovmor in R'opea. This was the first widespread conversion, or virtually contiguous with that of the Unreformed Highest Church, whose largely intellectual missionaries, *Amis de Dieu*, in addition to studying the New World, also converted many tribal members in the northeast colonies. Such en masse conversion had occurred earlier in R'opea but, according to scholars,

Rovmorians converted New World Natives on an *individual* level. Aviangelicals would now call this *knowing God personally*.... Is that clear?"

Pastor smiled at the blankness in response. "The history lesson is almost over," he said. Humor in his bespectacled gaze was more evident in the low lighting throughout the hall.

D&D, in back, applauded "Here here," he said. Then, in a more subdued voice, he said, "Maybe I won't be black after all. Native-Americle is looking better now." Some who understood his humor and reference laughed, or whistled.

Pastor said, "Some of those who converted were True People natives who had migrated to PencilsWood and EHio, but many did not convert. There were raids on Rovmorians both to kidnap and kill in heated rage and jealousy over their own territory. Most Rovmorians did not shoot natives because of their faith, but some were taken captive and learned native ways. Some of these had been very young and were later to encounter Rovmorians and achieve understanding of their roots—amazingly in many cases through translators."

The common gaze shifted once again to the roundtable. Parry waved his arms and smiled. Willie leaned over to Parry's table and said something otherwise inaudible to others. Subdued, the younger boy submitted.

"Now that we have origins out-of-the-way, it's time to bring in the *special* I spoke of earlier. Marion has also led me through some fascinating highlights on the history of the praise-chant. It turns out that chanting the praises of God, in various tongues, has an amazing cross-cultural history around the globe. Many believe, and there is some evidence for this, that Chris's tradition of praise-chant began on the She-bride islands off the north Celtic Coasts of R'opea. Marion and I watched a fascinating documentary, researched and recorded by a classical musician and composer several decades ago. Since then it's been reaffirmed, with additional findings and demonstrations. Our nation is full of under-acknowledged praise-chanting, mostly rural and reservation, but also in urban churches, of black, white, and native circles. Often gatherings to praise God occur by a river bank, where they call upwards in song of God's praise and blessing. Often, but not always, this can express in dirge-like forms."

He gazed round to see if this was as engaging as he found it. But Pastor, having their attention, was convinced that soon they would feel it as he had felt it, live, this afternoon in the basement of the Church on 11 ½ St., the church that was 8 ⅓ streets up the hill.

"Tonight we have among us, as special guests, some parishioners of the 11 ½ Street Church. We will hear the chants of those whose love, faith and hope is in Chris. Chris, who is himself Love. He is Faith. And he is Hope. These qualities are in the world, as we believe, through his punishing suffering, life, death, and resurrection."

Parry with ragged hair and wearing what he called bill-hilly clothes, leaned in to say to Willie, "Or as pop used to say, Chris-Jsus."

From the back Darren Dargwood raised his voice. "But weren't these supposed to be in the world before that? Weren't faith-hope-love always in the world?"

Pastor halted. He had been moving slowly before them as he spoke, sometimes with open hands. But now he stopped. It was a pause to heighten the effect of his answer, and he intended it so. But then he turned suddenly and walked along the Sharon Road windows toward the bank of Exchange Street plateglass where Darren Dargwood, the sad sack, habitually sat. Pastor Zettler came up behind him and Darren Dargwood turned, looking up, but Pastor was already squatting—not without stress to his knees—to be on a level with Darren's ear. Looking down, his glance snagged at the anklet on Darren's ankle. Homeless are being tracked? Was he a criminal? Maybe he wouldn't be voting after all? But there was no time to think of it just then. In a low voice he said, "He was crucified, killed, and came back from the dead in order to make the cosmos... before it was made."

"A suicide then?" asked Darren, his voice also low. No one heard what they were saying. A few leaned close but did not hear.

"A self-sacrifice, Darren."

"There's a difference?"

"A big one. Let's call it a selfless sacrifice. The suicide *wants* to die, perhaps disappear, destroy the world as one author put it. Destroy all who love him or her in the process. For in doing so these would never be seen by the suicide again. A selfless sacrifice not only wants to *be*, but wants *others* to *be*. This is what created the cosmos-seeding stars and all its obediently self-propagating, fruitful, inhabitants."

"...But what was Chris doing here—a man—then?"

"He is the image of God *without* the sin, killed here to save us from our fallen nature, and our committed sins. But the cosmos had to be created before creatures could live in it. The food we've been eating tonight is God's body, broken for us. According to all this—and you know from history—we've been eating food all along before the selfless sacrifice for our sins made by Chris. This 'In the beginning' creative *hopeful* self-sacrifice—*to create us, to have us live*—is why."

"...So it's all a symbol then?"

"No. It's real."

Darren looked at him. Darren said no more.

Pastor stood and went back toward the front, but as he did so, he shouted, "LET THE PRAISE BEGIN!!!"

Instantly people—men, women and children, scattered throughout the hall—stood up. There was a pause. Then a tall black men shouted.

A mighty propulsive shout! "Sing until the power of God comes down!"

Immediately, chanting cadence with profound musicality came up in the mission building—out of the mouths of people with various ethnicity, standing about the hall.

Tu looked back and nearly jumped up, startled, intense. He saw his parents on the edges, chanting praises in a tongue he had not heard before. His mother, standing two tables behind near the wall full of kids, was smiling at him with gaze of penetrating joyful love, piercing his psyche to depths he had not felt before. He felt himself melting into the sensation completely new, and yet somehow it was paradoxically familiar. It was a swooping, felling, fleeting, sensation of Love. He felt his eyes widen, his own smile returning her Love.

But he did not cry out. For her it would have been two years worth of a cry—for this was what his parents had been doing for two years while he was gone *—to 1900.*

The chanting continued, shouting, rhythmic, a seemingly endless repetition but with, somehow, mellifluous variation. Little movement accompanied the hall-rending excitement. The verbal pattern rose and deepened, increasing, but with decorum measured and sound.

The hearers, who had come to eat and hear a talk, sat with faces turned upward as though to glimpse open heaven, revealing its stars. Their eyes saw an old-fashioned cross-patterned tin ceiling lit with dim lights, but also in glimmers passing through the streets outside. They were in the presence of …*Something*.

Pastor did not know it, but more was to come.

Meanwhile, meters above ground on the monorail gliding soundless inches above its track, Pomala and Jayrai were talking about the chanting praise-shout, and sharing it streaming with Glindora on device. At the SoupMission phones of every type were sending out these exuberant praises, sending vital images of thanks and blessings into a virtual viral world. Beaming signal towers and satellites handed off vids across the globe.

All three were dressed for shopping, crisp and aglow in suits and bowties, the two girls having forsaken their casual wear to celebrate this outing with Pome's sister. And all were excited about the praises, talking talking talking, saying things like: *If we'd known*, and *How do we miss the good stuff!!* Pome and her sister were Grak Orthos, but the relation to Chris was firm among all believers and this was a great, if different, expression of the love all felt for Chris. "I'm gonna get me some-a-dat someday," said Jay laughing.

"No!" shrieked, Pomala, amazed. "Um, haven't you got mantras and stuff, though, to chant?"

"This is different!... So okay maybe not—but sheesh!"

"Sheesh!" squealed Pomala. "Jay! That reminds me of my dream!"

"We're here, girls!" said Glindora abruptly as the monorail slowed to a silent stop under the elevated portico beside an entrance for passengers to MammalZon's Mall Museum. "Let's have a good time here together without dreams and the like. Glindora was careful to add the like instead of saying *1900 or anything related to the dismaying disappearance of the 2017 kids for two years*. It was past. They were here now. *Be here now*, she thought. *Be here now*. Let the other go. *Please just be here now.*

"Girls," she said, "we've *got* to shop!"

As they were browsing and buying from shop to shop, suddenly Pomala exclaimed, "The Christmas Pup Tent!" She turned to Jay. "Remember that? There was one in the next universe below the mezzanine!"

"Let's get pop!" said Glindora hurrying them away toward the ShopSnack.

Then she proposed visiting a shop carrying things made of goose down on the next level. And there were still rounds of touring with the digital docent, and real docents wearing costumes from the 1960s, '70s, '80s, and ongoing. Displays and shops full of sacred texts like *How to Proceed in Business Being Really Trying, Who Ate My Cheese*, and *Hood Robin.* The last being advice and adventures explicating how to steal from the poor and give to the rich. Guides taught museum goers how material worship was done in these historic now individually dated bricks-n-mortars. MammalZon to the rescue! MammalZon was reviving it all!

They headed home as merrymakers full of buoyancy and cheer, colorful bundles and glittering bags; piled in seats around them, wafting perfumes and other pleasant scents destined to enhance the decorated body and face. They were sailing in the night-glimmer of passing cities, towns and suburbs; sailing, sailing past Sassalon, Pocley, Villesmith and Lost-Nation. Darkness along the route showed forth distant, dark and dreamy—each friendly golden-lit section, passing as darkness pursued again.

"But I have to tell you all about my latest dream, Jay. And it might be good for you to think about this, Sis. I noticed you were entertained by it earlier in Dr. X.'s session, but I really think you should listen and take this seriously, if you can."

Glindora was not prepared to do this. "I'm not sure I can," she said. Lightly she smiled but there was something else in her eyes, looking into Pomala's earnest blue face. Blue. Something she could not hide. *She* had let younger sister get away with too much craziness.

Pomala was silent. She looked at Jay.

"Is this about Gneis?" Jay asked.

"It is."

Glindora looked away. She was wondering if Jay —if Jay had been having these dreams as well. Of course Glindora was also thinking of Pomala's account of what these dreams referred to... and that Jay, at least in Pome's mind, was somehow involved. Glindora's dismay was growing. If Jayrai was somehow involved in this.... *So, this might be Jay's real question.* If Gneis might be a cult leader. And—if these kids really did need to get to the bottom of this in a real way.... And Cossyc was the only help for this kind of thing. And prayer. She could ask Bishop Sirifim about this.

Acting astonishingly sensitive and mature, and being freaked herself, Jay provided just a bit of relief for everyone. She said, "Pome, it's just a dream yes, but we can talk it over later. On the q-phone maybe?"

"...Yes," said Pome. "We could."

Everyone was silent for a time. The lights of Akropolis were glowing ahead, just off their shoulders, north and eastward. Each began looking down on her device. Jay put hers to her ear. "OMN!" She whispered, nudging Pomala. "Look at this." She grabbed Pome's device, put in the co-ords, and handed it back to her. Glindora was looking at the evening news. Soon she would switch to local. She heard Pome and Jayrai whispering.

She raised her head. "Is there something?" she asked.

Here's what happened while Pomala and Jay had been shopping and snacking in the MammalZon Mall Museum.

The shout!—cadenced chanting, and strange languages of praise in the SoupMission—all these had ceased. A silence fell over the company of the poor and homeless in the hall. It was noticed that—leaving pots and dishes mostly unwashed—Gretchen and her Sheltering Cares—Trice and Hibotchi, Shylane, Pristine, and others—had slipped out of the kitchen and were silently ranged along the adjoining wall. Big Flo and Bruster with two other volunteers were also there. Candace Parker's table was visible with Parry and The Girl, and next their table was Pastor's Roundtable full of young men.

When.

In the hush that followed mighty praises filling the SoupMission like windstorms ... *Ochquetit* stood up, Fabian's grandmother started. All eyes and devices turned to *Ochquetschitsch*. Pastor looked at her—surprised. Later the girls discovered that Sheree Kim's capture was responsible for this image.

Suddenly True People braves were on their feet, whooping, bending, bowing, and leaping among the people, tables and chairs. Willie and Parry were with them. They scattered in the movement which cast nothing aside, but was flexible, energetic, and full of an enchanting alien tongue that no one recognized but the teenagers at the roundtable. Tu, Fabian, and HB recognized the language but did not understand its repetitive words echoing into the hall, crashing off its tin cruciferous ceiling.

The group from 11½ Street Church stared, then took their seats as the Natives began. All were stunned. Later, people both local and far away all over the globe, shared videos from many angles. Experts in their respective fields did fine-grained analysis, down to a pixel, of high-resolution/definition and cultural explication, finding correspondences to everything imaginable—both human and AI. Every single bit and byte was taken into account. Meanwhile HBBBAII's magnificent Cossyc-built head was engaged in analyzing all things available and quantifiable to it.

It would be some days before the event could be brought to the attention of the Americle PresiDent because he was busy witting about the "phony moon landing," and proposing Americle send a mission to the sun in 2029.

But then the front doors opened and the two Quads—tall and small—entered, their olive-brown dimpled faces aghast. They looked from the whooping braves toward the kitchen at the same moment in which Pastor Zettler, standing before the counter glanced that way. They saw the giant enter the hall from the smoking kitchen. Evidently—and it was later proved—someone had left giant pots with fat on the gas burners. On high heat. By mistake. It was determined by witnesses and the Akropolis Fire Marshal's office that one of the kids (unnamed because under-age) must have accidentally turned the burners up high instead of off.

Smoke pouring forth, all eyes were on the giant standing booming out the code words of the Apokalup (rightly called *"The Unveiling!"*)

Smoke and Giant coming, Pastor fell back among tables and chairs with a clatter.

"Er," said Pomala in answer to Glindora's what's-up question as they glided through the night.

"Just something more at the SoupMission," said Jay with a quiver. "It must be old news by now, anyway. It's not happening at the moment."

They sailed on together. The lights of Sharon surrounded them. "Time to gather up, girls," said Glindora. She had not made it to local news yet. To Pomala she said lightly, "We've got miles to go before we sleep!" Glindora had parked at the monorail station and there was the disembarking and carloading still to do, plus dropping Jay off with her bags and packages.

"So, before coming to 2019, that's how we got back to 1900 CE from 1900 EE." Pomala said this to Jayrai on the phone. There was a long pause.

Then softly Jay said: "*Oh my Newfish oh my Newfish oh my Newfish.*" Silence.

Pomala said, "So... you've been quiet this whole time I'm telling you.... Do you remember any of it? You do remember the alternate universe—the universe next door, Tu called it."

"Tu said that?"

"When we were there, yeah."

Jay said, "And he hasn't said anything since then?"

"No. —But the prophet man at the SoupMission. Wasn't he like—?

"The 1900 Game Master," surmised Jay. "At least that's what HB says. He also calls him Grandmaster."

2017 thought it might be the Game Master. Only HB was positive. The others had their doubts but read (carefully) all HB had to say about his lone adventure in 1900 CE. He said his head analysis agreed—it was Game Master. Also he called him Showmaster and Big Fello.

Then HB said he had confirmation from the braves, including Willie and Parry. Only they called him by the name of Grandmaster. (They were sitting in the apartment with him, before going out again.)

The girls could not stay on-topic. As a result, their conversation was confused as each kept going back and forth between the dream, the universe next door, the chanting *and prophecy* in the SoupMission. And all the while they watched the videos from every angle captured on soup-mission crowd-sharing devices; Jay watching on her gizzzzzmo, Pome on babblet. And simultaneously they were texting Fabian and HB. Then Jay said they should include Quadrangi and Tu in the messaging because they had been there too. Just entering, Quadrangi and Quadri stood at the open door, mouths agape, eyes wide as the Game Master began to speak.

The end of the Game Master's message was seen as a capture in which the GM stood Dark and Broad at the front of the hall between soup counter and the crowd.

The Prophet was a massive man, rotund, immovable by any creature, man, or force but Himself. If one tried to take him by the arm they would feel it as Michelangelico's *DAVID* —scarcely moveable. He could lift a 1900 CE draft horse and throw it shrieking across the boulevard. His arms were as the limbs of a 300-year-old oak, his thighs like trunks of thousand-year-old cedars. His hands, balled in fists ere he began speaking, were like those of heavyweight champion Mohhammmed Eli in shining leather boxing gloves. He seemed a gigantic workman wearing filthy clothes—clothes that had been washed in carbon coke. You couldn't say what color he was. He was covered in coal soot.

His booming voice was mellow, deep and rich, yet compassing every timbre for the unveiling he gave forth. Even though they'd not seen him tip to toe covered in anthracite dust before, the A'ndians and 1900 CE could not mistake him. And like everybody, they stared at him.

Those eyes. No one could look away. They did not want to. They might, at the moment, wish ever after to see those white-flaming eyes and hear that majestic, deep, word-magnifying voice till the end of their days. For, as he sounded, *they forgot themselves*. Memory, however, was another thing: after he finished they would be filled with panicking dread for its memory echoing. This is the difference between memory and experience. The former, mentally digesting, is felt in the gut. The latter, embodied experience—gone forever.

Smoke poured out the open kitchen door with a smell of pots-and-grease scorching, but everyone had eyes and ears for him only.

He spoke to them. The hall was mesmerized, silent but for that speaking.

No one *thought* to record this grand happening in their midst. A few devices had been propped on tables as the earlier chanting ensued. Instead people partook whole, embodied, forgetful of babblets, gizzzzzzzmos, z-pads, q-phones and the like. What these devices took in was the full enactment of this great man, this magnificent being come from underground, from the coal seams, mines deep in the earth. His speaking, looks, movements, and disappearance all were recorded. But the giant did not, as this account suggests, vanish into invisibility. He simply went back into greasy black smoke billowing out of the kitchen. The audience began to cough and wretch. Then the fire alarm upstairs in pastor's apartment sounded, shrieking, repetitive, but the giant had already gone.

Slowly, in pain scarcely realized, pastor picked himself up out of the wreck of chairs he'd fallen into. After the great man's departure shouts and screams and chaos followed amid billowing blue-black smoke. Remotely—preternaturally—amid this chaos, pastor thought he heard a distant scraping, scraping, *scraping* of something moving across rock or pavement somewhere below. Later he thought that was wrong. The scraping had been outside the building, in the alleyway behind the smoking kitchen. But for now he was on his feet before the soup counter, trying to dampen these screams and shouts up-wailing beneath the sounding alarm—trying with mere hands, and mouthing of words scarcely heard. And people were pushing and running out the Sharon Road doors. Quad and Quadrangi were well ahead of them, running around the corner onto Exchange.

"HB says it's Grandmaster," whispered Pomala into the phone. "Did you see pastor tottering up, rubbing his elbows? He's an old guy."

"An old man," said Jayrai.

"Yo, Tu. I'm not going back to Cossyc for this or anything. It's projected on the wall and captured in the device. Take all this data and do something with it."

"Send it over. I've got the computer."

The two were talking—on phones. Something that almost never happened between HB and Tu.

"Okay," said Tu from his closet. He had already found the Mr. Mathematical Physicist and was busily inserting everything gleaned on the experience into the appe. He was starting on stuff found on the web.

Stationed on the couch in the apartment above the SoupMission, as braves were coming and going, HB thought, *There's just so much—too much—there*. Responses will have to be rerecorded, digitized and schematized with all the viral videos, then analyzed by an expert like Tu (as HB thought him); algorithmically harmonized, justified, bulleted, teased, crimped, stitched, soldered and sent to the space station in geosynchronous orbit around Mars where this sort of thing has its best chance for filtration of contaminants (no tweaking allowed.) *But Tu was his man!*

"I'm partic-lary interested in the GM's prophecy. Let me know if there's anything at all familiar about it. White Thang seems to think there is. I got my doubts. But let me know. I'll hang loose and let you get to work. And thanks, bro."

"No prob, girl," said Tu.

Tu?

"It sounds like what happened in HiTopOLis 1900 EE," Pomala was saying to him over the phone. [Reader, See more on this adventure in *SiXPointz HiTopOlis*.]

"Almost as if the giant workman or coal deliveryman or whatever he was had leaped across the giant chasm you mentioned between universes to tell us this."

"A centimeter," said Tu. "There's only the slightest distance between our universe and the next. Scarcely a breath. And there's one on the other side, too."

"Oh yeah. But do you remember HiTopOLis?"

"No. What is it?"

"Hmmm. Gneis said he was giving you dreams."

"Who's Gneis?"

"He's the dream-maker from the next universe."

"I must caution you that the multiverse is only a theory. But, really? I mean—there is one? An actual next universe, according to him? Dreams are too iffy, Pomala."

"Gneis says yes. And, well, I actually sorta remember it. We were there between 1900 CE and 2019 CE. I don't know exactly how that happened of course."

"No one would," said Tu. "They don't even know what energy is. Or gravity. Two very common entities. They don't know what time is or—

"Or potatoes once they get done being potatoes?" She was thinking of poop to calm herself.

"Well they've got the next stages for that figured down to a certain level. Maybe subatomic, but not sub subatomic. And techniques for measuring may cause break-up—smaller molecules harder to identify accurately because transmutation. And—they can't measure stuff we don't know what it is. And for instance, what does dematerialize mean? You can observe, measure, record (with changes), but what, I mean, is it? Where is it? Where does everyone, everything, go—except back to where it came from—wherever that is?"

"Yee-es. I think I see-ee what you mean…."

"But —I think I have had some pretty dense dreams, since we got back from 1900 a week or two ago."

"Dense?" Pomala wondered…. "Dense?"

"So yes. Some amazing information in these dreams. The kind of stuff any physicist, theoretical *or* experimental, would dream of encountering. That was a pun by the way."

"I knew that." Her voice was smiling. "They are from Gneis. I'm sure of it. He seems now to be interested in the *Hadesthon* and coordinates because Dah has no experimental hardware."

"Who *is* Gneis? How does he know such exquisite fresh-seeming formulas—and hardware?... I think I dreamed of a lab, amazing lab—heavy-duty. But mostly it was Maths of the richest densest, well, capture you can imagine. So who is he?"

"He's the son—or he was the son of—or maybe he still is the son of a physicist in HiTopOLis. SiXPointz HiTopOLis was supposed to be our neighboring neighborhood, so to speak. His lab was underground in order to to to..."

"In order to avoid interfering cosmic particles," said Tu.

"And guess what?"

"We interfered?"

"Exactly. That is, we just turned up there. We spent most of our time trying to get through to him so he could get us to go back. To our universe. We kind of blamed him for bringing us there."

"This is starting—starting to seem somewhat—sorta minuscule perhaps—familiar. Were there games, for instance? Games with kids? Say we were something. Dark matter. WIMPs, even."

"And they were MACHOs and RAMBOs and we actually helped the MACHOs make, or, that is, almost make BABY."

"Baby?" said Tu, just a bit embarrassed. Forgetting the potatoes he said, "Dark matter has something to do with making babies? This is quite...."

"Ha! Yes but it was a game. You played to bring the cosmos into being. It was so much fun! And Gneis played it with us. He was alive then."

"Was he in—some kind of wheelchair?"

"They called it an *eelie*, I think. You guys didn't really get their language, iirc. But I did somewhat. I think I kept getting better at it. And then there was wallpaper. I helped Jay with that."

"Wallpaper," said Tu, considering.

"It was made out of book pages. You spent a lot of time with the physicist, Dah. He was always slumped on the couch with computers."

A pause.

"Yes."

"So now all we got to do is figure out how to get Pastor and the SoupMission people to go make a hideout in the country. Some place to grow food and make huts and stuff," said Pomala. She was talking to Fabian over the phone, and simultaneously texting HB, Jay, Tu, Quadrangi, and Trice about various aspects.

Fabian said, "If I remember right, you were always getting into trouble trying to fix things, Pome. You better let Pastor handle this. You know?"

"But—"

"It seems the prophecy came to Pastor's mission and now we got to let it do its work. This is how things work. It's in the holier scripts. Religion knows all about how these things work. It takes bucket-loads of prayer and not eating and community prayer and not eating and all that."

"But—"

"Besides —we got to get back to 2017. See that text by HB? Look at that now."

"But—"

"Look, Pome."

A pause.

"So, Pastor does have all kinda rural connections and people and stuff," she said.

"And, *it's his job*."

"I wonder what the Bishop thinks?"

"That's a different denomination, but it might be interesting to know. However. This is way more important. —Who knows? …2017...." He said this thoughtfully. Like he was trying to understand. He looked over at the door to his grandmother's room. She was in there with the girl. It seemed to be dark in there. He turned off the light on the end-table to check. Yup, dark under the door. He began to whisper. "I don't know why but it just feels like that's what we should do."

"Look at Jay's message," said Pome.

Pause.

"I think not," said Fabian.

"You want to tell her?"

"Okay." Fabian texted Jayrai. There was an apparent back and forth.

"Now what's she say?"

"Look at that linkage."

Jay's message: *I told her -- and you won't believe -- politely -- NO. I told Ms. Kim we were busy getting back to 2017 and I didn't like being two years younger at school.*

"Oh-no," said Fabian to Pomala. "Wish she hadn't done that. Besides, Ms. Kim thinks it's all coSplay—all of it. Even Game Master."

Then they both saw what HB was saying to Jay about Sheree Kim's request for an interview.

HB's message: He/she's got like 50 people he/she can interview about the prophecy and all that viral stuff. She doesn't need us. So good excuse.

Fabian's message to everyone: but we need to keep the 2017 thing lying low. We *don't* want her nosing.

HB: Too much else going on at the moment. Kim Kim will cool on 2017, don't worry.

Then HB again: So what do you think now, Quad?

Quadrangi, as always, was reluctant to weigh in. His main concern was protecting his little brother, but the whole creep-factor....

Quad: I think hand-wavy. And what about the braves and --

He could not say "*the girl.*"

Holing up in her darkened shared dorm-cubicle at Sheltering Cares, Trice was just reading it all, not commenting. Gentle snoring surrounded their cots on the spacious partitioned floor but there were some tiny lights, like her own, aglow.

Sounds were similar in the SoupMission basement. Perhaps more explosive, here and there.

Pastor was out in the glow of the alleyway between the Third St. Complex and the backside of Sharon Rd. businesses; moving slowly past metal shelves where people left donations of canned goods.

These had been overturned earlier in the evening, cans rolling every-which-way when the Fire Department came stumbling in to quench the fire. This had proved unnecessary—both, overturned shelves and fire hose—because Gretchen had battled coughing fits and smoke to subdue the burner and quell hot metal pots in the slimy sudsy sink. The hose had not been used, for which everyone was grateful. Sheltering Cares kids had righted the shelves and brought in the canned goods.

Now it was late. All was quiet, save the hearts in the SoupMission, trying to sleep. The neighborhood psyche of FivePoints was disturbed all the way to the top of the apartment and condo complex, the gentrified houses along Sharon Road and environs. Some specialists at Cossyc were busily analyzing facets, categorizing, tabulating and musing, notably Dr. Rostof. And Dr. Neee, who at the moment was in one of the lounges reading copies of ancient texts borrowed from the Cossyc library.

Creeping past the metal shelves, Pastor saw the closed hatch framed between dark, hewn sandstone blocks. He stopped and looked away.

He must be in there.

Pastor Zettler stood awhile. It was chilly, he shivered.

Perhaps not.

He looked toward the old hatch, made of thick planks, darkened by years. He was almost wishing for one of those cigarettes of his misspent youth. That misspent youth during which school children had to kneel beside their lockers, heads bent and necks covered in case of nuclear attack. Akropolis, they said was number 5 on the bombing list— for being the rubber capital of the world. And Groverland was number 3 for being the steel capital of the world. Before rust transitioned Northeast Ehio. And medicine and artificial intelligence caught hold in these towns.

He looked up the alleyway where it began climbing behind shops lining the south side of Sharon Road. On the left-hand glowed rising condos and apartments beyond alley maintenance buildings. He stood against the wall, staring.

Then he heard steps behind and turned to look past the empty shelves. Through metal slats he saw a petite woman in pantsuit moving toward him. He stepped out.

"Another night-meeting for us, Pastor," said Sheree Kim. She came up to him, her gaze level. "Two in a row."

"Hello, Sheree." He said nothing more. She kept looking level. He returned her gaze. Silent.

"Pastor, would you mind telling me what's going on? What *was* all that?" Her voice was as petite as herself, yet serious and firm. She gestured toward the alleyway kitchen door.

Pastor smiled, a very slight smile.

"You were not there?"

"I did not miss it.... Quite a story."

Still again; he said nothing.

"And we have videos, of course."

"So you know then. I suppose you know all." Light from a streetlamp next the maintenance building gleamed off his glasses. She shifted her stance slightly.

"But you know I do not. The girl, the girl standing, for instance. That, that large, that large—filthy man.... Something crazy. I'm sorry—do I dis-respect. Is this disrespecting something you believe in? Or is it merely acting, players, coSplay? With special affects."

Pastor gazed at her perfect Osiian eyes, so serious. Serious about her work.

"You have it, Sheree. What you saw then, what you see in the videos is what it is." He thought a moment. "Unless someone manipulated those images in some way."

"They seem of apiece. You won't interpret for me?"

"It needs no interpretation." On second thought, he said, "You might look up interpretations of the various languages chanted—by the A'ndians and others chanting before them."

"I will but. But it's all crazy."

He said nothing.

"Look. Is it coSplay? I'm coming to you. Straight to you, Pastor. You are the—how do they say? —the horse's mouth."

He smiled. Not slightly but reflexively with humor, showing his line-perfect teeth.

Despite herself she laughed.

"Sht," she said.

With a nod and a smile she acknowledged, "You've got me back." Curiously she looked past him up the alleyway. Then turned and headed back toward the intersection.

When all was quiet, deserted, and he felt sure: he knelt at the hatch. The pavement was hard. Hard on the bony almost fleshless knees. On those knees, he murmured a prayer. Once, he thought, the hatch had been bolted on the outside. He was not sure when or if it had been locked from the inside. He gave a gentle push.

Fast and hard.

He looked at the giant iron hinges—three of them.

Pastor slacked onto his bony rump. *Ouch.* He leaned against the hewn stone foundation below the wooden clapboard wall of the SoupMission. If folks in the other cellar were sleeping—*could they be sleeping after this?* —If, when, they weren't there, say tomorrow, he could approach the coal cellar through the basement. That heavy door had padlock and hasp. He had the key for that somewhere in his study. He tried to visualize where. Maybe the drawer with the oddments, including seldom-used keys.

He let his legs sprawl and leaned against the hatch. Gave a gentle knock. Soft. Tentative.

A bolt began scraping against sandstone. Pastor sat up. The frame mostly outside, its hatch lowering. The giant now showed the whites of his eyes in broad blackened face, looking at Pastor. He smiled, an innocent smile like a baby's. The giant's teeth showed a bit. His eyes a'glimmer, eyebrows rising in delight, he seemed glad to see Pastor.

Taken aback, Zettler said, "May I come in?"

"Of course, Pastor. This is your house." The giant disappeared from the big rectangular hole, and Pastor saw faint glowing from inside.

He looked down, expecting the ladder. Below the hanging hatch door an old ladder made of rough-cut 2 x 4's descended a short distance to the compacted floor. Prone now, Pastor backed in, his feet feeling for rungs.

One could not easily describe the encounter, point by point, as though detailing steps taken to arrive in such a situation. First, there are social difficulties to express. After the initial surprise of invitation, Pastor was troubled, fearful of a glib approach.

While acknowledging that the building was someone else's house, the giant did not apologize for his presence there, or for eating the homeless food. Did not thank Pastor for anything. Pastor did think of this in passing as he sat absently in the sagging cot, the giant cross-legged on the floor beside him.

One thing—touched on vehemently in Pastor's heart—was the presence, the purpose of his presence here at the SoupMission. With difficulty he ventured... then stopped. He tried again. And stopped. Then, with anguish, Pastor said, "Why here? Why here with us who, who believe deeply such truths? Is a homeless man a, a, prophet? Have I mistaken? —Everything?"

There was no immediate verbal response. Amid the sooty tracery of scars in his features, the giant gazed at him tenderly.

"Oh!" said Pastor. "I *don't understand*! Why did you not say these things to, to, to —well CossycSystems, for instance? Why not to them? They need this so badly—this uncovering. Why not to *them*?"

The answering voice was deep, rich, mellifluous and mature. "I might have. I might have done. But I could not live there. I could not even get in. There were one or two who might have heard me. I do know Dr. Neee knows me, and he will see and hear of it. But I was not invited there. Here, homeless, I was invited. So here I must be heard."

Pastor had been gazing at the floor before him, listening. He wanted to take him in with his eyes but could not. Steady candleglow suffused the darkness. He saw the hatch was open when he glanced up from his seat on the cot. The alley glow also came in, softer.

"Invited?" he said. "Did Flo invite you? Was it Bruster, perhaps?

"You did."

"Me? You mean the need did? The homelessness?"

"You did." The giant held out his great hand. Pastor reached for it, a big scarred and calloused hand. He felt the rough calluses, the sudden frailty of his own smaller hand.

"You've worked hard in your life," said Zettler.

"I have."

There was silence, Philip Von Zettler gazing into his eyes. Irises large and dark and surrounded by white vitreous—as all human eyes are when healthy. Pastor began to notice the giant's eyes as though seeing eyes for the first time. He almost felt he knew how these eyes were put together. He seemed to be seeing the material intricacies of the mechanism of sight. Past the ganglion and down into molecules where the sparking photons signaled... signaling all the way through toward the visual cortex at the back of the brain. In so seeing—frightened—he marveled at the visual acuity of his own eyes in this sudden and exquisite unveiling. Then he was seeing the light of the giant's serious gaze. He'd never seen such light in such seriousness—only in fleeting joy or mirth.

"We will have to leave?" said Pastor Zettler.

"It is best if you do," said this dark giant covered in coal soot, grubby in flickering flame-light.

"Will you leave with us?"

"In a manner of speaking."

"You won't come with us?"

"I will be there... in another... I won't say form."

"But you will leave the SoupMission?... but only in this form?"

"Yes, tonight if you like."

Thinking of Sheree, Pastor said, "I don't know. Maybe. Maybe." He tried to think of everything. He could not get through everything, gazing at the floor. *Still he will need shelter!* He heard a noise and came out of himself.

The giant was already nearly whole-form out the opening above them. Then he was gone.

Pastor scrambled and climbed up the ladder. He looked out, saw the great man ebbing in distance, hurrying lightly, without a sound, up *up* Harkins Hill toward the intersecting road where Candace Parker had her apartment. As though moving to join Sharon Road near the historic martyr's house; and maybe beyond. *How lightly he went! How swift!*

At once Pastor climbed out on unsteady legs. That was the way they had to go, westward, but perhaps slightly south too, and maybe into CaShatan. His knees paining him, he ran after. Footfalls clapping the asphalt. Came a thought to speak of this on the short wave pastor's net. He ran up past the dry cleaners' rear door. The giant was gone and he'd never catch him. Never catch him. Never.

—*But*. But what would he do with him if he did?

Wrestle him to the ground? My knees are already bad. My back.

He began laughing.

He laughed with much humor, such delight!

Pastor was leaning against the side of the building by a stoop below the door of their FivePoints cleaners. Peripherally he noticed a light on inside.

Still laughing, breathless, he looked back down the alley and saw what he thought, in the distance, was a small figure of someone standing, then disappearing from the intersection with 3rd St.. Sheree?

The back door of the dry cleaners opened, cautiously. Bespectacled Mr. Yu peered out.

"That is you, Pastor Zettler."

"Oh. Yes. Mr. Yu, it's me." He was breathing heavily.

"Shall you come in?"

Pastor hesitated, surprised. He was surprised all over this night. "Why, yes. Certainly."

He stepped in and shook hands with Mr. Yu amid the great now silent drums of dry cleaning equipment. Overhead cables and lines hanging down toward ironing boards were lit by a single flickering fluorescence, pale overhead. Mr. Yu moved to close the door behind him and Zettler saw the LED timeclock beside it, where workers clocked their hours. All was quiet and still inside. This workspace was curtained off with snaking lines of bagged clothing and other cloth items, so that one could not see the front entrance and counter with cash register, card reader, and clothing collection stations where clerks would stand attaching numbers, scanning, and writing out slips. Pastor had been through the street entrance many times in his adult life but had never been back here before. The large room smelled of chemicals, cleaners and fresheners, artificial scents distinguishable from those of nature they imitated. Mr. Yu led him around through the clothing curtain to the front.

"Will you sit here?" asked Mr. Yu, indicating what must have been his place at the desk.

Mr. Yu pulled out a metal folding chair used by workers when resting, and sat across from Pastor. Pastor leaned on his forearms, hands clasped on the desk.

Then there was silence.

Out the large windows shone street lights of Sharon Road, but the interior light at the back had been shut off by this manager when they came forward.

"That was prophecy? You would say, formally? For true believers, Pastor?" Mr. Yu had not hesitated to broach the subject immediately.

"Yes. I now believe it was. Well, its fulfillment *only* will *prove* it prophetic."

"Yes. I understand. …Pastor, that is not why I asked you to come. To speak with me."

"No?"

Prophecy as an icebreaker?

"I wanted to ask you for counseling." Mr. Yu looked at him. "It is as though you were brought to my door."

About to agree to counseling, Pastor was surprised yet again.

"I was praying when I heard something. I looked out and there you were."

"Yes," said Pastor. "Response can be quick sometimes.... And you thought this encounter might be one, or part of one?"

"Yes."

Then Mr. Yu was silent. His look behind glasses was blank.

Pastor hesitated. Then ventured. "Was Tu surprised to see you and Mrs. Yu there tonight?"

"This is why I ask to speak with you."

Upfront, outside the plateglass, slow lights of a police cruiser went past beneath the glow of Sharon Road. Beyond, Cossyc campus buildings were visible from where Pastor sat at the managerial desk on the employee side of the collection counter. But he was looking at Mr. Yu and thinking of this problem.

"Tu has —no idea what you believe?"

"No. He does not... I think."

"May... May I know just a bit of your background and how you and Mrs. Yu came to believe?"

Meanwhile, Sheree Kim was on her way back to her own desk in the condominium shared with her partnering other. sWeetC would probably be working in the next room. Sheree Kim was not quite sure what the capture (or its quality) would be. She was certain it had a conversation to do with the event. She kept walking. To her device she said, "Buloxi, this recording is not for the Fog. …And, Buloxi, turn on the dishwasher. Buloxi, vac the floor! …And, *Buloxi*! No, I'm not sharing my feelings with you, you id!"

Not the first time Sheree had had to make decisions on the fly—on impulse she admitted—and then decide rationally, or even on the basis of conscience, what to do with it. She had one, she knew—. A conscience.

Hers was somehow embodied in the profession. And most of her colleagues went with what was right for their investigative careers. Better, she thought—what is right for true journalism, the profession. We are supposed to shine lights. Bring evil into the open. If it splashed wide, so much the better for them. For the first criteria, their careers. Why she did this to herself, this professional wrestling, she did not know. She hated introspection but was stuck with it. And conscience. Impulse coupled with story meets conscience—blah.

It was an old coal cellar someone had said. Some had said it was an old blue light distillery from early 20th-century public policy abstinence. Alcohol was illegal then. Sheree snorted inwardly. Would that have been something to report on? She kept walking up into the complex. Resisting the urge to put the device to her ear. *It's not like this pastor's the mayor—accountable to the citizenry.*

Or was it already too late for the conscience? —She had not yet listened, nor uploaded to the Fog. Oh please please don't think about *that*! Can I just listen first *then* decide? Thing was—she had not got a word of the coal-celler conversation with her living ears. Just murmurs, tonal qualities as she stood upright outside the hatch while a device more audibly receptive lay the pavement recording for her. Now what? What? Maybe that was good? Still time to decide. Oh god what am I doing in this profession? But I love it—don't take that away.

Was that the dry cleaners up there? Did the preacher go inside?

Where Did They Go?

"Mr. PresiDent, some people say you're a little kid disguised as an old fat man with yellow hair. What do you say to charges like this? Or that the FaMia brings prostitutes to the Gray House? How do you respond when they charge you with riding around in a wheelchair, smoking a cigarette with a long holder, having an affair? What do you think when the crowd cries, 'Burn this letter!' and 'Ma, Ma, where my Pa?' Mr. PresiDent, they want to know why you are always verbally punching down? If you are the most powerful man on earth, they say, you've got no right to punch at all. That the only one higher than you is God."

The PresiDent stopped a moment. He stared at Baunders. "It's all part of being PresiDent.... A lack of respect often goes with being PresiDent. I could die of ptomaine poisoning at any moment. And, before you ask,

Burni, I am not a crook! Also, I said it in the 80's, and I'll say it now, Make Americle great again!"

Did you notice that Tu's parents seemed to believe in Big Fello's religion? HB was e-mailing this morning. Fabian, Quadrangi, Jay, Pome, Tu —anybody. But this one went to Fabian only.

Yes, responded Fabe. Do you think we should ask him about that?

IDK. (HB)

Me neither. (Fabian)

"A couple things," said Pastor coming into the living room from the kitchen. He was wiping his hands on a towel.

"You said it wasn't my KP today," HB reminded him. *Uh-oh.* HB grinned. "Pastor," he said.

"Not that.... Maybe we could talk about the braves." He sat in the old Morris chair across from the couch, his back to the Sharon Road windows. "We haven't seen them this morning, for one thing—as you mentioned after starting the eggs. Speculations yes—but now what?"

"You said couple things."

"Yes. School or Cossyc?"

"Pastor-counseling. I need me some. Got any a-dat for me?"

"So you aren't going. No one is going, and still the order is out: go to school." *Or risk truancy—is that still something*?

"Pomala went to Cossyc and Jayrai went to school. None a dis will keep us from 2017 —if Tu can help it."

"But why 2017? Why do you …want to go back?" Pastor took courage.

"It was two weeks ago, not years. This 2019 ain't real. It's not real life."

Pastor stared at him.

Then changed the subject.

"I'm concerned they may find a way to move you out of here. We don't want that?"

"No way!!"

"Well, school?"

HB sighed and slouched further into the couch.

"You said it will make no difference to your plans." (Pastor was not going to think of these plans—absolutely not—and there was the OTHER THING.)

"Let me pass this um request by them."

Pastor repressed his own sigh. He stood. "Okay, I'll be in there. But I'll be back out, too. And we have work to do downstairs."

HB assembled all the addresses and sent out his missive. Copies to everybody.

Jay: in my experience -- gonna take us further out of the 2017 pipeline, headwise, socially, all that.

HB: Out of the pipeline?

Jay: yep. you start to get involved in class. right now? your gone.

HB: Don't you mean you're gone?

Jay: what ev. oops.

HB: Jay?

Jay was gone.

HB: Tu?

Tu: I'm working on it. I had another one of Pomala's dreams last night -- this morning actually.

HB: You get Pomala's dreams?

Tu: From her alt universe. It's a manner of speaking. Lots of good theory and calculus! You see I am carried away.

HB: We ARE NOT going to ask you to tell us about this. Just carry our ass back to 2017, K?

HB: Quadrangi?

Quadrangi: I'm in school, HB. So is Quadri. Bye.

Fabian, to everyone but Quadrangi: Suggest we stop talking 2017 to non-2017. The fam doesn't like it, friends don't like it, Quadrangi doesn't want to talk about it, wants to save Quadri from it, etc.. Saying though, I think the braves maybe helped convince Pastor 1900 CE, at least, is real. Maybe.

HB: But he still doesn't like it.

Pome: Trice seems kinda open to hearing about it but doesn't want to be —2017.

Pastor came out, again wiping his hands. Absently, HB thought, looking a question at him. Pastor seemed not to see the question, though he was gazing directly at HB. In the distance came gonging from St. Invincible's tower, and remote sounding of machinery from somewhere beyond the neighborhood. Was he listening to that? Pastor Z was not seeing him. Then he was.

"HB?" he said.

"Uh." said HB. "So we haven't quite got there yet."

"But what about *you*? This is about you, not them."

"Okay, I guess I can go. To school. Tomorrow?"

"Okay, tomorrow it is."

Pastor went back into the kitchen, thinking, *This is good, actually.*

It meant HB would not have to be considered at the moment (meaning tomorrow). Pastor had to get *down* and *pray*! All day! He hung up the towel beside the refrigerator and looked at the cupboard doors with paper-towel roll hanging above the sink. He did not see these things.

Tomorrow he wanted to have a private breakfast meeting with the adult volunteers, if possible. Most would want to do this on Spyke but that was not the way. Plus. *HE* had no way to do that. *Better get used to it now*. He was mentally addressing the volunteers.

What about the braves?

He stepped back to the door and stuck his head out. "Anybody seen the braves?" 1900 CE had not been accounted for since sometime last night, he thought.

HB was reading his gizzz, shaking his head.

Pastor went back, then came out to go into his study. Maybe he should call Candace.

"Uh oh," he heard HB say. "Pastor!"

"What?"

"The girl."

"What?"

"She gone, again."

"What?!"

"Gone. Fabe's grandma thought she was with him. He's on the wall across from the library. She's not. With him."

The phone rang. Pastor picked it up. It was Candace Parker.

FivePoints 2017 would be out searching the neighborhood for 1900 CE and the braves. *The girl*. Even Tu and Jay were there, Jay skipping right out of school—stealth mode. Tu, with the others, had been putting off the whole school/Cossyc thing, though he was leaning toward going back to Cossyc—but not to escape school. He thought it would be more interesting at the Systems' campus versus junior high. He remembered quite well where he'd left off the other week, also: algebra, English classics, history, geography—gym. So maybe it *was* an escape. But Jay had said history was history. So no problem there.

They conferred amid a remote background roaring of machinery. So: *spread out!* Meet back here at—whenever—soon. Ferret out the complex, the alleyway, up Third back of the po-leese part way up Exchange the other way, keep clear of the school on Bechtel! Go!

"But how 'bout the Gorge? asked the Jay—itching to see it.

"Holding us up," said HB.

"I don't think so, Jay," said Fabian. "We were just there with them night before last. Doesn't seem likely."

"But maybe the girl will want to see her memorial."

"I *really* don't think so," he answered.

They were back at the stone wall in half an hour, ready to report. It was a huge info dump on neighborhood doings—including an unfortunate inquiry at the FivePoints police.

"How was I to know?" protested Jay.

"Girl, you just too showin'-off!" said HB. "Of course they want all the goods on that story, stuff about the girl being gone. You didn't tell them they were 1900 CE or whatever, did you?"

"Not that dumb." She flipped back her streaky hair and glowered at him.

Pomala's white hair was draped like a cape of purity over her jacketed shoulders. Her breast pocket bulged with phone and z-pod, she was wearing her wool blazer. "Of course she didn't, you wouldn't." It was lightly said, soothing oil on these tempestuous waters. "Seems someone accidentally turned the summer cemetery music on!"

"Machinery's been going all morning?" Tu was speculating. He had been first on the scene at the wall after Fabian. "Perhaps the braves are back there watching things happen."

"Yeah, they like machinery; what's going back there?" HB cocked his broom 'do, staring off into the cemetery past trunks and naked stems. "Sounds like they're digging 300 graves at once."

"I think that's the next place to search anyway," said Fabian. "We should've started there."

A sudden silence.

Boom boom boom!

Then silence again.

HB had already turned and hopped down over the old stones. He was running toward the renewing sounds.

"They've been working since I got here, early this morning!" Fabian snapped shut on the phone message he'd been reading—another of his grandmother's. He jumped down and started after HB. The others were on it, too.

"Jay," I'm telling you!" HB flung this over his shoulder. "Watch out for that sneaky Sheree Kim." Jay came alongside.

"So?" she said.

"Pastor mentioned she followed him last night. She doesn't believe in the whole prophecy thing and wants to dig dirt—so watch out."

They were hurrying among gravestones, scattered in a loose group. Above them, remote on the left, the crenulated school building loomed large, and beyond that the tower and slate-roofed nave of the massive church—all visible through twining great dark limbs of oaks, elms, and maples. The kids below, glancing every-which-way, splitting up now and then to look behind newer mausoleums, and then the older more ornate; rejoining the party on the path leading them inevitably down along the stream toward the Civil War monument. The roaring drowned out dulcet elegiac mellifluous tones of music piped across the manicured grounds of this giant-tree-pillared GlimmerDale Cemetery. Then they smelled the fumes, saw the gigantic boisterous screeching machinery. Deafening. Three big yellow machines, plus piston hammers. Various kinds of deconstructive industry in progress. Beyond, a massive yellow dump truck trundled up a lane from the direction of Market Avenue.

"OMN!" Jay was screaming. "What are they doing!?"

No one knew really, least of all Jay. Then one of them did.

Pomala, she who quietly received the message from Glindora. This, she was sure, was the great stone, the old mossy ledge which Fabian, Tu, and HB—which the braves and 1900 CE found so important to all this business of 2019 not being 2017. She alone knew what was happening—and why.

Now, as they raced down into the streamlet's vale, all saw an emptiness left in the wake of energetic dismantling of circa 1769 braves' time-traveling rock. Around that emptiness moved strength, sounding iron and steel, bright yellow arms and monster scoop bucket-loaders attached to gigantic, roaring, gleaming machinery. And piles of sandstone-rubble—great stones, small stones, wiped clean and smooth in the struggle of uplifting and breaking apart. As they watched, drifts of rock powder, infinitesimal particles of diesel vapor and dust, hovered over the destruction. They were immersed, baptized, as though the sounding vibration would take them to pieces along with the earth and rocks and roots of trees downed and scattered, sawn.

On this side of the small stream, darkly flowing down toward Market St. entrance, flowing past beneath tall trees, and the gentrified neighborhood high above, 2017 stood together. Watching. Silent themselves amid the screeching, roaring and rending. Poor innocent rock. Poor ol' sandstone. Why'd anyone want to destroy this cool cool rock? They looked at one another, surprised, questioning. Except Tu, who looked blank.

Then everyone shrugged (but Tu, who still looked blank). They turned and walked back up the path over green green leaf-strewn autumnal turf, just wanting to get past the blasted energetic sounding of solid earth taken to pieces in the hands and arms of great machines, themselves made of ore and rock.

"What's that all about?" HB was first to ask. Murmurs of IDK, and don't know, and got me, answered from all but Pomala. She said, "The council decided against leaving the rock as is, I guess. There was a big discussion about it. Sis thought her side would win—because the Mayor's wife. —Mayor's wife was with them. I guess they decided they needed more grave spaces. But—"

"But what's so important to us?" asked Jay impatiently. "Why do you girls think it's so important?"

HB, too, and Fabian looked at one another.

"Tu?"

HB was asking.

Tu was silent, thinking about the night his father literally chased him down, followed him into the graveyard. The brief talk in the early a.m. before work this morning, the tender gazes of his parents in the mission the other night.

They waited him out. Then he said, "I think it has something to do with the braves' —with their, their, their maybe their...."

"What!" said HB and Fabe together. Was this stutterer Tu or not? But they were also thinking of that night: The scraped surface, clean-scraped of moss and dirt, and of the chiseled emblem—the careful outline, line-drawing, of a fish.

"Say it?" suggested Fabian.

"Religious belief," said Tu.

"Really?" said Jay, who had received an image from the boys of the scraped and symbolic surface. "What are they? Newfish people? BudIsts? Quacks? Some of those Chrisp Eople?"

"Xians, you mean," said Fabian smiling.

"Yeah," she said, "those."

Pomala had been hanging back, walking slowly, thinking of it.

"Did you see Sheree Kim with the machinery?" said Pomala, catching up.

"She was there?" asked Jay.

"It was the weirdest thing. Did you guys see?" She looked at the others shaking their heads. "Nope," said HB.

"She went right between two of those machines, waving at the operators. Then she captured some of the rock-moving and crushing. I guess she was streaming it."

"Brave," said Fabe.

"Very brave," echoed HB.

But Jay said, "What's so weird. It's for the LampPost."

"But then —*she tossed the babblet into the rocks!* For *crushing*. It's mashed to smithers. Then she waved again and stepped away. …She must have seen us seeing?"

"Maybe we'll be on the news, too," exclaimed Jay.

"Again," said HB.

"Maybe not." Fabian offered the possibility.

Jay rummaged through her gizzzzzzzmo for her capture of the scene. There was a figure, peripherally, coming up from the direction of the Market Avenue entrance. Jay zoomed on her face. "It's her," she said. "Look at her eyes—looks like she hasn't slept in three days!"

"Nice profession," said Fabian with unusual sarcasm.

Jay grinned. "Maybe I d'wannabe a barista. Maybe a reporter!"

"Can't find em," said HB to Pastor amid the bustle of the soup kitchen where volunteers were busy cooking, opening the great ovens, ladling tastes, washing dishes, scrubbing veggies, for tonight.

"You don't seem concerned? Candace says evidently the girl was not there after the initial bedtime."

Candace Parker had come beside them, a stack of rolled utensils in her hands. Pastor looked at her. "Maybe we don't need to worry?" He was asking, but hopeful.

She stood a moment, as though trying to apprehend. At last she said, "Perhaps."

HB wondered. Would she be praying? He had seen her on her knees that one time when Fabian came home.

...Big Fello's jury was still out on that.

Sheree Kim was *On* the news. On *Top* of the news: doing local and regional takes on the recent executive order. She had been in and out of schools, civic organizations, convenience stores and now BarStucks. Local pols had given brief interviews. When interviewing these folks—except for the historians—Ms. Kim had stipulated that there was only so much to say. The bits-and-bytes were abuzz with the latest ha-ha-brew, and it was best to signal virtue over this now because so much was in the planning, non-planning, or overplanning concerning foreign-policy and infracture-structure—as she called it (even sometimes online). Ms. Kim could be satiric. Often it was not detectable, however, except by smart people. She was sure of her smart people audience and readership, but equally sure of these regulars. It was a matter of tone, terms, and zeitgeist. For instance, was the tone dry, or smirky? Were terms exaggerated, or subdued? As for zeitgeist, she had no evidence but was intuitively convinced the prophetic coSplay was not Thanksgiving related. That means broad-based lampooning of anything to do with this holiday was permissible. At least she was considering it. The problem was, however, she could not find the players. Kim was relying on her own head—the thinkery—and what she took in to parse and analyze. Her head was enough, or at least it would have to do for now. She had destroyed the technological sensory organ (usual on the job), with heavy machinery. It, and Buloxi, had no conscience. Tech turned us into numbers, merchandise. Technology specifically designed with no conscience. Burnpage and Bozos didn't seem interested in reading Snicknedge's *Robot Diary*. (Kim had reviewed this book by an Akropolis author for the *Puffington Host*.)

"So what's to be the outcome of all these delightful seasonal cups here on display, now that Thanksgiving has been dismissed from our civic and religious lexicon?"

She was holding up her alternate device to the manager of BarStucks, Four Points neighborhood, (in Sharon, EHio).

"Well," said the manager, pulling back just a bit and hoping his bald head wouldn't reflect much fluorescence. He was of an older generation so he said, "well" instead of "so." Sheree was always quick to note usage. The manager was more than willing to engage with this question since he was a bit disturbed by this particular executive order. Many in his generation were, but he did not want to offend, either. He'd been careful, wondering if anyone—or who—might somehow be injured by what he was about to say. "I think we've considered this thoroughly and are ready to incorporate the order into our commercial enterprise... as soon as possible. The PresiDent, himself a businessperson, will understand if some towns don't get right on this, and, after all, we are free in this country. We don't need a nationally sanctioned holiday set aside to give thanks. What we intend to do locally, and I've talked with other Northeast EHio BarStucks managers—we intend to give our cups away. Remember, the religious, contrary to what you said, will continue to give thanks. Well, for us, perhaps the SoupMission down at FivePoints will have a use for these cups. Remember, these are not plastic cups, but paper, and will do no harm to the environment."

Kim said, "While we're here, let's talk a moment about the newly instituted non-compete contractual clause for your workers making the minimum. Is this something workers can no longer be thankful for? What is it about cappuccino that binds nondisclosure, makes it a secret worth depriving lowest-wage workers of a chance to work? Has it anything to do with harassment?" Her voice was characteristically neutral. Kim's viewers could not see her expression but the manager, who was himself under the non-compete contract, saw the mischievous challenge in her eyes (which she did not bother to neutralize). "Or if workers say something about coffee, does that mean no more service sector work for them? No more minimun wage?"

"…Well, as you said, it's true that there's not much time for this, Ms. Kim, but thanks for coming in to see what we think about the executive order for this holiday."

Sheree walked out satisfied, and began editing the interview down to size as she approached her tiny electric vehicle in the vast night-glimmering parking lot. The car sensed her approach via infrared signature and started at once. When she got to the door and reached for the handle, the car would unlock. Remembering her damned conscience, she was careful to use only what would not misrepresent the manager's spiel in this edit. So — it could be just a spiel— or it might not be. Who was she to judge him? It was the news, not a court of law. She was fairly certain the man was of that portion who believed news should be factual.

"I'll see you in my dreams? ...Again sometime...?"

"... Yes. I think maybe you will—or in another dream world you haven't heard of.—Or—

"—Or maybe I have?" Pomala was a bit disappointed. It was beginning to sound like they would in some manner be parting, now that Gneis's confirming message had been given her, and they were all to be on their way to 2017. Would Five Points, Akropolis, *the whole world* be going back? she wondered.

"Please thank Dah for us, as well," she said. Prophetic confirmation from the alternate universe aside, through his son Gneis, Dah had evidently given Tu the correct non-glitchy hidden coordinates in *The Hadesthon* to bring them back to 2017.

"So so we hope this will work," said Gneis. *"There's no guarantee. Yes, he has it all figured out and it's not hand-wavy as you FivePointers say, but still, things can go wrong.... And... there are other factors involved. But you know this."*

Pomala was silent. There was no noise in space, not in the Bubble Universe so colorfully vasty bright and brave. They were nebula—blue and brassy—sparkly bright amid the cosmos, but one thing they could share was thinking, intent, messages from one another—from an *Other* world—in dreams.

Gneis seemed to withdraw a bit, his stars gasses particles expanding.

"Wait!" She cried an inward yearning.

"Wait—What?" She knew he was distant, smiling. Remote and more remote.

"But why?" she asked, sharing her thought. *"Why have you done this? Helped us this way?"*

As from a great distance she sensed his thought coming. Coming to her.

"... There's an old saying in our universe.... 'Receive a good turn, do a good turn.'..."

In less than an experienced moment she felt his absence wrapped up in swift vacuum. Empty. Gone.

Up in her apartment not far from Pomala's gentrified house, Candace Parker lay in her dark room, a sparse gleam passing now and then across the ceiling.

They must be together, she was thinking. *She must be with Willie and Parry.*

Candace did not say to herself, Wherever that is. Instead, she thought: They are safe now. *She is safe.*

In the complex below, Sheree Kim was lining up her historians—e-mails to the lot. Tomorrow she would go into it more deeply—keep it going intentionally until the next reCycle. Another of her sardonic thoughts. Everything human happens over and over again wearing different cultures and clothing. Even the news. We appropriate Everything.

Also in the Third St. complex, Quadrangi and Hibotchi were going over it—Hibotchi in the Sheltering Cares, further up Exchange, toward downtown on Cheddar Avenue. Back and forth they were teaming it, creative as anything. And little Quadri had been consulted earlier in the evening of course. He was Kwad the KonkerEr—there was almost nothing he could not do. He wasn't invincible, but he was brave.

Gretchen was softly snoring away in her crammed office off the passageway not far from her kids' rooms. Moving lights of Akropolis 2019 passing on walls, the ceiling overhead. Every once in awhile she'd wake up, turn over and think of tomorrow's meeting and the prophecy and, and, and....

Below in the Third St. complex, Tu was in his closet thinking oddly un-Tu-like thoughts. Eyes staring at the crack of hall light beneath the bedroom door … zoning on familial and (weirdly) religious concerns…. The look on his face, had anyone chanced to see, was blank. Then Tu switched back to Tu-like thoughts as he went carefully over the dream calculations, with their far-flung abstract numerical incalculability (pictographic to those who had fled mathematics—virtually all who ever lived—according to databanks, algorithmic, keeping track of this).

This is what HB decided when he read Tu's latest briefing. And Tu was thinking—before reporting back again—he would have to warn them of.... *No*, he thought, *they remember what happened last time when we thought I had it. They've experienced me failing.* What in particular troubled him was: in his advanced *advanced* search of the InterWebs—no one *no one* had ever reported this kind of real-world episode while playing *The Hadesthon*. *No one*. He must share that before going any further with these people. These fragile people. He went back to multiplying the advancement of this search—just in case he missed something. No investigator seems ever to have appreciated the fact that there might be a connection between playing the game and the missing two years. It had only been noticed that they happened to be playing the game together—but that was it.

Further down the neighborhood, Pastor Zettler was on his aching knees in the study, door closed. Armpits sweating body odor, hands clenched reflexively together, muscles in his forearms taut, he prayed forcefully, sometimes in fierce anguish, once uplifted on a fleeting impress of joy, followed by his own silent adoration. He needed to know what to tell them at their meeting in the morning after sleepers left the shelter and HB went to school—all the grown-ups in the FivePoints community of volunteers. He wondered briefly how many that might be—enough to fill half the hall below? But his thoughts could not fill up with the detailed planning he felt this project greatly needed. The sole sure thing he had for them at this moment: all that would come. Again: Came a thought to speak of this on the short wave pastor's net. One thing: Maybe their lives would not be saved even so. They were not leaving the neighborhood of FivePoints in separation from it; they were not leaving Akropolis in flight for their lives. *No. Not at all. I don't exist to save my life*. Were this so he'd have to stay and send the others on. But his part, in obedience, was to lead. They were leaving because it was what The Maker wanted. The Maker wanted their trusting obedience. Pastor prayed they would give it if He willed. Then he stood and went into the living room to switch on the shortwave. He would call out to any available pastor on any band at this time.

Pome sat up late, typing feverishly. The room was softly, whitely lit from the only in-room source of light. Her computer. Her fingers ticked rapidly over keys, stopping now and then when she paused to take thought. *This*. This confirmation of the prophecy had been given by Gneis and, peripherally, from the more distant nebula called Mary Bala Jones. But now Pomala remembered everything of her experience with the SiXPointz kids and FivePoints kids in another universe, where Gneis had lived and died, and where, she thought, his family and friends still lived. All family and friends had bodies there but Gneis and his mother, Mary Bala Jones. Were they clouds of wisdom and witness of doings on their planet? With its multitude of lives living in that moment of 1900 EE? Was it still 1900? —or 1902? It was Jay who took courage to lead us back!!

Up in Sharon, Jay was frantic, trying once again—now with hectic energy—to contact BO. BO. BO BO BO. BO. *bo, how can you vanish? this is the interwebs. where are you? where*. Next she was going to buzz-cut her hair. Jay had been scouting the butch all over the internet, its entire history, various names, culture and other relevant minutia. She wanted to try the 'do. It would look good with that white streak in her brown hair.

Fabian lay awake in the room next to that in which his grandmother lay. He was thinking of the A'ndians from the 1700s. How amazing. He was more impressed with their feat coming out of the twinkle-transference, than with his own. And—amazingly also—evidently they were true believers. Willie and Parry *were*, he was certain. But for the True People braves to be believers seemed to him the real point of all their twinkling episodes. *You might expect 2017 to do it, but not circa 1700 anything.* They were NOT a part of the vaudeville circuit as we'd thought during adventures in 1900 CE. They were simply Time-twinklers. Willie, Parry, Eaglestreak and Walleye-stare. The Girl. Time-twinklers in a cosmic exercise of such massive strangeness and proportion—and yet—and yet it was like the altar call: So intimate that despite the bubbling praise and flames of holy fire on noisy rejoicing heads.... It was really quite intimate—not in noise for the outer ear, not in sensation, but that quiet still voice.

Yes. I am.

I am here with you.

Jay, up in Sharon, sent her last private message to Bo: so nevermind, bo. i'll see you in 2017. i'll look slightly different. She did not add, Dr. Boko thought it might be interesting and helpful.

New HAmsterdam Times; byline, Chesley Stalled:

"PRESIDENT WITTS, 'BUILDING INFRASTRUCTURE ACCORDING TO ANCIENT ROMAN METHODS A WASTE OF TIME.'

" 'We need planned obscelescence! (sic) They weren't smart enough to think of it.'

"Saying he had other things to think about, the PresiDent plans to veto the infrastructure bill."

Past Things First

Pomala slipped quietly through the back door and into the soup kitchen. She saw big Flo hanging out by the coffee pot and held out an envelope, with a smile. "This is for Pastor when he comes down."

Flo took a sip of her coffee, hand out for it.

Pomala smiled and waved and stepped back out into the alley. There was that, and she had left one also beneath her pillow. She began walking through mist toward the intersection of Third and Exchange Street.

HB said "bye" into the study and slipped out the apartment door. He had finished in the kitchen, carried his backpack full of books—the same he carried two years ago, or two weeks—depending on your perspective. Pastor would head downstairs for his special meeting with the volunteers, but HB wanted to avoid walking down with him, avoid the talking. HB needed some quiet, some breath discharge, some focus. *No matter what year it turned out to be: I'll see you later today* ***no matter what.***

Channeling Jayrai, he thought. *Stop that!*

She had seen her lovely white stripe buzzed off along with the dark remnants of her hair, and was now very pleased as she stepped off the bus. Jay saw HB in the mist... turning the corner onto Exchange. This was really going to bum HB! Unfortunately, it was also going to bug Tu, but she was sure they could live through it.

She was looking at the newest gizzzzzzzmo in her hand and saw Trice's message: "Are you there yet? :-)" As a line of passengers climbed off the bus, Jay stopped to text: "any moment." ;)." Then, with care, she slipped the gizzzzzmo next to the giant front tires of the purring diesel-engine bus, as the last passenger climbed aboard. She stepped back to watch the bus pull forward with a slight roar. It passed into the straight-ahead lane and through the intersection onto Bechtel. Jay looked into the gritty gutter. There was the gizzz's guts wrecked and sparkly in early light and mist. Maybe her new 'do; but that giz *wasn't* going with her! She hurried after HB.

There they were up ahead! Pomala's hair was blue flame again! — Everyone but Quadri lined up in the mist on the old stonewall, left side of the straightaway heading up toward downtown past the GlimmerDale. On the right were shops and the library, then empty shops and, further along, the FivePoints police compound. Fabian, Tu, HB, Pomala. With care exceptional for Jayrai, she watched both ways and crossed to the other side through traffic. Breathless she came up to them, saying almost nothing, and climbed up on cold rocks. She felt the cold through her cargo pants. The tips of her biomechanical fingers were sensitive to pressure and size, but not so much to the minutia of texture and temperature. She remembered CossycSystems were to be experimenting on ultra thin carbon for electronic skin with solar energy in 2018. She still had hopes of it even though they had not offered it to her in the last couple weeks of 2019. Part of their get-Jay-back-to-Cossyc-thing, she surmised.

They began to talk. Talk was a quiet jumble of exclamation, question, nerves and nonsense.

"What's with that hair!"

Jay had that dark buzz-cut with pale streak to one side. She grinned. "It's the new me."

"You mean to *2019* you."

"It won't got through, Jay!"

"Dr. Boko thinks it might be interesting."

Several voices cried. "*Dr. Boko*!?"

"E-mailed him we might be going back. Don't worry, I didn't say how or when."

"*But we are supposed to look, act, dress the same. That means hair!"*

Then someone (Fabian) had sense enough to say, "Maybe we better let Tu go ahead with our checklist or whatever we need to do?"

Tu looked at him, gave a brief respectful nod.

Everyone got quiet again.

They watched commuter traffic going slowly, quietly past. Some were speeding, of course. Trying to make the light. Nervous, Pome broke in: "When we get back, we'll still have Thanksgiving at home and at the SoupMission to look forward to! …But where will Quadri be?"

"We'll find out. Thanksgiving no matter what," HB. "The mission's not dumping Thanksgiving."

"Tu, what's the checklist," said Fabian. "Should we be sitting in the same order as last time? Have we got it right? Right—positioned across from the library."

Everyone got quiet again.

Tu said, "Let's stay calm, look at the image again. You've all got the same hardware and software as before?"

Everyone said some form of *Yep*. And they looked together at the image. All were wearing the exact same clothes. Jackets and jeans, cargoes, HBBBAH in his jumpsuit. Jay, only, looked different—too late to do anything about that!

"Remember," Tu cautioned. "Anything can make the difference. Nothing here but what was then. Doublecheck."

"Quad," they all answered, "Quadri," said Pomala.

Tu nodded. He did not want to bring that up. Or have it brought up, either. He looked blankly at them. He sighed. *The great physicist is slipping.*

"The great FivePoints scientist is slipping," said HB.

"We will go with what we've got," said Tu. There was a touch of irritation in his voice. Tu.

"So there are variables," he said.

"Right," said HB, "and we'll know we've been hit with one if it comes smelling like horse sht."

Tu continued. "The time variable, for instance."

"No duh," said Jay, thinking Big Time not little time.

Tu went ahead. "We are here on a different day and time in November, so it's micro variable. —November may not have anything to do with it. We aren't even sure *about* the day and time. The clock was striking 11—before midnight when we accidentally slipped out of 1900 into the alternate universe last time ... so we know my calculations did not, or may not have, worked right ... but the alt aliens have taken the blame for some of that, and their reassurance is um heartening." Instead of using their names, he was bound to call Gneis and Dah "the alt aliens" because that was most fitting to Tu's psyche. "We're putting trust in them because—it's all I got. We will use the 2017 version, and the other is toast. Pluto is back to dwarf as far as we're concerned. If that influences the go-back, we'll start over some other day with the new version. Maybe that's what caused all this. These alt aliens are flex capacitance for us, using *The Hadesthon* —which, btw, battery for same is in the same condition as when we started on this venture. They factored everything in, and so we go with that."

"We were playing other games, then too though," said Jay. "*The Hadesthon* —maybe just a bit too weird from now on. I'm not sure I'll play it again after all this."

Jay? Too weird? But this did echo deeply with the others. Also a few murmured amen's.

"Like I said—what we've got."

"Did the alt say anything about the missing Quad?" HB was asking. HB was just messing with him. Evidently HB cared if Tu's head would swell. "You being the scientist and all will not neglect to tell the folks over at HiTopOLis that things aren't quite the same in this regard." He grinned.

For his part, Tu was not about to bring up HB's own head. HB had not been paying attention to anything but gaming when they started this venture in the beginning. That is one factor.

"That is right," said Tu. Looking blankly at him.

"And that we all just happen to be here, no planning in it."

"That is right."

"HB!" said Jay. "Talk about showing off! We know you got bones to rattle! Let's get back to 2017!" And she was thinking again of Bo.

"So," said Tu, "I've given you the coordinates of the GM—that's me, you remember—and this is how to play the game according to the physicist—next-door universe—who created BABY™.

"He knows his stuff," agreed HB. "Now who's going to play for Quadri? Someone who wasn't playing this game?" He looked over it Jay, who said, "Problem solved! We were playing *Twinkle-in-Time* and *Wars of WorldCraft*—both. Not *The Hadesthon* that time.

"Wow!!" exclaimed three of them (all except Tu).

"Is this good or bad, Tu," asked Fabian.

Tu looked blank. He said, "Let's go with what we've got." He seemed to have finalized without much exchange. Mostly Tu had received. He did not interject—dreams were good if solely figures, formulas, diagrams and graphs. Otherwise—. And they could always try again.

"Settle back. At some point we are going to hold hands," said Fabian. He picked up Pome's hand.

The police drove by, nodding. The driver's side window was cracked as they passed up Exchange toward the compound. 2017 waved from the legendary wall as the morning-shift passed in their silent silver cruiser. It looked subtly softly gleaming in mist still haunting FivePoints valley this a.m..

These officers were not those who'd been having interactions with 2017; not the night shift, nor late afternoon. But they were familiar with the case, two males with a checklist on the regulation APF babblet for the morning round. "Aren't they supposed to be in school?" one asked of the other.

The other looked at the dashboard babblet.

"Not for another 15-20 minutes," he said. "We'll swing back around in a bit. They're up to something—maybe. But we'll see."

"Yeah. About 11 minutes till 8:30. And I really don't want to talk to them unless it's necessary. Half this intersection is nuts. Maybe the whole neighborhood."

On the wall the smart kid was saying, "Alt aliens say we make up the Time/Day discrepancy by playing exactly at 8:28 a.m., EST, our universe."

They looked at their devices: 11 minutes to go.

"So here we go," said Tu.

From him they felt no particle of suppressed excitement. Was it solely because the anticipation of each was so palpably strong? *It would happen.*

In a few minutes there would be no such thing as 2019.

Would it happen? 2019 does not exist!!

Would they leave behind the future—meaning the current present—for FivePoints, Akropolis, Americle, the entire world? Would they end up where they belonged? Would they *be,* or be particles in the Grandmaster's scheme of things? —Or the GM. Would they *be* in 1900 during the riots? Or with the Native Americles? Or be cavemen or... or... or...?

"There is no such thing as nothing," said Fabian.

"There's always something," said Pomala.

Tu said, "Device Open." He said, "Everybody on?"

"I am," said Fabian.

"Me too." (Pomala)

"Me also," said Jay.

"Me." (HB)

"Now," said Tu. "Be on your appes. Get set. Time to hack. First we use Quadrangi's appe as tested on the KitTen and backPedal all these devices. Every last one. I don't want a single bit or byte of 2019 anywhere across these gizmos. If you aren't willing to comply... well just leave the wall now. And I mean right now." He looked sternly at each in turn, then glanced at the time on his z-pod.

The library across the street was closed, of course, but the GlimmerDale gates were open all day till dark, there was still connection along the street. If all went well that library, with its wifi for babblets and such, would be open in another few minutes, November 3, 2017 after school. At that point in time, the sun would be going west behind Sharon Hill. Just right, he thought.

Suddenly, with surprise owing to their deep and committed concentration, out of nowhere Quadri, wearing jeans, jacket and black T, ran up panting and climbed on the wall between Pomala and Jayrai.

"I want to come!" he said. "I have to come, too!" He grabbed the hand of each girl. "Quadrangi wanted to come but Tu said he couldn't. I want to play *Twinkle-in-Time!*"

"Quick!" said Tu, "look at his 7qz.."

Pomala fumbled with Quadri's device as he got it out. Everything of his was already hacked. All along the wall the games were old again, the soSHmedia was ancient, some were missing entirely. Even the new PresiDent was gone from HB's screensaver. He grinned. He'd put the black-and-white PresiDent from 2017 on his gizzmo8 again.

"Quadrangi is a genius!"

"Are you sure? —Quad?" asked Pomala. "Sure you want to be in 2017?"

"If we get that far," said Jay.

"And no further," said Fabian.

"Yes! I'm going to 2017! I love you guys!" said Quadri.

"But you love Quadrangi!?"

"I do. I do!"

" 'K," said Tu, working his backPedaled device. To himself he said, One glitch kept happening. *—No!! No observing this. Just do and be.*

"Should we close our eyes?"

"Wish on the stars?"

"There are no stars, the sun's up though," said HB, meaning rising over the church and school behind them. Rising, in the thick of buildings, over trees, shining before them off windows across Exchange Street, off Cossyc campus windows high above the corner.

As Tu worked, there was silence, the Sun sIncing, then HB said "I'm playing the old game. This is for the birds, this waiting, Tu. Just do what you need to do."

"Like always," said Pomala with a smile. She was off looking for *CitiesUnderground.*

Tu was thinking, players need frustration, but not confusion, not disorientation. There's the game right there. That's how to encode.

There was silence, each lost in the game. Tu had started searching on Quantum Teleportation. Findings.

No one noticed short lean Kim Kim, looking down on his device, going into the library across the street.

"Wait till *Elevator 11, ThirdTier.*" (HB)

Fabian flashed him a grin.

"We's whomping your butts." said HB to his gizzmo8. (He was talking to Fabian.)

"Game ain't over," returned the other, intently playing his role.

They sat: The sun that had risen behind still sIncing, now off their right shoulders slightly ahead. Intent on gaming, no one noticed

"Lean in.... Here's a selfie," said Jay, showing them. "We're all here."

The wall was colder and harder. The sun was sinking in the crisp November air.

Tu closed his pod. "I've had it," he said. "See you." He got up and crossed through traffic toward the lighted library, calling back, "I love you, girls!"

"Ha ha. D'you hear that! Tu! Can you imagine!?" said Jayrai, flinging back her streaked hair. "Love you, too!" she called. "Tu! Tu! Ha ha love you, too, Tu! Thanks! See you girls," she said and hopped down. "The bus will be here. It's all set. Love you! Gotta date with my beau!"

"Who's that?" called Pomala. She thought she maybe knew, and wasn't quite easy.

"Not telling—it's a secret! Love you!" Jay headed for the intersection.

"Hey," said Quadri, "I'm not done!"

"But you're playing with your brother," said HB. "Go on, it's getting dark!"

Quad hopped down, holding Pomala's hand. He "loved" everybody out loud all the way across the street, still walking, holding Pomala's hand. She called back to the two teenagers. "Love you! Love you! Thanks!" and disappeared toward Third with her charge. There was Quadrangi, device in hand, coming down from Third between buildings, into the alleyway.

"OK, I give up," said Fabian on the sidewalk, turning to go.

"Yo! Course you do!"

"Love you, man," Fabe called over his shoulder and disappeared into lessening light on the busy street, calling back, "Thanks!"

"Yo!" said HB. He thought about it. Nobody's ever done that before. We just happened to be here and now everybody's loving everybody. What's up? Curiously he waggled his 'do. *Maybe my head will know the answer.*

If he remembered to check it when he got back through the twilight to Sheltering Cares.

"Thanks!" He called back to no one in particular.

—Maybe Big Fello?

Who knows.

Main Characters

Displaced 2017 characters
HBBBAH, *a.k.a. HB, a.k.a. Blake Griffin*
Jayrai, *a.k.a. Jay*
Fabian
Pomala
Quadri, *a.k.a. Quad*
Tu

SoupMission volunteers
Pastor Philip Zettler
Candace Parker
Gretchen, *a.k.a. Gretch, Sheltering Cares housemother*
Bruster, farmer, occasional volunteer
Flo
Hibotchi, *Sheltering Cares resident*
Trice, *Sheltering Cares resident*

FivePoints Akropolis police
Lt. Horace Hunch
Sergeant Benja Bench
Officer Wilhelmina Robust
Officer Slim Wilkes

CossycSystems engineers
Dr. Helda Vansing, *Quadri's examiner*
Dr. Van Helsing, *HB's examiner*
Dr. Neee, *Tu's examiner*
Dr. X., *Pomala's examiner*
Drs. Nicole Rostof and Baron deVill, *Fabian's examiners*
Dr. Boko, *Jayrai's examiner*

Native Americle True People, and 1900 kids
The Girl, Heirolynn, *a Rovmorian captive, a.k.a. Ochquetit, a.k.a. Ochquetschitsch*

S. Dorman

The *Meteu*
Red Fox, *a Meteu in training*
Eaglestreak
Walleye-stare
Willie, *captive from 1900, a.k.a. Digger-dog*
Parry, *captive from 1900, a.k.a. Girl-boy*

Others

Quadrangi, a.k.a. Quad, *Quadri's big brother (both boys are nicknamed Quad)*
Nandora, *Jayrai's mother*
Mr. and Mrs. Yu, *Tu's parents*
Sebastian Cruz, *blogger, a.k.a. Basti*
Sheree Kim, *journalist, a.k.a. Kim Kim*
Glindora, *Pomala's big sister, aide to the Mayor*

Dream people

Gneis
Dah
Mary Bala Jones

Assorted homeless adults and children. Assorted Sheltering Cares kids.

Stories in Order

Five Points Akropolis

SiXPointz HiTopOlis

DuOPolis